PRAISE FO.. ..UU. U...

But, oh, you've got to discover all the WTF and oh boy moments of this book. They are plenty and they are going to send you reeling and will make you read on until the very end. You won't be disappointed. You'll see.

—Leah

This book deserves more than 5 stars. I cannot explain it well enough how much I LOVE this series. Astrid can write awesome characters, amazing world building and she knows how to write an adrenaline filled fight scene!

—Kelsey

This book was just as incredible as the first two, I absolutely devoured it in only a few hours.

—Meg

The first half of this book had me so stressed. I didn't know what was going to happen, or what twists and turns it would take! And the end 🌑 had me in near tears.

—Mikaela

All I can say is holy shit girlie pop needs a break now. Sage has been through it again, again and AGAIN across these last three books, and *Ruby City* was no different.

—Devon

I really like books with insane plot twists and minor details and Astrid Cole did not disappoint.

—Pishi

Now this is book 3 of her series and I enjoyed every single page of this book. Duh, I cried I screamed I laughed and smile well her books make me feel all of it.

—Kari

Hold. On. Tight.

A wild run through the imagination! This book is filled with emotional growth and the MFC finding purpose. I'm here for the sassy banter and the wonderful twist and turns along the way.

Another exceptional read!! I'm ready for more!!!!

—Tarah

Ruby City focuses more on emotional connections and righting wrongs. It wouldn't be an Astrid Cole book without a killer plot twist or two, so you have been warned! I don't know where the story will go from here, but I'm booking my tickets now for *Opal City*!

—Nora

ASTRID, YOU NAILED IT! Again.

—Valery

RUBY CITY

ASTRID COLE

Hardback: 979-8-9881469-8-8; Paperback: 979-8-9881469-7-1; eBook: 979-8-9881469-6-4

Editing by astridcolebooks
Cover design by Kira Rubenthaler and James T. Egan
Book Design by Mayfly book design
Proofread by Kaitlin Devlin

Library of Congress Catalog Number: 2024913673

Author's Note

Ruby City contains trigger warnings and is NOT meant for readers below the age of eighteen. Some of these warnings include, but are not limited to: sex, drugs, rape, suicide, suicide ideation/planning, mental health, explicit descriptions of gore, death, and intense child-bearing scenes. Please bear these in mind as you embark on this crazy journey.

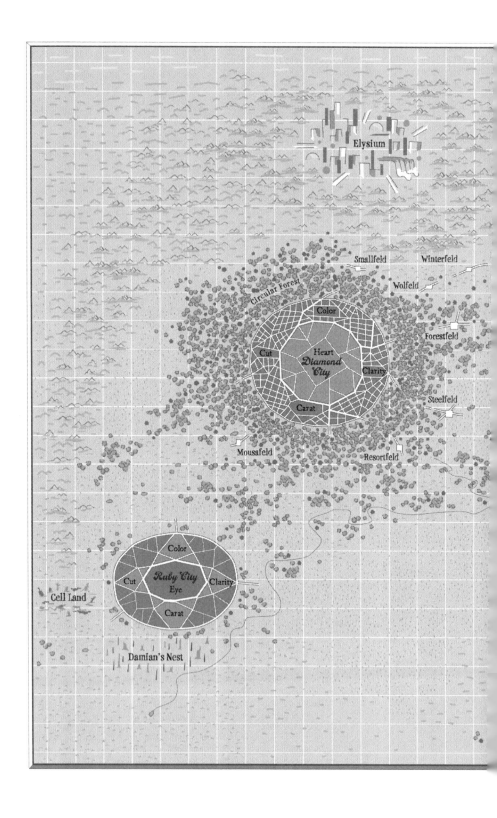

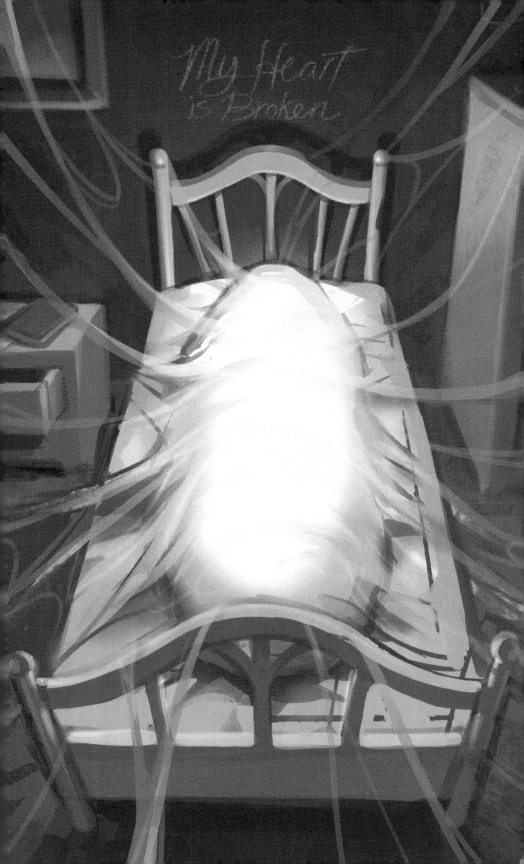

DIAMOND CITY CALENDAR

1 - Month of Birth

2 - Month of Love

3 - Month of Loyalty

4 - Month of Shine

5 - Month of Purity

6 - Month of Light

7 - Month of Flare

8 - Month of Innocence

9 - Month of Courage

10 - Month of Strength

11 - Month of Energy

12 - Month of Faith

To Mom,

Because we have a message for the world.

CHAPTER 1

Royal Academy vs. Cut University

There wasn't a doubt that Cut University had the best college fastball team in Diamond City. Possibly even the world. This was the school that trained and prepared athletes for their district's undefeated professional team, the Cut Porcupines. They *always* brought home the trophy every year. They always made a gambler's day. You'd be crazy to bet against them.

That's why Royal Academy didn't take Cut University for granted. Every player knew what they were up against. Ten versus ten, the matches random. No one wanted to play Number 18. That was Feodor Petrov, a huge twenty-three-year-old, who had more muscle than he did skin. He wasn't bulky by any means—he was just fit and fast. It was his skill that spoke the most on the court, the way he bashed those fastballs over the net with his fists and moved as if he knew where his opponent would hit next. He was going pro for sure—he'd be the Cut District's patron hero for many seasons to come.

As for Royal Academy, they had to win six out of their ten matches in order to bring home the gold. They were done being the outcasts of Diamond City. All four districts turned up their noses at anything that came out of the capital. No one wanted prissy princesses or beautiful princes in their entertainment—only in politics . . . if that. Allseer Louis had built quite the reputation for being a handsome leader, but looks weren't anything to brag about when the city needed help.

Well, it was time to change that. Heart wasn't all glam and no action. It'd show the rest of the districts it could put up a fight when it needed to.

The crowd was on its feet. The fastball court was ready for its first match. Twenty-four meters long and eight meters wide with a net across the middle. The floor was smooth, shaved concrete in neutral gray. The crowd brought the colors and the pride—red and gold for Royal Academy, and violet and pink for Cut University. It probably looked beautiful from up above, but no player was admiring colors nor concentrating on the crowd.

No way. Ruby couldn't stop to look at anyone other than her opponent. All that mattered was Feodor and the court. In fastball, men and women played against each other. While many experts argued that was a clear disadvantage, there were too many legal hormone therapies out there to level the fairness. Girls did what they could to be competitive, even if they had to work extra hard. There weren't many on the Royal Academy's team—Ruby was the only one.

And she was up against Feodor.

Ruby was already mentally prepared for it. This was the end of college fastball season, which meant that finals were right around the corner. Unfortunately, she had been unable to study for any of them. She had a mega World History exam next week, but that didn't matter when this game would determine whether or not Royal Academy would finally win a season. This was the *finals*.

"Ruby, Ruby, Ruby!" cheered her fans on the right side of the stadium. Ruby was a freshman, but she had already developed a reputation in the school. She could see all the handmade banners among the crowd—some for her—"You Got This, Ruby!"—and others for Feodor—"Crush The Bitch!" Perhaps security hadn't seen that one yet.

That was fine. Ruby was used to far worse. It didn't matter what people said about her—it only mattered what the final score was. She had to get to ten points first. That was it.

Ruby stepped forward onto the court. She had her tank top, short-shorts, and light sneakers. She didn't need a knee brace, but she did wear wraps for her wrists. It helped steady her fists, which she'd need to blast that ball across the court. It was seven inches in diameter and made of a plastic that felt like steel sometimes. Depending on the opponent, it had the potential to fly at the speed of light. Sometimes, Ruby couldn't see the ball—she had to feel it.

When Ruby thought too much about her chances and the craziness of the game, she lost her concentration, so she stopped. She walked out to her opponent and shook his hand.

Feodor squeezed it. Hard. His grip was a clamp, but so was Ruby's.

"Ready to lose?" he teased her.

Ruby said nothing. She called tails for the coin toss and won. She always served first. The referee gave her a ball, and Ruby took it back to the serving line.

"Ruby, Ruby, Ruby!"

Ruby looked out at the crowd. At their chanting. She had heard it so many times in her life . . . even if she couldn't remember anything before this year. Allseer Louis said that it was perfectly normal for someone suffering from amnesia. He never took her to doctors for fear that they would use her in unethical ways, but he told her she would regain her memories eventually. Whenever Ruby asked about her parents, he'd say they were killed in the Lolligo invasion thirty years ago.

An invasion that could have decimated Diamond City. The Lolligo were creatures worshiped by the Claritians as deities, and everyone had gotten a taste of why that day. But, thanks to a sound alliance with Emerald City, they had been able to stop the invasion and arrest the culprits. Ruby wasn't too sure what the situation was now, but the Lolligo hadn't been seen again.

Except, of course, for Herman and Tyrus. They were Louis' bodyguards and they were here to ensure the match went smoothly. Ruby had to admit she felt secure having them around. No one messed with seven-foot Lolligo that had arms the size of boulders and teeth as sharp as a shark's. By now, everyone had gotten used to Herman and Tyrus' presence, so no one paid them any mind.

Lolligo . . . Squid . . .

Ruby knew not to call them Squids. A huge insult, for sure. How did she know that?

"It's insulting . . . And he'll cut off your tongue."

Ruby was sure she had said that at some point. She couldn't remember when.

"Ruby!" Hayes hissed from the sidelines. He was her best friend, but sometimes he acted more like her manager. All her teammates were watching her. "Hey! Come on! Concentrate!"

Ruby looked at the ball in her hand. Right. She had to win this. She had to—

"RUBY!"

Ruby looked back up again. This time, there were no teammates on the sidelines. No Cut University players ready to annihilate Royal Academy. She wasn't even inside the gym—she was standing on a court outside, right beneath the bright sun partially covered by clouds. It was always raining in Diamond City, but summer was around the corner, and the humidity was a death blow to her hair.

Ruby sighed. She bounced the fastball up and down. She wasn't good enough to make it on the team . . .

"Aren't you going to serve?" Hayes called from the other side of the court.

Yes. Ruby did just that, hitting the ball over the net to Hayes.

Hayes was no pushover when it came to sports, and he rushed to deliver it right back.

Their volleys were good for amateurs. Just connecting with the ball was a big accomplishment. For some reason, that was Ruby's weakness. She was terrible at hitting things with her raw hands. Maybe if she had a bat or a weapon, it'd be easier. She felt like she could hit the ball every time, then.

"Ruby!" Hayes whined from the other side. "You're distracted again!"

Ruby sighed... again. She rubbed the back of her head as the ball went bouncing off the court and onto the grass. A few students walked by, talking to each other about finals. They stopped when they saw her. They just stared.

Ruby was sort of used to it by now. Once in a while, a couple of students would just stop and stare at her like that guy and chick were doing now. Typically, she gravitated toward Hayes's side for comfort and that's what she did. Usually, the students went away but these two were brave enough to approach her.

"Hey," one of them with thick glasses said. He was a red-head with freckles, of Scottish descent. Everyone in Diamond City had a pretty unique nationality. Nearly five hundred years ago, it had become a refuge for any survivors on earth. Nuclear Devastation between Russia and the United States had completely wiped out a lot of territory. Many places were still uninhabitable thanks to high radiation levels. "What's your name?"

"Why does it matter?" Ruby snapped, making it to Hayes' side at last. She adjusted the strap of her gym bag across her chest. "Are you going to interview me?"

"Please." Red-Head waved his hands. "My name's Charles. And this here is Kendra." He waved to his Black companion. She was pretty dark, but her skin was smooth and perfect. Her hair was straight and shiny, too, evidence that she had had it recently blow-dried. No matter how hard Ruby tried, she could never get her hair to look that nice. "And we—well—we wanted to talk."

"Better than staring, I suppose." Ruby crossed her arms. "Well? What did you want to talk about?"

"Would you and your"—Red-Head glanced at Hayes—"*friend* like to have lunch with us?"

Ruby looked at Hayes, who shrugged his shoulders. They were done with their classes for the day, so hanging out for a little bit couldn't hurt.

The four headed to the cafeteria together. This was finals week, so there weren't as many students around as usual. Royal Academy was a pretty exclusive school to begin with, with admissions at a measly thirty slots per semester. Smaller classes meant more one-on-one time with professors. As a result, graduates became the high-end working class in Diamond City, taking jobs at the palace or at a big corporation in one of the districts. In the eyes of the common folk, Royal Academy graduates were over-privileged snobs.

For lunch, Ruby always went for pizza. She ordered an entire pie for herself then sat down with her three companions. Hayes loved boba tea and ramen, and their new friends grabbed bento boxes big enough to feed a whole family. Of course, it was nowhere near as impressive as Ruby's ability to down all that dough and cheese.

"Hungry much?" Charles mused.

"I'm hungry pretty much all the time," Ruby admitted, picking up her third slice. "That's why I always carry snacks." Her favorite was Fruity Tarts. They were more of a breakfast item, but they hit the spot no matter what time of day.

"Yet you look incredible." Kendra eyed her shoulders and biceps. It was always hot and muggy in the capital, so Ruby wore short sleeves or tank-tops when she could. "Do you work out?"

"All the time," Ruby replied, taking a huge bite of pizza. She loved when she scored a particularly big piece of pepperoni. "In fact, I'm going to the gym after this. Hayes is coming with me, too."

Hayes shook his head. "I can't keep up with her. I just do the treadmill for a few minutes and then I watch her embarrass all the guys there. I mean, Ruby can bench *four* plates on each side of the bar. That's forty-five pounds each, *plus* the weight of the bar which is another forty-five."

Kendra gasped at Ruby. "You can bench 405 pounds?"

"Are you an Enhanced?" Charles asked her.

"No," Ruby said.

At least, she didn't think so.

"You have to be an Enhanced," Kendra said pointedly. "No human girl can bench 405 pounds!"

To be fair, Ruby had been working up to it for a whole year. Those first few days at the gym had been tough. With some work and consistency, however, she had improved on a lot of the major exercises. She had also gotten into running in the evenings, sometimes through the capital to see all the landmarks like the palace, the entrance to the Royal Amusement Park, the complexes, and the training fields.

Sometimes, she stared at those fields endlessly. It all looked so familiar to her. Louis always said they were memories from her past life, from before the amnesia had set in. Ruby only wondered what other memories she had that she wasn't remembering. Perhaps going to school was the reset button she had needed . . . but that didn't stop her from wondering from time to time.

"Can I ask you something?" Kendra leaned forward, bento box forgotten. She was at the best part, too—that tempura shrimp looked extra crunchy and greasy. "Are you, by any chance, the owner of a pizzeria?"

Ruby arched a brow. "Owner?"

"Yeah." Kendra reached into her bag to rummage for her phone. On it, she had saved a news headline from the Cut District. She very eagerly showed it to Ruby.

Two For Pizza At the Top Again! Owners Candice and Olivia Fraser Credit Their Aunt, Sage Arpine

And beneath it was a picture of . . . Ruby?

"Can I see that?" Ruby snatched the phone from Kendra's hand and started reading the article written by some local Cut journalist.

Two for Pizza was awarded Cut District's best pizzeria by critics for the thirtieth year in a row. Not only is it the district's go-to restaurant for a filling meal any time of the day, but the innovation they bring with their pies is dazzling. Flavors like the Hippo—all of the toppings, even bananas— the Beat Box—the perfect blend of beets and chocolate— and the Minefield—every raisin imaginable on dough—are just one of hundreds of options at this delectable hotspot.

"Our aunt, Sage, taught us everything there is to know about running a business and making awesome pizza," one of Two for Pizza's owners, Candice Fraser, says. "And we make sure never to sacrifice quality for quantity."

"That's what we try to teach our children," Olivia Fraser says. "You have to work hard to achieve great things. And our aunt was in this business for a long time. She started it right after the Unification War."

Candice and Olivia revealed that Sage Arpine was an Enhanced. Under Allseer Kilstrong's rule, Enhanced weren't given a lot of free reign in the districts (many were enlisted in the military), but Sage's obvious love for pizza kept her close to home. When asked about Sage's whereabouts, Candice and Olivia claim that she has long retired.

"We have her legacy to uphold," Candice says. "And that's what we plan to do."

There was more, but Ruby had stopped reading. She had seen Sage's picture in the article. Her mind was still trying to process that Candice and Olivia's aunt looked just like *her.* There was no doubt: Ruby looked like Sage, so Charles and Kendra had every reason to ask if there was a correlation.

"That can't be Ruby," Hayes said, taking the phone next. "I mean, we know it's not. Ruby is a freshman at Royal Academy. She's nineteen years old. Isn't that right, Ruby?"

"Yeah," Ruby said slowly. But even Hayes knew that Ruby suffered from amnesia . . . and there was so much of her life that she just didn't know. Maybe she really did have a hefty past . . .

But wait. Wouldn't Louis have told her? According to him, Ruby had been a palace girl all her life. A terrible accident in the training fields had knocked her in the head. This didn't coincide with Sage at all. Besides, if Ruby were Sage, how could she have forgotten 151 years of her life? That's how old Sage was, according to the article. That didn't seem likely, either.

"Damn." Ruby rubbed her head. Why couldn't she fucking remember?

"Maybe you're related," Kendra suggested. "A long lost twin or something. Why don't you go talk to those two chicks at Two for Pizza in the Cut District?"

Ruby thought it'd be a good idea to ask Candice and Olivia about her . . . origins. If she wanted to know more about her past life, then Two for Pizza seemed like a solid place to start. That would mean that Louis had lied to her, though . . . that Ruby was no palace girl . . . that she had been a warrior in the Unification War all this time.

The war that had united all four districts in Diamond City 133 years ago. The first humans, using a Lolligo's blood, had become Enhanced, or superior warriors. They, led by the Optimum, had overthrown the corrupt district Overseers and established unity. Ruby had read all about it this year in one of her Diamond City history courses, and nothing seemed to trigger her memory.

Ruby had a hard time finishing her pizza. Her head was pounding. She was so terribly confused. Then Charles went on to talk about some show called *The Rainbow in Me* and that made Ruby nauseous. God, she didn't even know the show, but she swore she had heard it from somewhere before . . .

"Isn't that an old show?" Kendra asked Charles.

"Yeah, but it's really good," Charles admitted with a slight blush to his cheeks. "It's about this dude who claims he's straight, but then falls in love with someone unexpected. It's won a ton of awards. I think they're doing a thirty-first season, believe it or not—"

Ruby got up. She drew heads as she bee-lined for the door and stepped outside for some fresh air. She held her head, trying so hard to remember where she had heard of that show before, but nothing came up. Before she could cry and scream about it, Hayes was at her side. Kendra and Charles followed.

"Ruby?" Hayes said, rubbing her back. "Are you all right?"

"Why can't I remember?" Ruby hid her face and shook her head. "Why can't I fucking remember anything?"

"Don't force yourself. It was a terrible accident."

"Wait." Kendra stepped forward. Her hair bounced with every move she made. "Are you suffering from amnesia? For real?"

She and Charles glanced at each other, as if they had discovered a pot of gold. Ruby didn't really want to engage with any of this drama right now. She needed the gym, but more than that: she needed to speak to Louis.

Ruby had to do this strategically. If she was, in fact, Sage, then Louis had lied to her. And if he had lied to her, that meant he wanted to keep her a secret. The question was why. Was there someone or something after Ruby? Was someone persecuting her?

Asking Tyrus and Herman would be the wrong move, too. Those two Lolligo were loyal to Louis and would tip him off of Ruby's insecurities immediately.

It looked like Ruby would have to sneak off tonight. She knew how to scale the palace walls because she did it every night for fun. She loved sitting on top of the highest spire and just looking out at the capital, at the biggest Ferris wheel she had ever seen. Sometimes, sightseeing helped jog her memory . . . but never enough for her to truly remember her past. It was Sage's picture that had Ruby's mind in a whirl.

She completed her workout without knowing what she had done. Today was squat day, so she had hit legs pretty hard, but she had failed to record her numbers. All she could do was stare into space and ignore the guys when they asked her for a spot on the bench. Hayes was on the treadmill like usual, going at a snail's pace. He was busy texting their new friends in between watching Ruby's behavior.

"Wow, you look really distracted, Ruby," Hayes said after Ruby called it a day. "And you look a bit pale."

Ruby cleared her throat. She shook the protein in her bottle. "I am. And ... um ..." She looked around for Herman and Tyrus. She found them across the courtyard, hanging back like they were instructed to do by Louis. "Can you give me a ride to the Cut District? Maybe at midnight?"

Hayes's eyes widened. "At midnight? Why?"

"I'm not sure I want to tell Louis what I'm doing."

"Ruby, *why?*"

"I don't know," Ruby said curtly. She really didn't want to explain herself right now. "I just feel there's something wrong."

Hayes snorted. "Because those two idiots told you that you looked like Sage?"

Ruby had a snapshot of the picture on her phone. There was way too much of a resemblance. Perhaps it wasn't a coincidence that everyone kept staring at her around here. It was as if they knew something that Ruby didn't, but weren't allowed to say anything because they'd get in trouble. Was Louis forcing everyone to keep quiet about her?

Ruby didn't like all the uncertainty that this was bringing. While she had blindly trusted Louis before, now she didn't know what to think. The doubt was driving her crazy, but her sense of dread was growing out of control.

"Promise you'll wait for me?" Ruby said to Hayes as they left campus. "In the parking lot."

"Ruby, my parents will kill me!" Hayes hissed at her.

"Aren't your parents never home?"

They were soldiers, who had been deployed to the Carat District last month. Apparently, there was some sort of trouble brewing there. Hayes didn't know much because it was all confidential. Louis didn't like to talk about it, either.

Hayes sighed angrily. "All right. I'll wait for you. But don't leave me hanging—got it?"

Hayes was more nervous than flustered. If his parents found out he was sneaking out of Heart at night, they'd kill him. A pretty boy like Hayes was on a tight leash for a reason. Back in his high school days, Hayes boasted he had dated the entire cheerleading team and had sex with each member, boys included.

Ruby didn't care much for Hayes' past because he was reliable and helpful in the present. He always reminded her when assignments were due and took notes on her behalf in class. Ruby loved history, but sometimes her mind was around *Defenders Unite!* and she'd start doodling. Besides, Hayes was willing to change and do the right thing, and that's how Ruby knew he'd be waiting for her at midnight.

For Ruby, it was her only opportunity to escape. Tyrus and Herman were always on her ass. Why did she get the feeling that Sage was supposed to be a secret?

Ruby had two options: She could keep quiet about her endeavor or press Louis' buttons during dinner tonight to see how much she could get out of him. She would have to tread cautiously because the last thing she needed was even more security. Louis had kept her out of laboratories, but that could quickly change if she showed signs of insubordination.

Ruby looked up at the palace. It was definitely straight out of a fairy tale. Whoever had designed it was truly trying to escape the horrors of everyday life. Heart was one big fantasy unless you were living in it. Then all the politics, people, and problems were very real. And there was plenty of that to go around here, protests and demands for more government support across all four districts. The palace had gone into lockdown a dozen times this year already.

Ruby's suite was all the way at the top. She lived by herself, but came out to dine with Louis in his private quarters every night. They used that time to catch up with one another and tell stories of their day. Ruby talked the most because she had learned so much history the past year. She noticed that Louis would just sit and stare at her with a dreamy gaze, as if he was listening to her every word but thinking of something else at the same time. Ruby didn't find it creepy at all. She only wished she could read what was going through Louis' head in those moments.

Everything about her past, perhaps?

Ruby picked a modest dress with sandals like she always did. Servants braided her hair, but nothing too fancy. Ruby lived at the palace, but she was no royal. Even Louis didn't dress like a king would.

He was in a simple shirt, a white button-up, and slacks. Servants were moving like ants all around him, setting up the massive dining table adjacent to his bedroom. There were chairs there for all his council members, but on nights like these, it was only him and Ruby.

"Ruby!" Louis grinned and waved like a school boy. He was 148 years old. His features had matured slowly over his long life as an Enhanced, so now he looked like a middle-aged man. There were a few grays here and there, but nothing to slow him down physically. He still trained with Ruby once in a while, and when the public allowed it, they played fastball. Not that Louis needed to be fit—that's why he had Herman and Tyrus with him at all times. The Diamond City military was pretty significant, too, although most of their troops were from Emerald City. Ruby had never met any of them personally. She saw them train from afar, from her balcony, but that was it.

Ruby bowed her head. "Greetings, Louis."

"How are you doing?"

"Fine. Last week of finals, so I'm pretty relieved."

"And you're well on your way to becoming an expert historian?"

Ironically enough. Ruby knew everyone else's history but her own. She supposed there was nothing wrong with admitting that out loud.

Louis sighed. "Indeed. Just give it time, Ruby, and you might start to remember."

"Am I an Enhanced?" Ruby asked him.

Louis stared at her. Ruby clenched her fists and braced herself. She couldn't believe she had blurted out that question. It suggested she was questioning her physique and wanting to know the truth—damn it, why had she opened her big mouth?

"I met some new friends today," Ruby added quickly. "And they were all shocked that I could bench 405. Is that ... normal for a nineteen-year-old?"

"It's not." Louis chuckled cordially. He sounded a bit relieved, actually. "You are definitely strong, Ruby, and you do have Lolligo blood within you."

Oh.

Oh.

But wait.

Ruby had Lolligo blood in her? So she was an Enhanced?

Ruby shook her head. "And you didn't bother to tell me this?"

"I didn't think it made a difference," Louis said honestly. "And I didn't want you worried or bogged down by the fact. I want you to live a normal life. But now that you've asked—well—I thought you should know."

Something was definitely wrong. Louis looked nervous as hell now, as if someone had flipped a switch: his face got all white and he started blinking faster than usual. These were not questions or concerns he was comfortable addressing. That's how Ruby was able to conclude that bringing up Sage would be a horrible idea. Instead, she checked her phone to make sure she and Hayes were still meeting up tonight.

Now she *really* needed to go to the Cut District.

"I understand, Louis." Ruby nodded her head. "Why you wouldn't want me to know what I am. Maybe it would have distressed me further."

Louis exhaled a huge air. He sounded awfully grateful Ruby wasn't demanding more information. "Of course." He cleared his throat and wrapped an arm around her shoulders. "Now come—why don't we eat?"

He sat her down and laid her napkin across her lap. Servants came by with a printed menu. Today was French Onion Soup for starters and filet mignon for the main course. Creme brûlée for dessert was a must.

"So, some guys got jealous, did they?" Louis chortled pleasantly.

"Guys always get jealous when chicks do more than they can," Ruby said absentmindedly. She wasn't going to get any more information out of Louis regarding her past right now. She was going to have to wait until she met Candice and Olivia. They'd be sure to tell her more.

It sounded so ridiculous when Ruby thought about it, though. Here was a long-lost aunt showing up in their lives when Sage had allegedly retired in the Cut District? That's what didn't make any sense...

"...And so it'll be a long night for me. I'm telling you that guy is a nutcase."

Ruby looked up. Louis was cutting his steak with a rather stern frown. "What?"

"The Emerald City Allseer," Louis said bitterly. When he scowled like that, he truly did look like an old man. Even his curls weren't as bouncy as usual. "I don't like him at all."

"Why?" Ruby said. "I know a lot of my classmates are dying to get into colleges in Emerald City. They say the city has tripled in size the past thirty years and wiped out poverty. Damianos Damaris—"

Louis jumped as if someone had shocked him. "Stars, Ruby, I told you not to say his name!"

"Can you help me understand why you don't like him, then? Perhaps you can learn a thing or two from him."

Louis flared his nostrils. "Really, Ruby? This is the guy who's salivating to take over Diamond City."

"Wouldn't he have taken over already, then?" Ruby said, thankful she was wearing sleeves on her forearms. She had a feeling Louis wouldn't have been too happy with her new tattoo. "He controls the military, doesn't he? All the Enhanced he sends our way are from there."

Am I from there?

"I'm scared," Louis admitted. "Very scared. What if he kills me, Ruby?"

"Like I said..." Ruby analyzed every twitch in Louis' body closely. He was definitely in clear distress over his future meeting with Damaris. "If he was truly here to kill you, he would have done so already. Just listen to what he has to say. I mean, he is the one sending us funds, right?"

Louis didn't respond to that, but *yes* was the correct answer here. He went back to cutting up his filet mignon a bit too thoroughly. The knife and fork squealed against the ceramic plate.

Ruby didn't understand it. Here was an Allseer that was more than splendorous with his wealth, and Louis was all hot and bothered by him. If anything, Louis should have been asking for more money. So many of the districts were suffering shortages and unemployment. As a result, prices and taxes were through the roof. The poor Overseers couldn't do much when they weren't receiving any aid from Heart itself. Perhaps it was Louis who needed to interview the Emerald City Allseer.

"Just ask him for help," Ruby said again. "It sounds like he'll give it." She finished her mashed potatoes and sipped on her cherry soda.

"Right," Louis said tightly. "So... any plans for tonight?"

"No," Ruby lied. "Just going to watch *Defenders' Unite!*" She made sure to avoid Tyrus and Herman's eyes. For some reason, she had the feeling they could read her mind. Lolligo were huge and a bit mysterious, so who really knew what their true potential was?

There wasn't anything else worth talking about, so as soon as she finished dessert, Ruby got up and left. She walked to her room as quickly as possible, before she was interrogated about her evening plans further, then closed the door like she always did. The Lolligo stood at attention in the hall, ready to execute whatever commands Louis gave them.

Ruby, on the other hand, changed out of her dress. She pulled on a shirt—loose—some pants—spandex—threw on a jacket, and zipped up her shoes. These were her favorite sneakers, perfect for scaling the roof. That's what she planned to do until it was time to flee to the Cut District with Hayes. The Lolligo never imagined she had such skills, and no sniper ever saw her all the way up here.

Her favorite spire was thirteen hundred feet tall. The highest point in all of Diamond City. Ruby could see so much of it from up here, but what she was especially interested in was the training grounds below. There was a private runway in the back for important people like the Emerald City Allseer. Ruby saw all those ships on the horizon coming in like moving stars across the night sky. She wondered what it was like to ride in one of them.

The ships were all black and sleek, a shiny light metal that allowed them to travel at over five hundred miles per hour. Those things could raid the Outskirts in no time, surely. To this day, Louis told Ruby that no one had truly explored all that the Outskirts had to offer. Emerald City was miles away and their reaches touched on a lot of eastern territory, but not all of it. Not all the way to the Atlantic Ocean, which was the closest massive body of water to their side of the North American continent.

Ruby wouldn't have minded taking a nice trip around the Outskirts. Louis had mentioned some exploration ventures in the future. Maybe after she graduated from Royal Academy, she'd do just that. It'd be so cool to rent one of those skimobiles and just ride over land. No city, no buildings—just land. What sort of wildlife was out there? Ruby had never even owned a dog. When she had asked Louis for one, he told her no. No pets allowed in the palace.

Hayes had a pet, though. An aggressive Doberman, Hamilton, who apparently didn't like people very much. He was always muzzled, especially when there was family over. But, he had seemed to take a liking to Ruby. He actually followed her commands and kneeled every time he saw her. Ruby wasn't sure how, but something as simple as eye contact got Hamilton to stop barking. When Ruby asked why the family kept such an aggressive dog around, Hayes had responded with "for protection."

As Ruby thought of pets and what Louis would say to a hamster, she watched the Emerald City airships touch down. It was hard to see him from so high up, but Ruby spotted the Emerald City All-seer right away.

There was no question *that* was the Allseer. Not because he wore fancy suits with long capes, either—in fact, he was in a simple suit with silver chains—but because his aura commanded attention. His long beautiful hair was swept to the side, some of it braided. His eyes were outlined in kohl, so they stuck out on his face, like a beautiful porcelain doll that no collector could afford to buy. His skin was pale and smooth and spotted with the right amount of glitter, a master at applying makeup.

On either side of the Emerald City Allseer were two young men that looked a lot like him. The resemblance was uncanny, as if they had inherited all of his genetics. One had his hair combed back, showing off his angular features. The other had his hair pushed to the side, long like his father's, with the other half of his head in a buzzcut.

The three of them looked like they belonged on a stage. They certainly commanded attention and anxiety from everyone. Not just Diamond City, either—but from the soldiers who filed out after them. They were Emerald City soldiers, who were ready to fight at a moment's notice. Not like Damaris and his sons needed it—those were three people Ruby wouldn't want to challenge to any sword-play—because they showed the world that their word was law and no one was going to change that.

Maybe that's why Louis was so petrified. Ruby had seen the Emerald City Allseer plenty of times before, had written full reports on his history, accomplishments, and skills, but she never tired of him. He wore a new outfit and hairdo every time he came to visit Diamond City. Ruby was so mesmerized that she wasn't sure she would ever be able to hold a conversation with him. That beautiful face was too extravagant and royal, stealing all her concentration. She'd want to gaze into those intense eyes forever, possibly touch his body and every muscle he had beneath his clothes. Not because there was a sexual attraction, but because Ruby admired beauty, something she wasn't very privy to.

The same went for his sons—they looked like his personal assassins. Ruby saw the way their eyes swiveled this way and that, surveying their surroundings, even if they had been here many times before. They were always assessing who might be a potential threat, especially when their father stepped forward to shake Louis' hand.

Emerald City brandished dark green and silver, a stark contrast to Diamond City's red and gold. Louis was dressed far more royally than he had been during dinner: in that pure white jacket with gold trimmings, he looked like an expensive doll that would break with a single blow—

Ruby froze.

One of Damaris' sons had spotted her.

The one with the half buzz cut.

Holy shit—he was looking right at her! The dark eyes were boring right into hers, taking her in, and searing her into his brain as real and not fake. Neither he nor his twin drank—didn't do drugs—so he wasn't seeing things: There was a woman crouched on the very tip of that tall thirteen-hundred-foot spire, balanced on the balls of her feet as if she were practicing yoga.

Startled, Ruby nearly fell over. Actually, she did topple a bit and she grabbed onto the spire to stop her plunge south. She hit a small railed platform below, took a few steps around to gain her balance, and gazed out at the fields again.

To her horror, the twins were gone. The Emerald City Allseer was looking right at her now, and the way his eyes widened made it hard to determine if he recognized her or if he was shocked there was someone clinging from that spire.

Fuck—fuck! Now Ruby would never be able to use that lookout again!

Now the entire training grounds was in an uproar. People down there were probably thinking assassin. Louis hadn't gotten a good look at her because he was barking orders. Pretty soon, the choppers would be on her ass, if the Emerald City Allseer's sons didn't get to her first.

They were scaling the goddamn palace as if they were acrobats.

Ruby had to admit that was impressive. Even she had never done it from the ground up. Now she was going to have to jump because there was no way she'd be able to climb—they'd catch her first. Louis would know she was escaping her room at night, and she might possibly be thrown in a prison forever.

That couldn't happen—not until she spoke to Candice and Olivia about Sage.

So Ruby jumped. She heard everyone's gasp as she gave a little flip then landed twenty stories below onto the palace roof without shattering a tibia. This was the craziest, fucking thing she had ever done, but she had to run—*now*—and she did it fast.

Perhaps Ruby looked like an acrobat now, too. She was flipping and jumping on anything she could find—mini spires, balconies, tiles, and walls—and scrambling to get away from her pursuers. As the twins caught up to her, they opened fire on her—actual bullets whizzed by her.

Ruby was so thankful for these sneakers—had she worn boots, she would have twisted an ankle. She also would have been shot a few more times. Damn, those kids were good.

Eventually, Ruby finally made it off of the palace. She landed on the street with another crash and a tumble. She had two bullets in her leg and another in her shoulder. She raced for Royal Academy, weaving in and out of streets that she knew so well, and found Hayes waiting for her by the campus parking lot as promised.

Hayes wasn't alone, though. Not only was a muzzled Hamilton looking out the passenger seat window, but Charles and Kendra were in the back, too.

What the hell?

Hayes gasped when he saw Ruby running. "Ruby?"

"Hurry!" Ruby slid into the backseat, pushing Charles and Kendra into the corner. "Floor it, Hayes!"

"W-what—why—?"

"Do it!"

20

Hayes screamed when gunshots rained on them. Hamilton twirled in circles on the seat, clearly wanting to bark. If Ruby didn't do something, they were going to be shot up.

Ruby climbed over to the driver's seat and floored it herself. She had only driven a few times for fun, but she knew her way around the controls pretty well. For example: she hit the ascension button, and they took off into the air. Damaris' twins were quick, but they sure as hell couldn't fly.

"R-Ruby!" Hayes croaked. "You're bleeding . . ."

Right now, Ruby concentrated on getting them the hell out of there. The entire capital was on alert, but no one knew for who or what. That's what allowed Ruby to race out of there without being stopped by officers, soaring over Heart's border like an eagle to escape the chaos.

Ruby looked behind her, searching for any pursuers. To her immense relief, there were none.

"Holy . . . shit . . ." Kendra croaked, looking out the window. Her hair was still perfect, though. "What was that?"

How the hell was Ruby going to admit that she had been spying on Emerald City atop a spire? At the moment, all she could say was, "You were right."

Kendra and Charles both blinked. Hayes was crying. Hamilton just stared with large dark eyes.

"I-I'm an Enhanced," Ruby admitted. "I-I have Lolligo blood. I mean . . . I just jumped thirteen hundred feet and got shot three times."

And I'm still alive.

21

CHAPTER 2

Two for Pizza

Ruby had no idea where she was going now, so Hayes had to put in the coordinates for the restaurant in the GPS. Two for Pizza was somewhere in the Cut District, but Ruby couldn't distinguish the blurs of all the buildings they were zipping around in the sky. Plus, she was dizzy.

Now that adrenaline was dying down, Ruby thought she was going to be sick. She asked Hayes to take over the controls and rolled over to Hamilton's seat. Hamilton whined and pawed her shoulders. Ruby collapsed.

"H-hey . . ." Charles leaned over. "Are you all right?"

No response meant Ruby wasn't doing too well. Hayes finally got them down to street level. It was still a sheer miracle that no one had followed them or that a cop hadn't pulled them over for speeding through air traffic.

"Let's pull over and get her some water," Kendra said from the backseat.

"Or how about a hospital?" Charles croaked. "She's been hit! Look at her shoulder—"

But Charles stopped talking. That's because the bullet that had been lodged in Ruby's body popped out on its own. There wasn't much of a wound left behind, either.

Despite quick regeneration, Ruby still felt fatigued, though. Maybe there was something else in those bullets that she couldn't see. It dragged her down, as if someone had tied ropes around her wrists and ankles and pulled her deep into an ocean. For a few moments, she blacked out.

When she woke up, Hayes was still weaving through the streets of the Cut District. The two in the back were still arguing about taking her to a hospital.

"We can't do that!" Kendra was exclaiming. "Isn't it obvious to all of us now? If Allseer Louis never told Ruby about her origins, it's because he wanted to keep her a *secret*. If we take her to a hospital, we'll be exposing ourselves!"

"But she looks like she's about to die!" Charles exclaimed.

Ruby opened her eyes. When she stirred and Hamilton gave another whine, everyone knew that she was very much alive.

"I think we need to stop at a hotel, then," Kendra said quickly. "She can rest there. Clearly, she's in no life-threatening danger— she doesn't even have a scratch."

Perhaps, but Ruby was still in a daze. Hayes was speeding through the Cut District and all sorts of colors were flying by them. Mostly pinks and purples. Store signs flashed in their faces, but Hayes was going too quickly for Ruby to distinguish what they were. She had definitely never seen "regular" streets before. Everything at Heart was always so measured and careful... Out here, people had more liberty to do what they wanted, interview who they wanted, and wear what they wanted. It would have been nice to sightsee all that the district had to offer, if only Ruby could keep her eyes open.

Eventually, Hayes came to a stop at some low-key motel. Rest Inn was small with only fifty rooms and it was a miracle it hadn't closed yet. Right across the street was the Porcupine Inn, the official hotel of the Cut District's number-one professional fastball team. Ruby really did sit up to see that.

It was beautiful. A tall, sleek building with balconies for every room. A hologram of the entire team shined on its surfaces, capturing the live faces of all ten players. Ruby had heard that it was nearly a thousand Diamonds just to stay there one night.

"Fifty Diamonds, and we all pitch in at the motel," Hayes said, parking the car at last. Ruby still had her head turned, staring at the Porcupines' preferred place to stay with longing. "I'll get us a room. *Two* rooms," he amended.

Hayes got out. He looked left and right a lot of times. He must not have put it past his parents to track his every movement. Who knew what sort of secret bug they had implanted in his body when he wasn't looking.

Hamilton bumped his muzzled nose against Ruby's chest. He whined and wagged his stubby tail.

Ruby felt so bad for the dog. If she were muzzled, she'd die of asphyxiation. It was hard enough to breathe when the thrill and anxiety from that chase had yet to die. She reached up to search for the clasps.

"So." Kendra cleared her throat. It was interview time. "Are you going to explain what happened, Ruby?"

"They saw me at the top of the palace," Ruby replied softly. She couldn't stop thinking of the look on Damaris' face when he had noticed her. A man who never even broke a smile in interviews or lost his composure in the fiercest of duels looked like he had seen a ghost.

"Right," Kendra said. "Because you can *climb* all the way to the top. And that never struck you as odd?"

Ruby shrugged. "No. I'm not really familiar with a human's limitations. I know they don't climb buildings for fun, but I couldn't help it. I'd feel so trapped at night."

"Fair enough. So you were at the top . . . doing what, exactly?"

Watching Emerald City arrive. The Allseer and his sons, so

royal-looking, as astute as hawks. Ruby should have known it would only be a matter of time before they spotted her. She had almost paid the price for it, too. If they had caught her, would they have imprisoned her?

"I can't go back," Ruby said quietly.

"Obviously," Kendra replied. "Not only did they catch you, but isn't it obvious by now? You're *Sage*, Ruby."

Ruby shook her head. That still didn't sound right to her. Sage was over 150 years old—how could Ruby have lived that long and not remember it?

"Something happened," Kendra said. She leaned forward, closer to Ruby, as her large dark eyes widened with a certain realization. "Something—"

"This is dangerous."

Ruby turned her head. It was hard to see Charles because he was directly behind her, but she glimpsed his face.

Charles looked stricken. He was so pale that someone might have died. Sweat trickled down his face even though the AC was blowing right at him. He started a little shake and then let out a little whimper.

"We're in trouble, aren't we?" Charles croaked. "We've helped a prisoner escape!"

"Yes," Kendra said patiently. "And in this case, it's a good thing. Ruby, who is really Sage, *is* a prisoner. Her memories of her past life were wiped. The Allseer was taking advantage of her." She never stopped looking at Ruby. "Did he rape you?"

"Stars, no." Ruby grimaced at the thought of it. "He ... never made any moves. Actually, there was a time he tried to kiss me, but he stopped. I don't think it felt right to kiss an amnesiac."

"That's horrible!" Kendra exclaimed. "I remember when Charles first tried to kiss me—I was uncomfortable, too!"

Charles hit her. "I thought you liked me, you goof!"

"Dude, I still needed way more time to decide that." Kendra shook her head. "But that's not what we're here to talk about—don't you see that we're on a mission?"

"Why are you always living in a goddamn fantasy world?" Charles scolded her. "This isn't a game! We can be arrested and imprisoned for all our lives!"

"We're doing a good deed, Charles." Kendra patted his leg. "We're helping someone reclaim their memories and their life."

Ruby still didn't get it. What on earth had happened to her if that was the case and she had forgotten her past? And if Louis had known all this time . . . then what on earth were his intentions? Why had he kept her a secret? Why had he kept her from her true family?

At last, Ruby got the muzzle off of Hamilton. She glared at him, warning him, and Hamilton didn't even bark once. He just licked his lips and sat down on the floor in between her legs, looking up at her with those shiny black eyes.

"Why did you do that?!" Charles exclaimed when he noticed the dangerous dog was unbound. "Hayes said he was a monster!"

"He's not." Ruby got out of the car because she needed to walk. Hamilton trotted along right behind her, licking her ankles in thanks for freeing him. He had a chain collar, but the leash was still in the car. Not that he needed it—he didn't stray far from her. He just needed the bushes and a little bit of grass to do his thing.

Ruby stood by on the sidewalk, making sure no one intervened. It was pretty desolate here. Judging by how empty the parking lot was, everyone preferred the Porcupine Inn. Perhaps people were pretty wealthy in the Cut District and didn't bother with the lower-end establishments. Or maybe it was just this area in particular that repelled tourists. Ruby didn't see why that would be the case because it surely didn't feel dangerous. The homeless weren't allowed to make camp on the streets and were swept away, out of sight.

Ruby heard a bell, and she turned to the front entrance of the Rest Inn. A couple had just stepped out of the office. They didn't look too happy.

"Where are we supposed to go now, Elias?!" cried the woman. "We don't have enough money for rent! WHAT ARE WE SUPPOSED TO DO?!"

The woman broke down crying. The man, who must have been her husband, tried to soothe her. It seemed they had been scraping the bottom of the barrel when it came to living on their own. With no jobs, they had no money to pay anything.

"Stay, Hamilton," Ruby said to him.

Hamilton was just sniffing around, minding his business.

Shortly after, Hayes returned to the car with room keys.

"We got lucky," he declared, stepping over to Ruby and the other two who finally joined them. "They're willing to lend us a room. The owner was telling me they're about to close this place up—they can't compete with the Porcupine Inn. They feel bad for us, though, so they'll look the other way tonight."

"How sad," Kendra said softly, looking down the street. "What was up with that couple there, though?"

"Looks like the motel was their only safe space," Hayes said, looking after them, too. "Maybe all the other motels are too expensive—"

A gunshot made them all jump. Hamilton started barking like crazy.

A second gunshot.

Ruby could see the bodies from here. The couple was dead, face-down on the pavement. A gun hung loosely in the man's hand.

"Oh, FUCK!" Charles exclaimed, hands on his head. "H-HE JUST SHOT HER! A-AND THEN HIMSELF! Call the police—h-hurry—call the police—!"

The motel owners rushed out to see what was going on.

Hayes backed away slowly, pure terror on his face. He looked to Ruby and then the free Hamilton, but said nothing about his dangerous dog on the loose.

"Get inside the room," he croaked to Ruby. "They can't see you here, Ruby—get inside!"

Ruby took the keys, but she didn't move as quickly as she should have. Fear kept her rooted to the ground as well. Shock, unlike any she had ever felt before, even when the Allseer's sons had spotted her, washed over her like a wave. Tears burned in her eyes, but they didn't fall.

"GO!" Hayes exclaimed.

Ruby backed away slowly. Her breathing was so tight. She wasn't getting enough oxygen into her brain. There had only been two gunshots, but she kept hearing them in her head. There must have been over fifty in there.

How could the man have done that? How could he have killed his wife? And then himself? But why?

Hamilton was jumping all over the place, but he wasn't barking. He was trying to get Ruby's attention, to remind her that she had a motel room to hide in. Room 131 was right down the hall—in front of the pool—but Ruby couldn't see the numbers. Somehow, Hamilton did. He scratched at the door as Ruby collapsed on the welcome mat.

She lost all the strength in her legs. This time, the daze was different from the one she had experienced on the way here. She could see, but she couldn't. The ringing in her ears drove her mad. She clutched her head.

Hamilton licked her hands. He put his paws on her shoulder for support. He stood there and stared at her until she calmed down.

Ruby could see the flashes of red and blue across the pool's surface. The police were just on the other side.

Ruby didn't have the strength to climb onto any rooftops right now. She also couldn't watch because she'd be seen again. The police would ask what on earth she was doing up there. Climbing was taboo.

Ruby didn't want to see anything anyway. She went into the room with a vigilant Hamilton on her tail. She didn't even have any extra clothes to change into. Nevertheless, she showered.

She paid no attention to all the rust in the stall or the cloudiness of the mirror due to poor cleaning sprays. This was night and day compared to what she was used to in the palace.

Suddenly, all of that glamor seemed so . . . minuscule. Frivolous. Gold-plated versus standard countertops. What did it matter when two people were dead?

Nothing but pity stirred deep in Ruby's belly. When she crawled into bed, she didn't cry. She let the tears run silently because she didn't want to startle Hayes, who came in about an hour later to check on her.

"Ruby?" he said carefully, closing the door behind him.

"Are they dead?" Ruby asked, facing the sliding glass doors. There was a nice view of the pool.

"Yeah."

"What were their names?"

"Elias and Johanna Westbrook," Hayes said, taking a seat on the opposite bed. "I overheard the owner tell the officers what happened. They were desperate . . . had nowhere to go . . . and now that the motel is closing, well, they were stuck."

"Why couldn't they find jobs?"

"Ruby, you know better than anyone that it's not that easy. Especially in the Cut District—there are a lot of businesses closing. So many people are leaving because everything has become so damn expensive. Even owning a place here is a lot. I guess Candice and Olivia are the exceptions. Maybe Sage is good luck or something. Sometimes, that's really what it comes down to."

"It shouldn't be like that," Ruby said softly. "Everyone should be given a chance to make it. It shouldn't be based on luck."

"I agree," Hayes said. "But you know that things have been tough in Diamond City."

"How much longer do they have to continue this way?"

Perhaps Ruby sounded like a child asking these questions. To some extent, she was one. She couldn't remember anything past the last year. Maybe she had seen all this growing up into an adult here, had gotten used to the destitution and poverty, but she couldn't feel for something she couldn't remember. She couldn't comfort herself with the excuses of old because she didn't know what those excuses were. She had to learn them all over again, and apparently, "Life is all about ups and downs" was one of them.

Hayes gazed at her earnestly. But he was just a college student, too. Pampered all his life by parents who served in the military and answered to the Allseer.

"Louis didn't want to talk to the Emerald City Allseer," Ruby said softly, still staring at the pool. "I told him to get advice. Maybe Damaris can give him a few pointers. But I sensed an intense hatred within Louis."

Hayes took off his jacket and ruffled up his hair. He did this whenever he had bad energy to expel. Sometimes, it was just to look cool, but that wasn't the case here. He sighed and closed his eyes. "I don't know what to tell you. I know even less than you do about politics and what the dynamics are between those two."

"Maybe I should have stayed to talk to Damaris myself."

"Ruby, it's not in your place—"

"Then in whose place is it?" Ruby snapped. "Louis clearly isn't doing anything about all the problems in the city! If businesses are closing and the districts are suffering, then it's up to the Allseer to fix it! He has enough funds to gold-plate the entire palace, but not enough to help out a stinking motel like this one?"

"Ruby," Hayes said patiently. "Don't you know by now? Allseers are all the same."

"Clearly not. Clearly not if Emerald City is doing well and don't you fucking deny it."

"Fine. Emerald City is doing well. But this isn't Emerald City, Ruby, and you're not the goddamn Allseer. So what can you do?"

Ruby sat up. She was in a tank top and spandex, so her arms were bare. Hayes stared at them in the dimness of the room, the cuts in her shoulders and biceps. Right now, Ruby could care less about aesthetics.

"What can I do?" Ruby said, looking at him at last. "What about the people? Are we all slaves to the Allseer, Hayes? We have to shut up and suck it up because we're measly people?"

31

Hayes was staring at her. It wasn't because she was in skimpier clothes, either—he saw her in tights all the time at the gym. And yet, now, he was looking at her as if he had never seen her before. What was going through his head that he wasn't voicing? Was he finally acknowledging that Kendra wasn't as crazy as she sounded and that there was a possibility that Ruby was Sage?

"Yes," Hayes said at last. He cleared his throat. "We are."

"Then we need to kick Louis off the throne," Ruby said simply. "We need to hire someone who is actually going to do something."

"And how are we going to do that? We're college *kids!*" he emphasized. "We don't even have our education yet, much less a rebel following to oust a worthless Allseer."

Ruby had to think about that. And because she couldn't sleep, she stepped out onto the pool deck and sat in a chair. Hamilton lounged by her feet. One time he even jumped in for a swim. Despite the fact the motel was closing, the pool still looked nice.

"Wow," Kendra said, watching her from the gate. She was in a tank top and underwear, too. She and Charles must have been pretty close if they were that comfortable in the nude. Ruby supposed she was the same way with Hayes—they were always together and never judged each other, either. Although Hayes had been commenting Ruby was becoming a bit too "manly" lately. He didn't like too much muscle on women. Not that Ruby gave a shit. "No sleep, Sage?"

Ruby glared at her. "I'm not Sage."

"Who are we kidding here, Ruby? Of course you are."

"If I am, then I'm truly fucked in the head, aren't I? I can't remember a goddamn thing."

"Shit happens." Kendra shrugged her shoulders. She was drinking coffee from a plastic cup. Had she made that in the bathroom? It looked like diarrhea. "My dad walked out on me and my mom when I was just ten. The cruel thing was that I was old enough to remember him. I didn't want to be a basketball player. I liked math and numbers. I graduated top of my class in the Carat District before getting my acceptance letter into Royal Academy."

Ruby was impressed.

"But I accepted my father leaving," Kendra said. "I'm doing what I love."

Ruby snorted. "And what's that? Running away from the very college that accepted you?"

"Hey, even I believe everything happens for a reason."

Ruby felt for her phone in her pocket. She was surprised that Louis hadn't come after her, but it would only be a matter of time. She asked Kendra for her number then wired her 50,000 Diamonds.

Kendra gasped. "What the—?"

Ruby threw her phone in the pool.

"Ruby, what are you doing?!"

"Can you do me a favor and wire that money to the motel owner?" Ruby asked. "I just don't want any traces of me directly."

"But they're going to know it's *me*!" Kendra said angrily. "Because now the owners know we're together! The four of us are staying in these two rooms!"

"No, they don't," Ruby said. "They never saw you last night, did they? They only saw Hayes, and I don't think he told his parents he was running away with friends."

Kendra sighed angrily. "They're going to put two and two together. My mother is already going crazy, and Charles was supposed to show up at the lingerie shop this morning. He works there," she said quickly when Ruby arched a brow. "They're going to know the three of us ran away, and there's a possibility you joined us."

"*Possibility*," Ruby stressed. "But nothing's for sure. Plus, the owner doesn't really know I'm here, does he? The three of you could be random strangers I met in my escape and that's exactly what you are. That money is from the Allseer, and I think the motel needs it more than I do right now. If they're truly a haven for people like Elias and Johanna, then they need to stay open just a little bit longer."

Kendra gaped at her. Ruby headed toward her room to change. Hamilton trotted up behind her.

It was time to head out to Two for Pizza.

uby, Hayes, and Charles waited for Kendra in the car. Once she came out and nodded at them—she had transferred the money to the poor owners as asked—it was time to go.

"You've got balls," Charles grumbled from the backseat. It was hard to tell which one of them he was talking to until he mentioned names. "Truly, Ruby. I mean, you practically gave your life savings away to a total stranger."

"It's not my life savings," Ruby said. "I didn't work for that money. I was just a plaything for Louis to gape at during dinner at night."

"So . . . Sage." Kendra puffed out her chest with pure confidence now. She fixed one of her pigtails as she said, "If it's really you, that means you own the pizzeria. That means you really do have a lot of money."

"Maybe," Ruby said softly. "But I guess . . . it belongs to my . . ." She cleared her throat. It was tough for her to say these women were family when she didn't even know them. Amnesia wasn't their fault, though. "Nieces."

"Oh, boy." Kendra rubbed her hands. "We're onto something, Charles! I think I might change my major to criminal justice or something!"

Charles snorted. "Please. A coincidence doesn't mean you're an excellent investigator, and that's what all this is: a coincidence. You weren't actively looking for Sage—you just happened across someone who looks like her on campus. You and half the student population there."

"But I recognized her from the article," Kendra said proudly. "*And* I was brave enough to approach her. It was my keen eye *and* bravery that got me the privilege of this adventure, Charles. And the funny thing is criminal justice is *your* field."

"Shut up! I totally saw the news article—you were just brave enough to ask. You know I'm terrible around chicks—I'd much rather talk to guys."

"Have you *seen*, Ruby?" Hayes said. "Her biceps are bigger than my thighs."

Charles scowled. "She's a girl, Hayes, regardless of how big her muscles are. Don't be a fucking misogynist."

"I'm not!" Hayes argued. "I just don't associate females with having large muscles, is all."

"Why?" Charles sneered. "Because they have to be all slender and pretty for your dick?"

"I didn't say that Ruby wasn't attractive—because she sure as hell is—I'm just telling you what I prefer. Or can I not do that, either?"

"It's that black-or-white thinking that's dangerous," Charles said. "Maybe you should watch *The Rainbow in Me*."

"I'm not watching that manly-girly shit!"

"Why is it 'girly'? Because it's about love? Fuck you."

"Can you please stop?" Kendra said to Charles.

"Ruby is Ruby regardless of what she looks like," Charles stated, still glaring at Hayes. "That's why we should all accept her as is and move on."

"Now I really want to see this through to the end," Kendra said excitedly. "Because I know that Ruby is more than just Ruby. Maybe even more than just a measly pizzeria owner, too. Because there were rumors in Heart that Sage Arpine was the *Optimum*. I mean, no one really knows that for sure—other than the Allseer, military, and those that know her—but can you imagine?"

Ruby looked over her shoulder at Kendra. She shook her head. "I'd rather not talk about it."

"Why?" Kendra said. "Wouldn't that be cool?"

"The Optimum?" Hayes said, driving them out of that hotel at last. He was still red in the face from his argument with Charles. "I thought that didn't really exist. I thought it was a Claritian thing."

"Ha—no way! I mean, yes, Claritians worship her, but for a reason! Just like they worship the Lolligo. The Optimum supposedly is a hybrid between Lolligo and human. It was her blood, supposedly, that created Enhanced, too."

"Why don't we cool it? I think we've all had a shitty night and we need to take things easy." Hayes offered Ruby a wayward smile.

As if that would repair the damage his hurtful words had caused. Not like Ruby cared.

Ruby said nothing. She was too busy looking out at the passing shops. This was a regular, everyday street, and more than half of these were closed. She read some names like We Know You Want a Puppy!; Swim Time!; Tae Kwon Doe; Lily Flowers; Vendors' Corner; Flip-Flop Flop-Flip; Oh, My Lucky Stars!; Nails For Life; and Vivi's Noodles.

"This looks familiar," Ruby said.

"I'm sure it does!" Kendra said happily. "You probably walked these streets all the time."

And then, at last, there was Two for Pizza. They opened at eight in the morning, so there was already a long line of customers waiting for breakfast cheese and dough. It was impressive. While it looked like a ghost town everywhere else, people seemed to really congregate here.

"Come on!" Kendra was the first one to fly out of the car as soon as Hayes parked on the side.

Ruby stepped out with Hamilton on her heels.

"Ruby!" Hayes whined. "Put the muzzle on him!"

"Hamilton doesn't need it. He knows how to behave and not bite people."

"No, he doesn't! I can get in trouble, damn it!"

Ruby snapped her fingers in Hamilton's face. The dog sat down and followed every movement. There was no way in hell that Ruby was putting that muzzle on any animal's face. All that Hamilton needed was a strict owner and a treat for positive reinforcement. Charles was right—Hayes was a pussy. And a jealous one at that. Little shit couldn't even bench a plate.

"Either way, we can't bring him inside," Hayes said.

"So you'll wait with him out here," Ruby said.

They had a line to make now. It'd be half an hour, more or less, until they reached the restaurant. Ruby took her time looking at the street, at her surroundings, and noticed Kendra watching her very intently.

"Well?" she pressed. "Anything?"

"That's not how amnesia works," Charles grumbled.

"Actually, it is. People who suffer from amnesia tend to forget short-term memories—not long-term. Memories of the past are more likely to be retained."

Right now, Ruby wasn't registering anything. She kept looking at the sign every minute to see if the "Two for Pizza" sparked a memory in her brain, but nothing. Had she designed that logo or hired someone else to do it? The two pizzas, one on top of the other, with the simple font? It looked like something she would do . . .

As she edged closer to the door, Ruby grew more nervous and afraid. She braced for some searing pain to explode in her head. Maybe she'd even pass out. Ruby rubbed her arms.

"I'll wait out here with Hamilton," Hayes said carefully. "Tell me if you meet Candice and Olivia."

Once they were inside, Ruby was too shy to go around asking for the owners. Charles went in her stead because she was too busy taking in the restaurant itself, how small and cozy it was, how some people sat to enjoy themselves while others were simply here for pickup. The right wall was all white and lined with pizza portraits, each with faces and dressed with different toppings. She noticed the pepperoni trail from the door all the way back to the kitchen. The left wall was all red and that one had a title: "How it Started".

The first picture was the one from the news article that Kendra had shown her. It was of Sage and another girl that Ruby had never seen before. The next few pictures showed Sage with other family members through the years, apparently. Eventually, there was one that caught Ruby's attention.

It was Sage, Candice, Olivia, and . . . the Emerald City Allseer? They were all in the same photo.

Kendra stepped over for a closer look. Ruby's eyes scanned each of those faces.

Nothing.

Then she saw another photo with a guy who had a small afro. A few more photos later, Sage was no longer present. Now it was just Olivia, Candice, the guy with the afro, and Damaris with the twins.

Wait . . . did the twins belong to Sage?

"Hey." Charles returned to Ruby's side. "So I spoke to the manager and he said that the owners aren't here. The manager's name is Micah, who is apparently Candice's son."

When Ruby turned, she found a tall young man looking straight at her. He was dark-skinned with large eyes and a buzzcut. It looked like he was trying to grow out his beard, too, but he was still too young for a chin full of hair. Nevertheless, he had sharp features and an intense gaze. This was one guy that didn't play around and knew how to run a shop. Clearly, if the line was moving along and customers were finding seats in an orderly manner.

"Who are you?" Micah asked Ruby.

Ruby took a long time staring. This was a young man she wouldn't possibly remember because he was born long after Sage's "retirement". Ruby's retirement. Whatever it was.

"My name's Ruby," Ruby finally said, moving up in the line. Kendra and Charles kept close to her. "I-I saw your news article the other day. You guys won best pizzeria thirty years in a row. So I wanted to try out the pizza here—"

"Do you know where Sage is?" Kendra asked. The confidence she exuded was incredible, as if she had known Micah for years.

Micah blinked. "Sage? No. I mean, she's not here right now. She's—"

"Retired?" Kendra finished for him. "Do you really expect us to believe that? Because this person right here"—she grabbed Ruby and pushed her to the front, like she would a child she was about to present to the world— "is no one other than her, my friend! This is Sage—"

Ruby shoved Kendra so hard that Kendra toppled to the floor. Everyone turned around to watch.

"I-I'm not Sage," Ruby said quickly, to Micah, whose eyes were getting bigger and bigger by the second. Micah might have never met Sage in person, but he certainly knew what she looked like. In fact, his eyes made a slow and obvious pass to the photographs on the wall.

"I'm not Sage!" Ruby exclaimed.

Perhaps what she wanted to say was, *I don't remember Sage. I don't remember anything, so I can't be that person.* And maybe there was some truth to that, but there was another side to the story, too.

There *were* people who *did* remember her and *did* know her. Clearly.

"Then how the hell do you look just like her?" Micah demanded. "Sage is my mother's idol! My mother worships Sage as the greatest woman who ever walked the planet—I grew up seeing your face all my life!"

"Where is Sage now?" Kendra interjected, clambering back onto her feet. Charles helped steady her. "If you're saying all this, then she's obviously not here with you. Or else, you wouldn't even be contemplating the idea of Ruby"—she waved at Ruby again—"being her, would you?"

If this were any other time, Ruby would have been greatly impressed by Kendra's ability to put two and two together so quickly. Unfortunately, right now, her blood pressure was rising and she was about to explode. A small sheen of sweat formed across her forehead.

"Can you follow me?" Micah glanced at the nearby customers. If he said any more, he'd be giving away family secrets that weren't for public ears. "Let's go to the office."

Kendra and Charles went to follow, but Micah frowned.

"Not you two—her."

"They come with me," Ruby said. "Honestly, if it wasn't for them, I wouldn't even be here. They're very vested in the whole situation. There's the possibility that the Allseer—"

Kendra clamped a hand around her mouth, shushing her. She laughed nervously. "Yeah, sure, Ruby." She cleared her throat and nodded at Micah. "That private room, please?"

The office. It was behind the kitchen with a perfectly thick door for these kinds of intense conversations. As soon as Micah filed them all in there, Ruby spoke at once.

"Where are Candice and Olivia?"

"They're at the capital," Micah replied. Sweat was also trickling down his face. He grew nervous about something or maybe he was starting to realize that Ruby's presence at the restaurant wasn't a coincidence after all. "There was a disturbance there, according to them. Damian had come by to talk to Louis when they spotted someone at the top of the palace. I'm not sure they could affirm who it was, but . . . was it you?"

"You must feel pretty confident that it's me if you're asking," Ruby said quietly.

"This was her office, you know." Micah picked up a frame from the desk. This one had a picture of Sage with the girls. He showed it to her. "And this was her . . . you."

"Fine, but you still haven't answered our question," Kendra said. "Where is Sage now?"

"She's missing!" Micah blurted out. "But—God—don't tell my parents I told you! It's supposed to be top secret because someone took her and we don't know who! We already investigated the palace, but we didn't find any traces of Sage there. Plus, Louis has been sending search groups all over the city. Even Damian sent his sons to scour the city and nothing."

"Dude, she's right here!" Kendra exclaimed, patting Ruby's shoulder. "And she's been living at the palace all this time. Louis must have hidden her in the closet or something or maybe even a secret tunnel that no one knows about." Kendra looked at Ruby. "Care for any confirmation there, *Sage*?"

Ruby rubbed her head. All she could remember at this point was Louis' dazzling smile and the time she spent at the palace, in a room, recovering, having conversations with him and the Lolligo . . . She had never been allowed to train with the military, but she had gone to school and used the gym. Had to be home by eight o'clock, always . . .

"Well?" Kendra pressed.

Ruby took a seat. Charles' phone blew up with a call from Hayes.

"Hey, um, you guys," Hayes said. Ruby could hear his voice, and so could Micah, who looked up. "There's something strange going on out here. There are these old-school vehicles coming down the street, driving around like nothing. They have wheels, so I think they're from the Carat District."

"Is that normal?" Kendra asked Micah.

That's what Charles and Hayes must have been thinking, too. This was an everyday affair, so no need to worry. They didn't panic until people jumped out of those cars with intentions that were far greater than just sight-seeing.

"What the hell?" Micah went out to investigate, but he got an onslaught of customers that flooded into the restaurant for cover. Hayes and Hamilton hadn't wasted any time, either. Gunshots popped from outside, followed by vicious laughter.

"We've got to get the hell out of here!" Charles exclaimed, grabbing Ruby and Kendra by the wrists and hauling them down the hallway. "I didn't realize that Diamond City was this bad—holy shit—is there no peace?"

Ruby dislodged herself because she needed to get to Micah and Hayes. There wasn't anything she could do about the gunshots other than ensure she wasn't in the line of fire. She had to dodge and shove people to grab Micah by the back of the shirt and then pull Hayes to her side. Everyone was going in the same direction, so Ruby and her companions followed the wave until they got to the trash bins outside. People were climbing the fence and jumping over it like their lives depended on it.

"Ruby!" Kendra waved at her from her hiding spot in the corner. "Over here!"

"Are we seriously under attack?" Charles croaked.

It seemed like it. Ruby witnessed another dozen or so of those vehicles pull into the back street. Basically, all these customers had run right into a trap.

"I brought you this," Kendra said to Ruby with stars in her eyes. She revealed a dagger. "Got it from my parents' stash."

"Are you crazy?!" Charles exclaimed at her. "A dagger? Are you fucking kidding me—against guns?"

"Don't you get it by now?" Kendra grinned. Her eyes couldn't sparkle any brighter. "This is Sage, the Optimum. And she's going to save us all."

CHAPTER 3

Escape

Except Ruby didn't remember how to fight. Her training sessions with Herman and Tyrus weren't enough to grant her victory in a situation like this. So many bodies were jumping out of those cars, and Ruby couldn't exactly tell if they were human or not. Probably not.

"Don't you all get it?!" Charles exclaimed from behind Ruby. His face was as red as his hair. "We're all doomed! We don't stand a chance of getting to those vehicles and running away in one!"

And he was right. In the face of these attackers, Ruby froze. She had the gifted dagger in her hand, but she had no idea what she was supposed to do with it. Tears welled in her eyes from fear and uncertainty. She and her friends were about to be captured by these thugs, and there was nothing she could do.

No one knew who these guys were. They didn't even look human. The veins squirming around in their skin said they were some caliber of Enhanced, but who had turned them into one? Even Tyrus and Herman, Lolligo themselves, couldn't turn humans into Enhanced directly. It had to be a hybrid. Ruby knew that now... somehow.

"Ruby!" Kendra exclaimed as the thug-looking crew got closer. "Do something!"

Ruby noticed a gash across one of the attackers' eyes. Every one of them had one. Were they a part of some gang? If so, someone at Heart had allowed them to gain a whole lot of steam. They had weapons that annihilated concrete and human bodies alike. Those guns looked like something the military would use. Ruby got to witness one particular demonstration: One of the Scarfaces seized a woman and blasted her foot clean off her ankle.

The scream was enough to send the rest of the crowd into a frenzy. Ruby grew confused, and so she dropped the dagger. She did nothing as those gangsters stomped over, seized them all—even Hamilton—and pulled them onto the street.

"RUBY!" Kendra exclaimed again. She was the only one who seemed to be calling for her amidst this chaos. Micah still wasn't sure who the hell Ruby was, Charles was screaming, and Hayes was stunned into silence.

An innocent midnight getaway had turned into a nightmare.

Scarfaces cuffed them all like police would criminals. These cuffs were different, though—they had little spikes that cut into skin and drew blood.

Ruby felt each one of those tiny teeth sapping away at her strength like a leech. It left her groggy and dizzy. She staggered on her feet as she was pushed along in the crowd and crammed into these large trucks stationed on every street corner.

There was nothing inside the trucks. The space was enough to accommodate thirty sitting people, and the Scarfaces pushed for forty. Micah, Hayes, Charles, and Kendra huddled close to Ruby. Hamilton was still outside, barking like mad.

"What are you doing?!" cried one of the Scarfaces. "Shoot the damn dog already!"

"No . . ." Hayes croaked from next to Ruby. "H-Hamilton . . ."

"I don't want to be wasteful! We can use him, too."

"Then knock him the fuck out!"

There was a crack and a whimper.

44

Hayes screamed.

The next moment, one of the Scarfaces threw Hamilton into the truck.

His brains were oozing out of his skull. One of his eyes was bleeding. Saliva dribbled from his mouth as his breaths slowed.

"G-God," croaked a woman seated on the other side of the aisle. "Just put him out of his misery!"

Hayes drew Hamilton into his chest. His hands were cuffed, but he did what he could to hold his dog close.

Hamilton's mouth rested on Ruby's wrists. He gave another low whimper.

More tears welled in Ruby's eyes. She stared at the dying Hamilton as he used the last bits of his energy to comfort her. His tongue came out to lick her wounds. So slow and weak . . . His saliva stung against the cuts. Ruby didn't grimace. She just smiled at the poor Hamilton, who was still gazing at her with large eyes. The licking never stopped. Eventually, Hamilton whimpered in pain. He yelped, too.

"Poor thing!" cried the woman. "Someone just kill him already!"

"Shut up!" Hayes exclaimed. "He's not dead yet!"

Clearly. Ruby could hear snapping bones in his body. The poor dog was truly suffering, but she couldn't find it in her to end his life. She sobbed to herself instead.

"I'm sorry," Ruby croaked dismally. "I-I couldn't do anything . . ."

Micah was hyperventilating. Charles had his head in his knees. Kendra was looking over, eyes zoomed in on Hamilton.

"Where are they taking us?" another captive asked.

No one knew. Everyone screamed when Scarfaces shut the door to the truck because it plunged them into complete darkness. Some people got up and banged against the walls. It was futile—there was no way they were going to be able to tip this truck over. And even if they did, they'd have lasers pointed at their faces as soon as they breathed the fresh air.

Hayes cried. Charles screamed louder. Ruby couldn't hear Kendra, but she could feel Hamilton convulsing in her arms. She cried, too, holding him even closer, feeling just a little bit jealous that this would be all over for him soon while she'd still be alive to deal with this hell. As she sat there in the pitch-darkness and her own misery, Ruby wondered if this was how Sage would have reacted. There was no way the esteemed Optimum would have been this much of a coward. Ruby was so afraid, though . . .

Soon after, the truck turned on. Seconds later, they were moving.

"WHERE ARE THEY TAKING US?!" a captive screamed. "Fore-fathers, someone help us!"

"Where is the goddamn military when you need them?!"

Scarfaces were driving. They were going. Somewhere.

The screams from the people were driving Ruby insane. They might have lessened at some point, but not in her head. They got louder in there, throwing her into another daze where she became even more useless.

Hamilton was still in her arms. She could feel him breathing fast. His heartbeat was right against her leg.

Ruby didn't understand it . . . but she believed she was getting it confused with her own. That was her own heartbeat, out of control, muddying up all her thought processes.

There was a bang. Ruby jumped. She looked up and noticed that someone had torn a hole through the ceiling of the truck. Everyone stopped screaming now.

Ruby gazed up at that hole. From down here, she could see the bright blue sky. It was only noon. They must have been driving for a couple of hours already. It was hard to tell if they were still in Diamond City because Ruby couldn't see what was around them. She braced herself for one of the Scarfaces to jump in with them, but there was nobody up there. So what had created the hole?

In the blink of an eye, something tore open another one. Ruby wasn't sure what it was, but it was coming from the inside—not from above. In the light shining into the truck, Ruby saw the confused expressions on everyone's faces. Everyone was looking to and fro for whoever was doing that.

In just seconds, there were five more holes.

At long last, Ruby saw tentacles. They whipped back and forth in the air. Ruby traced them to the source and she looked down at her lap?

Hamilton gave a fierce bark. That's because his next attack was even stronger: Using ten tentacles, he grabbed onto the roof and tore it wide open. All that fast wind blew right in, making people scream and scurry from the hole. That gave Hamilton an opportunity to tear an opening in the wall of the truck, too.

"HA!" Kendra exclaimed from Ruby's right. "I KNEW IT!"

Ruby didn't have a clue what the fuck Kendra knew, but it couldn't have been Hamilton sprouting tentacles from his back like a Lolligo. That was a skill only Tyrus and Herman had. Plus, Hamilton had regenerated?

"H-he's not a dog!" Ruby cried to Hayes, who was too stunned to speak. "What is he, Hayes?!"

Hayes couldn't answer. The next second, the dying Hamilton was on his feet and leaping out of the truck like an acrobat. Once outside, he used those ten tentacles from his back to grab onto the moving vehicle and stop it in its tracks. Ruby heard the Scarfaces cry out from the front. Other trucks swerved around them.

"GO!" one of the captives screamed. "THIS IS OUR CHANCE— GO!"

Their truck was at a complete stop. People flooded out as Scarfaces realized what was going on. When Ruby touched ground, she saw the two Scarfaces at the wheel had been impaled through the forehead. It wasn't enough to kill them, though—Ruby could still hear their vitals. Plus, the trucks coming up behind them stopped and more Scarfaces jumped out with guns.

"GO!" that same captive yelled. "DON'T STOP RUNNING!"

Except they were in the middle of nowhere. There was nothing but flatlands all around them. They were pretty much open targets out here unless Hamilton could become a big enough distraction. For some crazy reason, he could grow tentacles out of his back and use them to swat at their enemies. That didn't make him immune to their lasers, though.

"Kendra!" Charles yelled at his partner, who went racing toward Hamilton. No one knew what the girl was doing until Ruby spotted a few runaway captives with those laser guns in their hands. A group of them had seized the weapons from the Scarfaces thanks to Hamilton and were using them for defense. Kendra was one of the brave ones practicing her aiming.

Ruby hung back with Micah and Hayes. They couldn't do much—since their hands were still tied—other than run. Those valiant souls with guns were doing a pretty good job of holding the Scarfaces back, but it wouldn't be for long. More trucks were arriving—another twenty or so—at *least*—and there were no nearby towns in sight. No signs of help from anyone else out here. The situation looked dim.

"Run!" Kendra and Charles finally caught up to them. Hamilton was hopping in the distance. It looked like one of the Scarfaces had blown off his leg, but that was regenerating, too. Ruby still didn't know what was going on.

"This is crazy!" Charles was shouting with his disheveled hair, but someone had taken care of his binds. Somehow, Kendra had gotten the keys from one of the defeated Scarfaces. "This is fucking insane! We're open targets out here, and those things—those *Scarfaces*—aren't human!"

People were screaming from afar. The ones who were too slow to keep up. Ruby wasn't sure how much longer she could keep it up, either.

She collapsed on her knees. She hit the ground and curled up on the dirt. She wanted to cry, but hands shot out to pull her back up. There was no way they could stop now.

"Over there!" someone called out from up ahead. "We can hide!"

Amazingly, there was an abandoned town in the distance. Ruby knew that a lot of them had failed to function because of the isolation from Diamond City, while others had picked up because of their close ties to Emerald City. While some were starting to flourish, it was obvious that ones like these didn't stand a chance.

In this town, there was nothing but decrepit buildings. Grass and weeds were up to everyone's knees. Rusted cars had been un-used for a long time. Based on the models, these were over a hun-dred years old.

Just where on earth were they?

No one looked for signs as the small group that had managed to escape capture scattered to find cover. Ruby was still tripping over grass, with Hamilton bumbling up right beside her.

"The electronic building over there," Kendra called, pointing at the All Tech Needs office.

It was over thirty stories tall, most of the windows shattered or moldy. When the group rushed inside and took its first breath, it smelled like old newspapers. The paint was peeling, lobby chairs were on their sides, and the dust was inches thick.

"So sad," Kendra said, panting with that laser gun clutched in her hands. It would have been cool had a gang not used them to kill and arrest a bunch of innocent people. "Did people just up and leave?"

"What the hell's wrong with you?!"

Everyone looked to Charles, who was hyperventilating. His fists were clenched and he looked ready to strangle someone.

"Seriously!" he spat at Kendra. "How are you taking this so lightly? How are you enjoying yourself as if this was some kind of fucking game?"

Kendra stared. Even her pigtails were still perfect.

"You're having the time of your life, aren't you?" Charles spat. "Prancing around with daggers and guns as if this was a real life video game! You really need to open your eyes and realize that our little midnight rendezvous at the capital has become *hell*. We should have *never* left the capital, and now because of your stupid investigation, look at where we are." He waved his hands all around him. "This empty town with no food. How are we supposed to eat? How are we supposed to survive?"

Maybe there was a vending machine nearby. Ruby saw one in the corner of her eye, but all the glass was punched out. Someone had had the same idea before evacuating and calling it quits in this town. In the other corner, she saw a flag perched on the wall. The colors were red and blue with a circle in the middle.

Techfeld.

"Looks like we'll have to figure that out," Kendra said quietly, her lips in a slight pout. "But arguing about it right now isn't going to do us any good. We have to find higher ground because we're still not safe here—"

"I'm done."

Charles turned around. His head high and shoulders back, he marched right out of the lobby with conviction. He wasn't going to bother giving an explanation as to why he was leaving, either.

"Where are you going?" Hayes croaked.

"To hang around anyone but you. My best friend is a nutcase, you look like you're lost, that fucking dog of yours is a monster, Micah is an unfortunate soul who might never make it back home, and Ruby is a coward. Sage, or whatever the hell her name is, can't do shit."

"Hey!" Kendra yelled. "She's not a coward! She just doesn't remember!"

Charles wasn't hearing any of it, though. He pushed through the glass doors and didn't look back once. Whose group he was going to join now, no one knew.

"Hate to admit it, but he's right." Hayes couldn't stand anymore. He had to take a seat on the floor in order to talk. This was going to sap the last of his energy. "About everything. What are we supposed to do now?"

"We have to get back home," Kendra said.

"Kendra, we don't even know where we are! We were driving around for miles! We could be somewhere far south and off the map!"

"I know we passed Mousafeld," Micah said. He was clenching and unclenching his fists at his sides. "I saw the Ferris wheel."

"What's Mousafeld?"

"It's another town. I know because my parents talked about it all the time. They said that's where the Warlord and all the Diamond City exiles had set up camp about sixty years ago. Since then, it's grown pretty powerful. Diamond City has restored trade with them..."

"So it's a friendly camp?" Hayes raised his head with hope. He didn't look anywhere near as miserable now. "So if we get there, we'll be all right?"

"*If* we get there." Micah kept shooting Ruby these sideways glances, as if hoping she'd jump in and confirm their doubts. "I'm pretty sure those Scarfaces are out there patrolling for us. It won't be long before they check here."

"Where do you think they were taking us?"

"They were from the Carat District. I know there were some serious gang situations there."

"My parents were deployed there," Kendra said. "And I don't mean to cut this conversation short, but maybe we should find a place that's not the lobby of a huge building to rest in."

They could also search for food on the way to the top floors. Ruby let the more energetic Kendra handle that. Hayes didn't look like he could enjoy any food at the moment, even if he was starving. In fact, he rushed to a bathroom to throw up. Hamilton was sniffing up and down the hallway, poking into cubicles. If he wasn't barking, then there was no danger around.

No, this place was completely empty. Even so, it didn't look like people had left here in a hurry or under any kind of emergency. There were no personal belongings and no damage that wasn't due to environmental elements. Kendra did manage to find a vending machine with age-old snacks that Ruby had never heard of.

Cheesy Twists and Mr. Chocolate Twists didn't sound very appetizing.

Ruby withdrew into one of the offices on the thirtieth floor. She was all the way at the top of the building now. All-carpet meant the dust in here was unbearable. She could see clouds of it with every step she took. She settled in a spot next to the corner window, just to look out at the street below.

There was a closed-down tea shop and a hamburger joint right across the block. Farther down was an oriental marketplace that still had its banner swaying in the wind. All the tents had been packed up and stored somewhere, never to be used again.

Where had people gone, Ruby wondered . . . Had they all moved to Diamond City? Had the Allseer accepted them? Or had they taken refuge with the Warlord in his camp?

Damianos Damaris. Ruby knew all about the man who had been arrested for treason against Allseer Kilstrong then exiled for his crimes. Actually, he had run away. He had gathered followers in Mousafeld and eventually created enough of a force to confront the Allseer and kill him. He had kidnapped Louis and his late sister, Agathe, as a result. The Diamond City council had taken over instead, but they hadn't lasted very long in power. The infamous Warlord had returned and put Louis back on the throne. Eventually, he had abandoned his nickname and created a new image for himself as Allseer of Emerald City.

Damianos . . . that was his picture on the wall in Two for Pizza. He, apparently, had been close to Sage.

Ruby didn't remember him at all.

More tears ran down her cheeks.

Sensing her distress, Hamilton bumbled into the room. He sat right in front of her, beneath the glow of the setting sun.

Ruby marveled at what she saw: no wounds. No brains hanging out. Hamilton was whole and healthy, as if he had just left his house. The two dark eyes pierced hers with confidence. His sleek, powerful body was braced for any future battles. His little stubby tail moved back and forth on the carpet.

"Don't you have any questions?" Ruby asked him softly. She wiped her eyes. "How can you be so relaxed about everything? Y-you're not even a . . . um . . . dog anymore."

How? How on earth had that happened? Hayes would have definitely told Ruby about his dog being able to grow tentacles and give kidnappers a run for their money. He would have done more than just muzzle Hamilton in public, too.

Hamilton blinked his large eyes. He lowered his head and sniffed her wrists.

Ruby's wounds had just finished healing, although she had the scars from those bands all over her skin. She wasn't too sure what Hamilton was trying to tell her.

Or maybe she just didn't want to acknowledge that it was her blood that had done that to him. He had been licking her wrists. *She* had changed him into a monster.

It was too much for her, and Ruby didn't have a lot of energy left, so she fell asleep.

R uby had a strange dream, but she chalked it up to her hectic day. Of course it made sense that she'd dream about working at Two for Pizza. She had Candice and Olivia at her side. Damaris' twins—whose names she didn't even know—where there as well, helping.

"Darling?"

Ruby heard someone calling her from the front of the restaurant. She couldn't see the face, though.

"Darling, are you here?"

When Ruby opened her eyes, she had her head against the window pane. She was in the same curled-up position from last night with Hamilton by her side. Hayes was here, too, fast asleep. He must have made his way to her at some point after accommodating Kendra and Micah.

Ruby rubbed her face. Her entire body was sore. Her jacket was raggedy and bloody, and there were holes in the spandex of her pants. She must have gotten these yesterday at some point. There was one awfully close to her crotch.

Ruby looked out the window. She could see the sun rising from the horizon. It must have been early morning. Ruby hated dawn. She much preferred dusk. She had taken plenty of pictures of the sun setting from the top of the palace. In darkness, she felt free. It looked like her secret place was no more.

"What the hell? You actually *decapitated* them?"

"I was tired of their fucking bickering. Did you see the shit they pulled on us yesterday?"

Ruby's eyes widened. She knew she wasn't seeing wrong. There were three guys down on the street—Scarfaces—and they were standing in front of a pile of bodies. Another Scarface was bringing in another body from an adjacent building. Ruby knew exactly who that was. She wouldn't mistake that red head anywhere.

"Let me go!" Charles cried out. "You fucking monsters—all of you!"

The Scarfaces didn't need lasers to deal with these pesky humans. They had powerful swords, ones that sliced through necks easily. All they had to do was throw Charles to the ground, hold him in place, and let gravity do most of the work.

Shleck.

"Stars!" Ruby croaked, covering her mouth. She stared at the still twitching head on the sidewalk. The lifeless eyes seemed to bore right into her own from so far below.

"H-Hayes!" Ruby called to her partner, trying not to panic, but her heart rate was shooting up and she was starting to shake like crazy. Hamilton was already awake and he started barking immediately.

Hayes jumped. He hit the desk behind him then looked around, startled, before his frightened eyes landed on Ruby's face.

"Shh!" Ruby put a finger to her lips. Hamilton had stopped barking. He ran out to alert Kendra and Micah in the room across from theirs. "T-they're out there! I-it's not safe!"

Ruby grabbed Hayes's hand and pulled him away from the window. She wasn't sure if it was in her head or not, but she thought she heard voices and creaks from the lobby below. What if there was another group of Scarfaces in here searching for more survivors?

By the time Ruby and Hayes made it into the hall, Micah and Kendra were already there. Micah looked like he had been asleep—there was a dark spot on his forehead—but Kendra was fully alert, clothes and hair intact as if kidnappers hadn't been chasing her all day yesterday.

"What's going on?"

"You didn't see them?" Ruby croaked.

"No! See what?"

"Those guys are here! A-and they've killed a bunch of people!" Ruby was going to break down crying again. She just couldn't get the picture of Charles' head out of her mind—his frozen expression, his still face, when just last night, it had been twisted with frustrated fury.

"Don't panic," Kendra said. "That's rule number one. We have two options: we can either hide here or make a run for it—"

"Run?!" Micah said angrily. "Are you kidding me? If they're here by the hundreds, what chance do we stand of outrunning them?"

"They came in from the east," Kendra replied calmly. "Clearly, because I didn't see them from the west. And believe me—I was patrolling the whole night. If they had come from the west, I would have seen something."

Micah ran back to his room to confirm that. Ruby followed. When she pressed her face to the glass, she didn't see any Scarfaces prowling this side of the building.

"I-I don't understand," Hayes stammered, with his hair all greasy and matted, evidence of the particularly hellish experience he had undergone. There were a few tears in his jacket, too. Ruby wondered if those were from Hamilton. "What do they want? Where were they taking us?"

"We don't want to find out," Kendra said. "But we do have the option of making a run for it. How far away is Mousafeld?"

"It must be over fifty miles!" Micah exclaimed. Panic was starting to rise. Despite how close he was to Candice and Olivia, he obviously had never fought for his life before. "We're not going to make it there! Plus, we're all human! Who's an Enhanced other than"—his eyes found Ruby—"her?"

"Then we have no choice," Kendra said. "We hide and pray to the Lolligo that they don't search the closet. Which is it going to be?"

"Why are you asking *me*?"

"Who else am I supposed to ask? If we're going to decide, let's decide now, as a group."

"Are they in the building?" Hayes asked.

"They might be," Kendra said. "But who knows—"

"Can I have your gun?" Ruby asked Kendra. "I'll go check it out. We can't risk going down there together if they really are in the building. If they're not, then maybe we can hide if we just hold out for a few more hours."

"Ruby, no!" Hayes rasped. "You can't go alone!"

"I can survive, you can't." Ruby looked to Kendra. "Please let me have the gun."

Ruby sounded so confident, but she was about to pee her pants. Her hands were shaking, too.

"All right," Kendra said. She stepped forward to show Ruby the gun. "The safety's off once you pull back this notch. Then all you have to do is squeeze the trigger. There's a scope here, too. If you look through it, you can pick up infrared light. In other words, you can detect bodies and movement a lot easier since this traces heat."

Ruby's stomach dropped. "They can do the same to us?"

"If they have these weapons, yes."

"Don't fight them," Hayes said to Ruby. "Please. If there are too many, pull back."

"Oh, and here." Kendra had the dagger.

How on earth had she recovered that?

"I got it when you dropped it earlier," she said matter-of-factly. "It's yours, Ruby—*Sage*. The Optimum could do anything with a dagger alone. Isn't that right, Micah?"

Micah just stared.

"I don't want the dagger," Ruby said patiently. "Can you please hold onto it until we're in the clear?"

"We don't stand a chance," Kendra said. "Not against those lasers. Plus, you have ultra healing. You can get up and close with lesser risk. Please just take it."

"This belonged to your parents—"

"*Take* it."

Ruby pocketed it. She clutched the laser gun. She looked at Hamilton.

"Please stay here with them," she said quietly. "If anything happens, please defend them with your life."

"We're stuck on the thirtieth floor," Micah said. "Where are we supposed to go if someone finds us?"

"The emergency exit," Kendra said simply. "We can find our way out of the building."

They seemed to have it figured out, so Ruby took her leave. Hayes started crying. Ruby did, too, but she didn't let anyone see her. She had no idea how to fire a gun. She had no idea how to defend herself in the face of so many enemies. One-on-one, she had plenty of experience. She had sparred with Louis and even Tyrus and Herman so many times. Against a dozen or so of those Scarfaces? She didn't even know where to start.

Ruby's thoughts were vicious. They didn't let up as she took the stairs to the first floor. They didn't allow her to see or hear anyone that might have been close by. She was an open target and so very vulnerable to attack. What if one of the Scarfaces was waiting for her right outside the staircase door?

There was a small little window to peer through. Ruby pressed her face to it and scanned as much of the lobby as she could.

Her breath hitched.

Five intruders. Ruby glimpsed them on the other side of the lobby. And if she held her breath and really strained her ears, she could hear them talking . . . sort of.

"Are we really supposed to search *all* of these buildings?" someone was asking. Probably a Scarface. "This is going to take us weeks. There are thirty floors in this building alone. Plus, how do we know the missing sacrifices didn't take refuge in another town?"

"We don't," replied another. "We're just doing a quick sweep of the premises. I don't see anyone camped out on this floor, do you?"

"What if they're on the top floor?"

"Let's check there next."

"What if they're on the twentieth floor?"

A sigh.

"Do you get it?" said the first Scarface. "This is going to take forever. I say we let them rot here. There's nothing around for miles, anyway. We, on the other hand, don't have a whole lot of time to waste. Don't you want to see the birth?"

Birth . . . what birth?

"Look, we caught like ten of them this morning," reasoned another one of the Scarfaces. "And I really doubt that they spread out that much. Desperate people stay in groups, right?"

"Sounds to me like you lazy bums just don't want to do a thorough search."

A *boom!* made Ruby jump. She quickly realized that one of the Scarfaces was firing their gun at the ceiling. The lasers were powerful, but they couldn't penetrate all the way to the top floor. This was just for show, and maybe to scare any victims out of hiding. There was a pause that followed the blasts, and Ruby made sure to keep absolutely still.

"Don't hear anything," the Scarface who fired said. "So what do you boys say we get out of here?"

There was another pause. They must have been listening for movement. Micah, Hayes, and Kendra were too far up to be heard. It was Ruby who really had to hold her breath. She dropped to the floor, which was a terrible tactic if those Scarfaces decided to take the stairs all of a sudden, but she couldn't hold herself up anymore. She listened to them leave as more tears ran down her cheeks.

Charles.

Ruby didn't move for hours. Even when the Scarfaces were long gone and the sun was coming down to signal yet another done day, Ruby held her position. She had the gun in her hands and the dagger in her belt. She had weapons, but didn't know how to use them.

Eventually, Ruby got up. The three upstairs never came down to look for her because they were probably waiting for her signal. Right now, Ruby had to make sure no one was lurking outside the building. With a deep breath, she exited the staircase.

She crossed the lobby, looking at the mess of debris and drywall those Scarfaces had left behind. She got a closer look at all the plaques All Tech Needs had awarded their employees in the past.

The years were from before Diamond City's unification, and the people in those photographs were probably dead. One face in particular caught her attention, though. It was of a woman with dark hair and a cutting expression. It was no wonder she had won Employee of the Year ten times in a row.

Margaret Atwater.

Ruby was pretty sure she had never heard of that name in her life. Nevertheless, the face surely seemed familiar.

To think that nearly a hundred years later this building would be a refuge for a group of college kids. Or that some powerful gang would be bursting through those front doors employees had used so many times in the past. It was a bit sad, actually. Ruby wondered what sort of history this town carried, and if there was any way to bring it back to life ...

Ruby stepped outside. To her surprise, Micah, Hayes, and Kendra were already waiting for her there.

"How did you get here?" Ruby said to them at once, running up to their circle. "You said you'd wait upstairs!"

"Well, we did," Micah said, arms crossed. "And when we didn't hear back from you, we decided to use the emergency exit to take a look around ourselves."

"We swear that someone had captured you," Hayes said worriedly. "Since you never came back."

"I was waiting to make sure they had left for good," Ruby mumbled. She was annoyed, but at least they were well.

"Seems like they have." Kendra ambled down the street. "I'm just a little worried ... where are the other runaways?"

Ruby hesitated. She didn't know how to tell them that Charles ... was no longer in one piece. He was dead, a sacrifice for some sort of "birth." Hayes sensed that there was something wrong, but didn't ask.

"Where's Hamilton?" Ruby asked quietly.

"He's sniffing around," Micah replied. "Checking to make sure that the coast is clear."

"Well, isn't this what we wanted?" Hayes waved his arms at the emptiness around them. "Everyone left! Gang included. So we can go, too . . . right?"

Micah shook his head. "Mousafeld is too far. Even if we can make it there by foot, what are the chances we won't be seen? We're sitting ducks out there."

"Aren't we sitting ducks out here, too?"

Techfeld was a large town. Actually, it was more like a city. Downtown was a world all on its own. There was plenty of exploring to do and there was a chance they could survive based on the scraps they found. Maybe some restaurants had left behind non-perishables . . .

"That still doesn't solve our long-term problem, though," Hayes said with a scowl. "We have to go somewhere, do something. I mean, we can't be here forever! No one knows we're here . . . W-we all have lives!"

Micah glared at him. "You think? God knows what's happening in Diamond City! Maybe it's a total shit-show there, too. Right now, all we can do is survive. Maybe we'll find a working vehicle or something we can use to get us out of here."

Kendra nodded. "Then we should start looking, shouldn't we?"

CHAPTER 4

Techfeld

Techfeld was one of the first civilizations built after worldwide Nuclear Devastation. A lot of the towns and villages of the Outskirts were from that pivotal time humans had resurfaced to see the damages left behind by war. Issues between Russia and the United States had been brewing for many years, until a territory dispute in a European nation had pivoted them against each other. This time, with more than just words and threats.

In 2272 AD, the world had changed forever. People had crawled into their underground bunkers to wait for the fighting to stop and the radiation to subside. It had taken hundreds of years, and by then, war had leveled entire cities and rendered large portions of the world uninhabitable.

Ruby had studied all of that history in school. So many survivors had written of their times stuck underground and just how much of a hell it had been. Domestic abuse, drug experimentation, and full-blown homicides had wiped whole families out. Sometimes, the worst of humanity persevered. But in others, the best survived and gave their children a future.

Ruby came across one such bunker in downtown Techfeld. It was an underground laboratory, actually, hidden away in one of the office buildings. If Ruby hadn't taken the time to look through all the journals and manuals that had been left behind, she would have never noticed the trapdoor behind one of the desks. Just when she thought she'd be running into people down there, she found nothing but empty rooms and debris. There were beds, closets, dressers, and a kitchen area. This was just like the pictures in all her primary sources. It was so musty from the lack of ventilation. Ruby couldn't linger long without starting up a cough.

"At least we know we have somewhere to go," Hayes said from above, holding out his hand to Ruby. "You know ... in case those thugs come for us again."

"Not sure I'd want to stay down there." Ruby reached Hayes's side on ground level. They were in a room stacked with crates. From the mess inside this building, no one had been intending on using that bunker in a long time. It was hard to believe that people had actually lived down there for hundreds of years. Radiation levels wouldn't have been safe aboveground.

"Me, neither," Hayes said softly. He gazed at Ruby with uncertainty. Perhaps he was wondering what life would have been like in that time. Royal Academy didn't sound so bad now. Then again, they were no longer on campus, either. They were fighting for their lives just like these people in the past had. He crossed his arms and sighed, portraying his obvious worry.

Ruby certainly couldn't blame him. She could almost read each of the thoughts going through his head: survival, death, and torture. She, he, Kendra, and Micah were all in the same boat, struggling to get through day after day in this abandoned town. So far, they had been here for three months. Ruby always counted the dawns and dusks, so that's how she knew. No signal meant no communication. They didn't have their phones, anyway.

But Hayes's worry extended beyond their own safety. Like Ruby, he had seen what the Scarfaces had done to the others. After three months of rummaging through these ruins, they had run into no other survivors. That meant everyone who had fled from the truck had either been caught, killed, or was still in hiding somewhere. Kendra was determined to find stragglers, but Hayes had witnessed the truth.

One he had yet to tell Kendra and Micah.

"We have to tell her that Charles is dead, Ruby," Hayes croaked. He was visibly shaking. The sun was about to set, but this room didn't have any windows so it was always dark and damp. It certainly didn't help their spirits. It pulled Hayes down to the ground and he cried.

Ruby picked him up by the collar and dragged him out of the building. Now that they were in the Month of Innocence and fall was coming, the weather was a bit on the cooler side. That and the hardness in Ruby's gaze helped to calm Hayes.

"I think Kendra already knows," Ruby said. "Or if she doesn't, it's because she hasn't seen evidence."

"But *we* saw it, Ruby. We should say something."

This was a debate they had often. Ruby was tired of engaging with it, so she took the initiative to do what she should have done long ago—she just hadn't wanted to burst Kendra's spirits.

Kendra was so proactive in securing the town and making sure it was safe. Learning her best friend was dead could very well be a catalyst to emotional distress, but Hayes was right—it was better just to say something—

"Ruby, wait!" Hayes grabbed her arm. He was hyperventilating. "M-maybe we shouldn't!"

"Are we going to or not?" Ruby snapped. "Please make up your mind."

"Y-you're right." Hayes wiped his eyes. "What if it breaks her?"

"Isn't it better that she knows the truth?"

"Yes, but, I think they were a couple or something."

"They sounded more like friends to me," Ruby said. Either way, Hayes was absolutely right. If Ruby lost her best friend, she'd be devastated, but she'd want to know the truth.

"Let's just do it," Ruby said. "It would be the right thing to do."

She started her trek down the street. Hayes hesitated greatly. Eventually, and not wanting to be left alone in an empty, creaky shopping center, he caught up.

"At least it is cooler." Hayes rubbed his arms. The summer in Techfeld had been brutal. He was still peeling in some places from bad sunburn.

As for Ruby, she wore tank tops no matter how cold it got. With all the walking and exercise they had been getting these past months, it was the most comfortable piece of clothing she owned. Once in a while, she did come across some tank tops in closed-down shops from the clearance rack customers of old hadn't bothered to inspect.

"Aren't you scared?" Hayes asked Ruby. "I mean, how can you be so serious? So stoic? Especially at a time like this . . ." He sighed. "Aren't you worried about what will happen when we return home? Nothing's going to be the same. We still don't know if Diamond City is in one piece or not."

No, they didn't. At the same time, Ruby felt confident that Diamond City was fine. The Emerald City Allseer had come to visit and surely he wouldn't have let those goons take over. Three months later, Ruby was expecting airships to find them at any moment. Candice and Olivia had to know that Micah was missing and that the Scarfaces had kidnapped a lot of people from the Cut District. So if Damaris hadn't sent anyone to look for them . . . then what did that mean?

A few blocks from the Bunker Building was the Crystal Light Complex. It was full of apartments for Techfeld's workers from many years ago. Most units were empty, so Ruby, Micah, Kendra, and Hayes had moved right in. They had all agreed to return by sundown, so there was a possibility that Micah and Kendra were already here—

There was a shrill yell. It pierced the silence, swallowed the wind, and shook the grounds. The yell sounded like someone was dying. Hamilton's barks soon followed from afar.

Ruby and Hayes glanced at each other before taking off. They rounded a few more blocks before they found Hamilton jumping up and down, unsure if he should fetch Ruby or rush back inside the laboratory and rescue the in-trouble couple.

But the couple didn't need rescuing—they both emerged in one piece. Their legs shot out this way and that as they scrambled out of there. They were both holding their noses, and then Micah threw up on the grass.

"What the hell's going on?!" Hayes yelled.

"D-don't go in there!" Kendra halted him. "T-there's some pretty fucked-up things in there! It *reeks!*"

Dead bodies? Seemingly. Ruby didn't care for Kendra's orders because Kendra wasn't her boss. Ruby ran right past her, drew the dagger just in case, held her breath, and barged into one of the most unsightly scenes she had ever seen in her life.

Those couldn't be bodies. Those looked like mounds of . . . goop. Fleshy, bloody goop that was still sizzling in what appeared to be heaping amounts of radioactive slime. Ruby felt it burn her eyes and then her nostrils, even though she was holding her breath. The room was fuzzy, as if the air was thick and warped. Ruby left immediately, blinking the dizziness out of her eyes and growing fearful at the vomiting Micah on the grass.

Kendra and Hayes were both leaning over him.

"How much of that did you inhale?" Hayes cried at Micah.

Apparently, enough to knock him out. After losing all his liquids, Micah collapsed. Kendra and Hayes had to haul him out of there. Ruby was still staring at the laboratory.

"Science of Tomorrow". That's what the sign on the grass said. It had long since stopped blinking.

As the pictures of what she had just seen settled into her brain, Ruby covered her mouth and squeezed her eyes closed. It was as if she had taken a snapshot of the inside of that building. She could see every detail, every heap scattered around the floor as if someone had been dumping garbage there for years. She could even see the face in the corner, the one sticking out from in between a tangle of arms and legs. All the skin had melted, dangling off the skull of what was once human. But it was obvious to Ruby that that human had been through its fair share of transformations.

Lolligo. Those things were Lolligo.

But how had they gotten there? Or had someone just thrown all the corpses in one spot?

It was Ruby's turn to throw up. She wasn't sure if it was from the radiation poisoning or her nerves. She hugged her knees and shook viciously. She couldn't hear Micah's groans anymore.

Hamilton came trotting up behind her. He didn't sit because he was still far too agitated to get comfortable. He kept sniffing the air, knowing that there was trouble in the distance.

When Ruby composed herself, she stood up. To her horror, she felt someone coming.

Someone was coming.

Indeed, from the north. From Diamond City's direction.

Ruby stumbled back. Hamilton started barking, but realized that would give them away. He whined instead, indicating to Ruby that they had to *go*. That the intruder coming their way was no Scarface.

They were Lolligo. And they were no Tyrus or Herman, either.

Ruby ran. Hamilton followed. Eventually, they reached the trio still limping toward the Crystal Light Complex.

"G-go!" Ruby croaked at them. "Hide! We're not here alone!"

Perhaps it didn't make sense to Kendra, who had spent every waking moment securing Techfeld, but Ruby knew, without a doubt, that these Lolligo were headed right for them. In a do-or-die situation, Kendra didn't ask too many questions, thankfully, and neither did Hayes.

Ruby grabbed Micah, threw his vomiting form over her shoulder, and took the lead in the race to their complex. It was small enough to camouflage between the rest of the buildings on this street, and was Ruby ever glad for the shelter it provided.

"Scarfaces!" Hayes croaked as they burst into the lobby. "Did they find us?"

Ruby gave Micah back over to them. Kendra gazed at her earnestly, clutching the laser gun to her chest. That wasn't going to do much against any enemy that found them.

"Get back to the rooms," Ruby said. "I'll be on the roof."

She went for the stairs. It was fifty floors high, but her legs were equipped enough to make it there in just ten minutes. Ruby hadn't slacked in her training at all these past three months. She had recruited the others to join her, too. They had found enough food and non-perishables to fuel their workouts. Clearly, there was so much more to discover and so much more that could potentially find them, too—good and bad. Ruby wished she could say that the intruders happening upon their town were rescuers, even if it was Louis sending Herman and Tyrus after them, but it didn't seem like it. Lolligo weren't known to be very friendly. Even Herman and Tyrus had a hard time saying "Good morning" to her during breakfast.

When Ruby made it to the top of the Crystal Light Complex, she took cover behind the rail. She peered out, ready to dodge if one of those Lolligo noticed her and shot at her.

As she had suspected, she saw two airships hovering by the Science of Tomorrow building. They had come in from the north, which meant they had come from Diamond City . . . or at the very least passed it on their way here. Or maybe those particular airships were native to this area and were performing their usual rounds of the perimeter.

The longer Ruby watched them, the less likely that seemed. These ships were coming in fast. Their design was also nothing like what Ruby was used to in Diamond City. These were equipped for war, loaded with guns and other unseen weapons. They touched down in the distance with a light rumble. A lengthy moment later, Ruby heard voices.

"Is there anybody here?"

They were talking in Lolligo. Thank the Forefathers she had practiced this language with Tyrus and Herman on a daily basis, so she understood every word.

"No way," responded another. "No human has set foot in this place in years—clearly."

If those were Lolligo wandering through the streets, then what chance did Ruby and the others stand against them? They'd be over-run in minutes.

Even so, it didn't seem like the Lolligo were here for a takeover. They didn't have any foot soldiers to clear the city, and the Lolligo who had left the ship didn't stray far.

Ruby decided to investigate further.

"Hey!" Kendra joined her up on the roof. Hayes must have stayed with Micah. "Everything all right? What's going on?"

Ruby held out a hand. "I think I'm going to need that gun. Just in case."

Kendra blinked.

"You stay here and keep looking out. If anything goes wrong, you grab the others and run the other way. Got it?"

Kendra usually complied with whatever Ruby said, so she gave over the gun without question. She watched her jump off the side of the building like Ruby would a bed. Ruby landed on a balcony halfway down then jumped the rest of the way to the street.

Gun in hands, Ruby started toward Science of Tomorrow again. She had Hamilton at her side instantly. She wasn't planning on en-gaging any Lolligo, but she had a feeling she wouldn't be able to avoid a confrontation. At some point, she had to communicate that this was her territory.

Ruby had no experience fighting enemy Lolligo. She had battled Tyrus and Herman only in a scrimmage match, and the only rea-son she had walked away with all her fingers and toes was because Louis would be watching them like a hawk. He didn't allow the Lol-ligo to harm her in any way, even if Ruby did have lightning-fast regeneration. He didn't like her doing anything crazy or strenuous, and if keeping her hidden and locked up was the reason why, it made sense. Now, it was a sore disadvantage.

Ruby headed east, circling around Science of Tomorrow. She wasn't sure what kind of strategy she was employing here, but a head-on attack was dumb. She wanted to be subtle and calm because something told her these Lolligo weren't here to eat humans.

They appeared to be more fearful than predatory. They only covered a few blocks before they stopped their search all together. They were panting and making strange hissing noises. They sounded like a defeated fastball team after losing in the first round of the finals. Ruby couldn't get a good look at them, but she sensed three Lolligo in the group.

"This is it?" one of them croaked. "This is where we're supposed to stop?"

"I told you, Xeno: We need to go to Diamond City! We have to ask the humans to help us, particularly those hybrids! If the rumors are true, they can do *anything.*"

Xeno grumbled. His accent was thick, making his Lolligo nearly impossible to understand. "I refuse to ask humans for help."

"But they're not humans, Xeno. They're hybrids—*part* Lolligo. And they can intuit the battlefield so much better than we can."

"You don't get it, do you, Jamie?! They *live* with humans, so that's what they are!"

"Then you're no better than the Isolationists!" snapped the Lolligo named Jamie. "That's the fucking point!"

"For Prime's sake, forget politics! Can you please explain to me how a little human is going to topple Rhett? Who, by the way, is a total fucking hypocrite when he says he wants to stay away from humans but then creates an entire army of them!"

Ruby shrank to her haunches. She leaned against a wall as she listened to the two Lolligo argue with each other. The third one was strangely quiet.

"DON'T LOOK AT ME LIKE THAT!" Xeno barked at Jamie. "The Prime is just a damn name—not a god! That's the problem—we've given way too much clout to some stupid position, and it's clearly gotten to Rhett's head."

Ruby knew that the term "Prime" was reserved for the top Lolligo in their civilization. It was the equivalent of the humans' Allseer, according to Louis, who had never spoken much on the subject but had admitted to this:

Samson, the previous Prime, had been dethroned. Was possibly dead. That had been the reason for the Lolligo attack on Diamond City thirty years ago. Emerald City had fought them off, but would they be able to do it again? Apparently, the "Isolationists", or the Lolligo that were reluctant for any human contact, were employing the use of some human hybrids themselves. Also, based on what Ruby had just heard, these Lolligo were extremely reluctant to ask any other city for help. Was it pride? Or was it fear? Emerald City had probably made their terms clear: No Lolligo or else.

Ruby gazed at Hamilton, who gazed right back at her. He didn't seem to have any opinion on the matter. His ears twitched every time Xeno raised his voice.

"I CAN'T BELIEVE THIS IS HAPPENING!" Xeno roared in the empty city.

Stupid or smart? Ruby wasn't sure, but instinct told her this was the best time to make an appearance. She got up and turned the corner before doubt could stop her. Now she was in full view of the three Lolligo standing in the middle of the street, right in front of an old tanning booth.

As soon as the three Lolligo saw her, they stopped their shouting and whipped up their guns. They were steady and braced for attack. Xeno would have pulled the trigger had it not been for Jamie who waved him down.

"Don't shoot," Jamie said to Xeno. "Look, she's friendly."

"Friendly?" Xeno snarled. "Give me a break! Didn't we think there were no more humans here?"

Ruby put her hands up. Her Lolligo was decent enough to communicate that she wasn't here to fight them.

The three Lolligo gaped at her. Even the third one, who didn't speak and hardly reacted, looked shocked. Ironically, he was much taller than Xeno and Jamie—he looked like the tank of the group. One arm was as big as Ruby's body.

"My name is Ruby," Ruby said steadily, in Lolligo. "And I'm a hybrid."

She had no idea if that was true or not, but there was a chance it was. She went with it, since that seemed to be what these Lolligo were looking for. It really made them stiffen, as if she had declared herself a rabid animal instead.

That's when she noticed the egg strapped around Tank-Lolligo's chest. She knew that Lolligo were asexual and reproduced once every hundred years. She had no idea whose egg that was, though, since Lolligo died after coughing it up.

The Lolligo were here for refuge, clearly, but a helping hand in their feud against the Prime was a plus. Tank-Lolligo looked like he was about to cry, more out of relief than fear at this point.

"Y-you're a hybrid?" Jamie said carefully. The amber eyes scanned her from head to toe. "And you can speak Lolligo? Who taught you?"

"Tyrus and Herman," Ruby replied smoothly. "They're the Lolligo who work for Diamond City."

The three Lolligo glanced at each other. Ruby could tell that the names were familiar to them.

"Stolen by that pretty-boy Allseer!" Xeno croaked to his team. "Remember? Those were the two we sent out to spy on the Optimum when she was in Winterfeld!"

"They're our friends," Jamie said to Ruby, making the other two hiss.

"Don't tell her that!" Xeno barked. "We don't know if we can trust her!"

"I need your help," Ruby said.

That cut any of their arguing immediately. They whipped back around to her.

"Diamond City was attacked a few months ago," Ruby said in Lolligo. She had to speak slowly and articulate the words she was comfortable with. "My friends and I were visiting the Cut District when these strangers came out of nowhere. They attacked us, tied us up, and took us away. The only reason we escaped was thanks to Hamilton." She waved at Hamilton, who was sitting in the middle of the street as if he were watching a soap opera. "He drank my blood and transformed into some mutant."

The Lolligo eyed Hamilton closely, as if assessing whether or not he'd be an ally, too. If humans could employ canines on their police forces, then why couldn't Lolligo?

"My blood can do that to other living things." Now Ruby sounded like Kendra. "Because I'm a hybrid. But I'm the only person in this town. We're so lucky the attackers left when they couldn't find us. Still, we're stuck here. Can you please help?"

The Lolligo glanced at each other again.

"I know that the Lolligo went through a civil war," Ruby went on. "And I know you guys are hurting. But if you help me, I'll help you."

"You can't even help yourself," Xeno said with a sneer. "What can you possibly do for us?"

"My name is Ruby, but I'm really Sage," she said confidently. "I have ties with the Diamond City Allseer, and my husband..."

There was no denying those photographs at Two for Pizza. It was more than obvious that Sage and Damian were a couple, possibly married. Ruby took it and ran with it.

"My husband is the Emerald City Allseer," she finished. "And he can help you."

"If he can help you," Xeno said with that same sneer, "then why isn't he here helping you now?"

Ruby fought the stinging in her eyes. Truthfully, she had no idea what was going on in Diamond City. What had become of that attack by those Scarfaces? If they had overrun the entire city, then going back there now was suicide.

"A lot of humans were taken by the Scarfaces," Ruby said quietly. "The Scarfaces seem to have something out here of worth. I don't know what it is. But I'm hoping that if I can defeat their base, then maybe Diamond City has a chance of bouncing back." She cleared her throat. She clutched her gun tighter.

"Did you see anything suspicious on the way here?" Ruby asked them.

Jamie finally lowered his gun. He studied her some more before shaking his head. "No. We landed here because it was the most secluded town of all. No humans. These 'attackers'—do you know where they went?"

Xeno turned to gape at him. "Are you seriously considering helping her?"

"She offered to help us, so why not? We have nothing to lose by joining forces with a hybrid. In fact, I think we're pretty damn lucky."

Xeno scoffed. "Give me a break! She's just a human—"

"I know Sage," spoke Tank-Lolligo at last. He was half-turned from Ruby, just in case she got any ideas to attack the egg around his chest. But the more he looked at her, the more comfortable he seemed to become. "Sage was Samson's roommate. He told us about her, remember? She's the Optimum."

"Wait." Jamie whipped back around to Ruby. His eyes were glistening like a pair of jewels, interest fully piqued. "*You're* the Optimum?"

Ruby's lip trembled. She dropped the gun from her hand. She couldn't believe she was breaking down in front of Lolligo, but all this talk of Sage was tearing her apart.

"Y-yes," Ruby said. "That's me." She wiped her eyes quickly.

The Lolligo were staring at her. They were wondering, perhaps, if humans malfunctioned on a frequent basis. Unfortunately, they did, because Ruby felt so very broken right now.

Ruby couldn't remember *anything*. She had no idea who Samson was. She had no idea what sort of relations Sage had had with him, the Lolligo, or even her own husband. It was scary to think there were so many years of her life that had vanished into thin air, almost as if they no longer existed. In Ruby's world, anyway.

"Show us then," Xeno challenged.

Ruby's eyes widened. She took a step back. Hamilton got up.

"Show us that you're the Optimum." Xeno stepped forward. "I'm going to attack you and you're going to throw me on my ass."

"Xeno," Jamie said worriedly. "Please don't."

Hamilton started barking. He attacked, but Xeno blasted him and took care of him quickly. A hot, steaming pile of guts and blood, Hamilton twitched on the street.

Ruby could hardly believe what she was seeing, but she shouldn't have been so distracted. Xeno smashed her over the head with his gun and then pinned her to the floor. That was all he had to do to prove his superiority. Ruby could have gone for Kendra's dagger, but she was too slow and Xeno blasted her hand off.

Ruby cried out. She curled up on the street. Her state was nowhere near as bad as Hamilton's, but it felt so much worse.

Xeno spit on the ground next to her. "Pathetic. You're no 'Optimum'."

"Xeno!" Jamie ran over. He shoved Xeno out of the way and crouched over Ruby. Fear twisted his features, but Xeno didn't let him mourn long.

"Let her go," Xeno said. "She's a nobody."

"N-no way—look! She's regenerating."

Maybe so, but Ruby still felt like a nobody. She laid there, feeling empty and defeated because she truly didn't know anything. How could she be a person without her memories?

"SHE'S WORTHLESS!" Xeno exclaimed to Jamie. "YOU FUCKING IDIOT! We should just put her out of her misery!"

Jamie pointed his gun at him. "Stand the hell down," he said calmly, slits-for-nostrils flared like a snake's. "We're doing no such thing. You don't have to be an ass to everyone you meet." He turned back to Ruby, who started shivering.

She wasn't sure what happened next, but she blacked out. It was as if her mind did it on purpose to shield her from the world that was being so cruel. It was a defense mechanism to ensure her emotional health recuperated as well as her body. It certainly helped.

The next time Ruby woke up, it was dark. To her shock, Jamie was sitting next to her on the street. He had his legs crossed like a big kid listening to their teacher read from a book during story time. He had his head lowered, too, chin to chest. Perhaps he was meditating.

Ruby sat up. She noticed Hamilton lying next to her; his ears shot up when he noticed she was awake.

"I didn't want to move you." Jamie opened his eyes, too. "Just in case it disrupted your regeneration."

Ruby rubbed her face. She didn't realize she was using her rejuvenated hand until she noticed her glove was missing.

Then she gasped. She remembered *everything*—she remembered Xeno! Shit! Where was he?

Jamie held up a hand. "Sorry about that. He's an asshole."

"Asshole" in Lolligo was *Kilesee*, apparently. Ruby knew that now. It didn't soften the blow to her self-worth, though, because everything that horrible Lolligo had said was right.

Ruby was worthless.

Ruby hid her head in her knees. She didn't have the strength to ask where the Lolligo had gone. Had they returned to the ship? Or had they killed her friends?

"You said there were others with you," Jamie said softly. "We should look for them."

Ruby didn't say anything.

"Look, I know humans are sentimental and I'm sorry if we insulted you. Xeno is very upset, which makes him really mean to others. There's no excuse for his behavior, but he's an asshole by nature." Jamie stood up. He got a bit closer to Ruby. Surprisingly, Hamilton didn't bark this time. Either he had learned his lesson or he had grown close to Jamie in the time Ruby had been napping.

"Why did you stay with me?" Ruby asked quietly.

"I wasn't about to leave you here all by yourself and vulnerable," Jamie replied. "While I admit you and your friends have done a pretty good job of securing this old raggedy place, who knows what can walk through these streets at night." He offered a small smile.

Ruby had never seen a Lolligo smile before. Tyrus and Herman were always so serious. Lolligo didn't have a lot of lips, so Ruby saw all of Jamie's teeth. They were sharp like a shark's but long like a wolf's.

"If you stayed with me, does that mean you're interested in helping me?" Ruby sighed. "But what help can I possibly offer you?"

Jamie offered his hand. "Best not to talk about it out here. Follow me."

Not to his ship—he must have figured it'd make her feel too uncomfortable—so he reeled her back into a coffee shop. He must have been staring at it the whole time he had been meditating. Unfortunately, all the coffee machines had rusted out by now. The best Ruby could do was one-hundred-year-old nuts. She was used to eating age-old food by now.

"Would you like some?" Ruby turned to offer some to Jamie, who was fiddling around with some contraption in his hand.

It was a small metallic sphere. When he pressed the button in the middle, it configured itself into a refrigerator.

Ruby's jaw dropped.

"Lolligo don't mess around when it comes to technology," Jamie admitted. "And we never underestimate humans. You've been to Winterfeld, right? The humans there must be all geniuses if they can create such advanced gadgetry. Last time I checked, they had invisibility shields so any airships flying over their town can't see there's a full-fledged population of people beneath them."

That was the thing—Ruby didn't fucking remember. She just didn't know, and remembering that she didn't know made her upset. Hamilton whined a bit, pressing his nose to her leg. That was to calm her down. Then he turned his attention to Jamie and wagged his stubby tail because he was getting a treat, too. He actually stood on his hind legs in excitement.

"Found your new best friend?" Ruby said to Jamie, wiping her eyes.

"Dogs are very intelligent animals." Jamie took a seat at a booth as he opened the refrigerator. He handed Ruby a carton of orange juice then pulled out a bottled caramel frappuccino alongside a can of whipped cream. One was for him and the other was for Hamilton, who had both front paws on the table. "And this one is especially astute. I know that he drank your Cells, but still."

"What are you looking for?"

Jamie's fingers were kind of big for the bottle, but he got it open like a pro. He shook his head. "Refuge, like you were. We were driven from our home. Exiled."

Osemas. Exiled. Right.

Jamie looked up to make sure she was understanding. Ruby supposed she wasn't doing too badly with the language barrier.

"I'm sorry," Ruby said, sliding into the seat in front of him. She put her orange juice down. "I was honest when I said I wanted to help you. Um . . . can I ask you a personal question?"

"By all means."

"I know that Lolligo are asexual and they reproduce every hundred years. They spit up eggs and such . . ." Ruby cleared her throat. "Tyrus and Herman are my friends, so I know this. But I never asked them if they lost their memories. Do you lose your memories?"

Jamie hesitated. Not because he didn't want to tell her, but maybe he had been through his fair share of trauma when it came to starting a new life cycle. "It depends. Some of us do, completely. To make sure we always know what our mission is, sometimes friends or superiors leave a recording of who, what, when, where, and how. Some of us remember naturally, while others never do recover their memories of their pasts."

Ruby dug her hands into her eyes. It was all she could do to hold back her cries.

"Allow me to guess that you, too, reproduced and haven't recovered your memories?"

"No," Ruby croaked. "Not a one! I don't remember anything or anyone—even how to fight!"

Jamie actually chuckled at that one. "Perhaps I harbor some good news: We don't forget how to fight. Maybe it takes a bit to come up to speed, but fighting is like instinct. By the way, who is 'Damianos Damaris'?"

Ruby looked up. "What?"

"That name on your forearm. I did read it correctly, didn't I? My Lucidum isn't the best, but I am pretty well versed with how the letters sound."

"Jeez." Ruby shook her head. She wasn't sure how to feel about the tattoo she had gotten some months ago. Ironically, it had had nothing to do with love or memories—this was purely out of admiration for a man who had been through it *all*. Exiled, hated, betrayed, glorified, and now loved. All of her classmates were salivating to get into Emerald City. Additionally, he was one of the best warriors on the planet. Ruby had watched him duel Sword Devil, who had been crowned best blade master of all time. Looking back at it now, she wasn't sure what, specifically, had driven her to get his name on her arm, but maybe there was a connection from her past life.

Or maybe there wasn't.

"That's the Emerald City Allseer," Ruby said. "My husband. The one I don't remember."

CHAPTER 5

Compromise

The orange juice from wherever the Lolligo had come from wasn't bad at all. Jamie had some doughnuts in his backpack, too.

A Lolligo that carried around sweets? Ruby was amused.

"Who knows where life will take us," Jamie said, sipping some more of that caramel frappuccino. Hamilton had already devoured an entire can of whipped cream. He would have done the coffee, too, except caffeine was highly toxic to dogs, even ones that were part Lolligo. "And if these are my last days, I want to make sure they count."

"We can make it through," Ruby said optimistically. "I mean, I've managed so far. An amnesiac girl who doesn't remember anything fighting for her life?"

Jamie opened a powdered doughnut. "Just give it time. It seems like you've yet to meet your husband after your awakening. I'm curious: why didn't he have you with him?"

All that Ruby remembered was Louis. And all she knew was his keeping her a secret. The capital had gone into lockdown so many times, but it couldn't have been all because of protests and anti-Louis marches. It made sense now, of course ... but Ruby did wonder about Jamie's question. Why hadn't Damaris—Damianos—Damian?—kept her with him? Unless he couldn't have. Maybe he hadn't had access to her. That was a possibility, too. Ruby hadn't come from an egg—she must have been tied down or in critical condition or . . . something.

"Have you tried drinking his blood?"

Ruby choked on the orange juice. Some of it dribbled from her lips as she pictured herself growing fangs and ripping out Damian's throat.

"What?" she croaked.

Jamie nodded, as if suggesting she should start eating more vegetables. "Sometimes the right Cells can spark our memories. Cells carry more than just strength and physical enhancements." He waved at Hamilton, who was eagerly eyeing that second can of whipped cream in the refrigerator. "You may not be aware of it, but the beast is more fine-tuned to you than you think. To me, as well, since we are 'siblings' now. Related, anyway." Jamie looked up at her. "And your husband is a hybrid, correct? If he has Cells, there is a possibility that he can help you regain your memories."

"This is so weird." Ruby shook her head. "Why?"

"We are mutants, Sage. The blood and Cells of a Lolligo harbor so much potential. With our Cells, we were able to create hybrids, who then created Enhanced. While humans haven't studied this extensively, Enhanced have a more—forgive me—'enhanced' perception of the world and each other. Call it a sixth sense, if you will. Again, it's an area that remains largely unexplored, but definitely one worth noting. That's why hybrids are so dangerous: they are the perfect blend of Lolligo and human—the middleman—and they can create armies that'd be willing to die for them."

Like the Warlord and his rebels? Ruby wanted to say, but she knew that was incorrect. Most of the Warlord's rebels were Enhanced who had worked for the Allseer. Those Enhanced were created using Wren's blood, a hybrid the Allseer had kept in captivity. The Warlord and those Enhanced had shared no blood. That meant the rebels had followed him out of sheer loyalty.

Incredible.

"Is there something wrong with me?" Ruby asked quietly, staring at the empty carton of juice in her hands. The name was in Lolligo. The letters looked like slithery worms. "If I can't remember?"

"You're lucky you woke up at all," Jamie said. "We don't know much about hybrids, but if we share similar life cycles, then I have to say I'm impressed. You didn't become an egg, so you must have gone through some kind of hibernation, possibly. Perhaps you were in a coma?"

Ruby rubbed her temple. Maybe.

"Don't worry about what you can't fix." Jamie deposited the whole doughnut into his mouth like he would a piece of candy. "We'll figure it out eventually. Right now it'd be a good idea to round up those friends of yours. They're probably worried sick about you."

Ruby was surprised they hadn't gone looking for her yet. The sun had just set, and it was pitch-dark out there. Jamie finished his coffee, pressed the button on the refrigerator to compress it back into a sphere, and stood up.

"We're at the Crystal Light complex." Ruby didn't have any qualms saying that. She got friendly, peaceful vibes from this Lolligo. "This way."

Just a few blocks. Sure enough, Kendra and Hayes were standing outside, fighting like hens, debating on whether or not to go looking for Ruby.

"It's dark!" Hayes choked. "And she's supposed to be here by now!"

"We must stick according to the plan," Kendra replied. "Plus, we're weaponless."

"Forget that! Let's go look for her and see if we get some eyes on her—what if those Scarfaces kidnapped her?"

"I doubt Sage would allow herself to be captured."

"How can you be so sure about this? And stop calling her Sage—"

Hayes stopped when Hamilton went bumbling up to him. He whipped around and found Ruby right away. He also spotted the Lolligo that took up most of the sidewalk and gasped.

Kendra dropped to her knees immediately.

"Praise the Forefathers!" she cried with her hands in the air. "It's a Lolligo!" When she realized she was the only one on the floor, she grabbed Hayes and pulled him right down beside her.

"Oh," Jamie chuckled, amused. "I forgot that humans revered us. The Forefathers, anyway. They were brave souls, creating each of the districts in Diamond City. Not many Lolligo are willing to mingle with humans. Well . . . it did get them killed in the end."

"Ruby?" Hayes got to his feet and scrambled over to her. He could care less if there was a seven-foot Lolligo towering over him. He exhaled in relief at the sight of her. "Thank the Stars. We were so worried about you."

"They weren't Scarfaces, as you can see," Ruby said, trying hard to forget her pitiful encounter with Xeno. "This is Jamie. I'm not sure he can speak Lucidum very well, but he's been very kind and helpful."

"I don't speak Lucidum, I'm afraid," Jamie said. "But I do have a translator."

Of course he did. He pulled it out of his pocket and spoke into it. Then he extended it to Hayes.

"*Greetings, human, my name is Jamie,*" it said.

"Oh . . ." Hayes' eyes widened. He looked up at Jamie, who nodded, and then took the translator out of his hands. His own shook as he pressed the button and spoke into it.

"*Hello, Jamie, my name is Hayes,*" said the translator after Hayes finished.

Kendra was on her feet by now. She was trying so hard not to stare, but she couldn't help it. She bowed her head when her eyes had lingered for too long. "Thank you for saving Sage's life."

She had to say it to the translator. Jamie shook his head.

"It's not a problem," Jamie said cordially. "Sage offered to help us in exchange for helping the three of you. I heard that someone attacked Diamond City, and it's the reason you're stranded out here right now?"

"Unfortunately," Kendra said as Hayes snatched the translator from her.

"We need to get back to Diamond City." Hayes fumbled with the buttons, but he got his message across. "Can you transport us there?"

Jamie hesitated. That's because he and Ruby had already agreed on their next course of action.

"We can't go back yet," Ruby said to Hayes. "We don't know what's going on there. I think it'd be better if the Lolligo and I can find the Scarfaces' hideouts."

Hayes gasped. "Are you *kidding* me? Ruby, that's suicide!"

"Actually, it's a good idea," Kendra interjected.

"Why?" Hayes sneered at her. "Because we'd be heroes? That's what you want, isn't it? Oh, how I know you already!"

"This isn't about heroism. Strategically, it's the best move we have. Whatever is happening in Diamond City is because of what those gangsters are doing. Who knows what it is." Kendra looked at Jamie with large eyes. Tears of joy welled up in them. "If we have the Lolligo on our side, then what's to stop us from being successful?"

"How about there are *hundreds* of Scarfaces?"

"Are they Enhanced?" Jamie asked Ruby; he had the translator back in his hands. After Kendra and Hayes, it was a miracle it still worked. "These—er—'Scarfaces'?"

"I don't know," Ruby replied honestly.

"That's fine. I'll go talk to the others and see what they come up with. Why don't you rest—?"

Gunshots made Jamie and Ruby jump. They were too far away to startle Kendra and Hayes, but the two stopped bickering when they sensed something was wrong.

Ruby didn't even glance at Jamie—she took off. There was the possibility of more stragglers trying to escape from the Scarfaces. She thought of the long line of trucks driving out of Diamond City, the people trapped inside, the ones that were probably long dead by now. Ruby hadn't been able to save them, but she could do something about these new ones if she could make it there in time.

Ruby glimpsed something flying over her. She stopped running, startled to see that Jamie was swinging high above the streets with tentacles for lassos.

He settled on a nearby antennae to look at her. "Come on." Without hesitation, he sent one of those spindly limbs after her, caught her, and threw her into the air.

Ruby screamed. She clutched a nearby Techfeld flag flapping from the top of a skyscraper to stop her descent and hung onto it for dear life.

"Jump!" Jamie exclaimed.

Jump—right—Ruby had done it before from the top of the palace—so much higher than here—but her legs stiffened and fear overtook her completely. The worst part? Jamie grabbed her again and threw her another block or two across the town.

"JUMP!" he exclaimed again, as if he were her coach.

Ruby made a much better landing this time, but her legs were still wobbly. She wanted to cry because she wasn't prepared for this, but Jamie didn't care about her feelings. Perhaps swinging around like an ape were basic Lolligo skills, and anyone who dared to call themselves a hybrid could do it.

Damian's sons had done it: They had scaled those palace walls like jumping spiders. Wait—Sage's sons—*her* sons—

"FOCUS!" Jamie boomed, tossing her again.

This time, Ruby flew through the sky like a torpedo. She had another Techfeld flag to latch onto to break the fall, but instead of stopping, she swung. She flipped to cover another block and then she landed on the street.

Ruby's heart didn't stop that vicious pounding for another ten minutes. She bent over to steady her breaths and control the adrenaline soaring through her veins.

When she calmed down somewhat, she was able to lift her head and gaze up at the All Tech Needs building. From here, she could see the expanse of the Outskirts. There wasn't a single trace of civilization in the distance. The only thing that caught her eye was the trio of hover cars that had clearly come from Diamond City.

Three families—maybe four—were driving by. But something was wrong because the cars had stopped and all the men had guns pointed at the menacing Xeno right in their path.

"STOP!" Jamie roared at his violent companion.

Xeno didn't fire when he heard Jamie's voice, but the humans sure as hell got him. Now it was Ruby's turn to quell the hostility on the humans' side. She waved them down as half of them screamed at the monsters duking it out on the ground. Two of the men didn't have any intention of stopping their fire, so Ruby had to shoot their feet with Kendra's laser gun. She nearly hit one of them, too, making him curse. She would have annihilated his toes.

"Stop!" Ruby exclaimed. "Just stop shooting for a second!"

All the humans stared at her. Twelve of them. Aside from the handful of men with guns, there were elderly, women, and children in the group. There were two in white robes in the far back—they must have been from the Clarity District. The entire caravan was surprised Ruby was as human-looking as they were, but it was evident she was far from normal.

Ruby raised her hands. They were shaking like crazy. She heard the shouts between Xeno and Jamie in Lolligo.

"They're just humans!" Jamie was arguing. "For Prime's sake, do you have to attack everything that moves?! Just relax!"

"They're *humans*," Xeno spat. "What the fuck do they know?"

Jamie threw out his hand. It wasn't his fist that landed—it was some sort of energy that knocked Xeno on his ass.

Xeno didn't falter, even in the face of his friend. "Really, Jamie?" he hissed. "You're a human-lover now, eh?"

"Just be quiet!" Jamie didn't turn his back—he didn't dare—he just glanced over his shoulder to make eye contact with Ruby.

"Praise the Forefathers!" said the two preachers in white robes. "*Lolligo!*"

The humans froze. As that word sank into their heads, they lowered their weapons. The women stopped crying. The oldest children were no more than thirteen. Acne was attacking their cheeks.

"Are you all from Diamond City?" Ruby asked. Her voice was croaky like a frog's. She had to clear her throat.

The humans just stared at her some more. All the cars were still on, humming with life. Ruby dared a glance at the horizon, but she was too far from Diamond City to see any of the skyscrapers.

"Yes," answered a brave woman. She was tall, thin, and wearing bulky clothes. Then Ruby realized that this was no woman—this was a man who knew how to manipulate his looks. The perfect eye shadow said he was from the Color District. He had his wife, who was actually dressed as a man, and their children, who were too young to express themselves the way they wanted. Or maybe the couple were master artists who used each other as canvases. "My name is Pedro, and this is my wife, Paige. These are our children. The rest of the folks are also from Diamond City. We ran because there's been an invasion."

Ruby fought to keep it together. Her eyes passed over the rest of the group still holding their breath. The preachers were still on their knees, prostrated in the face of these Lolligo.

"The takeover started months ago," said another one of the humans. This one looked hand-picked from a college campus, possibly from the Cut District because he was dressed so properly and neatly. Tears were running down his face. He held his girlfriend's hand. "We had to hide and survive until we found an opportunity to escape. It was all thanks to Randall."

Randall must have been the guy in police uniform. It was all-white armor that had done its job deflecting the Scarfaces' lasers.

"What's going on?" Ruby croaked. "In Diamond City? I-I don't understand!"

Where was the military? Where was Louis?

Where was *Damian*?

"We don't know," Pedro said steadily. "But something isn't right. Those Scarfaces took over way too easily. They've been fighting all of Diamond City's forces. Emerald City has gotten involved, and it's really thanks to them that we were able to find an opportunity to escape. There's a war going on right now."

"Your turn," Paige said to Ruby. "Who are you?"

While the question was for Ruby, all eyes turned to the Lolligo that were still yelling at each other. No one could understand what they were saying but Ruby.

"Stand down, Xeno!" Jamie exclaimed. "And try to be more understanding! We're all struggling here!"

"My name is Ruby," Ruby said over the noise. "And I was one of the first the Scarfaces targeted. Well, I was at Two for Pizza with my friends."

"The Cut District was hit the hardest," Randall said. He was still staring at the Lolligo. It was hard to believe that the crazy preachers in the back had been right all along. "It was as if those *things* were on a mission. Still are. They seemed to be looking for someone."

At last, Hamilton caught up to Ruby. Everyone looked at him. The college couple gasped, as if they were delighted to see a friendly face, even if Hamilton looked ready to devour him. It was strange, but Ruby thought she could read each of their minds: *If there's a dog, then this has to be a safe place!*

"So you're here with others, too?" Randall pressed. He relaxed his stance a bit, but didn't let his guard down all together—not with the Lolligo still yelling. "And . . . um . . . Lolligo?"

"Yes," Ruby said steadily. She fought to keep her composure as her brain processed the situation. "We've been stranded here for three months. We've managed to secure the town . . . for now."

Which was a miracle. The Lolligo looked far more menacing than any Scarface.

"S-so we can stay here?" the college couple asked tentatively.

"Of course," Ruby said.

"How do we know we can trust you?" the elderly woman asked. She had plenty of experience in life, so she knew not to give in to friendly faces so easily.

"You don't have to. You can get back in your cars and move on. My—er—friends will move out of the way shortly."

Jamie pushed Xeno further into the ground. He looked like a parent discipling their kid, shoving him across the field to make way for the crowd. With Xeno still fuming in the dirt, Jamie turned to the humans and said with his handy-dandy translator, "We are sorry for the embarrassing display, humans. None of you are hurt, are you?"

It certainly didn't appear that way, but the old man next to the elderly woman collapsed. Everyone around them gasped.

"Travis!" cried the old woman, falling to her knees next to her husband.

"Move, move!" Jamie cried, rushing over to them.

No one had to understand him in order to do as he said—his presence made them scatter like ants. The two preachers started a vicious chanting that no one could understand in the rush and confusion of the next few moments.

Ruby watched as Jamie flipped the old man onto his back, took out a syringe from one of the many pockets in his coat, and stuck him with it.

"Ruby," Jamie said hastily, checking the old man's reflexes now with a little light. It was possible he could hear every one of the old man's organs just by proximity. "Can you please get all these people settled?"

That wasn't going to happen any time soon. Watching a Lolligo work as an EMT was like watching a shark nurse a human back to health. The preachers' chanting was loud but completely unheard.

"TRAVIS!" wailed the old woman.

Jamie fumbled for his translator. He said, "Elderly one, if you don't settle down, you'll also suffer a heart attack. Your partner will be fine."

"Oh, great!" Xeno spat from far away. "So now we're adopting a human?"

Jamie picked up the old man like he would a big doll and threw him over his shoulder. Then he walked away. He didn't look anyone in the face and didn't shoo the old woman, either. While she had to follow for the sake of ensuring her husband's safety, the others looked uncertain. One of the college kids peed his pants.

"Can everyone come with me?" Ruby said.

"And how do we know we can trust you?" one of the men with the guns spoke up at last. This one was bald with hard eyebrows. After Ruby had nearly fried his toes with her laser, he had no qualms about aiming his weapon at her in self defense. "We're supposed to trust you and a couple of monsters?"

"Praise the Forefathers!" the two preachers on the ground said. "He knows not what he speaks!"

"Like I said," Ruby went on calmly, "you don't have to trust me. But I am offering you a safe place for the night."

No one was going to argue with that. Ruby and Hamilton were much more attractive than the Scarfaces. In one smooth motion, the refugees got back in their cars and followed her through the city.

Ruby walked with Hamilton as the three cars drifted behind them. No one sped off. Everyone was busy looking at the buildings, at what they'd be calling home. There wasn't much to brag about, but at least it was safe.

Hayes and Kendra were still waiting for Ruby outside of Crystal Light. They were shocked to see working cars pulling up on the street.

"What the hell?" Hayes breathed. "Are all these people from Diamond City?"

Introductions were next, and Kendra took the lead. Ruby didn't have any leisure time when she was eager to get back to the Lolligo's ships. Those were still parked behind Science of Tomorrow.

"Is Micah doing all right?" Ruby asked Kendra as she downed a bottle of water. Stars, she was thirsty.

"He's a little sick," Kendra admitted. "But I think he'll be fine."

Ruby would have to ask the Lolligo about the horror she had found in that laboratory. Her mind was going at a hundred miles per hour right now, so she couldn't focus on that for too long. Priorities, such as Travis' condition, replaced any other concern trying to tear its way to the forefront of her mind.

Ruby announced she'd be back. She made to take off when Hayes grabbed her arm.

"Wait!" he called. "Where are you going now, damn it?"

"To see the Lolligo," Ruby replied. "Please stay here."

"Why do I always have to fucking stay here?"

Ruby shrugged her shoulders. "Then don't stay—follow—but don't hold me back."

Ruby wasn't in the mood to play babysitter, so she left the angry Hayes in the dust. She ran and Hamilton followed. She couldn't jump like Jamie could, but she did utilize her speed to cross the twelve blocks she needed to reach the docked airships at last.

Two of them. One must have belonged to Jamie and that Tank-Lolligo while the other belonged to Xeno. It was a sheer miracle that Xeno was still lingering around here despite how much he obviously hated humans. Perhaps he put his loyalty to his companions before his distaste for the enemy.

Ruby and Hamilton started for the ship called *"Luse"*, or "Light" in Lolligo. She suspected that was Jamie's and she was right: he came down the ramp to greet them and wave them inside. He hadn't taken off his coat or gotten comfortable so he must have been working nonstop for the past hour.

"Is Travis alive?" Ruby asked fearfully, reaching him.

"Yes," Jamie said happily. "He will be fine. I performed an angioplasty and he should be up to speed in no time."

"You're a doctor?"

"No way. These are basic life skills. It's important to know how our bodies function so we can repair them at a moment's notice."

That's because all these Lolligo had the technology. The inside of Jamie's ship looked like a science lab from Royal Academy, equipped with fume hoods, medicine cabinets, and body scanners. Ruby tried not to show any fear, but she grew terrified all of a sudden.

Travis was lying on a table, a pillow under his head and medicine in his vein, with his wife sitting right by his side. Jasmine was her name. She stood up to thank Ruby.

"Don't thank me, ma'am," Ruby said, glancing at Jamie, who was reading through a human anatomy textbook like a novel. "I'm no doctor."

"Of course I have you to thank," the old lady croaked. "If it weren't for you, my husband would be dead! Poor old Travis has been suffering from heart disease, you see."

"More specifically, coronary artery disease," Jamie said, still reading through the pages. All he needed were some glasses to complete the scholarly look because those eyes didn't need the aid of any magnification devices. Ruby had heard a rumor that Lolligo could see in the dark, but she had never confirmed that for herself. "But that is an easy fix once we get rid of all the plaque narrowing the arteries. Apparently, it's a disease humans die from in great numbers every year. However, there are procedures out there to cure it." Jamie looked to Jasmine, as if wondering why her husband had never looked into getting one.

"He was afraid of the risks," Jasmine explained nervously. "A-and the procedure was too expensive—our health insurance didn't cover all of it. We would have had to take out a reverse mortgage on the house, but then what would become of our children? We're going to die anyway . . ."

"What about becoming an Enhanced?"

Jasmine snorted. She dabbed at her eyes with a handkerchief. "That's only for military folk. While some people have gone in for some 'enhancements' to their overall builds, who can afford that? Much less a full-body transformation? Only the wealthy."

"So you cured his heart disease?" Ruby asked Jamie.

"Not yet," Jamie said. "But I most certainly will."

Jasmine started crying.

Jamie dropped the book. "Are you all right? Goodness, what's the matter—?"

"It's fine," said Ruby, who explained that they were tears of joy. Or so she had thought.

"This is all fucked up!" Jasmine declared. "So fucked up! I love Diamond City with all my heart! I remember the stories passed down from my grandparents on how Diamond City used to be before there was a fucking Allseer! Right before those bastards let power get to their heads, there was peace and unity between the districts! For the most part, it was each district for themselves, but the Allseer grew more and more powerful and started acting more and more like a tyrant!"

"Marchello," Ruby said.

Jasmine nodded, wiping her eyes. "That's how it all started. The first fifty years were great, but then there were rumors of corruption. We started hearing about the so-called 'Warlord's Rebellion'. We were all fooled, made to believe that the Warlord was evil, when it was *Marchello* who was evil!"

Jamie arched a brow. " 'Warlord'?"

"Damaris—the Emerald City Allseer!"

Jamie glanced at Ruby, who said nothing.

"I don't understand why Damaris didn't take the throne," Jasmine mumbled dismally. She was quivering on her stool now. "Instead, we let another Kilstrong take power. The sad part is there is nothing we can do about it."

"So you think it's Kilstrong that's the problem?" Jamie asked curiously.

"Clearly, sir. Ever since we established an Allseer—a tyrant—things have gone to shit! It's like dealing with a parasite over our heads. The sad part is it doesn't have to be this way because Damaris makes it work in Emerald City. Clearly. Things are so much more affordable over there."

"So why didn't you move?"

"What for?" Jasmine said. "We're old and withered, at the end of our rope. We didn't want to go through the trouble . . . but if I had a chance, I would. I can't live like this, with all this stress!"

"Where are your children?"

"We don't know." Jasmine's eyes welled with more tears. "We don't know if they made it out . . ."

"I'm sorry," Ruby said quietly.

Jasmine peered at Ruby closely. The room grew uncomfortably silent. Ruby didn't like how she was being scrutinized.

"Why do you look familiar?" Jasmine said, brows drawn. "What did you say your name was again?"

"Ruby!" Hayes was calling her from outside. Ruby really didn't want to deal with him right now.

"Have I seen you somewhere before?" Jasmine pressed.

"Maybe you know my face from Two for Pizza?" Ruby offered meekly.

"Really?"

"Um, yes. Some people know me as Sage."

"STOP, STOP!" Hayes yelled from outside. "I'm here for Ruby—I'm a friendly!"

"FUCK ME!" shouted Xeno. "You've got another human out here, Jamie! Are you hosting a party now or something?"

Jamie sighed. He rubbed his temples for some short-lived relief. "Please excuse me." He turned and left before Xeno blasted Hayes' head from his shoulders.

"Wait," Jasmine said to Ruby, "you're Sage Arpine from Two for Pizza? Oh, no wonder you look so familiar! I was a regular there, remember?"

Ruby sucked in a breath. She clenched her fists. "No," she said. "I don't."

"I bought pizzas there all the time. We had a conversation about *Defenders Unite!* once. I think it was your favorite TV show, even though it had been banned by the Allseer. Did you hear? It's making a comeback now! All new Defenders and all." Jasmine smiled. "My children were into collecting all the toys, so my grandchildren are getting into it, too." She looked concerned. "Why do you cry, darling?"

Darling ... darling ...

Ruby held her head. "I-I don't remember anything. I have amnesia ..."

"Oh ..." Jasmine's expression fell. "I'm sorry to hear that. My aunt had anterograde amnesia, which means she had trouble retaining new information. We went through quite a bit with her. While her amnesia got progressively worse, as it had to do with age and disease, maybe yours has a fix. Did you suffer any kind of trauma? Perhaps it takes a while for the brain to heal."

"What's your name, darling?"

Red and gold. A lot of red and gold. Ruby remembered a throne room of sorts—at least she thought she did. Or was that her just thinking about the Diamond City flag?

"Don't strain yourself," Jasmine said cautiously.

"Sage?"

Ruby turned her head when she heard someone calling her. She noticed there was another Lolligo standing in the room now. He had come in through the side door, probably after hearing her voice. Clearly, he seemed to know her, even if Ruby had no idea who this Lolligo was.

This Lolligo was nowhere near as big as the other three. He looked like an adolescent Lolligo, maybe in his thirties, since he hardly reached six feet. He was still muscular, though, with amber eyes and sharp teeth. He looked like a humanoid squid, no less intimidating, but more sentimental than usual.

Ruby had hardly seen a Lolligo smile, but she had never in a million years seen one cry. She hadn't known they were capable of it. Tyrus and Herman had never shown any emotion. Clearly, Jamie and the others didn't understand it very well, either. But this Lolligo, for some reason, actually cried. Actual tears welled in his eyes.

"Sage?" he croaked.

Sage . . . Sage . . .

The voice was familiar. Ruby thought it was familiar . . .

"Don't you remember me?" the Lolligo croaked. "It's me—Samson."

Ruby stared. She knew that Samson was the Prime who had lost the civil war against the Isolationists, and was—allegedly—Sage's roommate, but nothing more. Not even what his favorite cereal was.

94

Samson rushed to the counter. Ruby and Jasmine were both stiff as boards as he fumbled for a syringe. Ruby had no idea what he was doing until she saw him stab his own vein with that huge needle and withdraw a tube of blood.

Ruby ran. She was nearly screaming as she pushed past Jamie, Xeno, and Hayes, who yelled, "RUBY!"

That wasn't her name—goddamn it, that wasn't her name! Her name was Sage—she was Sage—but she didn't remember—she didn't want to remember!

Samson threw out a tentacle that would have knocked Ruby over had it not been for Kendra's dagger. She had a laser gun strapped to her back, but the dagger would do just fine.

Why was this so familiar to her?

Ruby knew why.

She and Samson used to do this all the time. They used to spar together, and she'd always lose. But if she wanted to stay away from that blood, she had to win.

"Stop fighting, girl!" Samson exclaimed. "Are you kidding me right now? You forget everything but how stubborn you can be!"

"Leave me alone!" Ruby croaked, hand shaking around her weapon. "Leave me alone!"

Never. Samson wasn't going anywhere until he won, so he swiped at her again.

Ruby jumped back, startled by the tentacles that would break her in half if they caught her. Tyrus and Herman would never dream of doing this. Louis would strangle her if he caught them doing this, but that's the thing: He wasn't here. This was all Ruby now, fighting for her life, and as useful as adrenaline was keeping her on her feet, she wasn't fast or strong enough to evade Samson for long.

"S-stop!" Hayes cried from the sidelines, still trying to evade the massive Squids holding him back. "Why are you attacking her?"

Ruby used the dagger to block another swipe from Samson. She had to jump back to avoid a second tentacle. Samson growled in frustration.

"Foolish girl! You haven't changed!"

"STOP IT—"

"Shut up, boy!" Samson threw a wad of slime to cover Hayes' mouth. "It never fails, does it?" he snarled at Ruby. "You always pick the whiny ones, don't you?"

Ruby used her dagger again, but then Samson used a third tentacle that flew right at her chest.

"You always keep your left side open!" he called, knocking the wind right out of her.

"Wow," Jamie breathed. "She can fight. Look at her, Xeno. She actually dodged Samson a few times. I mean, she's down now—"

Ruby shoved the dagger up through Samson's tentacle.

That did little to nothing because Samson quickly dislodged it. This was his chance to win now that Ruby was still on her back. He withdrew all his appendages and jumped right in front of her.

"No!" Ruby cried, throwing a punch, but Samson caught it. He dropped the needle as he caught her second fist, too. He held them both in his overly-large hands. Even the muscles on his forearms were bigger than the legs on an average human.

"Stop it!" he hissed at her. "Stop acting like a brat!"

Ruby sobbed.

"What's the matter with you?!"

Ruby deflated. Hayes was trying to talk, but he had slime across his mouth.

"We think she's lost her memories," Jamie said, observing her with worry. That's not how Optimums were supposed to behave. "At least, that's what she told me."

"I can see that!" Samson spat. He got down to his knees so he was eye level with Ruby, but he didn't let go of her fists. "The question is why? Why don't you have your memories? Did that little shit Louis pull you out of hibernation early?"

Ruby furrowed her brows. She looked up at Samson. "H-hibernation?"

"Yes! You were hibernating for thirty years! Didn't he tell you?"

Ruby cried again. Samson let go of her hands so Ruby could use them to hold her face.

"She was hibernating, sir?" Jamie said quizzically.

"Yes," Samson said. "That's what Louis told me many years ago, before I was reborn." He took a deep breath. "She was in a cocoon. The Warlord's doctor confirmed there was a body inside that cocoon, breaking itself down and then rebuilding itself from scratch. Similar to what Lolligo go through when they—*we*—reproduce. Only her rebirth took a much longer time than ours. It's far different from ours, too."

Ruby clutched her head. She sobbed.

"Stop crying, damn it!" Samson shouted. "You are the Optimum—act like it!"

Hayes was screaming, trying to say something. His face was redder than a tomato by now.

"Your name is Sage," Samson said to her. He had some kind of device in his hand. It looked like Jamie's translator, but this was a phone. A communication device. "And you have a husband and two boys. You told me this a long time ago. Louis knows it, too, but I think he was a bit jealous. He must have ripped you out of that cocoon before the Warlord could get to you."

He gave her the communicator, placing it in her hand. Then he picked up the needle full of blood from the ground.

"These are my Cells," Samson said to Ruby, offering her the syringe. "I gave them to you a long time ago. If you take them again, there's a chance it can help with your regeneration. There's a chance that your memories will come back faster."

"Do you think they'll come back naturally?" Jamie asked.

Samson shook his head. "I don't know. It's obvious that the hippocampus didn't develop as it should have. Her memories are lost, her reactions are clumsy, and she's emotional as hell—*praise the Forefathers*—stop crying!"

Ruby did. She had the communicator in one hand and the needle in the other. Samson didn't inject her with it.

"You'll do it yourself when the time is right," he said, standing back up. "Jamie, would you mind accompanying her back to the complex she and the rest of the humans are staying at? She needs to rest. Tomorrow, we start training."

Jamie arched a brow. Xeno gasped.

"What did you say, sir?"

"Are you deaf?" Samson spat at him. "We train her. She is our best option for survival. You said she wanted to compromise, right? Well, let's do it. We investigate where these 'Scarfaces' are, and in return, she can help us overthrow Rhett."

"This is ridiculous!" Xeno snarled. "I don't mean to undermine your decision, sir, but she's just a whiny coward."

"Sage is no coward," Samson said steadily. "She is a warrior who unified the four districts of Diamond City. She is far from being a coward. She can help us."

"She can hardly fight! She forgot how!"

"She will relearn. I will train her."

Xeno shook his head. "We're doomed. We're *fucking* doomed—"

Ruby stabbed her arm with the needle. Everyone whipped around to watch her inject all the blood into her body.

Ruby wasn't sure if this was going to work . . . but she did know one thing.

She was sick and tired of being called a coward. And she was sick and tired of being talked about as if she were a little girl. If she was going to save her family and her city, she had to get stronger.

And Samson's blood was the first step to that.

CHAPTER 6

Acceptance and Preparation

amson, it's Sage, said the very first message on the communicator. *Are you there?*

Are you safe? was Samson's reply to it.

Yes, Sage said. *What's my favorite food?*

The boiled egg. You found Herman and Tyrus. Are they eggs now?

Yes. I didn't know Lolligo did that.

Well, now you do. I didn't know either until I got here.

I love you.

I love you, too, Sage.

Please come, Sage said. *I want you to meet Castor and Pollux.*

Are they well? Samson asked.

Yes.

I'm not sure how, but why am I not surprised?

What do you mean?

Your babies would be the ones to survive, Samson said. *Those hundred years we lived together showed me that you are something special, Sage.*

Actually, it wasn't me, Sage said. *It was Damian's sperm.*

I would love to see you, but I cannot. I have been in the middle of a civil war here at home. Some of us want alliances with the humans. Others complete isolation. Similar to what's happening in Diamond City. Except, while it's political for you, it's racial for us. Some Lolligo despise hybrids and don't want them anywhere near here.

Is it true that the Lolligo want to dominate us? The humans?

Yes.

You want unity, Sage said.

I want our races to get along, Samson replied. *You and I were able to prove that much.*

What can I do to help?

Nothing. I think you have enough on your plate.

Lolligo hate humans, Sage said.

Terrified.

There has to be something we can do.

Right now, there isn't, Samson said.

Emerald City wants to defeat the Lolligo, Sage said. *Damian says they're the enemies.*

Yes. I suppose, in a sense, we are. Some Lolligo want a complete raid of Abloudor. They want to level all human settlements to the ground.

Is that why you took Wren? To learn how to defeat hybrids?

Yes, Samson said.

Maybe we can do this the peaceful way?

That's what I'm trying to do. But, Sage, listen: Diamond City and everything around it is dangerous. The Outskirts have been ravaged by unknown forces and it's only going to get worse.

Then Samson said, *Don't go alone.*

Ruby had no doubts about her family.

Not anymore.

She must have read the messages over a hundred times that night, to be sure she memorized each and every one. Two names continued to pound in her head like a drum.

Castor and Pollux. Castor and Pollux. Castor and Pollux.

Those were her sons' names. The twins. The ones who had spotted her on top of the palace.

But the thing was, no matter how much Ruby said them in her mind or out loud, no memory of her boys ever came back to her. No memory of her round belly or giving birth to twins. No memory of ever holding them in her arms.

Ruby sighed.

Hayes was in the corner of her room, watching her intently. After finally removing the slime Samson had pasted across his lips, he could talk. He hadn't said much, though. He had just watched her all through the evening as Kendra got the newbies settled into their rooms. At some point, he had gotten up to take a shower, but had failed to dry his hair. It was a bit poofy now. It was as if he had wanted to be as quick as possible to make sure Ruby didn't jump out her window or do anything crazy. He wanted to remind her of one thing.

"You're not Sage," Hayes said heatedly. "And even if you are, you're no longer her. You're Ruby—a new person, a new life—not some Optimum!"

Ruby said nothing. With the communicator still in her hand, she settled into bed. Despite the truth resting on her chest, she felt calm. Accepting. Perhaps a bit of longing, too, because her children were out there . . .

"Are you listening, Ruby?"

"Hayes, I really need time to figure this out," Ruby said adamantly, staring at the ceiling.

"There is nothing to figure out!" Hayes exclaimed. "You are a brand new person—do you know how many people would kill to restart their lives?"

Ruby scowled. "Why are you acting this way?"

"Because I see the abuse!" Hayes finally got on his feet. He waved his arms, upset. "I see the fucking abuse, throwing all these responsibilities on you because of something you did in the past. Well, we're not in the past anymore—we're living in the present. You have a new life and a new love—*me!*"

Ruby snapped her head to him. Hayes was panting like crazy.

"Don't look so confused!" he sputtered. "Y-you know I love you, Ruby!"

"Hayes." Ruby sat up again. She was fully alert now. She put the communicator aside so that she had his undivided attention. "Hayes, no—"

"What do you mean 'no'? You don't have any feelings for me? At all? A-aren't we friends—didn't we kiss?"

"We kissed," Ruby admitted. She could never forget that time they had pecked each other on the lips after the gym, but that was only once. Hayes had nearly peed himself and never done it again in fear he wasn't good enough . . . for her. Perhaps he could worm his way into every cheerleader's bed, but Ruby was no prissy teenager. They had settled as friends in the meantime, except in moments like these when Hayes claimed there was something more between them.

Ruby scowled. "You can't possibly expect me to figure all this out right now, can you? Of course I still value and care for you, but I have a past that I'm responsible for. You can't be that selfish and expect me to forget all of it. Didn't you hear what Samson said? I was pulled out of hibernation early."

"And what proof do you have of that?" Hayes snarled. "What proof do you have that you were in hibernation to begin with?"

"It's obvious that I'm not human and it's obvious that Louis was trying to keep me a secret. Plus, I look like Sage."

"But that doesn't mean you're her!"

"Then what the fuck does it mean, Hayes?" Ruby got to her feet this time. The anger was bubbling in her chest, threatening to spill out of her in waves. "What am I, then? Half a goddamn person? Is that the kind of person you love? Then you're no better than Louis. He tried to kiss me once, too, but worst of all: He *knew* who I really was. You didn't, but if you truly loved me, then you'd want me to be whole again. You'd want me to seek my lost memories, but you're scared that I won't care about you when I remember I have a husband and two kids."

Hayes' eyes welled with tears. He lowered his head, fingers in his hair. He gave half a sob. "Of course I'm scared . . ."

"I'm sorry," Ruby said, unsure of how to handle this. "I don't know what you want me to say. This wasn't your fault, nor mine. You should be mad at Louis for leading everyone on. Had he done the right thing, I'd be in Emerald City with my true husband—not stuck in this damn hellhole."

Hayes clenched his fists. He probably wanted to tear someone's throat out for the way his love life was evolving. All the time and attention he had given Ruby back on campus seemed to be for naught. That was incredibly selfish, but Ruby could see it all over his face. When he noticed, he changed his expression. But he quickly realized that Ruby's was right—this wasn't their fault. He didn't give up, though.

"But you still have a choice," Hayes said. "You can still choose to love someone else. Let's face it: You don't remember anything about your husband. How can you stay with him if you don't love him? How do you know you love him—because your past self did? Well, what if you don't anymore?"

"Hayes," Ruby said patiently. So, so much patience. "Hayes, stop. Just stop. I haven't even had a conversation with the man and you're already planting doubts in my head?"

"I'm trying to save you—save *us*—"

"THERE IS NO 'US'!" Ruby roared.

Her voice shook the room. The silence that followed was deafening. There was no doubt everyone in the building had heard her.

"There is no 'us', damn it," Ruby said again, angrily. "We're friends, Hayes. We just got to know each other this year. You've been there for me—and I value you greatly—but I'm going through a pretty fucked-up time in my life right now. Please don't be selfish and impose on me in this vulnerable state, when I'm half of a person walking around on two legs. Maybe I was reborn, but that doesn't erase my past and who I used to be. That wouldn't be fair to Damian, would it?"

"Can you at least give me a chance?"

"Aren't you listening?!" Ruby exclaimed. "How would you like it if your wife went missing and ran off with some scrawny kid because she didn't remember you? I'd be devastated!"

Hayes was about to argue that, too, but Ruby had had enough.

"Get out," she said. "Get out right now, damn it."

"Ruby—"

"GET OUT!"

Hayes finally got the hint. He knew when he had lost the battle and when arguing with Ruby was no longer going to give him the results he wanted. So he closed his mouth, turned around, and stepped out. Not without punching the wall, though.

Ruby was way too riled up to get back into bed. Moreover, she had Samson's words in her head—*"You always pick the whiny ones, don't you?"*—and she wondered if Damian was whiny, too.

No way. Damian was anything but the whiny type—he was an Allseer who knew how to govern, how to make his city flourish, and how to give people hope. Regardless of their marital status, Damian was someone Ruby looked up to. Wanted to be like.

She caressed his name on her arm. So ironic . . . she had gotten that tattoo before she even knew he was her husband.

Ruby stepped over to her window. She opened it and jumped out into the night. The air was crisp in the month of Innocence, but it was still hard to breathe. Ruby's chest was tight from all the stress to begin with. Her intention was to see Samson and have a conversation with him, but she noticed the lights on in one of the shops across the street.

Ruby walked over. It used to be a clothes store. She could still see the traces of "Glorious Fabrics" where the sign used to be. The previous owners had packed up everything they owned, it seemed, except for the empty racks inside. Ruby could see them lined up against the wall. It was a miracle there was any power in there. Ruby saw the generator next to the door.

"Look, Paige!" a voice sang from inside. "I think it's that Ruby chick!"

Two small children poked their heads out from behind the door. They found Ruby and ducked back in.

Curious now, Ruby walked up to the store and took a better look inside.

Paige and Pedro were a couple from the Color District. Paige looked like a man and Pedro looked like a woman. Ruby was confused because she couldn't tell who was truly what, so she wound up staring longer than usual. The family of four did the same to her.

"Sorry to intrude." Ruby finally forced her eyes from their faces to the peeling walls. There were posters that said, "All Your Clothes in One Place!" She asked, "Are you guys all right?"

"Oh." Paige blushed some. She had short spiky hair and pecs and arms that would fool anyone into believing she had a healthy dose of testosterone in her body. Perhaps she and her partner were both on some sort of hormone therapy. They sure looked the part despite their preferred pronouns. "Y-yes, we're fine. We hope we're not being a bother."

"Are we?" Pedro asked. He had a long coat, tight pants, and flats. But his hair was long and the makeup was extraordinary, so he really did look like a woman. Ruby couldn't tell if he had breasts or not.

"Of course not," Ruby said, still fighting not to stare. "I'm curious, though—what are you guys doing here? Did Kendra not accommodate you well enough at Crystal Light?"

"Oh, no, it's not that!" Paige waved her hands. "We were just looking around and we were curious if we could actually use any of this stuff."

Rickety racks? Ruby said in her mind, but Paige shook her head again.

"There are plenty of clothes in our room," Paige said. "There's everything there. We were just hoping to set up our own shop here. I'm a seamstress, see?"

"Are you?" Ruby looked to Pedro, who shook his head to confirm he wasn't gifted like his wife in that regard.

"I just sell her stuff," he clarified. "It's pretty impressive, actually."

Pedro still had his phone. Although there was no service out here, all the pictures were still in his camera roll. He had them organized into albums and started with the first in the list titled, "Make it Fit".

Basically, it was the same design over and over, but for all sorts of body types and shapes. Ruby could spend hours looking at the pictures of every type of person she could imagine in Diamond City, so she took a seat. There were over three thousand images for the first album alone.

The next album was titled "Medieval". This one had big poofy dresses and knight armor from the Old World.

Ruby's first question was how practical all these designs were in today's age, but the Color District made anything work. Sometimes, they threw festivals, parties, or galas featuring wear from a certain time period. For many people (resident and not), it was an escape from everyday life, while for others, it was a dream come true to shine in the spotlight. The competition must have been fierce, even for those who were talented in this sort of field. Ruby's doodles in history class were terrible.

"Impressed with what you see?" Pedro said excitedly.

"Phoebe used to give me her feedback all the time," Damian said with a sad smile. "She'd approve. I always trusted her judgment when it came to fashion."

"Yeah." Ruby looked up at the ceiling. There was a particularly dark water stain in the corner. Looking through designs sure felt familiar to her . . .

"Really? Oh—I have wedding gown designs, too!"

A book of them. Full of them. It was an explosion of white and glitter like some sort of angelic prophet.

Ruby remembered . . . or she thought she did . . .

"Are you from the Color District, too?" Pedro asked her.

"No, I'm from Heart." Ruby grimaced, as if she was in pain.

"Actually, I'm from the Cut District. I own a pizzeria called Two for Pizza."

Paige gasped loudly. "Wait—are you Sage Arpine? W-we met once! Don't you remember?" She turned to her husband. "You see? I *knew* she looked familiar!"

"We've met?" Ruby said, panting a little.

"Of course! I was a little girl then, but yes! My mother would take us to that restaurant all the time. Gourmet pizza at low costs was always the perfect way to eat at night! Do you remember me now?"

"She's not going to remember you," Pedro snapped. "You were a little girl then and you look like a man now."

Paige held her breath, waiting. She actually pushed back her hair so Ruby could get a good look at her face.

"Sorry," Ruby said softly. "But I really don't remember . . . There's a lot I don't remember."

That's not why she was here, though, so she changed the topic.

Ruby gave the phone back to Pedro. "So you guys owned a shop in the Color District and you want to reopen it here. How do you plan on doing that?"

"Well, Kendra did a good job of gathering whatever supplies were leftover at Crystal Light," Paige went on. "So there are some fabrics to work with. She also mentioned she found the town's power grid and that she'd be working on a way to restore power to this place."

Ruby arched a brow. "Really?"

"Yes. I think that old man—Travis—used to be some sort of electrician. Maybe he can help out."

"So you want to make clothes for everyone . . . for free?"

Paige shrugged. "Kind of useless to ask for money, isn't it? I mean, as long as we have food, shelter, and a place to stay, I don't mind. I'd love to dress up people, especially those Lolligo. They could use a bit of help with those drabby clothes they like to wear. For such divine beings, you'd think they'd be a bit more—"

Paige stopped at the look Pedro was giving her and she blushed. "What? Lolligo *are* cool! And they *are* real—those Clarity people were right."

Pedro rolled his eyes. "Whatever. They're still just monsters to me."

"What about you, Sage—er—Ruby?" Paige beamed. "Why did you change your name?"

Ruby lowered her eyes. "I guess I started a new life."

"Makes sense. Pedro and I wanted to swap names when we got married, but we swapped genders instead. I wanted to know what it was like to play the male role, so I transformed."

"Fully?"

"Yes," Paige said brightly. "Penis and all. Actually, it's Pedro's penis."

Pedro rolled his eyes. "And I love tits, but could do without the whole child-bearing. I let Paige handle that one early on."

"Do you have children, Ruby?" Paige asked.

For the first time since walking into the store, Ruby's eyes lit up. A smile spread across her face. She straightened in her chair and puffed out her chest as she said, "Yes. Their names are Castor and Pollux."

R uby spent the whole night talking to Paige and Pedro. The kids never went to bed, either. It was nice to bask in the hope they'd be able to spend their lives here in peace, doing what they loved without the pressures of society or the clutches of inflation. Once in a while, Ruby thought of the couple from the motel.

While the Diamond City stragglers spent their days exploring the town and brainstorming ways to get it up and running again, Ruby and Samson trained until the sun set. That meant hours out on the grounds. The crisp fall air was nonexistent when Ruby was fighting for her life. It was more like a scorching hell now.

Samson wasn't afraid to crush her bones or knock her out. Sometimes, Ruby wondered if he was trying to hit her head on purpose. Whatever his intentions, though, he was relentless. Plus, he was young, fast, and vibrating with an energy that Ruby couldn't dream to match. Perhaps it's what made Lolligo so deadly or—in the eyes of Claritians—divine. Fighting a Lolligo was like fighting one of those gods from Greek mythology, except Samson was no myth. Ruby had a lot of work to do if she was ever going to win any battle, and by the time the month of Innocence came to an end, she hadn't clenched one.

Ruby was a bleeding heap on the ground every single day.

Despite their ugly argument the other night, Hayes came out to watch her. He was a great cheerleader, but tended to get a bit too aggressive with the cursing and name-calling whenever Samson hit Ruby too hard. Samson wasn't going to tolerate that sort of hooting, so it wasn't long before he sent him to explore the Outskirts with Xeno and the tank Lolligo named Bruce.

The three hopped on some scooters and did some scouting and searching for any signs of those Scarfaces. They came back with maps, checkpoints, and other abandoned towns in the area. Eventually, they decided that it'd take more than just a few days to truly explore all the land around them, so they packed up and prepared for a week-long adventure.

Of course, Hayes absolutely refused to go anywhere without Ruby, but he didn't have a choice when Samson knocked him over the head and threw him onto the scooter like luggage.

"Seriously." Samson frowned at Ruby as Bruce revved the engine and took off, Hayes strapped down like a wounded animal. "What is it with you and these boys?"

"He's not my boyfriend." Ruby frowned back. "And he never used to be this whiny, either. He's upset that he's lost his shot with me, so he's throwing a tantrum."

"Good. He deserves to be put in his place."

"You don't think I'm being unfair . . . do you, Samson?"

Samson made a face. His teeth were too big for his mouth, so his top ones were always poking his lower lip. "Unfair?"

"Yeah," Ruby said. She already knew that ignoring her past was wrong, but she wanted Samson to confirm it. He seemed to be right on almost everything. "I have a new life now ... so why not give Hayes a shot?"

Samson snorted. He cracked his knuckles and swung his arms. He was getting ready to pummel her anew. He didn't have anything but pants on, so Ruby could see every muscle and cut in his torso. They were three times the size of hers. "What 'new life', Sage? Just because you went into hibernation doesn't mean you're a brand new person. Losing your memories doesn't mean you forget about your family and all your past trials. It doesn't erase what you've already lived. On top of that, I don't believe you actually have amnesia—I think your brain hasn't finished developing—and it was very fucked-up of Louis to pull you out of that cocoon early. The next time I see that boy, I'm going to decapitate him and offer his head to those two preachers over there."

Right. The two preachers that were standing at the end of the street, bowing in reverence to Samson. If they got too close, they both got a wad of slime over their lips. It took Kendra hours to scrape it off.

"Don't let your puny human emotions get in the way," Samson said to Ruby. "And especially don't let some horny boy toy with your emotions."

Ruby laughed.

"You know he wants sex with the most powerful woman he'll ever meet. And knowing you, you're probably looking for some coochie time, too."

Ruby's cheeks blew up. "Samson!"

"Tell me I'm wrong."

"N-no—I haven't even thought of it, actually."

It was sort of the truth. Ruby was attracted to boys, but she had never had sex with one. In this lifetime, anyway—*obviously*—because the time hadn't been right. Perhaps there had been too many distractions. She had been dodging Louis for one.

"Well." Samson pounded his fists together. "After this beating, you won't even remember what a vagina is."

It was times like these that Ruby grew jealous of Jamie, who stayed inside the *Luse* all day reading books on human health and looking over Travis as he recovered. Ruby thought she'd much rather play doctor and scholar than to get her arm torn out of its socket or to have both of her feet crushed because she wasn't fast enough to dodge Samson's hammers. He could shape-shift his entire body into anything, even a blanket that choked the hell out of her until she passed out.

Ruby would wake up on a table next to Travis, an IV in her vein. Not that there was anything special in there—just basic fluids and vitamins—but it did help her feel better. When Samson didn't knock her out, Ruby took some recovery tablets before crawling back to the complex for food and rest. She'd always pass by the two preachers on the way, who never failed to pray for her and bless her efforts against the Lolligo.

"Another hard day of training?" Travis asked her. He was sitting up on his table, a book in his lap. Jasmine was sketching something in her journal. Hamilton was sleeping on the floor on his side, legs spread out for everyone to trip over.

"I think I'm traumatized." Ruby rubbed her forehead. "And feeling a bit sick."

"I remember my fastball days," Travis said. "I was on my school team. I played for the Cavaliers in the Cut District."

"Really?" That got Ruby's interest. She sat up as Samson walked by and said to Travis in Lucidum, "Do *not* get her started on that fastball nonsense. She's a terrible player."

"Hey!" Ruby exclaimed. "I'm not *that* bad—I can hold my own."

Samson snorted. "Please. You have terrible hand-eye coordination. You have a good grip, and your fists are a force to be reckoned with, but you miss more than you hit. Thus why you get beat up so much by me."

"Please, sir," said Jamie to Samson, "can you cut her some slack? A whole month of training, and she's managed to stay alive and improve. Certainly that warrants some recognition?"

"It most certainly does not. 'Staying alive' does not win battles."

"Aren't you being just a little bit harsh?"

"Don't tell me you feel sorry for her just because she has two boobs and a pussy."

Travis' eyes widened. Jasmine started laughing. The two of them had learned an impressive amount of Lolligo thanks to being here all day with Jamie, enough to know what *osemee* and *isi* meant. Those were words Samson must have used quite a bit.

"You can't feel sorry for her," Samson said to Jamie, whose lips were pursed into a tight line. If he had skin, he'd probably be blushing a bit now. "Positive reinforcement, yes, but Sage hasn't done anything to warrant that reinforcement yet, so no compliments until she does. And 'staying alive' is not enough."

Defeated, Ruby fell back on the table.

"Sage does have one strength that has nearly toppled me in the past," Samson went on before Ruby lost all her drive. "*Nearly.* And that's her sword."

Ruby raised her head. Samson walked away. He went down the hall to his room. Hamilton got up to watch him return with a sword.

It was a blade as thin as paper but as powerful as any steel wall. It was over four feet in length. Not only that: It was made of Slainium, the only known metal that could destroy the Cells in a Lolligo, hybrid, and Enhanced. It was perfect for Ruby, who took it and gripped it in her right hand.

For some reason, Ruby's confidence swelled. She knew how to shape-shift like Samson—sort of—but she felt better when she didn't have to concentrate on her body. Moving this blade around was different than fighting with her bare hands.

"But we're not there yet." Samson took it back before Ruby could protest. "You still have so many basics to learn. Sometimes you won't have your weapon. You'll have to know what you're doing with your bare hands alone."

That meant another month and a half of pure hell. Ruby was pretty stubborn about the unfairness at first, but if she wanted to improve, then she had to be a bit more open-minded. That's what she learned from Travis before he was discharged from Jamie's ship and from the rest of the Techfeld residents whenever Ruby took a walk through town. Their desire to survive fueled Ruby's desire to be better. By the month of Strength, a full two months since Ruby had started training with Samson, she managed to walk away with only a scratch.

Samson never told her he was proud, but Ruby was thrilled with her progress. She could take laps around Techfeld, jump from the highest skyscrapers without fear, and hold her own against Lolligo. She even took on Xeno when he returned from one of his excursions.

And that, by far, was the scariest fucking battle of her life. Xeno beat her up, but at least Ruby had gotten two solid hits. According to Jamie, she had broken one of his ribs.

"She's still a weakling," Xeno spat to Samson after another scrimmage with Ruby. He had knocked her on her ass again.

"Give her time," Samson said patiently.

The only one who was quiet about all this training was Bruce. The tall giant didn't care about quarrels—only that Lolligo egg he carried around everywhere. According to Jamie, a very special friend was going to hatch soon.

"I think they've been friends since the beginning of the New World," Jamie said one night they were having dinner together. Samson was cooking. Ruby didn't pass out in her training session that day.

"The . . . *scene* at the Science of Tomorrow building," Ruby said softly. "Were those Lolligo?"

Ruby hadn't failed to warn everyone, including the Lolligo, about what she and the others had found there. From what she knew, Jamie had taken care of the mess since he had a special hazmat suit that protected him from the heavy bouts of radiation.

"Indeed," Jamie said, sipping some wine. "As you know, or surely suspect, Lolligo are humans. Well." He cleared his throat. "Some more than others. Nevertheless, the radiation mutated humans who left their bunkers when the environment wasn't safe.

Imagine that a lot of people tried to leave their underground hide-outs when supplies were running low. Some ran off and never came back. Some did come back and were horribly sick. The ones who did mutate were analyzed and studied by scientists who might have had a role in helping the mutations along."

"You mean creating the first Lolligo?"

"Yes."

"But there were many," Ruby said, playing with some crackers on her plate. She was waiting for Samson to finish that incredible-smelling stir-fry. "Not just one or two."

"There are all types," Jamie admitted.

"Do you remember your past life?"

"As a human? No. Only very few of us have memories of that life. It was so long ago. It's been five hundred years since that nuclear war."

"You don't trust humans," Ruby said.

"Heavens no," Jamie said. Samson was cutting more onions on the counter. "But we don't want to mistreat them, either. We also think it would be beneficial to have them as allies. I still can't believe the humans here have managed to restore power to the entire town."

It was crazy, but true. There was no gasoline or any other means of acquiring energy, so the Lolligo had helped out a bit in that department. They had created their own form of self-sufficient energy called Surgium that never ran out. They carried it around in small compartments that looked like batteries. Jamie had taught Travis and that Diamond City officer, Randall, how to use it without blowing themselves out of existence, and the two had managed to reconfigure Techfeld's entire power grid. Their next project was restoring cellular service so they could communicate with their families back in Diamond City.

"They sure are smart," Jamie said as Samson poured another bottle of teriyaki sauce into the pan. "If only humans weren't so destructive."

"Or backstabbing," Samson added.

114

Ruby wasn't really sure what Samson was talking about until she returned to Crystal Light later that night.

At first, she was quite distracted by all the lights flickering on and off in the buildings around her. Their group of fifteen had already cleaned these streets and constructed actual storefronts for clothes, shoes, electronics (from junk they had found lying around), and art. The college couple, Gary and Tiana, were engineers who had created a whole new nameplate for Crystal Light that read, "Home, Sweet Home".

Cheesy, but Ruby wasn't about to burst any bubbles. She took a moment to gaze at the words. They blinked in different colors, powered by Surgium.

Then Ruby turned around. She could see Paige and Pedro's shop from here, too. They had gone all out, outlining the door, windows, and even walkway with blinking lights.

People in Diamond City usually did that in the month of Faith, the last month of the year. New Year's was a big deal for everyone. It symbolized yet another year of life on this planet, but for Diamond City, it meant so much more.

After living in bunkers for so long, humans had surfaced to find nothing but death, destruction, and adversity. Humans had fought each other for control of the planet and would have wiped each other out had it not been for the saving grace of the Forefathers.

Those four Lolligo that the Claritians honored in their churches had created the Diamond City districts. They had given humans a place to stay and equipped them with the tools and weapons necessary to survive in this brutal world. Only those humans had turned against the Lolligo, martyring them and driving them out of the city. The Lolligo, however, had left behind gifts in those districts . . . hybrids. And one of them had been Sage, the Optimum, who had fought to unite the districts under one rule.

Thus, Diamond City had been unified. A year later, it celebrated its first birthday. Ruby only remembered the festivities for 132, and those had been grand.

Louis and Ruby had gone to every party imaginable at Heart,

from concerts to galas to ballroom excursions. They had toured the capital, ridden the ferris wheel, and watched the fireworks from an airship.

Perhaps Ruby had done all of it before, but she couldn't remember.

Ruby sighed.

Ruby took the stairs to her floor. She forgot she could use the elevator now and she'd be sure to remember that next time because her legs were about to fall apart. No tablet or IV was strong enough to cure her wounds from Samson's beatings.

Ruby wished there was something that could give her her memory back. Anything with the brain, however, was dangerous and intensive. Not only did the Lolligo not have the necessary equipment for that kind of experimentation, but Samson refused to hear any mention of it.

"Naturally," he'd say. "They'll come back naturally . . ."

As Ruby trudged down the hall to her room, she heard noises coming from next door. Loud noises. That was Kendra's room.

"D-damn . . ." grunted a voice that did not belong to Kendra. "Wow . . . so tight . . ."

Ruby recognized Hayes, but she wasn't sure what was happening. She got closer to listen, wondering if Hayes was in pain. He sounded like he was.

"Squeeze harder!" Hayes cried out, then Ruby heard a small gasp.

It was a female. *That* was definitely Kendra. But what were they doing? Having sex?

"Wow, Aunt Sage," said a voice that made Ruby jump. "I didn't know you were a pervert."

Ruby whipped around as if she had just been caught stealing the palace jewels. She scurried back from Kendra's room as if a snake had just flashed its teeth at her. It was the startled look on her face that caught Micah's attention.

Micah furrowed his brows. "Aunt Sage?"

Ruby wiped at her eyes. Horrible shame and guilt crept up her

116

body like a disease. She made for her room, but Micah caught up to her. "Aunt Sage, wait! I-I'm sorry! I didn't know you were into Hayes like that!"

Was that what Micah thought? That Ruby had been interested in Hayes and craved his attention? Ruby wasn't sure she had ever thought of sex or a relationship with Hayes. Even if she had entertained it, she had never taken it seriously. Maybe a small part of her was disappointed, but not because she had lost Hayes to Kendra—it was the *way* she had lost him. Hayes was loud enough to make sure Ruby heard every thrust—he yelled as he orgasmed.

Ruby lowered her head. On top of everything, Micah had called her a pervert. How embarrassing.

"Sorry," Ruby said quietly. "I didn't mean to . . . be a pervert."

Could anyone help listening to that noise? All the rooms on this floor were empty anyway, so the only one who heard it all was Ruby.

"Aunt Sage, wait!" Micah grabbed her arm. His eyes softened. "I'm sorry. I-I didn't mean to call you that."

"It's fine." Ruby wiped her tears. "I probably came across that way, right?"

"No, not at all. I'm sorry."

"Don't worry about it, kiddo. It's fine."

"I see that you're upset and I'm sorry. I know it's been rough for you, losing your memories and such. But for what it's worth, Damian loves you. A lot."

Ruby gazed into Micah's eyes. She tuned out the loud panting in the background.

"He went to see you in your cocoon every time he came to visit me and Mom," Micah said.

There was another groan from next door. "Suck my nipples, Hayes."

"Oh, for Stars' sake!" Micah dragged Ruby into her room. He shut the door, turned on some calm music, and sighed in relief. Ruby's light panels always came on at nightfall, so the room was already aglow in reds and oranges. "Finally. I can't think straight with all the moaning." Thanks to that and the thick walls, they couldn't hear any more sex. Still, Ruby wasn't sure she'd be staying in this room much longer.

"What were you saying about Damian?" Ruby asked.

"He came to see you, Aunt Sage," Micah said. "He'd come to Diamond City once a month to check up on Mom and Aunt Olivia. We never needed any money, but he always bought them gifts, paid off their houses, ensured the restaurant was doing well, and spoiled the living Stars out of me."

Ruby smiled. "Really?"

"Yeah." Micah beamed. "He showed me how to roller-skate and we went to this cool glow-in-the-dark rink they opened up in the Cut District. He bought me all the toys from my favorite TV series, got me my first phone, and taught me how to drive. Damian was more of a dad to me than my own dad, actually. My father's name is Geoffrey, but he joined the Diamond City military when I was young, so he's been away a lot."

"I see," Ruby said softly.

Micah nodded. "I played a lot with Castor and Pollux, too. We'd take trips around the entire district. One summer, we went to every water park we could find." He grinned at the memory. "They're like my older brothers. I wish I was half as good as them when it comes to sword fighting, but I suck at sports." He chuckled. "I just really like the pizza restaurant. When I turn eighteen, I'm going to take it up. My mother's going to retire and write books. Aunt Olivia, on the other hand, is an aspiring model in the Color District."

"That sounds fantastic."

"You'll come back to Diamond City, right?" Micah asked her. "To see everyone?"

"I'd really like that," Ruby said happily.

Micah had some pictures to share with her, so they spent the rest of the night sitting on the bed, scrolling through photos. Ruby's eyes teared up again when she saw her nieces, Damian, and her twins. Up close, they all looked so . . . different. Damian, especially, who was far more beautiful than Ruby ever imagined.

She'd only seen him in brief interviews, articles, and historical texts. Her top-of-the-palace ventures didn't count because his features were too far away to appreciate fully. But now that she could zoom in, which she spent a lot of time doing to each piece of his face, she could see that his features were perfect: straight nose, high cheekbones, full lips, and glossy hair. He wasn't overly dressed, either, even when he was sitting having pizza with the family on an ordinary weekend. Despite the smile on his face, however, there was a certain . . . heaviness in his expression.

"He'd stay with your cocoon for days at a time," Micah said to Ruby, who couldn't stop staring at Damian's face. "Mom would have to go by and make sure he was still breathing. He'd lay with you on the bed and talk to you as if you were awake."

"I don't remember," Ruby whispered.

"No one expects you to, Aunt Sage. You were hibernating in there."

"Do you have pictures of the cocoon?"

"No," Micah said. "It wasn't something I could take a picture of. Not that I wanted to, because it was so . . ."

"Sad?" Ruby said.

Micah nodded. "Yeah."

Ruby kept scrolling through photos. She smiled at Castor and Pollux, who were spitting replicas of Damian. Their expressions were much lighter, though, carefree, as if they were having the time of their lives. Sure, their mother was gone, but they had never met her, so the loss wasn't as detrimental.

"Castor is the serious, orderly one," Micah explained as Ruby zoomed in on their faces next. "Although they're twins, they're night and day. He hates losing. He's a bit of a brainiac, too. Very sarcastic and likes beating up on people inferior to him. He pulled a prank on Pollux once. It was a bit harsh, but he wanted to beat Pollux at the science fair, so he sabotaged his project by swapping the right chemicals with some wrong ones. I'm not too sure of the details, but I know Pollux's experiment would have blown up in front of the entire class. Somehow, Damian knew something was amiss and quickly found out what Castor had done."

Micah shook his head. "Castor never told us exactly what Damian did, but I heard from Mom that Damian locked Castor in a room and made him copy the Lolligo scriptures on humbleness word for word."

"Sounds fair," Ruby agreed.

"Oh, man." Micah grinned. He laughed a bit. It was wry, though, because he could only guess what it was like to be on the receiving end of Damian's wrath. A gentle, fun, caring father could turn into the devil himself if prompted. Micah didn't look like the kind to take any chances, because if Candice and Geoffrey couldn't discipline him, then Damian surely would.

"We all know there was much more to it than that," Micah said, amusement dissipating. "Castor was so traumatized by the experience that he needed counseling, and I don't think you get that from copying down a few scriptures. Let's just say he never mistreated his brother again."

"I'm not sure I would, either."

Ruby was amused. She turned to the other twin. "So what is Pollux like?"

"Pollux is a thrill seeker," Micah said. "Loves roller coasters and any kind of adventure. He hates the classroom and thinking too much, but he's super smart. Honestly, he sort of reminds me of you, Aunt Sage. You didn't like school too much, either, right?"

"No," Ruby said honestly. "Although my dream is to play fastball."

"Castor is a beast at it. He beats all of us. I think that if it wasn't for Damian, he'd be a pro."

"Why would Damian stop him from going pro?"

"Don't you know?" Micah said. "Castor and Pollux are the leaders of the Emerald City military. They're the ones who strategize all the moves. Well, you can imagine: Castor does the strategizing while Pollux executes the commands. Both in and out of Emerald City."

Ruby's heart swelled with pride. Her eyes welled with more tears. "Really?"

"Yes. I'm pretty sure that the Emerald City attack on the Scarfaces was all them. It sounds like they're struggling a bit, though."

Ruby zoomed in on her twins' faces again. She smiled as she studied them.

"Damian's done an incredible job with them," Micah said. "Mom and Aunt Olivia are always impressed. Despite the obvious grief he's experienced, he still parents them so well."

"He's depressed?"

"Aunt Olivia told me that Damian was very much into fashion. But since you fell asleep, he hasn't drawn a single design. He helped Aunt Olivia onto the big stage in the Color District, but he's lost his flare. Castor and Pollux also told me that Damian locks himself in his room all night. Never attends parties. Throws them for his officials, high officers, and even military, but never for himself."

Micah beamed. "But wait until he sees you, Aunt Sage—he's going to be so happy!"

"Does he like poetry?" Ruby asked.

"I don't know, but I'm sure he'd like anything written by you. Can you write poetry?"

"I can!" Ruby said excitedly. "I'm pretty good at it, too!"

CHAPTER 7
Ruby City

When nothing seemed to reach me
You shined through
All of my love squandered
Except for you

Times were rough
But it didn't matter
You kept me tough
and so I climbed the ladder

"Wow . . ." Micah grinned. It looked more like a grimace.
"What do you think?" Ruby asked eagerly.
He flipped to the next page in Ruby's little poetry book.

When I looked back, you were always there
A light in my night,
never a burden to bear,
but a heart of might

The love inside me grew
Every passing day it swelled and I knew
without you, I cannot live
And so my heart to you, I freely give

"I'm actually not a good judge," Micah said quickly. "I think it sounds all right."

Ruby thought these poems were pretty good. By the end of her tenth month in Techfeld, she had filled an entire journal. She wrote something dedicated to Damian every day. She doodled little hearts, angel wings, and boots on the margins because, according to Micah, Damian always wore boots.

"I think what's more impressive is your dedication," Micah said optimistically. He patted Ruby's back. "And your Castor-and-Pollux tattoo."

Ruby had gotten it behind her right shoulder just like Damian had. It was the same design, too: a pair of swords with their sons' names on top. Paige had used to do tattoos before becoming a fashion designer, so this had been no problem for her. All she had needed were some needles and ink to bring it to life, and after just a few hours, Ruby had her second tattoo.

Samson didn't understand it.

"Why do you mark your body like that?" he asked her one day during training. "Can't you just tell people you love them and be done with it?"

"I feel I need to express myself through art."

"On your body, though? Who can see that?"

Everybody, actually, since Ruby was in a tank top. She rolled her eyes. She stopped herself from saying something snarky like *Of course you wouldn't understand—you don't even have skin!* It just wasn't worth it. Samson would tear her to pieces, even more than he already did during their training sessions.

There was one thing Ruby did admit to him, though. After catching Hayes and Kendra having sex, she realized that humans were much more sadistic than she had believed. Samson just shrugged.

"I already told you," he said with a scowl. He was heading into the kitchen to start their dinner. "Humans are unreliable and they shouldn't take you by surprise. So very few of them are worth saving. I, however, am not God to decide which ones live or die. I just shield myself, you see."

"But you have to admit they're impressive," Ruby said, leaning against the wall. She was about to take off her boots when Samson sent her the nastiest glare on earth. "Sorry," she said quickly.

"Yes, they are impressive," Samson admitted, going back to his pot on the stove.

Impressive because the town had flourished. It hadn't taken long for the next round of stragglers to happen upon Techfeld, and Ruby and the Lolligo had been out there to welcome them just like they had the first group. It didn't take long for a population of fifteen to jump to thirty, then seventy, and then a hundred. A few women had given birth, too, but the Lolligo made sure to stay far away from wailing babies.

The screams hurt their ears, and Lolligo just didn't have the patience to deal with newborns. They hardly had the patience to deal with Ruby. To this day, Xeno still spit at her feet when no other Lolligo was looking. Ruby had pulled Kendra's dagger on him once for the disrespect and gotten her ass handed to her instead. Jamie was the only kind one, but even he shook his head when asked if he wanted to study week-old babies. Thank the Forefathers there were some doctors and nurses in town.

While everyone found refuge in Techfeld, the increasing number of runaways from Diamond City worried Ruby. She stayed up every night listening to stories of survival amidst the fighting between Emerald City soldiers and the Scarfaces. She braced herself for the worst—that Castor and Pollux were dead—and nearly threw up when she learned a major fight had gone down in the Carat District. Emerald City soldiers had been wiped out like ants, according to one witness who told the tale.

"Just what are they?" Paige asked Ruby one night at her store. "The Scarfaces? Can't be human, can they?"

It didn't seem like it. They were all the same, too, like an army of clones. Now that Ruby thought about it, they creeped her out. Scarier than that was the kind of power they held and how unstoppable they seemed to be. Just where the hell had they come from?

"Have you tried these kale chips?" Paige took a seat next to Ruby. They were in the backroom where she and her husband manufactured all the clothes. The racks were impressive. "The hydroponics crew are geniuses in my opinion."

There was an entire building just for indoor farming. A dozen or so of the Diamond City stragglers really seemed to know what they were doing when it came to plants and they had been fairly successful with it. Ruby had never seen an eggplant grow in just a month. The town had already gone through all the scavenged non-perishables, so hydroponics was their lifeline. Jamie pitched in once in a while to ensure the Lolligo didn't starve. They ate something close to ten thousand calories a day.

"Definitely a lot of smart people," Paige said, digging into the bag for some more. "I heard they want to build more underground tunnels just in case we get attacked."

Like the one in this very room. There was a trapdoor behind some boxes that led miles out into the Outskirts. Ruby had already deemed it safe. She wasn't sure how many people would make it here in an emergency, but at least Paige and her family had pretty high chances of survival.

"Something on your mind, Ruby?" Paige pressed.

The Scarfaces. They were the only things plaguing Ruby's mind right now. How long before they came knocking on their door? If the Emerald City military was equipped with the best fighters and they were being wiped out... then what did that mean for Techfeld?

"*Ruby* City," Paige said happily.

Ruby arched a brow. "What?"

"That's what we're all calling this place."

"Why?"

Paige rolled her eyes. "Why do you think? We all know you're in charge here. We all look to you for protection if someone comes to attack us. Check out this insignia I drew—I took a ruby and crossed two swords—"

"First of all, Techfeld is a town—"

"Not anymore," Paige said quickly. "A town depends on a city for sustenance. Why do you think all the towns in the Outskirts are nearly extinct? We, however, are self-sufficient. We don't need anybody else. We are *Ruby* City."

Ruby thought that was the dumbest thing she had ever heard. Techfeld was too small to be considered a city like Diamond City, but everyone seemed to be on the same page with the definition. While their population was peanuts compared to a true city, residents agreed that they were vastly developed now that they were using Lolligo energy sources and creating their own food, clothes, electronics, infirmaries, and even vehicles with some leftover parts they found in abandoned warehouses.

"I tried to convince them it should be called *Sage* City," Kendra said the next morning during breakfast. Everyone stopped by Jo's Yo-Go for coffee, smoothies, oatmeal, biscuits, and snacks. Lunch was at Meat Express from noon to two. Dinner was at some fancy ballroom not too far from Science of Tomorrow. Ruby always ate with Samson, so she hadn't been there in the evening yet.

Ruby shook her head. She stabbed her spoon into the huge bowl of yogurt with freshly-made granola. Someone was squeezing oranges in the back.

"Why do you say no?" Kendra said.

"Because it's not *my* city," Ruby huffed.

"Then whose city is it? Don't you see how people keep looking at you?"

"People always look at me."

Kendra snorted. She sipped her smoothie. Hamilton was tonguing up his Berry Goji Getaway bowl like he hadn't eaten in years. "Come on, Sage. Admit it."

"I'm not admitting anything," Ruby said pointedly. "We've gotten lucky and you know that. It'll only be a matter of time before those Scarfaces find us here next. Then we'll have to do what Emerald City and Diamond City combined couldn't do."

"And I'm sure you will," Kendra said, gazing at her earnestly. "Let's be honest: You've been training with the Lolligo. You've taken Samson's blood into your body. You're practically indestructible."

Ruby wouldn't want to put that to the test. She decided to change the subject. "So how are things between you and Hayes?"

Kendra shrugged. "Nothing different. I don't know why you keep asking me that."

"Well, aren't you a couple now?"

"Of course not. We've had sex a couple of times, but does that really mean anything?"

Hayes and Kendra's relationship was practically public knowledge at this point. Now that there were more people in their thriving "city", Ruby wasn't the only one who heard them at night or caught them banging in the bathroom. She wasn't sure what anyone else said about that very toxic relationship, but someone had to tell Kendra that Hayes was using her. Obviously.

Hayes was on a mission to make Ruby jealous at all costs. That's why he was having sex with whoever gave him permission, reverting to his old unethical ways from high school. Ruby didn't feel it was in her place to tell Kendra this and start a terrible war of dominance between the three of them, but maybe it was. No one knew *why* Hayes was behaving this way—just that he was—and it was up to Ruby, as Kendra's friend, to tell her there was foul play.

"Of course it means something," Ruby said gently. "Kendra, you're acting like you don't care, but you do."

Kendra sipped her smoothie some more. She was having the Good Morning, Mama. "No, I don't."

"Yes, you do. Please be careful."

"Are you saying this because Hayes admitted that he wanted to be with you but he's chosen me instead?"

"Kendra," Ruby said patiently. Hamilton barked and servers were ready with his second bowl of yogurt. "I'm married. You're the first one to tell me that my real name is Sage and that I have a past life I can't let go of. So this has nothing to do with me."

"It has everything to do with you," Kendra said steadily. "You might be married, but you still have feelings, Ruby. I know you're hurt that Hayes came onto me instead. You'd rather keep him isolated and all to yourself, wouldn't you?"

"Of course not!" Ruby snapped. "Damn it, Kendra, why do you have to be so stubborn?!"

Wow, Ruby really did hate these stupid love games. She got so angry that she walked away, deciding it was for the best that she didn't talk to Kendra for a long-ass time. She had spoken her piece, and there was nothing else she could do. Besides, more prominent problems came up.

While Ruby continued her training with Samson, the Lolligo and Hayes continued their excursions in the Outskirts. They were still searching for any signs of where these Scarfaces were transporting prisoners. It was on the latest trip that Ruby and Samson were alerted by police that there was movement on the north side of the city. That meant either more stragglers or Scarfaces.

Everyone always hoped for the first, but Randall didn't sound so sure this time. He spoke in quick, worried tones, utterly terrified that their newfound peace was about to come to a bloody end.

Ruby looked to Samson, who showed no expression on his face. She sought guidance from his amber eyes, but all she got was uncertainty in return. She didn't know how someone that was so powerful could be cowering in the face of opposition. Wasn't he supposed to be the Lolligo Prime?

Was, Ruby reminded herself. *Not anymore.*

Samson didn't say anything. He stood there in all his shirtless glory, a bit stiff for someone who was in imminent danger. Jamie came out of the ship to see what was going on.

"We're here for you," Jamie assured Ruby since Samson didn't seem capable of moving.

Ruby didn't waste any more time. She crossed the city, heading north toward the plains where she usually intercepted stragglers. The temperature was plummeting, which was usual for the month of Birth, but it wasn't snowing. Not yet. There was just this chill in the air that Ruby had never quite felt before. She was used to cold weather, but there was something especially piercing in the oxygen that she breathed. It felt like she was inhaling tiny knives that were cutting up her bronchioles and making her bleed from the inside out.

As she raced through the streets, Ruby saw faces peering at her. She saw people standing by on the sidewalk, unsure if they should hide or what they should do during an emergency. Many were hopeful they'd have new neighbors to welcome, but others already knew that the incoming forces across the Outskirts were not friendly.

Ruby saw them in the distance. They all had a scar across their left eye. That was the mark of their gang or maybe it had been part of their initiation. Whatever the case, they were one mind and one body now. They were all dressed in the same thick coats and carried the same laser guns in their hands. There were ten or so Scarfaces standing there, all looking up at the city with blinking lights, confused because they hadn't noticed such activity the last time they had driven through here. Or maybe they just hadn't noticed. On the ground in front of their feet were bodies. Judging by the hissing and the smell wafting from those corpses, they had just tested out their guns.

Castor and Pollux, Ruby thought to herself when gazing at those emotionless faces. She couldn't even tell if they were man or woman—they were just stoic, like dummies. Her hands were already shaking. She had her sword, but that wasn't giving her too much comfort at the moment.

"Ruby," Randall pressed. He was standing in a line of officers, who were confronting the enemy with a surprising amount of courage. As runaways from Diamond City themselves, they had already witnessed what these gangsters were capable of. "You're going to fight on your own? Where are the Lolligo?"

Ruby didn't know. She had to deal with her own fucking fears and get her head in the game or else she was putting a lot of lives at risk. She had to confront these Scarfaces in a peaceful, non-violent manner in hopes they wouldn't resort to fighting.

"Stay here," Ruby said to Randall and the rest of the police. They had twenty men and women—all human—in that thick battle armor with their own weapons. Against the Scarfaces, though? Ruby didn't want to take any chances.

Ruby stepped forward. She trudged across the Outskirts toward the Scarfaces, but she didn't draw her sword. Not yet.

"Who are you?" Ruby asked them. "And what do you want?"

As she got closer, she didn't see any vehicles. There weren't any trucks in sight, transporting anyone. It looked like these ten Scarfaces had strayed from the main group to deal with rebellious captives.

Hamilton whined from behind Ruby, who hadn't noticed him following until now. It seemed he was giving her a small piece of advice: She didn't stand a chance. When Samson looked like he was about to shit in his pants, what on earth could Ruby do?

It struck her, then: Had the Lolligo run into these Scarfaces on their way to Ruby City as well? God, she hated that name—

"Sage?"

Ruby stiffened and whipped around. She turned toward the person who had uttered her name. That was never a good sign—everyone who knew her seemed to want to kill her.

"Whoa, whoa, whoa!" chortled the voice. And then, from over the horizon, came the person at last. He seemed to pop out of nowhere. He came speeding right up to them and stopped next to the line of Scarfaces, a safe distance away from Ruby. "It is *you*! Bless the Forefathers—it's been so long, darling!"

He was in a long trench coat with massive amounts of bloodstains, as if he had been rolling on the conveyor belt of a meat grinder.

That was not normal.

Ruby took a step back. God, she couldn't remember who this

was. The man was nothing out of the ordinary—tall, thin, dark hair—but he did have amber eyes and a vicious smile. He looked like the kind to hover in the sidelines and watch the action go down.

"Don't you remember me, Sage?" The man frowned. The Scarfaces stood by, analyzing Ruby closely, perhaps recognizing her as the pesky prisoner that had gotten away. "It's Jared!"

"Who are you?!" Ruby exclaimed, frustrated.

"Oh," said Jared, scrutinizing her some more. "So you have amnesia, too. Cita was the exact same when she woke up, you know. She didn't remember a thing. As time went on, however, she slowly recovered her memories."

Cita? Who the fuck was Cita?

"Oh, sorry—you know her as Venus." Jared cocked his head. "But you don't remember that, either, do you?"

Tears burned Ruby's eyes, but she refused to let them fall. She was done crying about things she couldn't remember. This guy didn't seem bothered by the fact he had to fill her in.

"How sad," he lamented. "You should have recovered your memories by now. Just wait until the Warlord finds that his beloved doesn't remember him at all." He laughed loudly. "Oh, he'll be so broken! He already is, you know. Rumor has it he *screamed* at little Louis the night they caught you on top of the palace. If it wasn't for your boys, I think he would have decapitated the Diamond City Allseer."

As she pictured all that in her head, Ruby felt her feet sinking into the ground. She saw it all in her mind's eye: Damian screaming at Louis... horrified that Ruby had been kidnapped... and starting a brawl.

"He was supposed to die." Jared scowled. "That night, Sage, your beloved husband was supposed to be *dead*. Louis had set the whole thing up, you know, and I certainly don't blame him. My Enhanced were there to ambush him, but there was no containing the Warlord that night—he went on a goddamn rampage—and it's *his* fault that Diamond City is in shambles right now. How does that make you feel, Queen of Diamonds?"

" 'His fault'?" Ruby breathed. "How is it his fault?"

"He killed everything that breathed!" Jared yelled. "I think he slaughtered half of the guards at the palace and would have gone for more were it not for your two brats who stopped him! Little did he know, my Enhanced were prepared for a full takeover, and at long last, we have Diamond City in the palm of our hand. Do you honestly think that some half-ass militants who are more human than Enhanced are enough to fight *me* and my *true* army of killer Enhanced? They're not as daring as mine." Jared chuckled. "Those fools don't know what it means to wield power . . . and use it the way they're supposed to."

"What do you want?" Ruby said, ignoring the horrifying reality that this had been coordinated by Louis—what the fuck? "What do you want, Jared? Why are you taking innocent fucking people away and slaughtering them like pigs? What on earth do they have to do with anything? Don't tell me that was Louis' idea, too!"

"Didn't I already tell you?" Jared said patiently. "Oh, but you forgot, right? We are *hybrids*, Sage. We are the new race that will rule this world, the perfect blend of human and Lolligo. We can fight like mad dogs but win beauty pageants with our eyes closed. Your precious Warlord shut down all those experiments and even executed any scientists who thought of dabbling in them, so we are it. Well, *I'm* it, because it looks like you're as stubborn in this life as you were in your previous one. Still clinging to justice, are you?"

"I might be a hybrid, but I'm not a monster!" Ruby exclaimed, her ears ringing with the words *"race that will rule this world."* "And I don't turn people into Enhanced just for the hell of it."

"Yes, you *are* a monster," Jared said casually, crossing his arms. "We're all monsters here, darling. Some of us are just more subdued than others. But unlike you, I have embraced my nature and it is time to act."

"Where are you taking all these people?!"

"Does it really matter, Sage? You're going to die on this battlefield today, anyway. My Enhanced were complaining about some mutant freak they couldn't contain and—lo and behold—it's *you*."

Jared sneered. "While I would say Emerald City has a nice little surprise waiting for them, you'll be long dead before you see it. I only wish you could see the look on Damaris' face when he sees your dead body."

Jared clapped his hands. "Chop-chop, children. Kill her."

Ruby braced herself. Jared laughed like a banshee.

"Oh! And it looks like we have an audience!"

All of Ruby City was here. All one hundred-plus residents were here to watch the fight between Ruby and those ten Scarfaces.

Enhanced. They were Enhanced. Some time ago, they were humans. What changed that? Jared's blood? Seemingly. Ruby knew it took the blood of a hybrid to turn someone into an Enhanced. And even though Enhanced weren't as strong as hybrids, they seemed trained enough to stand toe-to-toe with one who was still learning how to fight.

Ruby eyed each one of her opponents. Whoever they used to be when they were human was dead. All that mattered to them was following orders. All that mattered to them was staying alive. To Jared, they were "children". But based on how they looked and behaved, they were dispensable. Anyone could become an Enhanced, lose their identity, and join Jared's ranks in exchange for a bit of power.

Terrifying. Ruby couldn't think about Diamond City right now, though. She couldn't think about anything if she was going to win this fight against ten opponents all at once. The only way to truly kill an Enhanced was to strike them with Slainium, which was what this sword was made of, but before she did that, she offered peace.

"You can go on without a fight," Ruby said to them. "You won't win against me."

"Oh?" Jared snorted. "Quite the confidence there, Sage. I guess you didn't forget how to fight, did you?"

Ruby wasn't about to give away the Lolligo. She kept her eyes on the Scarfaces.

"I didn't," Ruby said. She drew her sword, pointing it. "If you want to see for yourself, then attack me. Let's see what you've got, but the lot of you don't look like fighters to me."

Jared clapped, but this wasn't out of amusement—this was a command to his children. *Go!* he said with his scowl, and the Scarfaces reacted.

The ten of them charged her at once. They had no strategy. Easy.

Ruby jumped high up into the air. Thirty feet—non-human—so not normal to the people watching the fight. Even the Scarfaces couldn't reach her up there, so they looked up just as she unleashed a wave of energy that knocked them all off their feet.

Stunned by that move, the Scarfaces couldn't do anything to defend themselves against Ruby's next attack. This was her opportunity to skewer one of them, and she did so on her way down. Ruby drove her blade right through a skull, breaking through bone, then ducked all the swipes from the surrounding Scarfaces.

She was quick, agile, nimble on her feet, and didn't throw any attacks when there were so many bodies around her. She kept momentum in her favor, preferring to dodge rather than risk getting hit just because she wanted to knock down another opponent. She twirled out of that mess unscathed and braced herself for round two.

"Careful, children," Jared called with a tight scowl. "This one knows how to fight."

And shape-shift. Perhaps those Scarfaces were faster and stronger than the average Enhanced, but they didn't have the skill it took to grow limbs. Ruby used her left arm to latch onto the Scarface farthest from the group and jump right in front of him. She skewered him, too.

That was two down, but none of the Scarfaces were dead yet. If anything, they were learning all of Ruby's attacks and skills to better counter them in the future. Ruby watched their faces closely. There were no signs of confidence. They were all clutching their guns. Ruby never underestimated her opponents, but she knew now these Scarfaces wouldn't be able to keep up with her.

"SHOOT HER!" Jared roared.

That seemed to be the solution to everything. The lasers were powerful and blew through the ground, decimating mounds of dirt and snow. Perhaps to humans or even regular Enhanced, those beams of light were fast, but Ruby knew how to dance around them pretty effectively after having to evade all of Samson's hellish tentacles.

Amazingly, Ruby was at it for nearly an hour. She couldn't get close to the Scarfaces while they were firing lasers and they were depending on her to slow down eventually. That must have been their strategy against the military in Diamond City, too. It was impossible to get close to them while all those bursts of energy were going off right in her face.

"What are you going to do now, Sage?!" Jared taunted from across the field. "Attack them now, bitch!"

Ruby knew that she wouldn't be able to dodge forever. She also knew that those lasers could cut through physical objects like butter. She wasn't sure what was powering them, but she wondered how they would fare against Slainium.

Slainium was a resilient metal against itself. It was poison to Cells, just like these lasers seemed to be if they were cutting down Enhanced in Diamond City. Ruby had nothing to lose—other than her sword—by deflecting them, so that's what she did. She jumped to an area it'd be safe to try her tactic in and braced herself for the impact.

Amazingly, the blade deflected the blast. Ruby could hardly believe her eyes: That laser went flying backward. Ruby would make sure to kiss Samson later—maybe even get a tattoo of his face on her thigh (he'd kill her)—for this incredible weapon that just might save her life and all of Ruby City.

Ruby wasn't going to push the sword's limits, but she was going to use that rebound to her advantage. The Scarface who had shot it was confused, so he didn't stand a chance of ducking under his own attack. In seconds, he was a pile of bloody guts on the ground. Ruby made sure to grab his gun and then the rest was cake.

Dodge, shoot. Dodge, shoot. Dodge, shoot.

Ruby even got the two Scarfaces she had stabbed with her sword earlier. In just ten minutes, after a whole hour of dancing around the field, Ruby had defeated all ten of her opponents.

Cheers and hooting erupted from Ruby City. Ruby should have known better than to lose her focus, because Jared grabbed her from behind and pressed a blade to her throat.

"SHUT UP!" he yelled at the crowd—they hushed instantly. "SHUT THE FUCK UP, YOU LOUSY HUMANS!"

Ruby could have lost her head, but she noticed someone in her peripheral vision that made Jared freeze.

"Let her go," Samson said.

That was the distraction Ruby needed to duck, grab her sword from its sheath, and run it right through Jared's chest.

Jared staggered back, gasping. His eyes focused on Samson, who had his own gun raised and pointed.

Samson didn't hesitate to fire—Jared jumped—and Ruby followed him with her blade in hand.

"You annoying wench!" Jared yelled as he blocked her sword movements with a measly dagger. "You just don't die, do you?!"

"And neither do you, scumbag!"

For someone who didn't look like a fighter, Jared held his own surprisingly well against Ruby. He blocked her movements and concentrated on putting as much distance as possible between them. To Ruby's horror, there were more Scarfaces in the distance.

"I'd stop while you're ahead," Jared sniggered. "Do you really think you're going to win, Sage? Against *hundreds* of my precious children? My babies might have withered away, but these Enhanced will *not* die. Do you hear me?"

Ruby clutched her sword tighter. Jared was falling to his feet.

"If you kill me, they'll attack," he spat. "And even you and that ugly Squid won't be able to stop them. My children can overwhelm Lolligo. Would you like to see them?"

"You're going to kill us anyway!" Ruby exclaimed.

Jared held up his hands. He coughed on some blood as his chest wound took forever to close. The Slainium was turning his veins black.

"We won't kill you if you let me go," Jared said. "You want to save those humans, don't you?"

Samson caught up to Ruby and he fired his gun again. Jared had to scurry if he was going to evade that blast.

"I can't believe there are any Lolligo left!" Jared taunted with a hissing hole between his feet. "Didn't you lose some war or something? Are you the pathetic leftover that managed to escape Elysium? How fucking sad! All you Lolligo are big muscular brutes who can't even run a city! You can't fight much, either, because you're scared—you're fucking scared—"

Ruby lunged, but Samson held her back.

"No, Sage," he said in Lolligo. "It's not worth it. There are nearly fifty Scarfaces out there and only two of us. Xeno and Bruce are still not back. We may not win if we try our hand at fighting them." He turned to her. "It's better to live today and fight tomorrow. Xeno's found something and he's coming back with a report."

Ruby gazed into the amber eyes and believed him. She found comfort in his decision, so she softened her stance.

"You have their gun," Samson said, eyeing it in her left hand. "I can analyze it and create something to combat it. Looks like Slainium did a pretty good job of deflecting the blasts."

"He's going to die, you know!" Jared exclaimed as he inched backward. It was at a snail's pace, but he made progress nonetheless. "The Warlord will die."

"Don't listen, Sage," Samson said to her, seizing her face so she wouldn't look at Jared. He kept her eyes on his. "He doesn't know shit."

"They say he's in failing health," Jared went on. "How can't he be? After all the heartache the past thirty years, I think he's about to wither away."

No way. Ruby had watched him fight Sword Devil.

"Don't believe me?" Jared said casually. "He's bedridden at the palace. He can't go on without you, Sage. If you hurry, you might just see him die."

Was it true?

Ruby forced her face out of Samson's grasp so she could turn around. Jared was a speck in the distance now, his scooter forgotten on the ground.

"My beloved was in a cocoon, too," Jared said. "And even my own fucking kids died, but I didn't let that stop me. *Nothing* will stop me. And my beloved understands that, too: We will be unstoppable. But your Warlord? He's too *weak*. He's about to die any moment now."

Samson grabbed Ruby and slapped her. Hard.

Ruby was so startled that she fell on her ass. She looked at Samson, who shook his head.

"I fucking know you," he snarled. "Whatever thoughts you have in your head, you stop them *right now*. Understand? You're thinking of doing the very thing that that loser wants you to do. If you go back to Diamond City on your own, you'll be overwhelmed and you'll die.

"The Warlord is *not* in failing health. Do you think he's going to keel over when he knows you're out there?"

So why hadn't he found Ruby yet? If he was out there, searching for her, then why hadn't he come across Ruby City yet?

"He's trying to save Diamond City!" Samson yelled at her. "*Your* city, damn it! He thinks you're there, biding your time, but you are *not* going to fuck this up now by doing something dumb! GET UP!" He pulled her to her feet. He slapped her again. "Use your head and not your feelings for once! *Think*, Sage, for Stars' sake! How the fuck does Jared know the Warlord's in failing health?"

Hadn't Jared and his Enhanced taken over the city?

"He and his kin might be causing chaos, but they're *not* in control. Not yet. Emerald City isn't done yet. I know the Warlord, Sage—you might have forgotten, but I haven't. We spent too much time together in Mousafeld, and I know his tactics. I also know his drive. While he might be a bit depressed—boo-hoo, we all were without you—that's not going to stop him! He's going to fight with everything he has to get to you, and that's how I know Jared hasn't been able to take full control of Diamond City."

Samson snorted. "Bedridden? Give me a fucking break. If that were true, Jared would have killed him already. And if the Warlord was already dead, Jared would still tell you he's in failing health to draw you into a trap."

Ruby gazed at Samson. Her brain was taking a while to process all his words—his Lolligo was so fast—but it did.

She believed him.

When she turned her head, Jared was gone. So were the Scar-faces.

The cheering and hooting. It started again.

And this time, it didn't stop.

CHAPTER 8

Goodbyes

"RUBY! RUBY! RUBY!"
The cheers never stopped.
"RUBY! RUBY! RUBY!"

That's because the people knew how close they had been to losing their lives. The Scarfaces would have raided their city with ease and decimated them. Now, thanks to Ruby and her trusty Lolligo companions, they were going to live another day.

"Jeez," Samson muttered under his breath. He was picking up all the dead Scarfaces' guns from the ground. "I hate humans."

Ruby smiled. "They're not so bad. I can live with this."

"You can, but I can't. Some peace and quiet would be nice."

"Don't be such a grouch."

Samson glared at her. "You're not thinking of going back to Diamond City, are you?"

Ruby hesitated. But the answer was no.

"Good. My response stands: It's a trap. Right now, we have to figure out how we can defeat those Enhanced." He pressed something on his watch. "Jamie, come and pick up these bodies, will you? I am not getting my hands dirty."

"He called you a Squid," Ruby said.

Samson whipped around to her, nostrils flared. But when he saw her sincere expression, he must have realized she felt bad about the insult. To her, Samson was anything but a "squid". To Jared, though, it was supposed to be hurtful.

"It's insulting," Samson said crisply. "And you used to say it all the time."

Ruby was surprised to hear this. "What? Why?"

Samson's lip quivered. He looked like he had a stomach ache, but that was just him fighting back a smile. "Because you like to be a pain in the ass."

Ruby smiled, too. And that was as close to a compliment as she was going to get.

Samson didn't want to go anywhere near the group of humans, so he hung back.

Ruby, on the other hand, joined the ranks of all the people waiting for her by the city's edge. She got patted on the back, high-fived, hugged, and kissed by pretty much everyone. The preachers blessed her for defending them and "thanked the Forefathers" for sending them such powerful warriors in a time of need, especially Samson, whom they were starting to refer to as the Lolligo Prophet.

Ruby laughed.

A successful mission called for a celebration. Paige and Pedro knew just the spot, too. The college couple, Gary and Tiana, had opened up a club a few blocks away from Crystal Light. There was nothing to study, so why not invest in music and booze? They had a full-fledged stereo and some nice strobe lights for the rest of the evening. No one worried about the Scarfaces when the Lolligo were nearby and Ruby was in their midst. It was time to relax after those stressful few hours.

"How did you dodge all those lasers?" Paige asked her, impressed. Even her kids had seen the whole thing. They were bumbling around the club pretending to be her. "Weren't you nervous you'd slip up?"

142

"I was more nervous that Samson would cut me into pieces," Ruby admitted.

"I would be, too," Pedro said darkly. "I'm actually surprised the Lolligo haven't killed us all yet. They hate us."

"How about a drink?" Paige offered happily.

"I think I'll go with a soda," Ruby said with a smile.

Cherry soda was her favorite. Ruby thanked the waitress then relaxed in her chair. It was easy to do when Hayes was still far away on his excursion with Xeno and Bruce. His absence was a grand relief to them all. Kendra and Micah were more tolerable and much more amicable toward each other when competition wasn't in the way. It was no secret that Micah had been hitting on Kendra for weeks.

Ruby smiled. She watched Micah laugh at some random scientific fun fact Kendra had learned in her city travels today. Because they had a hair stylist now, Micah had gotten a nice cut and shave. Dressed in that plaid flannel with tight pants and boots, what girl wasn't looking his way? Other than the fact he was still seventeen, of course, but his birthday was coming up in a couple of months. Kendra was well aware of it and the way he was looking at her. She had been making much more eye contact recently.

Their company plus the entertainment made Ruby feel right at home. She was happy to see everyone engaging with each other from her plush chair in the corner. There was only so much dancing people could do at this late hour, so someone started up mini games and competitions.

First up was who could paint the best portrait of a Lolligo, judged by the preachers who waited outside because raucous music would "upset the Lolligo." They weren't wrong, though—Samson hated it.

Ruby laughed to herself. She watched Jasmine and Randall become the first contestants. They had bottles of paint at their disposal, and it was time to illustrate the monstrous Lolligo. Jasmine went with some green and silver since those were her favorite colors.

"An imperial Lolligo," she declared. "With a green and silver robe."

Green eyeliner, silver glitter. Perfect foundation on his face and gloss on his lips. Long black hair framed his face, touched his chest. That had grown a lot over the months. Silky, like a waterfall. Sage touched the strands gingerly. Then she rested her hands on his bare shoulders, the low cut of his top. He was incredibly beautiful. That sexy fairy man wandering through the woods . . .

"I think this is dumb," Micah grumbled. "We all know they're not divine beings—they're just some poor saps that were exposed to radiation."

"Still powerful, though," Kendra said.

"I will love you and cherish you forever," Damian whispered against Sage's temple. "And I will always be by your side to protect you. I will get stronger so that you won't have to fight, my Star."

"Damian," Sage said softly. "You don't have to fight my battles for me."

"I do. I absolutely do."

Sage reached into her pocket. Gertrude had bought her this Portable Projector, but Sage didn't need two. Defenders Unite! *was enough for her. Damian, on the other hand, loved* The Rainbow in Me.

They had only seen the first three episodes before the craziness started. The main character, Doug, had started to contemplate his true feelings for the cameraman. But then, at the end of the third episode, he had caught the eye of the dancer on stage. Sage wasn't sure what happened after that, but she had the whole season here.

Sage thought it was the perfect gift. She didn't remember downloading this, but this was an ideal dream, so she had.

Ruby looked at Kendra. Heart in her throat, she rasped, "I remember now!"

Kendra arched a brow. "Remember what?"

"The show!"

Kendra still wasn't getting it.

"*The Rainbow in Me*," Ruby said patiently. "Charles had said he was watching it, remember?"

"Well, not really," Kendra said. "The new season hasn't come out yet. Or has it? With all the trouble, I wonder if it ever premiered." She shook her head. "Probably not. So you used to watch it, too?"

"I . . . think." Ruby rubbed her head. "At least . . . Damian did . . ."

She had gotten him a Portable Projector. Wow, those things were rare. Ruby had always wanted one with all the *Defenders Unite!* episodes. Apparently, she had owned one in the past.

Kendra grinned. Beneath the strobe lights, she had all kinds of colors dancing on her skin. It was obvious that Ruby's amnesia was one big science experiment to her. Any time Ruby remembered her past was a reason to grow excited. "So you actually remember now?"

A little. Ruby could still see Damian's face and hear his words. It felt like something that had happened in the past, although Ruby couldn't be sure. Nonetheless, she clung to that memory where she had been one-on-one with Damian in some kind of forest. There had been snow at her feet.

"Jared escaped," Micah said to them, changing the subject. Maybe he sensed he wouldn't have a lot of opportunities to talk about it.

Ruby sighed. "He did."

"You're going after him?"

"I am."

Ruby would be sure to see Samson in the morning. Right now, she was so exhausted she had a hard time making it back to her room. After a quick shower and changing into some comfortable clothing, she grabbed the little book of poems she had been working on the past few months. She couldn't dream of rhyming words at the moment, but she did feel the need to write to Damian from the heart.

Dear Damian,

No poem today. I just fought Jared and his Enhanced, and my hands are still shaking. This was my first real battle after waking up. I don't re-member anything from before that time, but I do get snippets. You liked

*The Rainbow in Me, didn't you? You wore green and silver once. I'm sorry
I don't know more, but I want you to know I love you no matter what.
Everyone's told me what a great father you've been to Castor and Pollux.
I hope I'll be able to see you soon.*

Ruby hesitated.

*Please don't be disappointed in me. I've been trying so hard to remember.
I hope you're well.*

Ruby hesitated again.

Love,
Sage

Ruby closed the book. She put it on her nightstand then crawled
into bed. She didn't pull the covers over her just yet. She laid there,
staring at the ceiling.

She fell asleep right away.

The next morning, all was quiet in the complex. Ruby got up early
to talk to Samson about what Hayes and the other Lolligo had reported from their excursion. She thought she was all alone until
she found Micah waiting for her in the hall.

He was showered and dressed in different clothes from last
night. He must have gotten very little sleep.

"Are you heading out?" Micah asked her.

"I have to," Ruby said.

"I have a feeling they'll be here soon."

"They" as in Emerald City.

Ruby nodded. These people needed all the help they could get.
Micah was stating the obvious for other reasons.

"If you wait just a few more days, you can go together," he said.

"But that's just it," Ruby said softly. "There's no guarantee Emerald City is on their way. Plus, we're trying to intercept Jared,

wherever he is, and we don't have much time to waste if we hope to catch him."

"By yourself?" Micah challenged. "And those three Lolligo? Is it enough? Didn't you see how scared the Lolligo are of humans? They looked traumatized."

"Yeah . . . I know."

"Please don't die!" Micah blurted out. "I feel that it'd be better if you stay and wait than just rush out there like this! I know the Lolligo need you, but I don't want them to abuse you, either."

"I won't do anything reckless," Ruby promised him. "If things get tough, I'll pull back. I want to see what's going on first. Then, when I return, we'll be able to make a decision from there."

"Who's going to defend us if you're gone?"

"Don't worry. Jared won't be coming back, and I won't be long."

Micah's eyes welled with tears. "Aunt Sage . . . we haven't known each other long . . . but I can see why you're special. I can see why my mom and Olivia speak so highly of you."

Ruby bowed. "Thank you. You're not such a bad kid yourself. And if you're going to make a move on Kendra, I'd do it sooner rather than later."

Micah gasped. "What are you talking about?"

"I might be an amnesiac, but I'm not dumb. I see the way you look at her."

Micah was blushing like crazy. Even with dark skin, he was as red as a tomato. Ruby just laughed.

"I'll be back."

Ruby took the stairs for some exercise. She walked down the block leisurely, looking up at all the storefronts that would be opening for business soon. Jo's Yo-Go was already set up for breakfast. Ruby wished she'd be able to join them. Hell, if Emerald City was on their way here, Ruby wanted to stay and meet her family.

To Ruby, it was still so surreal. The warrior she aspired to be because of Damian's battle with Sword Devil, because of everything she had learned about him in her classes, was her *husband*. This was dumb, but she felt the need to ask Samson if she was really married. Micah had never mentioned "husband" nor "wife" when describing her relationship. Or did he need to? Were those tags really necessary?

She found him in the *Luse* analyzing the Scarface leftovers with Jamie. Travis's table, as well as Ruby's whenever she got torn to pieces by Samson in training, were both in use. Samson and Jamie always wore ultra Lolligo-sized hazmat suits just in case they were "contaminated" by human diseases. Ruby certainly didn't blame them—hybrids and Enhanced were still a mystery—but that meant she couldn't come in until they were done.

So Ruby waited outside. Xeno, Bruce, and Hayes still weren't back from their excursion anyway. They had taken their ship for this extra long and potentially dangerous mission.

Ruby took a seat on the ground. She rolled up her sleeve to caress Damian's tattoo. Seeing it comforted her. Knowing that he was close by gave her confidence. Even long before knowing they were together, Ruby had found him extraordinarily attractive. Sure, he was beautiful by nature, but Ruby couldn't deny the more intimate connection she felt whenever she looked at his face. Perhaps she didn't need her memories to feel that way—her heart and soul still remembered all.

Ruby wiped her eyes. She didn't understand why she was crying again, but the tears were coming. She had a horrible longing in her belly to be held and loved. She felt like she wanted to embrace someone, but she was too shy to express herself.

What the hell was wrong with her? Samson was asking her the same thing.

"For Star's sake, *what* are you crying about now?" he snarled as he stomped down the ramp of his ship. "That boy isn't even here to cause you any problems and you're still emotional!"

"Gosh, sorry." Ruby used her shirt this time. "I-I just can't control myself sometimes. When I try to remember things, I get overwhelmed with emotion. I keep thinking about Damian and I feel . . . sad. Then I look at you and I feel there's more to us than just training, too. We were roommates for so long, so I'm sure we went through a lot, right?"

Samson's eyes softened, but not by much. "I suppose we did."

"Can I hug you?"

Samson's eyes blew up.

Ruby got to her feet. "Even though you make me go through hell during training, I feel like I love you, too. Can I hug you?"

"N-no!" Samson sputtered. If he had skin, he'd be as red as Micah from this morning. "Stop being all lovey-dovey—it's not like you. Besides, we have a situation and you need to be focused."

"All right. Sorry."

"We've been communicating with Xeno and Bruce," Samson explained tightly. He was still making faces and brushing away embarrassment. "And it seems they've spotted something massive. It's over a hundred miles out from here, but they want us to see it. They don't want to lose track of it, either."

Ruby was still processing the "something massive" part. "Do you have pictures of what they spotted?"

"Unfortunately, no. I think we need to see it for ourselves." Samson nodded at her sword. "The Slainium in that thing can cut down anything with Cells, as you proved yesterday when you fought Jared's Enhanced. All the Cells in their body have completely shriveled up, which is a good thing for us. Xeno and Bruce are more than equipped to start blasting from the skies, but we'd like you to take a closer look."

In other words, they needed her small size and agility to navigate the grounds. Ruby didn't mind doing that.

"Do you think this *thing* is what Jared was protecting?" she asked.

Samson shook his head. "Don't know. I guess we'll see soon enough."

Ruby nodded and made her way to the ship. As she passed Samson to step onto the ramp, he extended his arms.

He looked like he was carrying an invisible whale. The strain on his face was painful.

Ruby arched a brow.

"Hurry up!" Samson sputtered. "Before Jamie sees us!"

"Sees us what?"

"Do you want a hug or not?"

Ruby's cheeks flushed. She grinned. While her hair got a bit frizzy at times, she did love her teeth. They were white, nice, and straight.

"Come on!" Samson hissed.

This was her chance to do what she had been plotting for *months*: Ruby rammed into Samson's chest on purpose and knocked him to the ground. He was a young Lolligo—nowhere near as massive as Bruce—but he was still thrice as big as she was. He was all muscle, too, so his body wasn't the most comfortable, but Ruby didn't care. With knees on either side of his waist, she made sure to squeeze his torso and smile into his chest.

Samson didn't chastise her, even though he was dirtying his shirt by lying on his back on the ground. He kept quiet, a bit tense, but eventually he relaxed. He patted her head like a dog.

"Oh, my!" sang Jamie from the *Luse*'s entrance. "Isn't this the cutest sight ever? Hold on—let me get a picture—"

"All right," Samson grumbled, pushing Ruby off of him. "Enough—"

Ruby kissed his cheek, and Samson's whole face really did turn red. All that pink muscle turned to the color of a seasoned cardinal, which beat Micah's blush by a landslide.

"Thank you, Samson, for everything," Ruby said happily.

CHAPTER 9

Cell Land

The trip that followed that display of affection was a strange one. Ruby felt content and confident, so she kept quiet in her seat. She liked sitting close to pilot controls so she could see how Jamie was flying the ship. Maybe she'd pilot her own ship one day.

Jamie was in a pretty good mood, too. His smile never faded, and it had nothing to do with the picture he had gotten of Samson and Ruby. For the first time since Ruby had met him, he seemed at ... ease. He knew, with a hundred percent certainty, that Ruby wasn't going to betray him. Perhaps there was a chance of survival, after all.

The only one who was stomping around like a child was Samson, who was still flustered from that kiss. He didn't admit it—he just complained about everything.

"The day that I don't have to deal with people's messes will be the day I grow hair," he grumbled, sweeping the floor where Ruby had, apparently, walked with her dirty boots. "And because Lolligo don't grow hair, that's never."

Ruby checked her boots. She didn't see any dirt on them. She couldn't imagine what Samson would say if Hamilton ever had a potty accident on the ship.

He liked to hang around the Lolligo a lot, but he never pooped out of turn. *Never.* Ruby certainly didn't blame him. She wouldn't put it past Samson to make the poor dog eat his own shit if Hamilton ever got indigestion from the ten thousand-plus calories he consumed every day.

"Sage wasn't that messy, was she?" Jamie asked innocently.

"Actually, it was you," Samson spat at him. "I've told you to wipe your shoes before walking around in the ship! Pretty soon, I'll be requiring all shoes off!"

Jamie sighed. "Sorry, sir."

"Just don't do it again!"

"Samson, are you nervous?" Ruby asked him.

The answer was yes, even if Samson didn't admit it. He just kept sweeping because it kept his mind entertained. Jamie, on the other hand, showed Ruby some pictures that Xeno had taken of their find in the Outskirts.

Ruby gasped. "What is that?"

Xeno called it "Cell Land". That's because all of the mounds and piles of body parts belonged to Enhanced, humans, and a few Lolligo themselves. It looked like a graveyard of corpses that no one had ever bothered to bury. Most disturbing of all, it stretched far into the horizon, larger than any trench Ruby had seen from World War I photographs.

Just what the hell was this?

It was only when Jamie got closer that Ruby noticed some kind of figure in the middle of it. From a distance, it looked like a plant with a ginormous mouth and tentacles in the ground. When Ruby zoomed in on it with her binoculars, there were pairs of amber eyes scattered all over it. But nothing compared to its gigantic mouth with razor sharp teeth that would cut through flesh like that of a shark's. Knocking one of those out, she had a feeling, would make ten more sprout in its place. Splattered all over its body were specks of blood from what Ruby imagined were violent feedings. Beneath the crimson, however, was something white. Gooey and sticky, like glue. Perhaps in an everyday plant it'd be the equivalent of nectar, but on this monstrosity, that milky substance could disintegrate rocks.

Was that a Lolligo?

"What is it?" Ruby asked Jamie, who had the answer to everything but that question.

"I'm not sure," Jamie admitted. "It looks to be some sort of deformity not too different from what we found in Science of Tomorrow. The strange part is the radiation levels are normal and the thing . . . well . . . is alive."

"Meaning it's cognizant?"

"Exactly."

It wasn't a wonder that Samson was so nervous. But then again, if this thing was a Lolligo, wouldn't it be easy to kill with their arsenal of Slainium?

"We're assuming it's a Lolligo," Jamie explained. "But we're not sure it is and we're not sure what the Cells in its body are like. Slainium is for Lolligo that are biologically like us. Mutants like what we found, however, are a whole different ball game."

"Is that why hybrids scare you?"

Jamie hesitated, but the answer was yes.

Ruby crossed her arms. She gazed at Jamie earnestly. "I don't understand. Samson kicks my ass in training, yet you're afraid of some measly Enhanced? I pale in comparison to you."

"Not exactly. If you truly wanted to damage Samson, you could. And if there were more of you? You could overwhelm us."

"Slainium is lethal to me, too."

"Yes," Jamie said. "But it takes a lot to bring you down. Even the Scarfaces didn't die right away when you hit them with their own lasers."

"What happened in your city?" Ruby asked. "It's called Elysium, right?"

This time, Jamie looked at Samson.

"The four of you were running away from this Lolligo named Rhett," Ruby pressed. "But how did he manage to drive you out? Did he turn the rest of the Lolligo against you or did he have some kind of weapon?"

Jamie looked down. Samson cleared his throat.

"Now's not the time to talk about it, Sage," Samson snapped. "We had an agreement: We help you with those Enhanced, and then you come with us to figure out a way to defeat Rhett. I have ideas that may work . . . but we have to focus on this first. Understand?"

"So this 'Cell Land'—what is it?"

"That's what we're going to find out."

Ruby thought it had to do with Jared, but the Lolligo weren't too sure. They finally landed some fifteen minutes later, right next to Xeno and Bruce's ship a safe distance away from Cell Land. They were standing by, Hayes in between them, looking tense and worried as they surveyed the globs of goop they'd be traversing soon.

Jamie got out first. Samson hung back, looking as timid as a student on the first day of school.

"Samson?" Ruby said.

"I'm fine," Samson said curtly. "Don't mind me."

Samson was afraid. Ruby wondered if Sage knew why. If she had her memories back, would she know why Samson was the biggest coward on the planet? Jamie had a guilty look on his face, too.

Ruby decided not to say anything about it right now. She kept her head down as she stepped past Jamie and joined Hayes, who was scowling with his arms crossed. He kind of did play the part of Lolligo-sidekick well.

Hayes looked her up and down. His scowl deepened, depicting his annoyance and his complete inability to do anything to rid himself of his new masters. Xeno was pacing up and down while Bruce waited for instructions from his Prime. He had that egg strapped around his chest.

"Just what the fuck is all this?" Xeno called out. He waved at the barren landscape featuring nothing but mutilated body parts. The closest pile of gore had arms, legs, and feet all viciously torn from the bodies they once belonged to. It looked like a butchery out here, but something else didn't seem quite right.

This was no accident like the scene from Science of Tomorrow. This was definitely someone's dumping ground. Ruby had seen the Scarfaces decapitate Charles. All these bodies were from Diamond City.

Ruby threw up. She'd munched on some pancakes on the way here, but they were on the ground now. Her stomach was bubbling up. Her arms were shaking, too.

"Hey!" Xeno hissed at her. "Keep it together, girl! We're depending on *you*, remember?"

Right. They were depending on her to do what, exactly? Clean up this mess?

Hayes snorted. "Really?" he said out loud. "On *her*? Well, she is the Optimum, so I suppose that makes sense."

Ruby didn't like how cold Hayes sounded. Sage would have said something—wouldn't have been vomiting her guts out to begin with—but Ruby didn't have the strength to reprimand him. She felt so minuscule that she didn't know how she was going to lift her sword again. After she finished throwing up, she glared at Hayes over her shoulder.

Not fair, she said in her mind. *So not fair.*

Hayes was a jealous son of a bitch. That's what this was about—wanting to steal her from her family and take her for himself—but Samson reminded her that now was not the time for emotional games.

Samson grabbed her arm and pulled her to her feet. "Focus," he hissed in her face. "Will you? Focus, damn it!"

"I'm sorry," Ruby said quickly, wiping her mouth. The bile on the floor smelled awful. "It's just this place is disgusting! What the hell am I supposed to do here?"

"That's just it," Samson said tightly. "By the look of all these bodies, this is the Scarfaces' lair. If I had to guess, this is where they've been taking all their victims. If I'm right, then Jared shouldn't be too far, either. We need to go in there and see what's going on."

Xeno cleared his throat. " 'We', sir?"

"Yes. We're not sending Sage on her own—we'll be right behind her." Samson nodded at Ruby. "Take the lead, see what you find. You can be far more discreet here than we can."

"And the other human?" Xeno bared his teeth at Hayes, who turned the color of sour milk.

Samson hesitated. Hayes still didn't know Lolligo, so he didn't know what they were saying about him. He could very well become the sacrifice he was destined to be.

"It's up to Sage," Samson finally said.

Ruby shook her head. She didn't want any liabilities. Moreover, she didn't want to put Hayes in danger.

Without saying another word, Ruby stepped forward. Her entire body was shaking. She had already thrown up everything in her stomach, so she didn't feel the need for a second round, but now she was hungry and dehydrated. She was hot and sweating beneath her jacket. She wiped her forehead and took a few deep breaths, but nothing helped.

There were bodies *everywhere.*

But why? What was the purpose of killing off all these people and stacking their bodies into piles?

Ruby drew her sword. She clutched it in her hand because she felt something was going to come out of one of those decomposing bundles and attack her. Some of the corpses looked like they were twitching. The ones that were high up gazed down at her, eyes blank. Some had twisted expressions, as if their final moments in life had been agonizing. Some belonged to children.

Ruby covered her nose. The closer she got to the heart of this mess, the stronger the smell of death and rotting flesh. Cell Land was a few acres big, so Ruby didn't know how much more she could see without passing out. Xeno hadn't reported any movement, but he hadn't done a thorough job investigating this, either.

There was a shuffling not too far away from here. Soft groans, too. A munching, as if someone were consuming bones.

What the hell?

Ruby got down. She glanced at the mounds around her, searching for nearby movement. When all was clear, she edged closer to the source of the noise. She kept her sword behind her as she peered around one of the body towers and nearly screamed at what she saw.

Ruby had seen it before, but now she was feet away from it. That plant-thing in the middle of this mess was actually a woman.

A huge *fucking* woman the size of a whale.

She was at the very center of the gore, her legs the size of tree trunks wide open, her belly about to explode from the abnormal amounts of eating she was doing. She just plucked whatever pieces were next to her and *ate* them. There was blood smeared all over her now, and that white goop was doing its job of digesting the pieces of flesh before it reached her mouth.

Ruby screamed. She just couldn't hold it in anymore—she screamed and ran. She completely missed the other voice that said, "Ah, I think we have a visitor," and just scrambled out of there because she couldn't take it. She rammed into a dangling torso and fell back on her ass, giving the Scarfaces a huge opportunity to grab her.

Ruby didn't let them touch her—she swung her sword like a crazy person, slicing a few faces and arms, but that didn't get her very far. She had no strategy, no sense, and no calm to escape from this hell with her life. All she could do was scream as those Scarfaces seized her and dragged her back toward that woman, but Samson and the Lolligo were there to blast them.

"Up, girl!" Xeno pulled her to her feet. "What are you doing, screaming like that?!"

"MONSTER!" Ruby cried, all out bawling. "There's a MONSTER!"

So ironic in the face of Lolligo, but that woman was far from anything human. Ruby couldn't stop crying no matter how hard she tried to compose herself. She was in the lion's den, and her life was on the line, but the surge of confidence never came, leaving a scared little child that very quickly became a liability. She crumbled against Jamie, who was the only Lolligo capable of holding her without throwing her away in disgust.

Then Ruby remembered something horrible. Suddenly, she knew why she was crying like this.

She had seen so much horror in her life, especially in the Uni-fication War. She had seen her friends blown to pieces by the op-position's weapons. She had seen an old lover of hers—August Vaughn—extract his own Cells and wither away and die. She had seen her sister, Wren, and her sister's pet, Taz, destroy the capital, Gregory's head in their clutches. But she had never seen a monster like *that*.

"What's the ruckus?" cried a voice from afar. At least, it sounded like it was coming from far away because Ruby couldn't stop crying.

"Stand down, you filthy hybrid!" Xeno exclaimed in Lucidum, pointing his gun at the figure that emerged to see more of his En-hanced in pieces. The Lolligo's guns might not have been powered by Slainium, but they were just as effective as blasting away bodies.

"Oh, my!" Jared gasped. "Lolligo have come to see me? And here I thought you had learned your lesson."

"And you call us monsters! What the hell is all this?"

"Humans," Jared said, without a speck of remorse, as if he was showing them his card collection. "But I like to call them trash. Use-less weaklings who don't really serve much of a purpose in society but whine and create gangs all day long. So we took the humans and brought them here, where they'll become part of a much grander purpose. Just please don't disturb Cita at the moment—she's busy consuming the last of the Enhanced we managed to capture. I think there were a few Emerald City bozos in the mix, too."

"What are you doing?!" Xeno sputtered. "*Why* is she doing this?"

Samson waved at Xeno to be quiet. They already knew the an-swer to that question. Maybe it was obvious to them, but Ruby was still lost, crying against Jamie's chest.

"She's consuming Cells," Jamie said quietly. "And this right here is her playground."

Jared smiled at them. "Smart. Ruby City, was it?"

Ruby looked up.

"The Venus Flytrap has to eat," Jared said matter-of-factly. Why did he look right at home standing atop a tower of gore? He had even changed into new clothes and combed back his hair. "Much blood must be spilled to finally eradicate the humans. Ruby City will be a *feast.*"

Samson fired at Jared, but Jared jumped back, laughing.

"You're going to have to be faster than that, Squid!"

Samson took him up on that challenge, firing like crazy. He never backed down because he was determined to take out that bastard.

The only problem was Cell Land was coming to life. Ruby could feel the rumbling beneath her feet. The groans that she had thought were all in her head were stronger now. They were coming from the corpses that were somehow alive. The smell of rot was intensifying twofold. It was so thick in the air that Ruby's eyes were burning.

Ruby stopped crying to stare into one of the faces. Glassy eyes and open mouth. The head started trembling. Fingers dripped with decay.

"Do you think there's enough Slainium in the world to defeat Venus?" Jared said from atop another pile. He scowled at them. "But who am I to dissuade you?"

"Retreat!" Samson cried in Lolligo. "We can't beat this thing from the inside!"

"Samson, no!" Ruby croaked, grabbing his arm next. "They're coming for Ruby City! W-we can't let them get close!"

"And how do you propose we beat them, Sage?! Not from here!"

"We blast it from the skies?" Jamie proposed.

But how? No amount of lasers was going to put a dent in this thing, was it?

Ruby looked up at Jared, who was laughing. He must have found it quite funny that the five of them didn't know what to do.

"Sage, no!" Samson yelled at her. "I know what you're thinking and it's a terrible idea!"

Ruby threw her sword. Jared was too busy laughing, so he wasn't even close to dodging it. He got a blade through his head, incapacitating him. Ruby jumped up to grab her sword right after Jamie blasted the body to pieces. More Scarfaces came out to attack, but the Lolligo could handle them.

"Fight them!" Ruby cried to Samson from atop the pile. She couldn't afford to waste any time on Jared now. "Hold them off—I'm going to see Venus!"

"YOU STUPID GIRL!" Samson roared. "COME BACK HERE AT ONCE!"

Ruby didn't need to. Perhaps Venus was bringing Cell Land to life with her freaky powers, but it wasn't fully functional yet. Those corpses were still too cold and stiff to do any damage.

So Ruby braced herself for the most wretched sight of her entire life once more. She used the corpses to jump toward Venus, who was munching on bodies as if she was consuming a stack of ribs.

She slurped on them loudly. She had over a dozen arms bringing corpses—some still in their Diamond or Emerald City uniform—into her mouth. But the mouth wasn't on her face—it was on her chest. A huge slit the size of a small building with a gazillion teeth shredding whatever was between them. Venus' head was too small for Ruby to get a good look at it.

Ruby supposed it didn't matter when she had a huge mouth to deal with. Two gigantic breasts stuck out on either side. The belly crumpled and twitched, as if the bodies within were still alive. Arms and tentacles swayed back and forth from the massive monster that must have weighed over ten thousand pounds. How had it grown this quickly? Ruby was certain it wasn't this big when she had sighted it with her binoculars.

Ruby was at a loss for what to target. Scarfaces were spilling in from every crevice like ants. Ruby had to dodge them and save her energy for what really mattered, but she just didn't know what to do.

A massive tentacle swung at her. Ruby jumped, but then more tentacles sprouted out from Venus' body and grabbed her, wrapping around her wrists and ankles. She dropped her sword and hit the ground, rolling on a puddle of that disgusting white gook. It burned her like acid.

"SAGE!" Samson jumped onto one of the nearby piles and fired his laser. He loosened the tentacles around Ruby, who scrambled for her sword on the ground.

She grabbed it and looked up. Past a few Scarfaces, she saw the head at last.

Venus was looking right at her. Every pair of amber eyes was focused on her. More opened up on the rest of her body, as if her brain was sending distress signals that enemy number-one was close by.

"RUN, SAGE!" Samson yelled at her.

Not yet. Despite her hissing skin, Ruby threw her sword and impaled Venus through the head. She prayed to God that would be enough—that skewering the brain would kill this monstrosity—but that was all wishful thinking.

Venus roared. There was a massive rumble as all the corpses around her roared, too.

"RUN!" Samson screamed.

There was nothing else for Ruby to do. She scrambled to her feet and fled Cell Land, bypassing as many corpses and Scarfaces as she could. Eventually, she tripped and twisted an ankle. She tumbled to the ground, grass and dirt and snow in her face and nostrils. She balled her hands into fists and clenched her teeth. She tried to still her breathing, but she didn't have any opportunities to relax—the Scarfaces were on her.

Ruby had to roll, dodge, and block if she was going to escape from this with her life. As she faced the dozen or so Scarfaces that surrounded her with their stoic expressions and marred features, she saw what was going on in the background.

The towers of corpses became one. Tentacles weaved in and out of the bodies like stitches in clothes. The appendages lashed out into the air as Venus gave an almighty roar that nearly ruptured Ruby's eardrums. Her sternum rattled in her torso, a few bones breaking from the force.

The Scarfaces were relentless with their lasers. Ruby did what she could to maneuver around their attacks and impale them from behind with her own blades. She grew immensely thankful for all her training with Samson, who had saved her life in more ways than one by now. The injuries from Cell Land were nothing compared to the ones Samson gave her, but Ruby was, of course, losing momentum. There were too many other factors distracting her here, like the Lolligo, Hayes, and if any of those military corpses that Venus had been munching on belonged to her sons or even Geoffrey. It was only a matter of time before one of those lasers hit Ruby's shoulder and then her leg.

Ruby blacked out from the pain. The burn was so intense that it felt like she was on fire. She wondered if this was the end and if this was what it was like to die. She braced herself for that final blow that would come at any moment now—she prayed with all her might that Samson had made it out of here alive—but all she heard was talking.

"Please don't kill her."

A woman's voice.

"She doesn't know any better, sweet children. Don't you see that even her own husband abandoned her?"

"SAGE!"

Ruby opened her eyes. In the distance, she saw a beautiful woman stepping across the field as if she were on a runway.

Tall, sharp features, full breasts, curvy hips, and shapely legs. Her hair was long and black, flowing in the wind. In her hand was Ruby's sword.

"GET UP!" Samson was screaming from somewhere. Ruby finally spotted him way back on the other side of the field, a dark speck. He had a laser gun he had confiscated from one of the Scarfaces in his hands, which he used to shoot at the woman.

The woman blocked his attacks with the sword. She did it so quickly that Ruby didn't even see her move.

"My goodness." The woman frowned. "These Lolligo just don't quit, do they?"

A thick, fleshy tentacle shot out of the woman's back and impaled Samson through the chest.

"S-Samson!" Ruby croaked, forcing her body to move. Despite all the Cells she had lost thanks to the Scarfaces, she was still in the middle of regeneration. She coughed up her own blood as she climbed to her knees. "S-Samson!"

Samson stumbled back. An impalement wasn't going to kill him, but Ruby was freaking out too much to remember that. Samson seemed to crumble in the face of this woman, who Ruby now knew was Cita.

The Venus Flytrap.

This was the woman who had been consuming Cells and using human bodies to fortify her own.

Venus didn't just sprout one tentacle—she sprouted ten. They all went for Samson, who finally hit the ground. He would have been dead were it not for Xeno who jumped in front of the attack. The tentacles impaled him instead and tore him to pieces like someone would paper.

He'll regenerate, Ruby kept telling herself as she staggered toward Venus. *He'll be fine.*

Venus grabbed the pieces and threw them into her mouth. It opened up into a huge bowl.

Ruby stopped. She stood there as she watched Venus chomp on Xeno like potato chips. The Scarfaces didn't bother attacking Ruby because they knew she was no match against their mother.

"RUN, SAGE!" Samson yelled.

Blood ran down Ruby's body. It didn't seem to stop flowing. She was losing vitality fast, but there was one last thing she could do.

There was no fucking way that bitch was using Ruby's sword to kill Samson. Ruby already saw the wheels turning in Venus' head, as if there'd be no better way to end Samson's life than by using the Optimum's most esteemed weapon. Venus' face returned to normal, lips full and voluptuous. She smiled down at the blade.

"I can smell the Slainium." Venus took a whiff. "This is a powerful weapon indeed—"

Ruby shot out her own tentacle and swiped the sword from Venus. Samson took this chance to blast her in the face. Jamie was running up to them from behind, but he was too far from Ruby to rescue her successfully. It was up to Ruby to flee, but she only had seconds to fly past the Scarfaces and evade Venus all together.

It wasn't feasible. Even if Ruby cut through a few Scarfaces, she still got blasted by them and lost tons of energy. She was facedown on the ground again, sword in her hand, as she struggled with a body that was pretty much useless. The worst part was that Samson wasn't going to leave her—he made a run for her, but then something made him stop mid stride.

All the Scarfaces stopped, too.

Ruby could hardly see. There was blood in her face. She might have gotten blasted in the head at some point because her brain was pounding and something slimy was dribbling down her cheek. She looked up, but all she made out in her hazy vision was a dark silhouette. She had no idea who that was, but she was trained not to cower in the face of enemies.

Whoever it was, they got down on their knees, too. For some weird reason, the Scarfaces weren't attacking them. Ruby wasn't expecting a pair of soft hands with long fingers to touch her face.

"Damian?" Ruby whispered. She didn't even know why she had. Perhaps he was the only thing on her mind right now before death.

He wrapped his arms around her. He brought one of his palms up to his mouth, as if he was sipping water, and drank what looked like blood. It was as crimson as Ruby's. Then the cut that had manifested in his hand out of nowhere seemed to disappear on its own because when he held her shoulder, there was nothing there.

"Damian?" Ruby said.

She saw his face now. Pale, angular, and framed by long locks of black hair. The expression on his face was tender. His eyes were shiny, full of tears. His mouth held all the blood he needed to give her, to replenish her wounds, so he kissed her. He made her drink it, and Ruby couldn't do anything to stop him.

She swallowed.

CHAPTER 10

The Ultimate Hybrid

The blood was thick and coppery. Ruby almost choked on it, but Damian released the pressure of his lips on time.

As Ruby swallowed, Damian brought her closer to his chest in an embrace. He held her as if she was his teddy bear. Maybe even his life support.

"Damian..." Ruby whispered.

She wanted to tell him that there were Scarfaces staring at him, but that's all they were doing. They seemed too shocked to move. They had spent the whole day fighting one hybrid but now there were two. Even Venus was looking over, wondering who Damian was.

"Oh, my..." Venus breathed. She had completely forgotten about Samson and Jamie at this point. "And who are you, handsome?" She looked him up and down multiple times.

It was easy to tell that Damian was from Emerald City based on his uniform. He had the insignia on his right shoulder—an emerald with a crown on top—and golden chains and latches on his jacket, belt, and boots. But, unlike Louis, he didn't prance around with a cape or crown to indicate his status. His clothes could fool anyone into believing that he was a regular soldier. He had a single sword at his hip and he unsheathed it in the face of Venus.

She couldn't stop staring. Pretty soon, she'd start drooling. She didn't care about the sword pointed at her face. She licked her lips a few times. She felt her breasts and closed her eyes, as if she was trying to picture what Damian's hands would feel like on her body.

Ruby got to her feet. She had her sword, too. She realized it looked a lot like Damian's, as if Samson had welded them both with his hands. She kept it up, unsure if she should attack the Scarfaces who were waiting for their mother's instructions. Venus didn't seem very inclined to tear a beautiful man to pieces.

"Well, well!" sang Jared. He came out of nowhere, waving his hands like a conductor in front of his orchestra. "At long last, the battle royal we were all waiting for, darling! And you are the star of the show, my glorious goddess." He turned to Damian. "My precious Warlord, you look as beautiful as ever. And here I thought you were dying of a broken heart." He glanced at Ruby with a devious smile but continued talking to him. "Did you finally reunite with your precious? What does it feel like to know that she doesn't remember anything about you?"

Ruby wanted to shout that wasn't true, but she didn't want to break Damian's concentration.

Damian stood feet before Venus. He braced himself, sword up, but never moved.

It was Venus who attacked first. With just a look, she sent these waves of energy across the field right at Damian. Ruby was pretty sure they would have sliced anything they touched to bits.

Damian didn't dodge. Yet he never got hit. He stood there in the same pose, eyes focused on Venus. He didn't glance at Ruby, and he sure as hell didn't pay any attention to the annoying Jared, who was clapping his hands.

"Careful, Warlord," he called. "Or you'll get eaten very quickly."

There was no way in hell Ruby was going to underestimate Venus, but that didn't seem very likely. Ruby quickly realized that Damian *was* moving—only no one could see it. When he swiped his sword, it looked like he was stretching or practicing his technique. Ruby never saw the arch of energy that cut Venus cleanly in half.

"My, the famed Warlord is powerful!" Venus exclaimed as she regenerated quickly. This time she used tentacles to attack Damian, but he still didn't move.

Ruby shouldn't have been surprised. She had seen the Warlord in action before, but this was in person now. This was against a true and terrible enemy, and he didn't waver once. While his eyes were intense, the soul behind them spoke stories about the sort of losses he had suffered. At this point, his heart couldn't take any more, so what was there to be afraid of?

Ruby hung back because she wasn't sure how to help. Even attacking the Scarfaces would have been a distraction to Damian.

When the tentacles didn't work, Venus resumed throwing blades of energy, but she never landed a hit.

Damian, on the other hand, wasn't going to hang back forever. He retaliated when an opportunity to do so presented itself. While Venus evaded his swipes at first, jumping around the battlefield like a ballerina, a few knocked her off her feet.

Ruby knew exactly what Damian was doing: he was wearing her out, attacking when he could, but keeping momentum in his favor, even when his blade failed to make contact sometimes. It was all about keeping his head in the game—that was more important than landing every hit.

Venus seemed to be falling for his tactics because she was starting to slow down. She was no fighter, either—she was used to swallowing people whole. She grew frustrated when Damian sliced her across the chest and then thigh with his sword.

Venus regenerated, but that was only going to get her so far. If she didn't damage Damian, she'd run out of energy. It was only when she realized this that Damian flipped a switch and went on the offensive.

He was insane.

When he flew forward, he moved so fast that he disappeared all together. From the frazzled look on her face, Venus had no idea where he had gone until he was up against her body, thrusting a blade right through her belly.

Venus jumped back before he could slice her in two. With her body amidst healing, she used a tentacle to lash out—Damian ducked, swerved to the side, then plunged his sword right into her chest. Cracking bones said he had caused quite a bit of damage to her sternum.

Venus screamed in frustration. She grew ten arms on each of her sides and went for another swipe, but Damian was already in the air. A ginormous tongue shot out of her mouth to impale him, but Damian disappeared. Not completely, though—his image remained, but his body manifested behind Venus's.

Damian impaled her once more. That blade had to be made of Slainium. Ruby wondered if it'd be enough to end her. Damian didn't seem flustered as he stepped back and watched her regenerate yet again. He looked ready to spend the entire week fighting.

Venus wasn't. She was desperate and it showed: she grew to three times her size, making herself an even bigger target. At the same time, she had more of the ground to stomp on and blow up. Her hope had to be that she'd crush Damian in that mess of limbs. Ruby didn't think a sloppy strategy like that would work, but she reconsidered it when Venus started throwing tentacles around. These had mouths and extra arms to grab Damian, who evaded every attack that came his way.

Ruby held her breath. She couldn't see Samson from here, but he had to be watching in awe, too. If Damian could move like that around Venus, he might even stand a chance against Samson.

Damian was so focused and confident on his technique that he never made a mistake. He even used some of Venus' tentacles as steps to get closer to her face. He struck her in the neck with his blade then used his weight to cut down into her belly. He dissected her in front of everyone to see, then jumped when Venus screamed and swiped at him.

"SAGE!" Samson yelled out of nowhere.

Damian looked up.

Ruby already saw him coming. Jared wasn't a warrior, either, but he was rushing across the field to use her as a hostage. One-on-one? This was Ruby's chance to end him.

Ruby used her sword to cut him down. Samson bumbled out of his hiding spot to blast away any of the Scarfaces that came to help their father.

"You worthless girl!" Jared yelled, clutching the huge gash on his side.

Ruby might not have been able to defeat Venus like she had hoped or save the lives of all these innocent people that had become part of a monster, but she wasn't worthless. She proved it by decapitating Jared and ridding Damian of any external threats.

It was just him and Venus, who didn't last much longer in this fight. While she might not have cared about Jared, his death still put her at a disadvantage. It toyed with her head and made her slip up against Damian more than once. Her final strategy was to grow even bigger and absorb whatever remnants of Cell Land there was. She was massive and overbearing, but Damian didn't let her size stop him.

"Sage," Samson said to her, drawing her close. "He's going to strike her in the heart. When he does, you need to jump up and get her brain. Understand?"

Ruby watched, mesmerized, as Damian danced around that flurry of tentacles like an acrobat. He used one to drive right into her chest. But then, out of nowhere, Damian changed direction. To Ruby and Samson's shock, instead of going for the heart, he flew through her jaw and brain, sword out in front of him like a spear.

"GO, SAGE!" Samson pointed at the spot between Venus' boobs. They were as big as submarines. "Right there!"

Ruby had to do the same thing as Damian and evade the tentacles. She seized up a bit, but this was a fight for survival. She grabbed onto one, got closer, and then got the surprise of a lifetime when the chest configured into one gigantic mouth and chomped on her.

But Damian had already inflicted major damage to Venus'

head. The mouth wasn't strong enough to munch. Ruby was in pitch-darkness, minus the light that snuck in through Venus' rows of teeth, and bounced unsteadily on a thick tongue. Nonetheless, she had the grounds she needed to jump and she flew straight up until she sliced right through Venus' heart.

Venus roared. Her whole body collapsed and fell apart.

Ruby found an opening to jump out, and she used her side and shoulder to burst through disintegrating muscle and tissue. Full of blood and guts, she rolled to the ground and crashed into something hard. She was surprised to find Damian already standing beneath her, waiting for her.

He wrapped an arm around her waist and jumped back, putting a safe distance between them and the monster. The Lolligo moved in to finish the job by unleashing as much of their lasers on Venus as they could. Ruby's heart broke for Xeno's absence.

Ruby started shaking. She dropped the sword in her hand.

Damian held her tightly. He rested his chin on her head as he watched the Lolligo finish Venus. The show here was over. The exhibition was done.

What was left of Venus' body just slumped to the ground in a massive heap. Ruby didn't want to think about what would have happened had this monster made her way to Ruby City. She couldn't feel any more relieved that it was over, but Ruby was so emotionally drained that she cried.

Damian held her face. He didn't have any gloves on, so Ruby felt his smooth skin. For someone who fought like an expert, his hands were pristine. Each of his fingers had a ring. There was a bracelet around his wrist with ten charms. Ruby thought it looked familiar, and that's what made her cry harder.

She couldn't remember.

She had drank his blood and she couldn't remember a thing. Was there something wrong with her?

"D-Damian," Ruby choked, clutching him harder. "I-I'm sorry! I'm sorry!"

Damian kissed her forehead. He wiped her tears with his thumbs. He held her so tightly that Ruby could rest easily. No one would attack her in this powerful embrace.

"Sage!" Samson came running.

Ruby didn't want to let go of Damian, so she didn't. She did pick up her sword, though, and finished cleaning her face. Stars, she was so embarrassed by how emotional she was being.

Samson looked from her to Damian. Like Jamie, he took a step back, but Ruby assured him it was fine. Damian didn't look like he was going to attack the Lolligo.

"P-please," Ruby said, oscillating between them both. "No fighting."

Samson had a look on his face that said, *We won't if he doesn't.* But Damian didn't make any moves otherwise.

"Damian, thank you." Ruby grabbed his face with her shaking hands and kissed his forehead. She went for his lips, too. She nestled her head beneath his chin and just basked in his presence for a moment.

Not alone, she thought to herself. *Never alone.*

"Castor and Pollux?" Ruby finally said. She looked up at him.

Damian was still caressing her cheek with his long fingers. His face softened even more at the mention of their sons.

"They're well," he said. His voice was smooth and not too deep. It was actually kind of pleasant to listen to. Ruby wondered if he could sing, too. "They're in Ruby City, waiting for you."

"How did you get here?" Ruby asked.

"I flew. Or, rather, my comrades transported me here. The residents of Ruby City told me where you had gone."

"Thank you." Ruby smiled at him. She kept an arm around him and he did her. It was strange, but standing next to him felt so right. Tragically, she couldn't remember a single thing about him other than that night with the green and silver. The lost memories destroyed her, but at least he was here now . . . and safe.

Ruby took her first steps forward. Damian was right behind her.

She made it to Samson, who was panting as if he had run a mile and looking at Damian in fear.

"He won't hurt you," Ruby assured him.

"Forgive us," Jamie pitched in. "But Emerald City has never been a friend of the Lolligo."

Ruby had suspected that much. It was Emerald City, after all, that had expelled the Lolligo from Diamond City over thirty years ago. She turned to Damian, who probably didn't understand what Jamie had said. She translated it for him, but he still said nothing.

"Although I feel, given our situation and the mess we've created, perhaps there is some merit to their distrust in us," Jamie went on, still studying Damian like a specimen under a microscope. "But we will discuss this once we leave this battlefield."

"Xeno..." Ruby whispered.

"What counts is that freak is finally dead," Samson snapped at her. "*Both* of them." He spotted Jared's corpse some miles away. "That is all. We knew the risks when we decided to help you, and there is nothing we can do about Xeno now. Diamond City can start to rebuild, and we can move on to the bigger problem on the horizon."

"Which is what, Samson?"

Samson's lip trembled. His breathing got tight. Jamie intervened and kept the peace.

"At home," Jamie said. "We will discuss this at home. I think you need a rest right now, Sage." He looked at Damian and said in Lucidum, "Why don't you come back with us as well?"

Damian bowed his head. He stuck close to Ruby, who wondered where his aircraft was. Or maybe his comrades had taken off in search of the Scarfaces. Were Damian's closest fighters Sage's friends as well?

Samson and Jamie reunited with Bruce, who didn't look very thrilled at their new hybrid ally. Ruby ignored them and turned back to Damian instead.

Ruby smiled at him.

Damian smiled back.

They held hands.

Ruby remembered seeing so many couples do this on campus at Royal Academy. While Hayes had made obvious passes at her, she never dreamed she'd be doing it with her rightful husband.

"Candice and Olivia?" Ruby said.

"At the palace in Diamond City," Damian replied.

"And ... Louis?"

"Detained until we get this situation sorted out."

Samson looked over his shoulder at them. By now, it wasn't a surprise to him or the Lolligo that Louis had played a grand part in this mess. The question was how much?

One of Damian's communicators went off with an incoming call. He took it from his belt and said, "Yes?"

"Sir, we've got quite the situation on our hands," said a female voice. "There is a mass number of those Scarfaces making their way to you right now. What do you wish to do?"

"We'll isolate them and defeat as many as we can. In the meanwhile, please ensure the area is clear of civilians. I'll be right there."

"You're going by yourself?" Ruby said.

Damian bowed his head. "If that is what you wish."

"The answer is no." Samson stepped toward them. Why the hell hadn't he left yet? Of course he was eavesdropping on Ruby's conversation with Damian. "Sage has done enough fighting for today. We need to take her back to the city immediately."

"Then please do so."

"You don't get to decide what I do, Samson!" Ruby yelled at him. "There's no way I'm going to let Damian fight by himself! All those Scarfaces? They're probably going apeshit now that Venus and Jared are dead!"

"That might be so, but you are in no condition to continue fighting!" Samson hissed at her. "You will get overwhelmed and become a liability. Do you not realize that you were blasted with Slainium lasers that destroyed a good deal of your Cells? You need time to regenerate."

"We need to help him! We *all* need to help him!"

"We can follow closely in our aircraft," Jamie said as a means of compromise. "And aid the hybrid in whatever he needs."

Ruby agreed to do that, but she still didn't want to let go of Damian. She held his hand tightly, afraid that she'd never see him again.

Damian smiled at her. His eyes glistened with longing. Behind the pupils was a vortex of emptiness.

Go, they seemed to say. *I'll be fine.*

So Ruby let go. But she couldn't take this feeling of loneliness, so she reached back out, but Samson grabbed her and hauled her away before she made contact.

"Come on," he growled in her ear. "We have to go."

They had to traverse what was left of Cell Land. Mangled body parts and pools of blood still littered the field. The smell was even more atrocious, as if someone had poured more of that white gook all over the place. It stirred up Ruby's empty stomach again and jostled some of the thoughts in her head.

She realized that Damian was about to face all the Scarfaces by himself. Even if he had allies, what were the chances he'd survive if he couldn't do anything to stop them in Diamond City for months?

"Something is not right with him," Samson declared as they continued to cross Cell Land to get to their ship. Hayes was probably still waiting for them there. "He didn't seem like himself at all."

"What do you mean?" Ruby asked.

Of course, Ruby couldn't tell. She hardly remembered the esteemed Warlord. All she was familiar with was his impeccable fighting style.

"Damian was a lot different as the Warlord and the Emerald City Allseer," Samson said. "Mind you, I never knew him personally, but he was ... much more intense than that. For starters, I expected him to accuse me of using you. He didn't become defensive of you. I was honestly expecting a fight from him."

"It's almost as if he's given up," Jamie said.

"What do you mean?" Ruby said. "He didn't 'give up'—he was fighting!"

The Lolligo didn't entertain any other comments on Damian's condition and that frustrated the hell out of Ruby. Now, she was worried about him. She didn't know what to think because she couldn't remember a damn thing about how Damian used to be. Micah had mentioned grief, but he hadn't mentioned a change of character. Or maybe Micah wasn't old enough to remember the old Damian, either.

"My God!" Hayes croaked from beside the two ships. Ruby was surprised he was still here, actually. Then again, had he run, he would have been an open target. He didn't know the Lolligo required to run the ships, either. "Y-you're actually alive!"

"Get in!" Samson barked as Bruce pushed Hayes into his ship.

Ruby followed Jamie into Samson's.

"Hurry and let's get the fuck out of here!" Samson yelled at Jamie.

"Wait," Ruby breathed. "Aren't we going to help Damian?"

"We can't, Sage! What can we do against the Scarfaces?"

Jamie was pressing buttons and the ship was starting up. Ruby was starting to hyperventilate.

"No!" she croaked. "You promised, Samson!"

"I promised to help *you*," Samson clarified. "Not the Warlord. We're fucking done here, Sage—we need to get back—"

Ruby grabbed her sword and ran. Jamie hadn't taken off yet, so she could still open the door, but Samson beat her to it—he blocked her with his huge body.

"*Sit down!*" he hissed.

"Get out of my way, Samson."

"Tell me what the hell you plan on doing to help him. Tell me how martyring yourself is going to make a difference, Sage."

"*We're* supposed to help him!" Ruby exclaimed. "And you're going back on your word!"

"This is survival!" Samson snarled. "Nothing else! The Warlord of old would have told me to get you the hell out of here!"

"But he's not the Warlord of old and he needs help, damn it! Just like you need help!"

"Exactly. I need you, Sage—"

Ruby drew her sword in Samson's face. "You open this fucking door right now."

Ruby only had an instant to make her move. If she fought Samson directly, she'd lose. So she had to dodge his swipe, roll on the floor, then throw herself against the window. She broke her shoulder for sure, cut herself up everywhere, but she made it outside.

Ruby crashed on the ground. She had Samson's screams and Jamie's hesitation right behind her, but her mind was made up.

She wasn't going to let Damian do this by himself.

Bruce's ship hadn't taken off yet, either. Bruce and Hayes must have figured something was wrong because they both came out running, calling for her. They had scooters to catch her, but Ruby didn't intend on getting caught.

Ruby ran. That, she could do. She had enough training under her belt to cross Cell Land without a hitch, pass right by Venus' carcass, and find what Damian's comrades had reported from the skies.

She found Damian standing right in front of a mass of Scarfaces. There must have been over a hundred of them. His fighters were hovering overhead, a dozen or so hanging from their ship to start shooting and aiding their Allseer in this battle. One of them couldn't help herself—she gasped when she saw Sage.

"IT'S SAGE!"

Ruby had no idea who all those people were, but they were all in Emerald City uniform, so perhaps they were old friends of Sage. Her eyes passed over each of the faces, but she came up blank.

She caught Damian staring straight at her. Perhaps he was searching for recognition on her face. There was no expression on his, so it was difficult to read what he was thinking.

Now wasn't the time to mourn her amnesia, so Damian turned back around and drew his sword in the face of his new opponents.

Ruby felt so horrible. She could only imagine what this was doing to him right now, all the trials and tribulations they had been through in the past just erased from her head. Ruby, for one, would be devastated.

"YEAH!" that same female voice roared from above. "GO, SAGE!"

It was just Ruby and the Scarfaces. She had done this before and she could do it again. Sure, the numbers were greater this time, but she had eyes in the sky. All of Damian's allies were circling the battlefield like hawks—there was more than one ship here now. To Ruby's relief, Samson and the Lolligo had arrived, too.

And so, Ruby and Damian attacked. They charged through the Scarfaces and weaved around all the blasts coming from their lasers. They never strayed far from each other, swinging, jumping, and rolling like a well-oiled machine. This all felt familiar to Ruby, so the movements became natural. Her confidence swelled, even as her face and body got splattered in blood. She was killing the Enhanced of Venus and Jared, but she was also liberating Diamond City from her oppressors. Without the Scarfaces, there was no one left to terrorize her.

What about Louis? Ruby asked herself.

Ruby had no idea what would become of Louis. She wasn't sure what the story behind him was yet. Hell, she didn't even know how Louis had allowed a monster like Venus and a crazy psychopath like Jared to run around unchecked.

All Ruby knew was by the time she finished off the last Scarface, she was exhausted. She collapsed on the ground, leaning on her sword, covered from head to foot in blood. When she looked over at Damian, he was as clean as a whistle. Not only had he avoided blasts and swipes, but he twisted around sprays of blood like a cat afraid of getting wet. With help from above—including the two Lolligo ships—Damian was able to finish off the last Scarface with ease.

No people. No civilians out here.

Damian sheathed his sword. Then he extended his hand to her.

Ruby was afraid to take it. She was so worn out and dirty that she felt like a flattened worm. Shame smashed over her head and drew her further into the ground.

All those people hanging from the airship jumped out. They landed on the ground as nimbly as gymnasts and waited for her.

Samson, Jamie, and Bruce hung back, watching and making sure Damian didn't run off with Ruby forever. Hayes probably had his face pressed up against the window.

"D-Damian..." Ruby croaked. She leaned even more against her sword, shielding her face from his soft eyes.

From all the eyes looking at her. All the faces turned her way, ones Ruby no longer recognized.

"Sage!" cried that same female, but everyone shushed her. This was the Warlord's moment.

Damian stepped over to her. His footsteps were so light despite all the heavy clothing he wore. He kneeled next to her and wrapped an arm around her shoulders.

"I-I'm sorry!" Ruby croaked. She was saying this to him *and* them.

Damian held her face. "Please don't apologize."

"It's not fair!" she cried. "It's not fair to you and it's not fair to them!"

"Sage!" That woman was relentless—she ran from the line and right toward Ruby. She was tall and muscular with flaming red hair. She had a short man bumbling at her side, unsure if he should follow or not, but they were either friends or lovers because he stuck to her like glue. The woman's freckles seemed to glow beneath the daylight. Her lips grew into a grin, even if Ruby's gaze remained blank. "It's me—Gertrude! And this is Tate—well, Turtle—you knew him as Turtle."

Ruby's eyes welled with tears. She shook her head.

Tate looked horrified. That expression quickly contaminated the rest of the line as one by one their worst fears came to light.

Sage had forgotten *everything*.

"It's fine!" Gertrude said quickly, before they made Ruby feel even worse about herself. "Micah told us about the amnesia. It's not a big deal, really."

Tate looked at her wondrously. "How is it not a big deal?"

"Why does she need to remember anything? She's still Sage. And very obviously she hasn't forgotten how to fight."

There was one warrior that Ruby recognized in the back: Sword Devil. Small and short, but she was ferocious on the battlefield. Sword Devil bowed in reverence.

"That show was spectacular," the oriental guy next to her said. He introduced himself as Tai. He had long hair in a ponytail and a smile on his face. The two women standing on his other side did, too.

One had short blonde hair and the other had long dark hair tied in a braid. The blonde one was crying tears of joy.

"It's *Sage*, L!" she sniffled. "It's *Sage*!"

Damian helped Ruby to her feet. He kept a light hold on her hand just in case she got dizzy. Ruby was pretty spent at this point, and using her brain to match names with faces was going to take the little energy she had left.

"Sonia!" said the blonde. "My name's Sonia."

"Margaret." The next woman bowed. She also had dark hair, but hers was in a bun. "You knew me as Mega Woman."

"Ramon," said the man after her with rainbow highlights in his hair. He bowed, too. "But I was called Rockstar."

"Eric." The next man bowed. "You knew me as Eye Candy."

"Cecilia—I was Clara."

"Bernard—Butch."

"Shane—Sailor."

"And I am Paul." He was the only one in white robes. Ruby had totally not seen him until now, maybe because he blended in with the snow so well. "I was the preacher in Mousafeld, oh great Optimum." He raised his hands to the skies. "Although she does not remember us, we remember her. And that is all that the Forefathers care about. We must face these tribulations with courage and hold our heads up high. The Lolligo have gifted us with a newly reborn Optimum. She is the ultimate hybrid."

Compared to Damian, Ruby was terrible. But she appreciated the camaraderie and what they were trying to do. Still leaning against Damian, Ruby smiled.

"Thank you."

"Why don't we head back?" Gertrude suggested out loud.

"Before we're caught out here? Don't know if there are any more undesirables leftover."

Ruby wiped her eyes again. She probably looked like hell. "Right."

Damian drew her against his body and pressed a soft kiss to her temple.

"You can come with us," Gertrude went on, as if she was talking about slumber parties and not tactics in the middle of a bloody battlefield. "Or with your Lolligo friends. Either way, I think we should all return to Ruby City."

Ruby would rather not leave Damian's side. She kept an arm around his waist as they walked across the field together. The line of warriors started to clap. That quickly turned into hoots and cheers. Ruby's cheeks turned red.

"Welcome back, Sage," Gertrude said happily.

CHAPTER 11

Old Friends

R uby got applause all the way to their ship. She kept her eyes down and her smile small. She didn't feel like she deserved this at all.

This ship was so much different than the Lolligo's. It was smaller and sleeker with a luxurious feel; it seemed more for transportation than actual combat. The finishes were crisp, the chairs were plush and comfortable, and there were quarters in the back for all the troops. Gertrude and Tate, apparently, had already set one up for Ruby.

"And I got you your favorite socks!" Gertrude sang happily. She bumbled over to a line of Wooly Socks laid out on the bed.

Ruby absolutely loved these. They were so soft on her feet and the designs were incredible. What really set her heart pitter-pattering, though, was the Star Raider image. There was a different pose on each pair. Ruby grinned.

"What do you think?" Gertrude asked eagerly.

"Can she take a shower first?" Tate scowled. "She's covered in blood and . . . mucous." He made a face.

"Right." Gertrude rummaged in the cabinet for some fresh

clothes. "It'll take us twenty-four hours to get home, so here are some pajamas."

Ruby lowered her head. "Thank you. Um ... ?"

"Gertrude," Gertrude said quickly.

Tate winced as if someone had punched him, but Gertrude was more than happy to remind her old friend what her name was.

"Sorry," Ruby said again. "It's just ... well ... It's been a long day."

"Go and wash up then."

The bathroom was small, but comfortable. Ruby enjoyed the tight little space where she could let her thoughts roam. She sat in the little stool in the corner for a while, hands crossed on her lap. She stared at her knees and then her feet. They were full of veins and a bit red from all the running she had done in her boots. She looked up at the spray of water, making sure it reached every part of her body. The blood was all gone by now. She had to scrub a few places for dirt, but it all washed out with soap. It smelled like eucalyptus.

Suave-Suave was an excellent conditioner, so it was easy for Ruby to untangle her hair. She gazed at her own reflection, the circles under her eyes from so much fighting and stress. She wasn't hungry, but Gertrude and Tate had a tray of food on her bedside table.

Ruby's eyes went directly to Damian, who was sitting in the corner of the room. He, too, had freshened up and changed into more comfortable wear. His hair was still wet and swept to the side, showing off his perfectly sharp features. His shirt wasn't buttoned all the way, either, so Ruby could see the top line of his pecs. He must not have wanted to miss a single second of Ruby now that she was here. He gazed at her fervently, taking her all in as if he was seeing her for the first time in his life. Perhaps, in a sense, he was.

Ruby blushed. Wife or not, she wasn't used to that kind of scrutiny. She was taken aback by how intense those eyes were, like two little whirlpools ready to suck her into the abyss the moment she made contact with them.

"Other than the amnesia, are you feeling all right?" Gertrude asked Ruby, taking a seat next to her on the bed.

"Oh, yeah." Ruby was thankful for the distraction. She had her food to fiddle around with, too, sparing her from Damian's stare for a little while longer. She opened up her sandwich and squirted ketchup until there was a thick layer of it. She couldn't eat ham and cheese otherwise. "I feel fine."

"Sage . . . what happened?"

Although Gertrude, Tate, and Damian were the only ones in the room, the rest of the warriors were in the hall, trying to listen in as much as possible. Ruby didn't mind recounting what she remembered when she first woke up.

"I think I was in a car," Ruby said. "The backseat. And . . . Louis was there. He kept talking to me, but I don't remember specifically what he was saying. He kind of looked nervous."

Tate snorted. "Of course he did. He took you from your fucking cocoon. You were supposed to stay sleeping another year or so. That's what Kevin said."

"Who's Kevin?"

"Our doctor," Gertrude answered, keeping that smile pasted on her face despite how disturbed she must have been inside. "Dr. X. He came by to see you every time we visited. You know—to make sure you were alive in there."

This wasn't the first time Ruby had heard she was in a cocoon for nearly thirty years. The idea of it was daunting. Seeing it was even worse, as Gertrude and Tate tried so hard to hide.

"How did I get in there?" Ruby asked.

"We think it had something to do with your giving birth," Gertrude replied. "Lolligo spit up eggs and die, so something similar happened to you."

"And Venus?"

Gertrude blinked. Tate looked surprised that Ruby would remember that much.

"Jared told me he'd had babies, too," Ruby said to them. "With Venus. But they died."

"Yeah," Gertrude said softly. "They did. Or, rather, we found their bodies shortly after we paid the Carat District a visit. The babies had wilted away. We're not a hundred percent sure why, but Dr. X said they hadn't received the right nutrition from their mother." She hesitated. "We think Venus never fed her children what they needed."

"And what was that?" Ruby asked wondrously.

"Blood," Tate said. "That's what you used to feed your children. Three times a day, too. We all thought it's what had contributed to your hibernation, but it seems that was going to happen regardless of how much of yourself you gave. After having kids, your body was on its way out."

"I know this is a bit personal . . . but . . ." Gertrude cleared her throat. "Do you get your period? Still?"

Tate's eyes widened. Someone coughed from the hallway. Damian remained staring at her.

Ruby's cheeks flushed. She tried not to look at Damian as she said, "I do, but only once a year. I just had it in the month of Purity."

"How long did it take for you to get it after you woke up?"

"Um." Ruby looked down. "A year. And why does that matter?"

"Well, Sage used to have hers in the month of Love," Gertrude said. "And we all believe that your period has a lot to do with your . . . being. Like, the very last period of your life cycle—technically—was the pregnancy, and that started the hibernation process. Thirty years later—which is the equivalent of when a human turns eighteen and becomes an adult—we all anticipated that you'd be waking up in the month of Light in the year 132. But Louis pulled you out months before that—"

"So you can get pregnant again?" Tate sputtered.

Ruby's face couldn't get any redder. "I . . . suppose."

"Sorry," Gertrude said quickly. "It's just you're one of a kind. You know that, right? Right now, you're the only female hybrid we know and your reproductive cycle is very different from an Enhanced's. You hibernated for thirty years, and we're still not sure if losing your memory is a part of that process or not. It's possible that Louis wrecked you by forcing you out of your cocoon prematurely."

Ruby looked back at her sandwich. It remained untouched.

Ketchup oozed out from in between the bread and cheese. "Samson said that was a possibility, too. But he also mentioned that some Lolligo never regain their memories."

"Or it takes them a while to," Tate said optimistically. "But you haven't gotten yours back yet."

"Like I said!" Gertrude said cheerfully. "The important thing is you're here now, Sage."

Ruby nodded. "I appreciate your support."

"Castor and Pollux are very eager to meet you! They are such handsome men now." Gertrude's grin got bigger and her eyes started twinkling like stars. "Just like Damian!"

"Y-yeah." Ruby kept her face down.

"Stop embarrassing her!" Tate hissed at Gertrude.

"Speaking of reproductive systems, did you know I managed to give birth to a son?" Gertrude touted.

"Oh," Ruby said. She saw the obvious excitement on Gertrude's face. "Congratulations."

"No, Sage." Gertrude scooted closer to her. "I actually had a *child.*"

"Were you not able to have children before?"

"Don't do this to her, Gertrude," Tate said softly, looking disturbed. "She doesn't remember."

Gertrude took a deep breath. "I know." She beamed at Ruby. "And it's fine. I used to be a biological male, so giving birth has been a pretty big deal. Then again, the transformation hasn't been easy."

Oh.

Ruby looked from Gertrude's boobs to her trim waist and to her shapely hips. She gasped, because she would have never been able to tell.

"Look." Gertrude showed Ruby a picture of a boy missing his two front teeth.

"He looks beautiful," Ruby said.

"I think you'd be proud!" Gertrude said excitedly. "He can fight, too."

"Has Sword Devil been training him?"

Gertrude chuckled. "Not yet. I'm afraid she'll slice off his head without meaning to."

"For sure," Ruby agreed. "I saw her fight against Damian. It was scary. More so than any of those Scarfaces, I feel."

"Sword Devil is a scary bitch, but Damian isn't afraid of anything." Gertrude sighed with pleasure, taking another glance at the Warlord. "And even after thirty years, he's still so good-looking, isn't he?"

Ruby found it a bit strange Gertrude kept complimenting Damian's looks (not that Gertrude was wrong—he was *hot*), but then it became apparent that everyone was afraid. Having started a new life, Ruby no longer looked like a seasoned adult. She was young enough to pass as a growing nineteen-year-old and beautiful enough to pick up all the men she wanted. God only knew who Ruby had been fiddling around with at Royal Academy.

"All right, that's enough." Tate grabbed Gertrude by the sleeve and dragged her out of the room. He already knew that romance couldn't be forced. Plus, the Warlord didn't need any help in the charming department, even if there were rumors he had lost a bit of his mojo. "We'll let them figure it out. So why don't you focus on how handsome *I* am instead?"

Gertrude was giggling. It made Ruby smile.

Thankfully, no one else asked her about her reproductive system as old friends took turns entering the room to see her.

Ramon and Eric were a couple, who apparently used to be bullies. Ruby was quite intrigued that they would say something like that to her, but they seemed eager to show her that they had changed and found love in the midst of all the fighting and turmoil. With each other.

"That's great." Ruby beamed. She had already eaten her sandwich so she was munching on some fruits now.

The next visitors were Cecilia, Bernard, and Shane. They were a trio that was always together and had come a long way in the attitude department.

Margaret used to be a bully, too, but ever since becoming Damian's advisor at the palace as well as leading the Emerald City council, she had turned over a new leaf. Margaret not only kept records at the palace, but she had started writing about her life. Apparently, her origins were in Techfeld.

Ruby was surprised to hear this . . . but then she knew exactly where she had seen Margaret's name before.

Margaret Atwater. Employee of the Year at All Tech Needs for ten years in a row.

It went without saying that Margaret was a ruthless woman, both in and out of the office. Ruby didn't remember her at all, but there was a reason Margaret was still alive and proud of the "settled down" and "decent" person she had become. She had accepted Damian would love no one other than Sage and wouldn't look at anyone else like he did her.

Or like he was doing right now.

Damian was staring at Ruby's right arm.

Ruby was in a tank top, so everyone could see her tattoos. She grew embarrassed, but she told everyone the truth: Damian's battle against Sword Devil had inspired the hell out of her. She had always known her way around a sword, but she had become especially interested in training after seeing Damian decimate his opponent.

He was so calm and collected, beautiful like a sword master would be, and an expert at his craft. That level of skill was so rare because humans didn't live long enough in their prime to achieve it. Even Enhanced weren't dedicated enough to master anything like Damian had. After 150 years of swinging his sword, Damian was a true prime. His lifelong dedication to fighting was what had pushed Ruby to defeat Herman and Tyrus on the training grounds one day.

"No way," Margaret breathed at the tattoo she finally noticed. "So you got that tattoo without even knowing he was your husband?"

"Yes," Ruby said, smiling at it. "I respect his skill. I also respect the way he governs Emerald City. Everyone wants to go there—"

Damian got up. Neither Ruby nor Margaret had been expecting

him to move so suddenly. They stared as he left the room and the warriors outside made way for him.

It seemed Ruby was the only one who didn't understand his behavior because the others said nothing. She looked at them quizzically, hoping for an answer.

"He's . . . going through a tough time," Margaret said quietly. If anyone knew him, it was her. She had saved Damian during the Warlord's Rebellion and stuck to his side ever since, even if she had never been able to worm her way into his bed. "Your hibernation destroyed him. Not that it's your fault, Sage—it took an emotional toll on all of us—but be patient with him."

"I understand," Ruby said quietly. She finished eating her fruit in peace. When Sonia bumbled into the room, things got loud again.

"Did something happen?" Sonia asked, sensing the tension.

"Please go see him," Margaret said to Ruby before stepping out.

"Can you pipe down?" L scolded Sonia. "Sage is still recovering and Damian's in a shit mood!"

"I'm sorry, but I'm not going to act like a grouch—like *you*! I'm here to cheer things up because life is too fucking short." Sonia planted her hands on her hips. "Even for us Enhanced, we have to make the best of things."

But Ruby couldn't stop thinking of Damian. She wasn't sure why he had gotten up and left like that—was he disgusted by the tattoo? Betrayed? Insulted?

"SHUT UP!" L yelled at Sonia before turning to Ruby. Wow, she was intense. Her hair was big and wavy, framing all the anger in her face. She looked Ruby in the eye and said, "I'm sure you're aware that while you were sleeping, we were taking care of business. We had to pick up and move on without you. I know it's not your fault, but try to be understanding."

"Give me a break—she *is* understanding!" Sonia argued. "And we have to be, too, because the poor thing lost her memories! She doesn't remember any of us."

"I'm sure she remembers how annoying you can be," L spat at

her. "But I'm not here to coddle anyone—I'm here for the facts." She stepped up to Ruby, who was a bit afraid of this intense woman. "Sage, it's been tough without you. It has been especially tough on Damian. Everything that he used to be is gone and hasn't been seen in thirty years."

Ruby's eyes welled with tears. "What do you mean?"

It was as Ruby feared. Micah had never seen the Damian of old, so he couldn't possibly know what Damian had been like before Sage's hibernation. If anyone else had noticed Damian's behavior, like Candice and Olivia, they certainly hadn't told their innocent son what extreme grief could do to a person.

"Please stop," Sonia said to L. "She doesn't deserve this. None of this was her fault."

"I'm not saying it was," L said, eyes burning Ruby to a crisp. "But these are the facts and you of all people need to know them, whether you remember your past or not. Damian was charismatic, sexy, and outgoing. Now, he is nothing but a shell. I think the only reason he keeps his head high is because of your dying wish to save Emerald City and raise your sons."

"L! Stop!"

L said nothing else. All the damage was already done—the ugly was out there—and now it was up to Ruby to sit there and wallow in it. Gertrude and Tate had heard the whole thing, but they didn't offer any words of comfort.

No one did.

For the first time in her life, Ruby longed for Ruby. She longed for the new life she could have had had she never climbed to the top of that damn palace. Perhaps forgetting her past had been for the best and starting anew would have been the restart she needed.

Hell . . . perhaps Hayes was right.

The hurt and grief Sage had left behind was too much for Ruby to handle. It pressed on her chest like a stone slab and choked the hell out of her.

All of a sudden, she wanted to go back to Royal Academy. She wanted to continue her studies in history, play fastball after class, hit the gym in the evenings, and have a pleasant conversation with Louis after dinner. What had been wrong with that? Why had she yearned for something more?

Ruby didn't sleep at all that night. All she could picture was the morose look on Damian's face in that lonely corner of the room. He'd had a little notebook in his lap, too.

What had he written in it?

CHAPTER 12

Planning Ahead

"**S**age!" Gertrude knocked on Ruby's door bright and early the next morning. "Are you awake in there? We're here—we've arrived in Ruby City!"

Ruby was awake, but she didn't want to get up. She didn't want to see Castor and Pollux because she didn't want to bring them any more heartache. Maybe it was better if they never met their mother, if they just remembered who she used to be and what she had done, feats even Ruby didn't know.

How could Ruby stand there and greet her own fucking children when she didn't even know who the hell she was? How could she be a mother like this? How would her sons treat their handicapped mother?

"Sage!" Gertrude sang.

"Coming," Ruby said, sitting up in bed. "Just ... give me a moment."

Ruby composed herself. She couldn't let her emotions and thoughts spiral out of control. She had to act like a Lolligo.

She pulled on a jacket, a pair of pants, and some comfortable boots. There were plenty of clothes in the closet. She had a few snacks from yesterday's dinner and a few new ones from this morning's breakfast on the tray outside. Gertrude went around making sure everyone was fed.

Ruby grabbed her food and quickly ducked back into her room before she was seen. She opened a drawer in search of paper and pen and found a convenient notepad ready for use. She sat on the bed and gathered her thoughts.

Castor and Pollux,

Ruby hesitated. What should she say?

I love you very much. I will find you soon.

Soon . . . but not now.

Love,

She hesitated again.

Sage

Ruby wiped her eyes. She left the note under the tray then edged toward the door. She listened for any movement outside. She knew the front entrance of the ship, but there was a docking station in the back. In fact, it's where the crew kept their scooters. Those scooters didn't look as sophisticated as Samson's, but they would have to do.

Samson, Ruby typed into the communicator, *meet me in the Circular Forest. We can complete the deal there.*

Ruby didn't know if this was a good idea or not, but there was nothing else to do. She didn't have the face or the heart to look her children in the eyes. She couldn't let them see her like some lost shell, sensitive to everyone and everything. Perhaps Sage was dead . . . and it was time to let her go.

Ruby glanced over her shoulder to make sure no one else was in the hallway. It sounded like everyone was either up front or outside talking to Ruby City residents eagerly anticipating the Optimum's return. Thankful for the distraction, Ruby made her way to the back, wondering which one of these rooms belonged to Damian, and pulled down the latch.

The door slid open. There were a lot of boxes, crates, and items stacked on the shelves. The scooters were all bunched up in the corner.

Ruby picked one. She pressed the ignition and the engine hummed with life. Perhaps it wasn't as powerful as something fueled by Surgium, but it would do.

Ruby took the scooter to the back door. She'd have to escape the crowd and head north if she wanted to get back to Diamond City. There was a good chance she'd be seen, but she was confident she'd be able to outrun anyone that tried to catch her. Right now, it was her best bet.

What are you doing? said the communicator.

Running away, but Ruby wasn't about to admit that. She just couldn't handle any more emotional trauma right now. If she saw Castor and Pollux, she'd break down. She didn't even remember them as babies. She didn't remember fucking *anything*. According to L, she was the reason Damian was moping around like a heartless man.

Another latch, and the final door between grief and freedom opened. The ramp flattened out against the ground. It was a beautiful sight, endless heaps of land. No people, no accusations, and most of all: no bloodthirsty, flesh-eating monsters.

Without further hesitation, Ruby climbed on to the scooter. She straddled the seat and clutched the handles. She braced herself then squeezed with her hands.

She took off.

No one noticed her leave. Not at first, anyway. Gertrude would probably come back to the room to check on her and then it'd be obvious that the back door was wide open. By then, fifteen minutes would have elapsed and Ruby would be miles away, cruising across the Outskirts.

The most wonderful part about it was that Ruby couldn't hear anything. No one was calling for her. If they were, the wind sucked up their voices. It was empowering. Ruby felt like she had just cut ties with Sage and she had become the new person she needed to be. It was the only way to free herself from this oppressive force that grew inside her with every one of Sage's acquaintances she met.

Ruby wasn't sure for how long she rode, but it was dark again when she reached the outskirts of the Circular Forest. This was the part she had completely missed in that truck ride with the Scarfaces. She had never crossed this forest alone. While she wanted to see the city, she had to wait for Samson to catch up.

Ruby slowed down after a few miles in. She could see all of Diamond City's high risers on the horizon, a beautiful foreground to the setting sun. The flashing lights and the dashing hover cars were enough to entertain Ruby's mind for a good while. They were enough to prove that a sense of normalcy was returning to the city after all those horrible battles against the Scarfaces. If Ruby went back … could she redeem the life she had left behind in Heart? Or was it too late for her now?

Ruby sighed. She didn't go too deep into the forest because she was tired. She parked her scooter and climbed off slowly, leaning against it for a moment so she could stretch. Her legs were sore from the ride, but a small stroll cured that. She gathered wood for a fire and lit it immediately. She always carried a lighter in her pocket.

Ruby took off her sword and rummaged for the snacks she had taken from Gertrude this morning. They were coming in handy right now. There were little tarts—blueberry and strawberry—that were more for dessert, but they eased the hunger pains a bit. Then she went for the breakfast bars. Those were especially filling because they were over a thousand calories each. They reminded her of Jo's Yo-Go and—curiously enough—of Hamilton. Ruby realized she missed her companion terribly.

Thanks to the thoughts of close friends and good people, Ruby actually fell asleep. She leaned against a tree with the sword between her legs. An open target, for sure, but she couldn't help it.

S omeone was caressing her hair. Long, cool fingers were brushing away the strands from her forehead. It felt nice. Whoever those fingers belonged to had really soft skin. They also seemed to know their way around hair because the combing didn't hurt. Sometimes Ruby's hair got so dry that she'd see stars when she used a comb much less her fingers.

But wait—who was touching her now?

Slowly, Ruby realized she had someone's coat beneath her head and a blanket over her body. She had forgotten how cold it could be in the winter. The fire did its share of heating, but the wind was cutting. In the month of Birth, even Ruby had a hard time sporting a tank top outdoors—

Ruby sprung awake. She looked up and found Damian sitting right next to her. He looked like he was here on a picnic. He still had that button-up from last night. It looked like he hadn't gotten any sleep, either. He had taken her spot against the tree and let her lie down instead.

"What are you doing here?" Ruby said, sitting up. "How did you find me?"

Damian chuckled. "I will find you anywhere, darling."

Ruby rubbed her eyes. They were incredibly swollen and itchy from lack of proper rest. Her body felt heavy, too.

Damian leaned forward a bit. He gazed directly into her eyes and said, "What did she tell you?"

Ruby straightened her jacket. She eyed her sword on the ground. "What?"

"L," Damian said. "What did she tell you?"

Ruby pursed her lips. She really didn't want to talk about it.

"Whatever she told you, it made you run away and that is not acceptable. She will be punished for it."

"You don't have to punish her!" Ruby exclaimed. "What she said was true!"

"What did she say?"

"It's because of me you've changed!" Ruby got to her feet at last. It put her a few heads above him at least. "I'm the reason you're depressed and I'm sorry! I can tell you're disgusted by me because you charged out of the room as if I was a disease!" She was panting now, looking straight into Damian's widening eyes.

This was the most emotion he had shown yet.

"Why did you follow me?" Ruby gritted her teeth and clenched her fists. "If you're so disgusted and heartbroken just stay away from me—I didn't choose this!"

Damian got to his feet, too. Ruby drew her sword.

"I fucking mean it!" she exclaimed. "Get lost!"

"I charged out of the room because I was overwhelmed by you, darling," Damian said softly.

Ruby blinked. Damian's expression remained hard. He looked like he was about to explode despite how tender he was trying to sound.

"You were overwhelmed by me?" Ruby said.

"I am very emotional."

Ruby snorted. "And here I thought all men were hardened assholes."

"Certainly not all," Damian said neutrally. "Although I am curious to know what 'men' you've dealt with. You aren't talking about Louis, are you?"

"A friend of mine, Hayes," Ruby admitted. "We were going to school together." She realized how strange that sounded. If she was over a hundred years old, how could she still be thinking about classes and boyfriends? Damian didn't make faces, though. "He tried to woo me, but it didn't work out very well for him. I quickly realized he was an asshole."

"I am relieved to see you think otherwise of me." Damian glanced at her right arm. "You got my name on your body. I asked you once if you'd ever respect me enough to get a tattoo of me." He smiled. "I finally got my answer, although not in the way I envisioned."

It was Ruby who started shaking now. She didn't remember that.

"And so I left the room because I couldn't handle my feelings," Damian went on. "Before you fell into hibernation, I was a heartless fool. But thanks to you and the letter you wrote me before you went to sleep, I did all in my power to change and become the very leader you saw in me." He chuckled wryly. "It seems I have done well."

Ruby lowered her sword. "You have." God, what should she say? *I learned everything there was to know about you in school? I admire everything you stand for?*

Damian took a deep breath. His eyes bored into hers. "All I could think about the past thirty years was the day you'd awaken in my arms. But that sniveling coward took you from me for an entire year. He played games with me, Sage, and might have even destroyed your memories in the process. It was all for revenge, I feel, to erase everything you remembered of me."

"Was it intentional?" Ruby asked softly. "I mean . . . how did he know pulling me out of hibernation early would do this to me?"

"He tried to steal you regardless. And because of his maliciousness and selfishness, I have lost you."

"You haven't lost me. I am still Sage . . . aren't I?" Ruby swallowed thickly. She felt like she had betrayed herself by saying that, but she didn't want to be an asshole to Damian, either. "Or do my memories matter?"

"Of course they matter," Damian said. He raised his arm and pushed back his sleeve to show her that bracelet he had been wearing during his fight with Venus. Ruby could see the tips of the sage tattoo as well, which she had seen before in his duel with Sword Devil.

And it finally hit Ruby.

Sage leaves. *Sage.*

"This bracelet," Damian said. "Do you remember when you gave it to me?"

"Stop," Ruby croaked. "That's not fair."

"I'm not trying to be harsh or belittle you. But if you don't remember our love for each other, then how can you still love me?"

"You're worried if I love you?"

"Of course," Damian said. "How can you love a person you don't remember? Do you love me because you're supposed to—because I'm your husband—or because you really do?"

197

Ruby turned from him. She wiped her eyes for what felt like the thousandth time in the past twenty-four hours. "Damian . . . I . . ." She bit her lip. "Please . . . just give me some time to deal with myself. I ran because I didn't want to see Castor and Pollux. Rather, I don't want them to see me like this. I know I'm handicapped, but there's nothing I can do about it—I've tried!" she declared, whipping back around to face him. "I've tried, Damian . . ."

Damian smiled at her. "I know you have."

"Promise me you'll give me time."

"I will give you whatever you need, darling. I am here for you."

"Damian, I have something I have to do," Ruby said. "Samson said he needed my help with something. I'm not sure what—something with the Lolligo."

Damian caressed her cheek. His fingers were intoxicating, but it was his eyes that Ruby got sucked into. "I will help you."

Ruby embraced him. Perhaps Damian wasn't expecting such a show of affection so soon because he stiffened. Nonetheless, he wrapped his arms around her, too. With her head tucked beneath his chin like this, Ruby could hear his heartbeat. It was low and steady.

"I read the poetry book you left for me," Damian said softly. "Micah had it."

Ruby looked up at him. "What did you think?"

"Terrible."

Ruby gasped. "What?"

Damian cleared his throat. There was an amused smile on his lips. "You were never a poet, darling."

"Who the fuck says?"

> " 'When nothing seemed to reach me
> You shined through
> All of my love squandered
> Except for you
>
> " 'Times were rough
> But it didn't matter

You kept me tough
and so I climbed the ladder.'"

Damian chuckled. "Pretty bad."

"Asshole!" Ruby pushed at his chest. "I wrote all that for you!"

"I know that."

"And you *memorized* it?"

Damian took her hand and kissed it. "I have memorized every-thing you've ever written for me. Even the letter before your hiber-nation. Would you like me to recite it to you?"

Ruby didn't think she could handle it. Damian shook his head.

"Not now—I understand." He reached into his pocket. He pulled out a small little notebook, the same one he had been work-ing on last night. "When you have a chance, I'd like for you to look at them."

"Them?" Ruby quickly realized that these were filled with drawings.

Of her.

All of them.

And the very last entry was Ruby sitting on the bed next to Ger-trude eating her ham-and-cheese sandwich.

Ruby looked up at him.

"I, on the other hand," Damian said deeply, "am a skilled artist."

Ruby snorted. "You're a godsend."

"Am I not? Who else is capable of fixing your hair?" Damian took another look at it. Apart from the bangs and flyaways he had been taming in her sleep, the rest looked like a bird's nest. "Let me guess: you braided it yourself."

"Who the fuck else is going to braid it?" Ruby snapped at him, taking off her tie. "Samson?"

Damian chuckled. "Come here, darling."

"I don't trust you."

"Then good luck doing it yourself."

One tug and one knot was all it took for Ruby to cave. She was usually much more stubborn than this, but she was desperate. She couldn't stand her hair in this state. She huffed as she stepped over to him.

She stood there as his skillful hands undid all the tangles and smoothed out the strands. With his fingers alone, he weaved the best French braid Ruby had ever had: not too tight, neat, and perfect.

"Well?" Damian purred.

"I'm sure it looks beautiful." Ruby patted her head.

"It does."

Ruby wasn't sure she could handle his ego right now. Nonetheless, it kept her entertained and made her laugh. She made sure to put out the fire then pick up his coat from the ground. She shook off the dirt, folded it, and gave it back.

"Thank you for coming to find me," Ruby said. "It means a lot to me."

Damian bowed to her. "Of course."

Ruby didn't see a second scooter. She was about to ask how he had gotten here when she noticed an approaching airship from afar.

It was the *Luse*. Samson.

Ruby took a few steps closer to Damian. She was thankful for the companionship because she was scared of what Samson had to accomplish. She was also not looking forward to the explosion for the "recklessness" she had pulled in running away.

Samson was marching down the ramp before it was even fully extended. He stomped right up to her, not giving a shit that Damian was right there, and hissed in her face.

"Are you *insane*?" he breathed at her. "What's wrong with you, girl? Did hibernation multiply the stupid in your brain?"

"I had my personal reasons," Ruby said icily. "And you obviously don't understand them."

"You're right—I don't—because the only thing I understand is that you ran off on your own without any provisions or plan and left *me* to deal with all those despicable humans in your city! You should have seen them swarming my ship as soon as I landed! I refused to come out, so Bruce and that other sniveling boy had to clear them out on their way to me."

Sure enough, there was Hayes looking down at her from atop the ramp. He seemed shocked that she was still in one piece. Then he lost all the color in his face when he realized that Ruby wasn't alone.

Her *husband* was here.

Damian stepped forward. He didn't look twice Samson's way, walking right past him as if he were used to having Lolligo around. Maybe he was since he had already dealt with Herman and Tyrus back at the palace. He marched up to Hayes, grabbed him, drew his sword, and stabbed him with it.

Actually *stabbed* him.

All the way through, too.

"The next time I hear," Damian hissed at Hayes, dangerously low, "that you were an asshole to her, you will lose your head. You don't mess around with vulnerable women and you especially don't try to fuck with the emotions of one who already belongs to me. You are *not* her lover, but I think you've already established that by having sex with Kendra."

Ruby gasped. How the hell did Damian know that?

"You think very carefully of your morals," Damian spat at the gurgling Hayes. "Because I don't tolerate that kind of abuse toward anyone."

Damian withdrew his sword and shoved Hayes right into Jamie's chest. Ruby didn't get a good look at the Lolligo up there, but Samson was standing right next to her and his lips were twisted.

But wait.

Ruby gasped again.

That was Samson fighting his amused look.

"Damian!" Ruby exclaimed as Damian returned to her side. He cleaned his sword on the grass with a scowl. "You don't have to do that!"

"Actually," Samson mumbled in Lolligo, "that was well deserved. There was something dirty about that kid."

"Do you agree with this?"

Samson's lips finally curved into a smirk. He said nothing,

though, as Damian grabbed Ruby's scooter and brought it into the ship without a word.

"Seriously?" Ruby said angrily.

"Let's go inside, Sage," Samson said, more calmly now. "We have much to discuss."

Inside the ship, there was a bit of chaos. Jamie was working to save Hayes' life while Bruce kept staring at Damian as if Damian were an alien.

"Um . . . s-sir." Jamie turned to Damian, too. He was speaking in Lucidum, but he'd had some practice the past few months so it didn't sound too bad. "Might I say you were most incredible?"

Damian arched a brow. Hayes was moaning on the table.

"Your fight against the hybrid as well as the Enhanced. You are truly a warrior to behold. We have been training Sage relentlessly and we are confident that with your help she will reach that level as well."

"What did I say about over-complimenting?" Samson scolded.

"Forgive me, sir." Jamie clumsily stuck a needle into Hayes' vein. "I acknowledge there is plenty of work to do, but he did just help Sage—and us—rid the world of that parasite. Thank goodness."

Damian bowed his head. And then he shocked the world by saying in Lolligo, "Of course. Getting rid of scum is what I do best."

Samson's jaw dropped now. Jamie stared. Bruce was so stiff he didn't look like he was alive.

"Since when do you speak Lolligo?" Samson sputtered.

"I have had plenty of time to learn," Damian said.

"Before or after running a country?"

"Both. After the civil war in your city, I knew I'd be dealing with the Lolligo in the future."

Ruby had heard of this civil war, but she wasn't too sure about the details. Only that Samson had been ousted from his position as Prime of all the Lolligo, with only a handful of followers still trusting in his ways. Apparently, those ways were to ally with humans.

Samson had to clarify a few details, though. Not all was as it seemed. This "civil war" that he had allegedly lost was much more serious than they had all imagined. He looked uncomfortable at the idea of saying any more on the topic, but he didn't have a choice if they were going to move forward as a team. He pursed his lips and looked to the side as he asked, "Do you remember Wren?"

" 'Wren'?" Ruby said. "That's the hybrid whose Cells were used to create the Enhanced in Diamond City."

"Right," Samson said slowly. "But she is also your sister. The two of you were estranged and didn't exactly get along. For good reason, of course—she was going around Diamond City taking back everyone's Cells. In other words: she was killing Enhanced."

This, Ruby had known. She just hadn't been aware that it was her sister.

"I took Wren the day she attacked the capital," Samson went on. "And I brought her to Elysium. That's the name of the Lolligo's city or civilization or whatever the fuck you want to call it. It was the first place we and a bunch of other Outskirts survivors erected after we joined forces. We thought we were building an ideal place, but then the Forefathers ran off to start their own districts. I think they were more interested in humans and pretending to be something they no longer were. Then, when the humans betrayed them, they turned around and sought help from Emerald City. Thus, they created the hybrids."

"Yes, but Sage—I—was the only one who actually united the districts," Ruby said. "Long after they were martyrized."

"You remember?" Damian asked softly.

"I . . . studied it in school."

"So fast forward some years and we have Wren." Samson snapped his fingers before Damian drowned in his misery anew. "I took her and brought her back with me, yes? While I had studied Sage's growth for a hundred years, I needed a live specimen to bring back to my people and Wren was it. Thanks to her, we figured out how to replicate hybrids."

Ruby gasped. "So what does that mean? You created more hybrids?"

"Yes. Using different human DNA we collected from our

ventures in the Outskirts, as well as samples we had from our own people, we were finally able to create our own hybrids."

"So now you have an army," Ruby said slowly, information processing. "And you're going to use that army to fight us? All the cities out here, I mean?"

Samson hesitated. "That's what *Rhett* wants to do. That's why he kicked me out. He wants to use the hybrids to take over, whereas I would rather make alliances."

"I don't understand, Samson—why do you need hybrids to fight? You're so much stronger than they are."

Jamie looked over his shoulder to see how Samson was going to answer this one.

Samson was doing that thing with his lip again. This time it wasn't because he was fighting a smirk. He looked greatly ashamed and distraught to admit this next part, but Ruby and Damian were official allies now, so he had to be truthful.

"There were only twenty Lolligo in the whole world," Samson said quietly. "Four of them were martyred in Diamond City. Seven of them were killed by Sage in the Outskirts. Herman and Tyrus are still alive. The Scarfaces killed another from our group—Ptolemy—and Xeno is dead, too. But me, Jamie, Bruce, and the egg over there, Vince—a friend—are still alive."

"So that means Rhett is the only Lolligo in Elysium?" Ruby said incredulously. And here she had been picturing an army of Lolligo. Their fear of hybrids and humans made sense—if they died, there'd be no more of them.

"Yes," Samson said. "It's the reason Rhett is so passionate about his hybrids. It takes many years to raise them, so he has an all-hybrid school there."

"Wait—so the Lolligo invasion over thirty years ago wasn't really by the Lolligo?"

If there were so few of them to begin with, it didn't make sense for the Lolligo to put themselves at risk. Ruby was right.

"No," Samson said. "What you saw that day were hybrids."

Ruby looked at Damian, who seemed to be processing all this as well. He had a hard look on his face.

"I need the two of you to infiltrate Elysium," Samson said flatly. "And take out Rhett."

"So apart from Rhett and the hybrids, who else lives in Elysium?" Ruby asked.

"There are some humans. But let's just say they're a bit—er—stuck up. They think a lot like Lolligo," Samson amended quickly. "But a lot of them are my friends and one in particular works at the palace."

"And what do you want us to do in the palace?"

"Kill Rhett," Samson said simply.

Ruby stared. Damian didn't move a muscle.

"How?" Ruby said.

Samson crossed his arms and left the room. Jamie remained looking at them, but said nothing. Ruby and Damian couldn't discuss their thoughts out loud because there was no privacy and Samson had one last thing to show them. He brought back a little vial.

"This is a concentrated dose of Slainium in liquid form," Samson said. "Basically, it's what I used to weld your sword, Sage. But I need you to ensure it gets into the bodies of every hybrid in Elysium. Once we take out the hybrids, we can take out Rhett."

"Why do we have to kill innocent hybrids?" Ruby sputtered. "Isn't the goal here to kill Rhett—not them?"

"Rhett hides behind those hybrids. They are loyal to him."

"You will allow us to take care of it." Damian spoke up at last. "And we will determine who to kill."

Samson shrugged. "Whatever. I just need Rhett out of there."

"Thank you for the information," Damian said curtly, wrapping an arm around Ruby's waist. "Sage and I will discuss it further after we rest."

"Good idea," Jamie piped up. Hayes had stopped moaning a long time ago to listen in. "There's a room for you in the back."

Damian directed Ruby right to it. It was down the hall in the corner, the least likely place they'd be overheard. Not that the Lol-ligo wouldn't try to eavesdrop, but Damian was taking all precautions necessary because he had an important message to relay to Ruby. So much so that he took out her book of crappy poems and ripped out a blank page. He wrote, hastily:

This is suicide. It is clear to me that Samson wants to eliminate us all.

Ruby stared at the words. She didn't know what to make of them, so she drowned in silence until Damian said, "We have to plan strategically. We cannot eliminate potential allies."

Ruby swallowed thickly. "I agree."

CHAPTER 13

Thirty Years

Samson wants to eliminate us all kept swirling around in Ruby's head. It froze her to her spot in the middle of the room and made her sigh. She listened to everything Damian had to say and then some.

"We will talk to Samson in the morning about details." Damian put Ruby's little book away in his pocket. "In the meantime, I feel it would be wise to get some rest."

That meant take a shower first. Ruby went to do just that, thankful for yet another moment of reprieve from this crazy world. Yesterday, she had met people she was supposed to know from her past. Today, she was finally with her husband on a Lolligo ship on their way to Elysium. The experience was a bit surreal, and sometimes Ruby wondered if she was daydreaming in class or dozing off after another *Defenders Unite!* rerun.

After drying herself and throwing on some of the clothes Samson had packed for her, Ruby exited the bathroom. She found Damian waiting for her by the window.

He was looking out at the passing night sky. Diamond City was right beneath their feet. He seemed entranced by all the neon lights, but he turned to her as soon as she stepped out.

"Your hair," Damian said.

Ruby arched a brow. "What about it?"

"It's wet and you're about to sleep?"

So Ruby had no choice but to march right back into the bathroom and allow Damian to dry her hair. Although she was annoyed at first, she lightened up when she acknowledged that he was doing this because he cared ... and loved her.

It showed in the way he glanced at her in the mirror. Although he said nothing as he worked, his glittery black eyes told stories.

"But wait until he sees you, Aunt Sage—he's going to be so happy!"

Damian's fingers passed through her strands seamlessly. No knots ... no pulls. Just nice hair after he was done drying it. Ruby wasn't sure it was intentional, but Damian kept a hand on her shoulder as he racked the blower. He had a ring on every finger, and they were cool against her skin. Ruby took a moment to study them, wondering if they meant something.

She noticed one was the Diamond City signet ring, which was what ex-soldiers from the Unification War wore. That was on his middle finger. On his ring finger, which was the most important one of all, was a simple band that looked like something he would receive at his wedding after exchanging vows.

Ruby's eyes widened. If that's what it was, then where was her ring?

Ruby turned around to look at him. She intended to ask him about her ring, but she wound up staring at him instead. Of course, Damian could see that she was blushing now, but Ruby wanted to study his face closely, the sharp features, straight nose, and full lips. She had kissed them on the battlefield. She hadn't quite felt anything then, but maybe it'd be different now. The only question was: would Damian allow her to?

"You don't have to," Damian said softly. "You don't have to do anything that makes you uncomfortable."

"What if I want to?" Ruby squared her shoulders. Her blush only got worse. She couldn't help it because Damian was so good-looking. This was supposed to be her husband, but Ruby didn't feel like she wanted to kiss him because of that. These were her "girly" feelings, as Samson would say, her desire for "coochie" time. Perhaps she had longed for Hayes at one point, but now she had the opportunity to kiss the hottest man on the planet.

Ruby felt so stupid because she didn't even know how to kiss. What she had done with Hayes didn't really count. And what she had done with Damian on the battlefield wasn't any better. A press of lips was a kiss, but it wasn't a kiss-kiss.

Even so, Ruby went for it—she kissed him—and it sent her heart soaring. Ruby wasn't sure if it was how soft his lips were or how his scent was shooting up her nose, but she was panting and she hadn't done much.

Actually, Ruby wanted more, so she did it again. She kissed him over and over to see what would happen. She thought she'd get used to it—that the fast heartbeat was a mistake—but each time felt like the first. As if she were taking hard liquor shots, her body got more and more tingly. Ruby's head was spinning.

"You look a little drunk, darling," Damian mused.

It felt like it. Was kissing him always like this?

Damian didn't push her to do more. He held her face, caressed her cheek, and studied her features like he seemed to be doing so much of lately. Perhaps Ruby looked a little different than Sage—younger—and he was still coming to terms with that. Damian looked like a middle-aged man and Ruby looked no older than eighteen. He was relaxed, but he didn't take charge, as if he was afraid of upsetting her or taking advantage of someone with memory problems. Ruby just wanted more kissing.

So she grew bolder. Ruby really pressed into his mouth, and then she captured his upper lip. She nibbled on it, tugged on it, and Damian did the same to her.

Now they were in a true lip-lock. Damian knew the angles, the movements, and how much time to spend in each position. As he entertained her mouth, he used his other arm to draw her closer to his body.

Ruby melted against him. She got a bit weak-kneed, but Damian lifted her onto the counter. He settled his body between her legs as they continued ravaging each other's mouth.

Ruby wrapped both of her arms around him and hung on for dear life. She met his tongue halfway, too—by accident, at first—but then it became part of the kiss. A little fire started deep in her belly and brought her whole soul to life. The kissing made her head spin, to the point Ruby didn't know where she was anymore.

All that mattered was him. His mouth and his tongue were relentless, but Ruby was no pushover. She could meet every lap, twirl, and thrust just as expertly as he could. It was the intensity that incinerated her and his scent in her brain that destroyed her neurons.

Teakwood and lavender. That's what it smelled like.

Then Damian's lips trailed across her face. When they reached her jaw and neck, Ruby sighed with pleasure. But even when Damian touched her clavicle with those puffy lips of his, Ruby didn't feel that he was trying to seduce her.

In fact, she didn't think this embrace was very sexual at all. Damian held her as if his life depended on it. He told her in so many ways other than words that he was here for her. It was nice to hold on to that feeling. It was nice to know she wasn't alone in this cruel world.

"I used to kiss you a lot, didn't I?" Ruby said, eyes half-lidded. Her arms were loose around his body now. His lips were awfully close to her breast. "We would kiss in front of the fireplace ... after you removed those horrible heads ... and then ... when we returned to Diamond City ... we'd kiss on the balcony."

Damian pulled back to look at her. His eyes were dark and ... empty. But his breathing got faster.

Ruby smiled at him. "You hated when I teased you."

Damian said nothing.

Ruby caressed his face. She made sure to run her fingers down his cheek until she held his jaw. Then she leaned in and kissed him again.

This time, she set the pace. She had all of his long hair to play with as she explored every inch of his mouth anew. She thought she was being pretty thorough. Despite the number of times Damian battled her, she still dominated the kiss. Maybe a bit too much.

"I'm not sure I can do this right now," Damian said breathily against her lips.

Ruby stopped. It wasn't his words that put a halt to her explosion of passion—it was what she felt between his legs. Clearly, this kiss had the very real potential of leading to so much more. While Ruby certainly wouldn't have minded it, she respected Damian's wishes and let him go. In fact, she was embarrassed as hell.

"Sorry," Ruby panted. "I didn't mean to make you feel uncomfortable."

Damian chuckled. "Do you think this makes me feel uncomfortable, darling? I want nothing more than to ravish you. But . . . I . . ." He sighed.

"It doesn't feel right?" Ruby finished for him. "Because I'm half a person?"

"Is that what you think you are?"

"That's what it feels like."

"Perhaps, it does," Damian said softly. "You haven't recovered all your memories, but that doesn't make you 'half' a person. You are very much the Sage I know. Nothing about you has changed."

"Except for the fact I don't remember you," Ruby said. She unbuttoned his jacket and slid it off his shoulders. She did the same to the long-sleeved shirt he had underneath. "And so I guess we'll have to wait until I do. And if I don't, we're over—is that it?"

"Of course not, darling. Our relationship doesn't depend on you recovering your memories—it depends on what *you* want. Do you want me? Or do you want a shot at a new life?"

"That's a stupid question, Damian," Ruby snapped. "I'm not fucking naive. I know I have a past with people I used to know. I'm just trying to figure out my feelings." She shook her head. "I'm not sure that has anything to do with the love we already share, because it's obviously still there. I may not remember everything, but I still feel. And despite how"—she bit her lip—"handsome you are, I think you're incredible."

Really incredible. He had an amazing body. All his muscles were defined, as if someone had sculpted them out of clay and sprayed them with shine. He didn't have a single scar, either. When Ruby touched his skin and trailed her fingers down that chiseled abdomen, Damian hissed.

"What?" Ruby said.

"The teasing, darling," Damian said patiently. "Remember? You touch me like that, and I'm supposed to just stand here?"

"Well, you're not going to have sex with me, so I guess so."

Damian chuckled wryly. He seized her hand before it did any more damage. It was way too close to the waistline of his pants. "No, no, darling—that's not how this works. You never get to touch me like you just did and expect me not to retaliate."

"I just wanted to feel your abs," Ruby said innocently, and Damian's nostrils flared.

"And I want to feel your breasts," he breathed, eyes blazing with passion. If he were a dragon, he would have burned her to a crisp by now. "I want to suck on them, too. I want to run my hands down that powerful body of yours and I want to eat you up alive. Then I want to thrust deep into you and make you explode. Then I want to rub my penis across *your* abs and cum all over you. How about that, darling?"

Ruby swallowed thickly. She had an excellent imagination, but she also learned that she had some kind of sexual instinct. For a moment, all she could think about was dominating her partner on the floor. Which was why, despite having no sexual experience in this life, she was a bit bold when she said, "You'll have to catch me first."

Damian gasped.

But if he was so uncomfortable, then it was best Ruby walk away. She understood his concerns perfectly so she didn't harbor any ill-will or resentment. This was all going to take time, which was why she didn't push for anything more, either—as wobbly as her legs were—and walked away.

It was so hard. Probably one of the hardest things Ruby had ever done. She stopped at the doorway and looked over her shoulder.

Damian was glaring her down like a lion. He looked ready to tackle her and take her on the floor exactly as he had described to her in vivid details. Ruby wouldn't have minded that, but she didn't want to make him feel guilty. Definitely no regrets . . .

So Ruby left and closed the door. She stumbled toward the bed, belly still pounding, and laid down. Now that her hair wasn't wet, she could sleep. At least, that's what she was hoping for. After that encounter in the bathroom, Ruby couldn't keep her eyes closed for more than two seconds.

So she grabbed the little notebook Damian had given her from her nightstand. She used the lights flashing by her window to illuminate the drawings. They were dated, starting all the way back to year 102. This must have been Damian's first entry after she had gone to sleep. He had drawn the cocoon with amazing amounts of detail.

Ruby held her breath.

It looked like a human-sized butterfly was sleeping in there. There was even webbing in the corners of the room, holding it down to the bed. It was impossible to see what was inside, though. Damian had only written four words beneath the sketch.

My heart is broken.

The rest of the pages were all cocoons. Damian wrote those same words over and over again. Eventually, there was a different picture. This one was of Sage making pizza. Her brows were furrowed and her hands were kneading dough. She looked intense.

I can't get you out of my head.

The next picture was a bust of Sage. It was eerie how accurately Damian drew these. The skill it took to pull off shading like that . . . They almost looked like actual photographs taken in real time.

You rarely smiled, but when you did, I made sure to capture every detail.

Sometimes, Damian snuck in pictures of Castor and Pollux. He had one of when they had first learned to crawl.

Little devils, the both of them. I'm sure they get this from you. I am always well behaved.

Ruby chuckled.

The next entry was of the Emerald City palace. Its spires were long and straight, unlike the whimsical touch Diamond City's had.

I can't rule without you.

Damian had drawn their friends, too. He had been halfway through Tate before giving up and writing, *I still don't like him.*

The next drawing was of a naked Sage. She wasn't in a sexual pose, though—she was leaning against a counter, arms crossed, smiling at him. Ruby blushed furiously at how well he had captured her small breasts, waist, and thighs. And even her... womanly parts. She noticed some tattoos, like the Diamond City insignia on her biceps, that she never knew she'd had.

I miss you so much.

The grief was real. And now that Ruby thought about it—after a long thirty years—how on earth was Damian even functioning?

The shower turned off. Ruby was only halfway through the book by the time Damian came out. He was in a soft shirt and pants. Like Ruby's clothes, they sported Paige's company logo, too: two p's inside a circle. Samson had stocked the ship well with human clothes. Damian's intentions were to leave, but Ruby didn't want him to.

"Please stay," she said softly.

Damian didn't hesitate to slip into bed next to her and pull the covers over them both. When he settled in, Ruby curled into his chest. She felt his damp hair with her fingers.

"You didn't even dry it," she noted.

Damian smirked. That meant he was getting ready to boast. "My hair is glorious no matter its state."

Ruby laughed. "That's true. You got lucky."

"Your hair is beautiful, too." He stroked it. "It just needs special care, is all."

Ruby closed her eyes. She still couldn't sleep, though. She had so many questions for him, but he beat her to it.

"Do you know how I longed to hold you like this?"

"I read some of your notebook," Ruby said, looking up at him now. "And . . . I'm sorry, Damian. I can't imagine what that felt like. I feel so ridiculous because I only remember some things. Did we . . . used to spar?"

"We did," Damian confirmed.

"And did I always beat you?"

Damian actually laughed. "No, darling. You're not remembering that part correctly."

"I'm pretty sure I kicked your ass."

"You are terribly confused."

"I'm not." Ruby giggled. She ran her hand down his back and settled on his hip.

"What do you remember of our time together?" Damian asked quietly. He drew circles on her cheek with the back of a finger.

Snippets. Maybe. But Ruby wasn't sure if they were real or not. She decided to talk about what she did know, what she had learned from her studies at Royal Academy, what Louis had said about Damian during dinner, and all the people she had met in Ruby City. Particularly, Micah.

Damian smiled. "He is a wonderful boy."

"He spoke very highly of you. He told me stories about Castor and Pollux and what an amazing father you are." Ruby nodded. She kept a hand on his side as she said, "It takes so much strength to do that . . . especially when you're still grieving."

"I'm not grieving anymore," Damian said quietly.

"Of course you are. You can't just get over this in one day. It takes time, Damian, and I understand."

"Do you?"

"Yes." Ruby kissed his nose. "So . . . are you up to date with all *The Rainbow in Me* seasons?"

"No," Damian said, smiling again. "Not at all. I haven't even watched the second season."

Ruby gasped. "Why not?"

"Not without you, darling."

"I think they're on thirty-one, aren't they?"

"Actually, not yet. They had to reschedule it due to the situation in Diamond City."

Ruby nestled back into his body. She fit him like a puzzle piece, so perfect that it was air tight between them.

Damian held her to his chest. His arms were powerful around her body. Then he started shaking.

Ruby knew he was crying.

CHAPTER 14

Mission

The next morning, Samson was in the middle of making breakfast by the time Ruby got up. They hadn't arrived at their destination yet. When Ruby looked out a window, she saw a gray sky and tons of clouds. They had already passed Diamond City and were heading over the Roaring Mountains.

"Did you get any sleep?" Samson asked her. It was a legit question, not because he suspected she and Damian had been having sex all night, but because there was plenty to talk about. So much to catch up on.

"Not a minute," Ruby admitted, pouring some orange juice into her glass. "But I did rest." She listened closely. She could hear Jamie and Hayes talking in the next room; the latter was still recovering. Beneath that, she heard the shower still going in the bathroom. That was Damian. He had to wash his hair again because polyester was the "bane of his existence." Unfortunately, Samson didn't have any satin sheets on board. "Is there anything about Damian I'm supposed to remember?"

Samson cracked an egg into the skillet then looked over his shoulder at her. "Like what?"

"I don't know. Like, what was he like when we first met?"

"You already know the answer to that, girl."

"Fine—I know we met in Mousafeld—but what was he *like*?"

Samson snorted. "An egotist with a passion for flare, seduction, manipulation, sex, and death."

Ruby frowned. "You make him sound like a bad guy."

"He was. Sort of. He was a brute." Samson thought about that word. "Or maybe a sensual brute. He was like a big child who threw tantrums if he didn't get his way. He also used you in his campaigns to win over the Outskirts."

"How did we fall in love?"

"I think he just wanted to dominate you at first," Samson said. "And you him. Then you had sex and got pregnant."

Ruby sighed. "There has to be more to it than that."

"Evidently. Unfortunately, I wasn't around to analyze your emotional development. Somewhere in between, you clearly fell in love. I do know you hit a bit of a rough patch when the Warlord got a bit too close to the female Allseer—I forgot the bitch's name—but you made up after that."

Ruby arched a brow. "Agathe?" Wow, even Louis never mentioned her. Ruby knew all about the female Allseer, of course, having read about her sheltered life and then controversial policies in history classes, but she hadn't had a clue Agathe and Damian were . . . together.

"Yes," Samson said. "The Warlord killed her for more than just show. It was personal."

Ruby's stomach twisted. "Did Damian . . . cheat on me?"

"Can we please stop talking about this?" Samson spat. "It was in the past! Everyone fucks up once in a while, including me." He huffed. "I should have never left you in Mousafeld."

But Ruby couldn't stop thinking of Agathe. Samson could see it in her eyes.

"Don't you dare ask him." Samson gritted his teeth. "That man has been through way too much heartache to be thinking of his past transgressions. Stars, I should have kept my trap shut."

Ruby didn't hold it against Damian, though. They had been through too much since. Besides, if her past self had forgiven him, then she had no right to stay mad. Not like she could even if she wanted to. When Damian finally joined them, she smiled at him.

Damian stopped to stare at her. He was as serious as always, but then his lips curled up when he saw her dreamy look was genuine.

Ruby couldn't help it. She did hide her face when Samson turned around, though—she'd never hear the end of it otherwise. She went back to her juice, fighting the blood that crept up her cheeks.

Maybe he does have a lot of flaws, Ruby thought to herself. *But that doesn't matter.*

"We are nearly at our destination," Samson announced, serving them plates of ham, hash browns, and eggs.

Ruby was used to Samson's exquisite cooking, but Damian looked impressed. He picked up his fork and knife to dig right in. For someone with so much muscle and energy, he surely didn't eat a lot. Ruby's plate was three times as big as his.

"Don't mind if Hayes joins you all, do you?" Jamie said, leading the very weak Hayes over to the table.

Hayes' wound had healed by now, but he looked like he had been run over by a truck. His hair was messy and his clothes were disheveled—he must have hastily thrown them on this morning. His eyes blew up when he saw Damian, who continued eating while looking through messages on his phone.

"A-and you're all just going to let him bully me around like that?" Hayes croaked, oscillating between the two Lolligo in the room. Bruce was still getting ready in his room. "He can just stab me and do whatever he wants?"

"Did you ever think for one moment that you deserved it?" Samson spat at him. He was sipping coffee at the table now. His pinky was always out. "Taking advantage of pretty much everything that can breathe?"

"I didn't take advantage of anyone!" Hayes exclaimed. "Is this seriously about Ruby—?"

"*Sage*," Samson corrected. "Her name is Sage, asswipe. 'Ruby' is a name that Louis gave her in an effort to hide her from everyone. It's like calling her by her slave name."

Ruby stopped. She hadn't quite thought of it that way before.

"She's not a slave—she's never been a slave!" Hayes exclaimed. "She was allowed to do whatever the fuck she wanted, all while living at the palace and being pampered like crazy! Who wouldn't kill for a life like that?"

"Listen," Samson said patiently, "because I'm only going to say this once. You don't take things that don't belong to you. Sage was *not* Louis' property. You don't take someone and hide them from the world because you want them all to yourself. If you truly love someone, you let them choose what they want in life, and Sage had no choice when she was at the palace. She didn't know she had two nieces working her pizza restaurant and she didn't know she had a family waiting for her in Emerald City. Do you get it now, dipshit? Or are you still looking at the picture through the lens of a twenty-year-old?" Samson snorted. He looked at Jamie. "Why are people so stupid at that age? Or is it a human thing?"

Jamie nodded his head. He said in Lolligo, "Impressive, sir. Your words."

"They're the truth."

Maybe so, but Hayes still didn't look convinced. He sat down at the table with a glare at Damian, who continued scrolling through his phone as if no one else existed, and a longing glance at Ruby.

You're better than this, he seemed to say with his eyes. *So much better. You can leave all this behind.*

Perhaps Ruby could. But even she acknowledged that what Louis had done was nothing short of selfish. She was sure that she could have a palace life just as easily by Damian's side.

"All right, well, we're nearly there," Jamie announced, heading toward the cockpit where Bruce was in communication with someone. "And so our first person of contact is a human by the name of Faye Sabine. She happens to be the Prime's primary attendant in the palace at Elysium. She hires all the ladies and gentlemen who work with her. We were thinking that the two of you would make fantastic maids."

Hayes gasped. Ruby did, too, but not because she'd be a maid—but because she'd be a spy among Elysium's royal class. This was supposed to be Samson's home, but it had been hijacked by Rhett, and Ruby had to play her cards right or else she'd be arrested and executed. The mission was already making her nervous.

"And how is becoming a maid supposed to help us accomplish our goal?" Ruby said.

"It's very simple." Samson cut his ham into tiny pieces as if his razor-sharp teeth couldn't shred anything they munched on. Ruby wondered if Lolligo were just quirky like that, but then Jamie always ate like a normal person. It was definitely a Samson thing. "You have access to pretty much everything in the palace. You can spy and assassinate others as you feel fit."

"So there are three classes in Elysium," Jamie explained. "There's the Prime at the very top, then the Lolligo, then the hybrids—who either serve as officials, officers, or soldiers—and then the humans, who do whatever job they can find."

"What about Enhanced?" Ruby asked.

"Enhanced are illegal in Elysium. Hybrids aren't allowed to share their blood and the Prime doesn't want them playing god, either. Their purpose is getting stronger, not deciding who they're going to turn."

"There is a tournament that is going to take place in the month of Light," Samson said. "Well, your month of Light—we just call it the summer solstice."

"How do you know this?" Ruby asked. "You haven't been in Elysium in a while."

"Because there's a tournament every year. It's when the strongest hybrids from the academy battle each other to the death. The one left standing becomes a 'Prime Warrior'. And this year, specifically, is an important one because it's the final draft." Samson swallowed thickly. He looked them all in the eye. "Rhett will have enough numbers to start a full-scale war against the Outskirts.

That's why we have to take out every single hybrid." He gave Ruby the vial of concentrated Slainium, placing it right next to her juice. "Before that can happen."

"And they're supposed to accomplish that as maids—?" Hayes got more slime slapped across his mouth to keep him quiet.

Samson peered into Ruby's eyes, as serious as ever. "Kill the hybrids," he said again. "Defeat Rhett."

"But . . . Samson." Ruby braced herself. "Not all the hybrids can be bad. They can't all be brainwashed and think that launching a war against all these cities in the Outskirts is a good idea."

"Perhaps not," Samson said softly. "But I will leave that choice up to you, Sage. If you strongly believe there is another way to stem the war, then by all means: do it. Perhaps you're right and there is a way, but you fail to realize that these hybrids are even more bloodthirsty than Lolligo. Even the Warlord loved playing games with power—I don't think it's anything we can help."

Ruby glanced at Damian, who was cutting hash browns. His face remained neutral. Perhaps that was his way of agreeing with Samson.

"There is a lot at stake here," Samson reiterated. "And I am trusting the two of you to do the right thing."

"So we go in . . ." Ruby said slowly, "and we put a stop to these hybrids somehow . . . but isn't your target Rhett?"

"Bring me his head." Samson picked up his coffee. "But I have a feeling that Rhett will be the least of our worries."

Ruby looked to Damian, who still hadn't spoken. Perhaps he had said everything he needed to last night. Samson wanted to eliminate *all* of the hybrids . . . including them. It was hard for Ruby to internalize that after everything that Samson had taught her on the battlefield, but she also knew she was a tool. Samson didn't stand a chance of making a dent in Elysium. No human maid would ever be able to accomplish defeating hybrids. Even an Enhanced wouldn't be able to pull this off.

Hayes kept trying to speak through the slime across his mouth. His eyes looked ready to pop from his skull.

Samson didn't care about what he had to say—he continued sipping coffee. He looked a bit lost in thought now.

Ruby finished her breakfast with a bit of difficulty. Her nervousness was only getting worse. She kept looking at Damian, who had his arms crossed and eyes closed. Was he meditating?

They finally passed the Roaring Mountains. Ruby looked out the window to see a huge city on the horizon, with skyscrapers twice as tall as the ones in Diamond City. They looked different, too: thin and twisty like perfect coils. A few hover cars shot back and forth. Larger airships were taking off into the sky right next to the building that Ruby surmised was the palace.

There was certainly something... *imposing* about the place. No Diamond City airship had ever been brave enough to lead an expedition across the Outskirts, much less to the other side of the Roaring Mountains. It truly was as the preachers from the Clarity District described: a powerful civilization that dwelled on the other side of the continent, run by the Lolligo and the people they deemed worthy enough to live with them.

Even Samson couldn't come any closer. Bruce landed right next to some shack hidden in a mountain pass. From here, Elysium looked like a mirage. With all the clouds and snow, Ruby couldn't quite tell if there was something there at all.

"Patrols don't typically extend this far," Jamie said to Ruby. "Do you see all that flat land?"

Ruby peered out the window more closely. There was a lot of flat land between here and Elysium. Almost like a no-man's-land.

"It's the equivalent of your Outskirts," Jamie explained. "Except we call ours Tribulation."

"That's pretty dark," Ruby said.

"No one can cross it without being gunned down. Anyone that leaves Elysium does so because they have permission and by aircraft. But any unauthorized person that steps foot on those lands typically dies."

"You shoot them down?"

"No," Jamie said. "They just die. Heat exhaustion... cold...

disease... fatigue... Any of the above. No one has ever crossed these lands into Elysium by accident."

"Except for the Lolligo." Samson sounded awfully proud. "We did. We built this city from the ground up."

"Are there underground passages or bunkers here, too?" Ruby asked.

"Pathways, yes." Samson nodded. "I had them built myself. And it was a good thing I did, because it's how I was able to escape. I'm actually the only one who knows about them."

"I guess it was a precaution."

"Very much so. Sometimes Lolligo are worse than humans."

"Do you remember yourself as a human?" Ruby asked Samson.

"No," Samson said neutrally. Jamie looked serious. "I no longer have those memories."

Bruce exited the cockpit. The ramp was down, and it was time to send Damian and Ruby on their way. The Lolligo waited for the two to descend before following them. Hayes was still having a hard time with the slime, so Jamie finally relieved him of it. This would probably be the last time they saw Ruby anyway.

Damian stepped up to the shack. It looked like a cozy cabin with a hearth for a fire and a bed in the corner. The dust said no one had been here in ages. Maybe not since Samson had run away from Elysium thirty years ago.

"I became an egg here," Samson said quietly.

Ruby noticed all the medical supplies on a table. There were scalpels and staplers. Rolls of gauze were stacked one on top of the other.

"We barely escaped with our lives," Jamie said.

"There's an underground tunnel that leads to a secret room in Faye's quarters," Samson said. "She will accommodate you there."

"Won't it be obvious we're new?" Ruby said. "And what about the language?"

"Everyone in Elysium speaks Lolligo."

"And won't it be obvious that she looks like Wren?!" Hayes

sputtered now that he had been granted the privilege of speaking. "That's her twin sister, isn't it, the one you used to create all these hybrids in the first place?"

"No one will notice," Samson sneered. "You don't think I thought of that already? Rhett doesn't pay attention to faces, and so long as Sage acts accordingly, she'll be fine." He flared his nostrils. There was no other way to do this.

Damian opened the hatch on the floor. Like Ruby, he didn't have his sword or any kind of weapon. He was in his clothes from yesterday minus the jacket. He must have figured it'd be hot as hell down there. Now that his hair was groomed, he had it tied behind his head so it wouldn't get in his face as he peered down at the dark tunnel that was miles long.

"Here." Samson gave over a small pack. That was for the trip. "Food and water until you make it to Elysium."

"How are we supposed to communicate with you?" Ruby asked.

"You're not. I'll know when it's time to move in."

Damian went in first. It was a good five-foot drop without the stairs. Ruby was careful as she lowered herself into the tunnel. She wasn't claustrophobic, but it was tight and stuffy. There was hardly any room to walk upright. At least it was better than the one beneath Paige and Pedro's shop.

Damian held out his hand. "Come, darling."

Ruby took it. She squeezed as tightly as she could. She looked up at Samson, who gave her half a smile from the entrance above.

"Be safe" was all he said before he closed the hatch. Hayes was still whining about how dangerous this all was.

"Damian," Ruby croaked. She could hardly see him. There was a faint light up ahead. "It's hard to breathe."

"Just relax," Damian said. "Control your breathing and try not to talk. Let's quicken our pace so we can arrive at our destination as soon as possible."

Right. Samson had said something about Faye's quarters, which made Ruby wonder just who she was to Samson. If he had built a tunnel leading from her room, then he must have truly trusted her during his time as Prime. Ruby wasn't even sure Samson trusted her that much.

The path was rugged and ill-kept. There were those tiny lights here and there that were powered by Surgium to help illuminate the space, but not by much. Ruby could picture Jamie or even Bruce sticking those up there as they blasted through more and more ground. This must have been their worst case scenario, fleeing their very own city with bounties on their heads. Ruby wished she could have asked them more about those dynamics, but she supposed she'd be finding out for herself soon enough.

Damian kept her moving. His arm remained around her waist the entire time. He only sipped a little bit of water and made sure she drank the rest. Out of a bag of snacks, he took one and let her eat as much as she could.

"Damian," Ruby murmured. "Don't be ridiculous. There's enough here for us both."

"I want you to be well," Damian said.

"Well, I want you to be well, too."

This journey didn't just take hours—it took days. After miles of walking, Damian and Ruby took a seat and rested. They remained curled up together, but didn't sleep. Ruby couldn't.

After the second day, the tunnel finally came to an end. At long last, Ruby reached the hatch that would grant her entry into Faye's room. She had yet to acknowledge that she had just crawled under Tribulation and arrived at Elysium, the esteemed Lolligo city that even the preachers in the Clarity District had yet to see with their eyes. It was exciting, but Ruby was too terrified to celebrate. She was a complete stranger in a foreign place with an extremely high probability that she'd be caught and put to death. She had hardly stood a chance against Jared's Enhanced . . . how was she supposed to fare against hybrids? An entire army of them?

Damian went first. He took the stairs and pushed up on the hatch—it opened easily. Then he took Ruby's hand and ascended with her in tow.

The fresh air was glorious. At last, Ruby could breathe. It was cool, too, which helped bring down her fever. She was thankful to see what looked like a closet. Damian had removed a box of shoes from atop the door. Faye must have been using it to hide her and Samson's secret. Ruby wondered if Rhett had officials search the rooms for any foul play.

And then Ruby smelled blood. She heard laughing. It was coming from the bedroom. She was about to ask what was going on when Damian wrapped a hand around her mouth.

"DAMN!" someone cried from the other side of the door. "This bitch is *always* tight! So, so good . . ."

There was a thumping. Ruby already knew what was going on, but her mind didn't want to acknowledge it. She kept making excuses—maybe it was something else—but there was no escaping the truth when time went on and the thumping got faster and the painful groans grew in volume. She saw it on Damian's face, in his eyes when they peered into her own and communicated that bursting out of here and being seen by the enemy would get them both killed. This was not a place they could afford to act out in, no matter how badly Ruby wanted to tear that rapist to pieces.

Ruby cried silently. Damian kept her head against his chest. He was shaking a bit, too. They had to stand there and wait. They had nothing but fancy dresses and robes to look at until it was clear.

Elysium was no paradise.

Ruby already knew it was going to be hell.

CHAPTER 15

Faye's Secrets

amian let Ruby go when the door to the bedroom slammed closed and a woman's sobs filled the air. Ruby was too shocked to move, so all she could do was stand there as Damian burst out of the closet and ran over to the half-naked woman on the bed.

It was a four-poster with the curtains drawn. The mattress was king-sized. There was a nice view of the city outside the window.

But none of that mattered right now. Damian picked up the sobbing woman and asked Ruby to get a fresh robe. He took her into the bathroom.

Hands shaking, Ruby looked through the racks in the closet and took down the first silk nightgown she found. Taking deep breaths and closing her eyes for just a moment, she edged into the room, footsteps absorbed by the carpet, and peered into the bathroom. There, she found Damian removing the rest of the woman's clothes and dipping her body into the tub.

"Could you get me some disinfectant?" Damian asked Ruby.

That must have been for the woman's wounds. There were plenty of bruises on her body. There was severe bleeding between her legs.

"God..." sobbed the woman, who clung onto Damian. "W-who...are you?"

"A friend of Samson's," Damian replied, dropping some epsom salt into the water. "We were tasked with finding you via the underground tunnel. I assume that you're Faye? I'm sorry to have walked in in such a bad time."

"No." Faye shook her head. "Don't be sorry...I would have suffered so much more without you."

"Who did this to you?"

"R-Ray." Faye cleared her throat. "That's his name. He's the Prime's pet and he struts around the palace like it, too."

"I understand." Damian poured some soap onto his hand and started washing her.

Faye rested her head against the edge of the tub. She squeezed her eyes closed and winced every time Damian touched a particularly sensitive spot on her body. The softness in her eyes said she greatly appreciated his attention.

"What is your name?" Faye asked him softly.

"Damian," he replied. "And that there is my wife, Sage."

"How lovely." Faye craned her head to get a better look at Ruby. "She certainly is beautiful."

"Oh." Ruby blushed a bit. "Thank you."

"She is, isn't she?" Damian scrubbed Faye's legs with a sponge. "I fell in love with her as soon as I saw her." He chuckled a bit. "I might not have known it was love at the time, but I couldn't get her out of my head. I became obsessed with the very thought of her. She was driving me insane. I knew I had to make her mine or I wouldn't be able to continue living my life."

"That is powerful," Faye admitted. "I'm not sure I've ever felt that way about someone before...even my lover now. And no," she quickly amended, "it's not Ray."

"I would like to think not."

"Finding your soulmate feels impossible at times, especially in a world with so much evil."

"Despite all my ill fortunes in life, I am very blessed," Damian said. "It took over a hundred years, but I found her. One day, perhaps, you'll find yours, too."

Ruby's heart wouldn't stop pounding. If anything, her cheeks turned even more red.

"How long have you been together?" Faye asked.

"Thirty years now," Damian replied. "And there isn't anything in existence that will pull me from her side, even if I were to die tomorrow. I believe there's an afterlife and I'd most certainly be with her as a ghost."

Ruby thought that was rather morbid and she wasn't sure if Damian was trying to be funny or serious. She didn't like how he was talking about death so casually. Faye had a better look at his face, but all she did was sigh.

When Damian finished scrubbing her, he lifted her from the tub. He dried her, and then Ruby stepped in with the antibiotic. She made sure to get all the bruises.

"Why are you here?" Faye asked softly. She looked much more thin and frail up close.

"I'm sure you can imagine why," Damian said. "Samson has sent us on a mission. He wishes to oust Rhett."

"I see . . . and how does he plan for you to do that, exactly?"

"We become maids," Ruby said. "Will you be able to sneak us in?"

Faye held her breath for a few seconds. It seemed she had been waiting for word from Samson for some time, but she had not been expecting a plan as crazy as this one. At least, not one with so many risks. "Yes . . . but it won't be easy. I'll have to come up with paperwork to make your identities convincing. Humans aren't allowed to enter Elysium without the proper connections or familial ties. Listing you as my own will be tough, but I have a few accomplices that might be able to help."

"You seem willing to put a lot on the line. Are you friends with Samson?"

"We are very close," Faye said. That was a statement that implied there was more behind the relationship than she let on. Damian and Ruby didn't need to know anymore for tonight—Faye was willing to work with them, and that was all that mattered.

"I'll give you the details in the morning," Faye said softly as Damian helped her into that silky nightgown.

Ruby went to change the sheets in the bedroom. She tried not to look at the bloodstains or the splashes of semen. This was so fucking gross, but she didn't make faces or ask any further questions about Ray. She focused on her task as Damian finally came out of the bathroom with Faye at his side. Once the bed was ready, Ruby helped him tuck her in.

"Feel free to use the spare bedroom," Faye told them.

While Ruby wanted to stay and watch her, Damian tugged her out of the room. It was best to give Faye some space, and after that horror show, Ruby needed a moment to process it in her mind.

"Are you all right?" Damian asked her in the hall. It was dark save for the small nightlight in the corner, illuminating all the sharp features on his face. His eyes twinkled with concern. It didn't matter how old Ruby was—no one was ever prepared for that sort of sight—but she was especially young and . . . *tender* without her memories of the past. It made her wonder if she had ever witnessed a rape before.

"I'm fine," Ruby said softly. "I just wasn't expecting that."

"I'm not sure anyone ever does."

Ruby studied the paintings of Elysium in the hall. Same artist, different colors. No matter the filter, from cool to gingham, Elysium was grand and majestic. Faye's "room" in the palace was more like an apartment.

"Do you want to talk about it?" Damian asked her.

"No." Ruby rubbed her face. "I've seen some pretty fucked-up things since I woke up. And while that one takes the cake, I'd rather not dwell on it." She caressed his cheek then went for the room next door.

This must have been the spare Faye had mentioned, but it was huge. It was more like a suite complete with a living space and kitchen. Better than the plush furniture and gold-rimmed counter-tops was the view outside.

They were hovering over an abyss. A steady stream of water fell into depths unknown.

"Whoa," Ruby breathed. That was miles deep, so far into the earth that she didn't see where it ended. Pure darkness swirled around down there, ready to consume whatever unfortunate thing—living or non-living—fell in.

"Darling?"

Ruby turned to Damian, who was still standing by the door. He didn't seem anywhere near as entertained as she was with their view. He probably had this and more in Emerald City. His main concern was obviously her.

"What 'fucked-up' things have you seen?" he asked.

Ruby didn't want to talk about it. At the same time, she didn't want to shun him out. She wished there was a way to say that without hurting his feelings. Perhaps it was better if she just took the emotional brunt of the experience and told him, but then Damian sensed her distress and shook his head.

"Forgive me," Damian said quickly. "It's just I want to break the face of whoever exposed you to such violence."

"Well . . ." Ruby said, looking back at the waterfall. "You already tore Venus to pieces, so I suppose that takes care of a lot of it. I think about Cell Land and all those people almost every second of the day. I saw her Enhanced execute my friend in front of me." Ruby crossed her arms and rubbed them. ". . . I did see a suicide shortly after I left the capital in Diamond City. It was the night I ran from . . . our sons. Looking back at it, it seems kind of silly . . . but I truly didn't know, Damian."

"Of course you didn't." Damian stepped forward. "That wasn't your fault. Where did you see this suicide?"

"Rest Inn," Ruby said softly. She watched the water flow into nothingness, although her mind was far away, drowning in the horrors of that night. The gunshots. "Elias and Johanna Westbrook."

She had gotten their initials on her left ankle. She didn't want them to be forgotten.

Damian wrapped an arm around her.

"Venus is evil," Ruby went on. "And so is Ray. They do what they do to hurt others on purpose. But Elias and Johanna? They weren't evil. They . . ."

"Were looking for a way out?" Damian finished softly.

"There are other ways out, Damian. I feel that there is always hope no matter what. Had they stuck around with me and my friends . . . who knows . . ." Ruby sighed. "Maybe they would have done well in Ruby City."

"Sometimes that's what people who are desperate need to hear." Damian kissed her forehead. He kissed her nose, too. "We need to be reminded that there is hope."

"I didn't get to them in time," Ruby whispered.

Damian lifted her head, forcing her to look at him. "That is not on you."

"I know."

"You have done so much already, Sage. You built a city out of nothing and kept so many people safe from what was happening in Diamond City. You truly never fail to impress me."

Ruby smiled. "I appreciate that."

"Kiss me."

How could Ruby deny him that? His lips offered a great reprieve from the evils of this world, and she sank into them. With the rush of water in the background, Ruby was living in a different time and place. She realized it was hard to get enough of him because all she wanted was more. When she was done ravaging his mouth, she knew there was so much more to move on to, but she controlled herself. Still, she was super red and panting by the time they withdrew their lips and tongues.

"How about some tea?" Damian suggested with a chuckle. He had fixed her hair in the tunnel, but his hands had done quite a number on it now. He brushed the flyaways back.

"Sure," Ruby breathed.

As he went to do that in their little kitchen, Ruby checked out the bedroom they'd be using. She felt a bit naked without her sword, but she did have Kendra's dagger she had stashed in her sock and the vial of Slainium that Samson had given her.

"What if Ray comes back?" Ruby asked Damian, who brought her a cup of lavender and honey with a hint of spice. Just one whiff and Ruby felt her sinuses opening up.

"I doubt he'll be back tonight," Damian said. "But if he does, we hide. We don't engage anyone until the time is right."

Ruby let him handle this one. She had to admit she was able to rest a lot better knowing that he was in the hall keeping an ear out for Faye and any intruders that might have been lurking outside. As Damian had predicted, no one else came to bother them that night.

It was a grand miracle that Faye was still alive. As one of the palace's head maids, she was clearly a target and an object of much desire. Hybrids couldn't bully each other, so humans were at the top of their list for entertainment. Faye explained that everyone in Elysium had come to accept his or her place as an inferior to the Prime. Humans were arrogant, but they took punishment without complaint.

"We are fortunate," Faye said. "And therefore we are grateful for what we are given in life. How many humans in Diamond City can say they live in the most fortified and advanced civilization of the New World?"

"So you're fine with all the rape?" Ruby said incredulously.

The obvious answer was no. But Faye wasn't here to complain to them—she was here to help them achieve Samson's goal.

And the first step was waiting. A lot of waiting.

Damian and Ruby couldn't do much without believable identities. Faye pulled whatever strings she needed to make it happen, to give them names and backgrounds so that they could become part of the royal work force without raising too many questions.

She knew how to navigate the Elysium population and politics, so Ruby trusted her.

She and Damian would wait in the apartment all day and come out to explore at night. They never told Faye about their ventures because their snooping was extremely dangerous to her and themselves. Getting caught would throw their whole mission off and might possibly get them killed. Samson had come up with concentrated Slainium, but the scientists here had probably done the same. How else did they discipline these hybrids if there wasn't some looming threat?

In their first round of exploration, Ruby and Damian split up. Ruby took the hallway left and Damian took the right. At night, the lights were dim, allowing shadows to build up in the corners. Ruby traveled without shoes to keep her steps light. With concentration, she could sense when someone was approaching from afar. The maids had finished all their rounds by now, so it was just whatever lingering hybrids were out here that Ruby had to be careful with.

These are the elite, Ruby reminded herself as she turned the corner and traveled down her very first hallway in Elysium's massive palace. The carpet was soft and plush. The walls were made of thick, shiny steel. An Elysium flag with black-and-white stripes was pinned in every corner.

After a few more twists and turns, Ruby came to a fork. On the wall between the two branching hallways was a grand painting of the palace at night. Whoever had done that was talented as hell. The details and shading were spot on. Ruby would have never guessed someone had painted this if it wasn't for the caption. Maybe "Ulysses Barclay" was a hybrid with a knack for art. Damian didn't look like the kind to draw many environments, but that looked like something he'd be capable of doing. Ruby was lucky if she could get a stick figure right.

As Ruby continued exploring what was the first floor of the palace, she made sure to memorize every detail. Hallways branched off, so she noted which ones she still had to see in nights to come. She kept track of all the rooms she passed by, located all the storage closets, bathrooms, and offices, and hid behind a plant when she heard voices.

Ruby held her breath. Thirty minutes in and this was the first time she had run into anyone. The voices were loud and laughing. There were three of them, although two stuck out above the third.

"Damn, Ilan! Her, too?"

"Of course. I've had my eye on her since I caught her bringing me a fresh uniform."

"That's because you got your ass whooped by Ray."

Ilan snorted. "I was just lying in bed. I asked her to join me, but she refused and ran out. I think she went to talk to the Faye bitch, so she's been avoiding me since."

"And where do you think she went?" asked that second voice.

"I don't know."

Ruby had to be extra still to make sure the trio didn't see her as they rounded the corner. They strolled right by her. Thanks to Samson, she knew how to make herself invisible. She glimpsed the three just as they left her line of sight.

They had white uniforms with long sleeves and two black bands on their right arms. That was the hybrid uniform, apparently. And those three were after one of the maids. Ruby knew the name.

"Sarah."

As the trio drifted farther away, their voices faded. Ruby didn't hear anything else. She had a name, and that was all that mattered. She'd be asking Faye about it first thing in the morning.

Ruby decided to keep going. She didn't run into any more hybrids, so she was able to cover a grand part of the first floor. In total, so far, twenty-four apartments that belonged to hybrids. The maids must have been on Damian's side.

Whoever had designed this place must have thought it was a good idea to separate the two species, like the two sides of a coin. Yet the two still made up the highest class in Elysium. This place still functioned like a well-oiled machine, with hybrids leaving their rooms during the day for training and the maids moving into their personal spaces for cleaning until the sun set. Ruby pictured it all in her head.

Unfortunately, Ruby never ran into Damian, so once she felt she had made it far enough for the night, she decided to go back.

Damian was waiting for her on the couch. He stood up as soon as Ruby stepped through the door.

"Darling?" he said. He was concerned, of course, but this was Sage. Memories or not, she knew how to stay off the radar. With a small exhale of relief, he pulled out the map he had been working on.

Ruby wasn't anywhere near as meticulous, but she did have the hallways memorized in her head. Together, they pieced the entire first floor of the palace, the room numbers, and where they had run into hybrids. Damian had seen some chick standing idly in a corner, but no one else. Ruby expressed her concern about the trio and Sarah.

Ruby had to contemplate how to approach Faye about it. The poor woman could hardly walk straight and had a hard time sitting down in a chair. Damian always had breakfast ready for her in the morning. He brought out the coffee and served her a cup.

"Thank you," Faye said.

Ruby didn't mean to stare, but she did. She took in every detail of Faye's face, the hard lines and dark spots on her skin from stress and bruising. Ultimately, as Damian served the waffles, Ruby decided not to ask about Sarah. She was concerned, however, over Faye's state.

"Maybe you should see a doctor," Ruby suggested.

"What good will that do me?" Faye said. "These doctors don't care much about rape victims. They clean you up a bit and then send you on your way."

Ruby gaped. "And that's it?"

"This is survival of the fittest. You want to survive? Stay out of trouble and out of the limelight. Although for some of us, depending on which hybrid targets us, it's impossible."

"So what you're saying is Rhett doesn't care about humans?"

"He doesn't," Faye admitted.

Ruby didn't make eye contact with Damian. She didn't have to. Her brain was coming to life and it started racing at a hundred miles per hour as she ate her breakfast. When she was done, she hardly knew what she had eaten.

Faye got up to get ready for another day of services. As Ruby helped pick up dirty dishes, Damian said, "I know what you're thinking and that is a hard no."

Ruby blinked. "What?"

Damian glared at her. "Darling, it's all over your face. You're *not* going to fix the system and you're going to endanger yourself for nothing. We need to concentrate on taking down Rhett, not embarking on a quest for revenge that won't see an end until we take out the one in charge."

Ruby turned back to the dishes and started scrubbing. There was a dishwasher, but those things never cleaned the plates right.

Damian stepped closer to her. He touched her chin and said, "Look at me, darling."

Ruby looked at him because she couldn't help it. She got lost in the darkness of his gaze and swooned a bit when she stared at his lips. Damian was serious, though.

"Promise me you won't do anything risky."

"I won't," Ruby said at once. "Nothing risky."

That was the truth. Just because she had lost her memories didn't mean she was dumb. She knew exactly what was at stake and how to conduct herself in a foreign place that wouldn't hesitate to kill her if they discovered who she was.

By the time Ruby finished cleaning up, Faye was out the door. Damian was vacuuming the rug and taking a chance to snoop through drawers and cabinets. Ruby would have said that was an invasion of privacy, but she did it, too. She felt determined to find out who Faye was and why Samson trusted her so much.

Of course, there was nothing here. Ruby wondered if security raided the palace often. Having any sort of evidence was dangerous, so the search was a bit futile. Damian was determined, however, to find proof of something.

After cleaning the floors, Damian started rummaging through furniture. Not just peeking into drawers, either—he felt for secret compartments or doors and cut up fabrics for hidden documents. A woman like Faye had to have some sort of outlet, and he was determined to find where she stashed her secrets.

"A journal, maybe," Ruby said, looking through all the clothes in the closet next. She touched the walls, glancing at the trapdoor by her feet every once in a while. She swore Samson would come bumbling out after them at any moment. He had to hold an enormous amount of trust in Ruby to not die of anxiety on the other side of Tribulation.

"Yes, perhaps," Damian said from the bedroom. "Although that might be a bit too obvious."

Ruby got to the shoe cubbies in the back. Taped to the top corner was a photograph of a woman and man. It was incredibly old, though, even if it had been printed on expensive, glossy paper. Once-vibrant colors had faded a bit and a few scratches adorned the edges. Ruby didn't have a clue who these two were, but she guessed they were relatives of Faye's . . . Perhaps her parents?

Ruby took the picture for a closer look.

For a human, the man looked like he was in his forties because he had some gray at his temples. His eyes were vibrant and full of life. While his expression was serious, his lips were curled in a slight smirk. He looked like the kind of guy that could win any argument.

The woman was a lot younger. She had golden-brown hair in waves. Her skin was pale, as if she didn't see the sun often. There was a softness to her features that indicated she was content with her life. Her grin confirmed that. This woman was a troublemaker.

And these two, Ruby concluded, were not related to Faye at all. They didn't even look like her.

Ruby turned the picture over in hopes of seeing a name and year. While Elysium didn't follow the same calendar that Diamond City did, she'd be able to gauge just how old this was. Nothing, though.

Disappointed, Ruby put the picture back.

When Ruby emerged from the closet, she found Damian sitting on the floor in front of the dresser. His sleeves were rolled up, so she could see the sage leaves on his right forearm. His rings glistened beneath the rays of the sun streaming in through the window. His hair was pushed to the side, flowing down his left shoulder. From the draw of his brows, Ruby could tell he was concentrated as he looked through a photo album.

"This is quite odd," he said, flipping to another page.

"What is?" Ruby stepped over.

Damian didn't say anything as his finger guided her eyes through each of the photographs. There was nothing spectacular about any of those photos, though. They were mostly from parties, award ceremonies, or hybrid tournaments. A few of them were of Faye and some of the maids. Her team, possibly.

But Ruby quickly caught on to something. While physical photo albums were a bit odd to have when there was a working computer in the corner of the room, also cycling through many nature shots of Elsyium and a rare aurora borealis taken late at night, there was something lackluster about this album in particular.

"There are photos missing," Ruby said.

"Indeed," Damian affirmed. "Nobody takes the time to print photos they don't care about." He waved at some random street shots and poorly-taken panoramas. "Faye doesn't seem like the kind of person to waste time and dabble in nonsense, not if she had a clear and obvious plan with Samson. Plus, these photos are all dated from thirty years ago."

"Thirty years ago." Ruby thought for a second. "So . . . from before Samson was expelled?"

"Right. And for someone who is loyal to Samson, there are no photos of them here whatsoever."

"Maybe they didn't take any pictures together."

Damian snorted. "Darling, please. The two are a couple."

Ruby gasped. Someone might have thrown a bucket of cold water over her head. "*What?*"

"It's so damn obvious. Faye loves Samson so much that she chose to stay in Elysium and help him return to power when the time was right. Even if it meant years of persecution and rape."

"But she love-*loves* him?" Ruby said, head still spinning. She had never contemplated a Lolligo and human in a romantic relationship before. Ew? "I-I mean, how is that possible? Lolligo are asexual."

"You don't have to have sex to be in love. And while Lolligo might not have penises . . ." Damian made a face. "They have fingers, don't they?"

"God." Ruby grimaced. But before she pictured Samson's fingers in between her legs, Damian said, "My point is it's obvious how loyal Faye is to Samson and there definitely wouldn't be any evidence of that here or in there." He nodded at the computer.

"Right," Ruby murmured.

Damian closed the photo album. He tucked it back underneath Faye's pants in the bottom drawer. He was still frowning. "I wish Samson would have told us more."

"What difference does it make? We still have to stop Rhett."

Damian looked at her. His eyes grew tender as he regarded her. A small smile crossed his lips.

Ruby blushed. "Why are you looking at me like that?"

"Because you are loyal, darling," Damian said. "And you believe that the people who claim to love you can do you no wrong. Samson means a lot to you, but he is also a man on a mission. Despite his physical appearance, that's what he is. He is human at heart and that means he can be as lying, scheming, and backstabbing as any of them. Do you understand?"

Ruby lowered her head. "I don't think Samson would get rid of us. Isn't that what Rhett wants?"

"I'm not sure that Rhett cares to get rid of anyone. He wants to clear out the people who might potentially hurt him, yes, but his focus is power and expansion. Samson, however, has had quite enough of hybrids. While he pledged allegiances with them when he was Prime, things are different for him now that he's been expelled. He might not harbor resentment toward humans, but it is unwise to rule out that he wishes to eradicate them *all*. Including you and me."

Damian had said that before. Ruby wasn't sure what to think of it still.

"You don't really know, do you?" Damian got to his feet. "Even when you were roommates, he hid so much from you. He was working on behalf of the Lolligo while documenting you. Your sister was the scapegoat for him and his schemes. He just wasn't able to maintain order here like he had been hoping and he had to flee."

"So his love and attention for me are all pretend?" Ruby said softly.

"Perhaps for now it is. I am not going to pass judgment too quickly, but I do want you to be prepared for the worst. I don't want you to get hurt, darling. You are a hybrid and the only female one at that. Potentially, you can still create more children."

"For how long? I mean—am I immortal?"

"Lolligo don't die, darling." Damian caressed her cheek. "They reproduce and go through cycles. You, I imagine, are the same."

"Wait . . ." Ruby captured his hand. "What about you?"

"What about me?"

"You haven't hibernated, have you?"

Damian chuckled. "No. Nor have I spit out any eggs, thankfully. Or birthed any cocoons. For males . . . I'm not too sure what our fates are . . . and while we live long lives . . . it seems we are meant to die."

"What?" Ruby breathed. "How do you know that?"

"Because I nearly died."

It was getting harder for Ruby to breathe. She had never associated Damian with death, even from before she knew who he was in relation to her, and it was devastating to hear him talk about it. It wasn't the first time he had mentioned dying, either, and Ruby wanted him to stop it. Jared had teased her about it before, too, but she hadn't believed it. Hearing it from Damian was world's different, and it made gravity press down on her like never before.

"How?" Ruby demanded. "How did you nearly die, Damian?"

"It was strange," Damian said. "And not many know this, but I was on a steady decline from the moment you entered hibernation. I attributed a lot of my weakness to grief and depression. Kevin examined me and determined that my Cells were simply withering away, almost as if I was being poisoned." Damian shook his head. "But no poison was ever found in my blood. It was clearly something else—a disease, or maybe even a side-effect from some unknown condition. I had to be there for our sons, so I fought through it. It was challenging, but I did it for your sake. I trained and led a relatively healthy lifestyle. But nothing I did ever seemed to slow down the rate at which my Cells were dying. No matter how strong I was, I knew I was dying inside.

"And then, that day in Diamond City last year, I saw you. I got so upset with Louis that I actually suffered a heart attack. My Cells have not been strong enough to sustain me and it seems I have degenerated a great deal."

"S-so it was true?" Ruby croaked. "You really were bed-ridden?"

Damian arched a brow. "Who told you?"

"Jared. H-his spies saw you, I guess—or it was rumors—I didn't believe it, though!"

"Not my best moment," Damian mused. "But it is clear proof of my decline. Our sons are men now—fully-grown adults—and no longer need me. Soon, they will be the new leaders of Emerald City. And you, darling . . ." He smiled. "You will be there with them."

"What about you?" Ruby asked immediately. Her heart was pounding so hard that it hurt her whole body. Tears were threatening to spill out of her eyes. "How can you just take this lying down? Can't Kevin figure something out? Isn't he supposed to be an expert?"

Damian said nothing.

"But you're so strong!" Ruby exclaimed. "You cut down Venus as if she were nothing! Y-you're even stronger than me!"

Damian cupped the back of her head. His thumb caressed her jaw. "I love you so much, darling. I can never give you up ... or pass on the opportunity to live with you. I don't know what life has in store for you or female hybrids, but I hope you will be around forever. This world needs you. Our sons need you to guide them."

Ruby yanked his hand off her. "Why the fuck are you telling me this now? Are you serious?"

"In the past, I was terrible about telling you the truth," Damian said. "I was scared, sometimes, to admit what I was or what I was doing because I didn't want you to reject me. But you have every right to know what's been going on, darling. I don't feel I am immortal by any means, although I am fighting so hard to find a way to achieve it."

"Oh, God!" Ruby turned from him. Perhaps she was blowing this out of proportion—because Damian in no way looked like he was dying—but she couldn't imagine a future without him. Now that he was here with her, Ruby had no question that he was the love of her life and that she had to fight tooth and nail to save him.

There *had* to be something. Out of all the research that Elysium had done on hybrids, didn't they know that this would eventually happen to their male population? There were tons of scientists here dedicated to hybrid research, so they had to have a serum that could restore Damian's Cells. Blood transfusions, apparently, weren't enough for him.

"It's happened to Enhanced," Damian said quietly.

Ruby crossed her arms. She was tense, but listening.

"The Cells your sister gave them have given them a longer, stronger life. But like with anything on this planet, those Cells eventually die. Enhanced are not spared the woes of aging. Male hybrids, seemingly, are similar."

"Maybe you'll be reborn again," Ruby whispered.

"I don't know," Damian said softly. "Perhaps."

The question was: did Ruby want to take that chance? Did she want to be the one waiting thirty years for Damian to wake up again? If that was the case?

And what if that wasn't the case? What if nature was cruel and ready to do away with him now that he had reproduced and raised children?

Ruby swore she'd tear nature to shreds.

No one was taking Damian from her.

CHAPTER 16

Reinforcement

I t was hard to sleep that night and future nights. It was hard for Ruby to concentrate on her nightly ventures, too. Sometimes, she felt like she was suffocating. After Damian's admittance of his "condition", the stakes were that much higher. Suddenly, Ruby was fighting for more than just her own life—now she was fighting for Damian's. She wanted a way into Elysium's laboratory, but leaving the palace was out of the question. That's why she spent the next few weeks snooping through every room she could breach on the first floor. She was curious to know what was in the average hybrid medicine cabinet and if there was a special set of pills or injections they were taking to keep themselves strong.

Once in a while, Ruby came across the hybrid trio in the hall. She knew that the leader, Ilan, was in room 117. She had seen him enter and leave with her own eyes, typically with a smirk on his face that made the mole on his chin look that much bigger. He trained on the grounds every morning, hung out with his fellow hybrids in the city in the afternoons, and came back to his quarters at night. While Ruby had never seen Sarah, Ilan still talked about her. It seemed that the girl was hiding from him.

Ruby breathed in and out. She hid in the darkest shadow behind the potted plant in the corner of the hall. The Mass Cane provided more than enough cover.

Ilan stepped up to his door and got his eye scanned. Just as the light beeped green and he stepped inside, Ruby pounced.

She slammed into him, knocked him to the floor, and shut the door behind her. She whipped out her dagger as Ilan raised his hands, startled at the intrusion.

"What the fuck?!" he exclaimed, panting like a mad dog as he scrambled back on the carpet. "Who the fuck are you?!"

"Listen and don't speak," Ruby said. "Or I swear I'll rip your fucking tongue from your fucking mouth. If you think you'll live anyway because you're a special hybrid, then let's see you regenerate from this." She raised the vial of concentrated Slainium. "I'll pour this down your throat so fast your stomach won't even have a chance to digest it before it kills you. Understand?"

"HOLY SHIT!" Ilan cried, as if Ruby were holding poisonous snakes in her grip. "Y-yes! What do you want?!"

"Is it true that hybrids age and die?"

It took Ilan a few minutes to compute what Ruby had just asked him. Someone as young as him couldn't possibly be thinking of death. But he had to know something if he was under observation and had his share of medical exams.

"O-of course," Ilan said, blinking rapidly. He was still staring at the vial. "I mean ... isn't that what happens to all of us? Even Lolligo have their cycles of life."

"Do you take anything special to stop that from happening?" Ruby asked. "Any vitamins?"

Ilan snorted. He sat up a bit, but Ruby didn't let him get too comfortable—she brandished the dagger again, and he shrank back. He glared at her, possibly assessing if he could take her. Ruby didn't let him get any ideas.

She flung the dagger and caught him straight in the eye. When Ilan cried out and clutched his head, Ruby stepped forward, recovered her blade, then tore the mole right off his chin.

Ilan turned red and started coughing. He actually pissed his pants then threw up on the carpet.

"Fucking answer me!" Ruby exclaimed.

"YES, YES!" Ilan yelled, vomit dribbling from his lips and blood gushing out of his chin. "But they give it to me at the lab! E-every two or three months, they pump our bodies with something called Reinforcement. It's supposed to help our Cells regenerate from daily wear and keep our bodies functioning at its prime. I-I'm not sure if there's any way to get some, though—"

"You're going to get some," Ruby stated, tightening her grip on the dagger. "Or I am going to slaughter you and all your friends on this floor. You like to pick on Sarah, don't you? I wonder where she is."

"A-all right." Ilan raised his hands again. His skin was regenerating, and it'd only be a matter of seconds before his mole was back. "Who the fuck told you?"

Ruby said nothing. She kept her face straight as Ilan confessed to his own sin.

"Don't tell anyone!"

That was a much more frightening possibility than death, it seemed. Rhett didn't care about humans, but he probably cared about honor and order. The last thing he needed was his hybrids acting like brutes. God only knew how much money hybrids paid doctors to keep their victims quiet.

Right now, Ruby didn't care about anyone else's morals—she wanted Reinforcement to work on Damian. She knew she was risking everything by doing this, but if this was Damian's life, she was desperate enough to execute whatever it took to save it.

"You don't want me to tell anyone?" Ruby said casually. "Then when's your next appointment at the lab?"

"Do you really expect me to steal that shit from there?" Ilan croaked. "Can you think about this for one damn second? Do you know how crazy tight security is?"

"I do. But even I was able to get in here, so I'm sure you can work something out. I don't care what the hell you do, but I expect you to cooperate and bring me some of those vials. If you can sneak around and harass maids, then you can do that much, can't you?"

Ruby frowned. "I better not hear you told anyone about me. It's none of your business where I'm from, but I don't like you. I'm only willing to spare your life if you do me this favor."

Ruby noticed his rack of guns on the wall. Unlike the ones Jared's Enhanced used, these were smaller and much more portable. Their lasers were probably equally strong, though. This was perfect for hybrids going on dangerous missions or who didn't want to get their hands dirty. They didn't need guns on a day-to-day basis, but they were trained on how to use them all the same. Ruby took one. She checked for trackers.

"I hope I'm making myself clear, asshole."

While Ruby was pretty sure she had him, she was still taking a huge risk. Nonetheless, there was no turning away from this now. She had to cross her fingers that Ilan would follow through with his promise.

Ruby whipped around and left. She returned to stealth mode once she was in the hall. A few twists and turns and she was back at Faye's quarters, but to her horror, she wasn't alone.

"Oh, Faye!" chimed a very familiar voice. Ruby didn't recognize the face, but how on earth could she forget *him*?

It was Ray.

"Faye, darling!" Ray called. He was knocking on the door. "Are you in there?"

Yes, Faye was. She was in her room, sleeping. Damian was probably still making rounds on his side of the palace.

Ray didn't seem to care there was no response, though. He was relentless as he knocked on the door. Perhaps he was used to entering through the balcony. Maybe he was going to try that next, but then he noticed that the door was unlocked. Damian always left it open so he and Ruby could return home without alerting Faye.

"Oh?" he purred. "Left it open for me, did you?"

Ruby grabbed her dagger. Without thinking, and for the second time in one night, she flung her blade. She got him in the temple.

The scanner on every door captured every movement in its line of sight, so Ruby made sure to keep to the floor. She crawled along the baseboards until she could grab Ray's boot. Then she pulled his twitching body down the hall and rounded the corner. This was one of her hiding spots, and she knew no camera could see her here.

So Ruby did what she had to.

First, she retrieved her dagger. Ray came back to consciousness, but not for long. Ruby stabbed him in the mouth, blade breaking through his vertebra and out the back of his neck. Then she got him in the stomach, where she twisted and turned until all those squirmy organs were mush. She stabbed him over twenty times before she was satisfied enough to move on.

Ray gurgled on his blood as Ruby threw down his pants. He let out a small moan and then a scream as Ruby sliced his penis clean off his crotch. She grabbed it from the floor and then stuffed it into his mouth to shut him the fuck up. His eyes were wide open.

"You piece of shit," Ruby said. She splashed some of that Slainium all over the stab wounds on his stomach. It seeped into his body immediately and started to hiss.

The smell was atrocious, but Ruby wasn't done yet. In the case anyone wondered why Ray was dead and what he had done to deserve it, she left a very clear message in his blood above his body.

By the time Damian returned from his venture, Ruby was already showered and ready for bed. She was sitting on the edge of the mattress, legs crossed. She was gazing at the window, looking out at the night sky with all its twinkling stars. She could hear the running waterfall from the balcony. She had an excellent view of it, too.

"There you are, darling," Damian said with a smile. He took off his jacket and unbuttoned his shirt. "Tell me . . . anything to report?"

Ruby looked at him over her shoulder. She gazed into his eyes then took her sweet time taking the rest of him in, too. He wasn't huge, but he was well built. She could see every cut of muscle on his body. She gazed at his abdomen, his fine hips, and his legs. He lowered his pants, but didn't take off his boxers. They slept together, but never naked. She knew he did it for her sake. She knew he did a lot of things for her sake.

"Is there something you wish to tell me?" Damian asked. Perhaps he could detect she was acting a bit strangely.

Ruby was numb right now. She didn't really feel anything. She wasn't happy, sad, or afraid. She just . . . was.

She remembered Damian and how he had tended to Faye. So loving and kind . . .

Ruby stood from the bed. She took off her shirt. She didn't have a bra on, so her breasts were out in the air. She took off her underwear, too.

"Sage?" Damian said, confused. He was panting, though.

Ruby laid back on the bed. She gazed into his eyes and communicated what she couldn't in words at the moment. She didn't feel like speaking. Not because she didn't have the energy, but because she didn't have anything to say. He knew what she wanted. If he wanted it, too, then he'd comply.

Damian took off his boxers. He was stark naked now and he was *glorious*.

That pounding in Ruby's lower belly got stronger. Her fingers curled on the bedspread ever so slightly. She arched her back just a little bit, wondering what it would be like to have *that* inside her.

Damian was as erect as could be. The tip of his penis nearly brushed his naval. It was obvious he couldn't control himself, especially when he was looking at a naked Ruby. It didn't matter that there was an obvious concern over pregnancy—Ruby's period was coming up in a few months—he deemed it safe enough to have intercourse and stumbled over to her.

Damian crawled on the bed to get to her body. When he reached her, he straddled her, a knee on either side of her hips, and looked down at her.

First, they devoured each other with their eyes. Then their mouths.

It was a kiss twenty times more intense than the one they had shared at Samson's ship. It made Ruby's heart take off and tingles unlike she had ever felt before surge through her body. She was so incredibly aroused at having Damian's tongue in her mouth and having his hands pass down her waist and over her hips that she thought she was on fire.

"Oh, darling," Damian breathed against her lips, saliva hot. "Do you know how long I have waited for this moment? To have you in my arms so I can make love to you?"

"I can only imagine," Ruby breathed back, licking his lips. "And that's why I love you."

Damian entered her slowly.

For Ruby, it was pure torture. She could feel him inside her, stretching her. She didn't know why Damian was taking his sweet time until a tear made her tense the hell up.

Ruby's eyes widened.

She might have had sex in her previous life, but never in this one. It seemed she truly was a virgin after all. It was the strangest moment of Ruby's existence yet. In fact, she wanted to cry from embarrassment. It was as if someone had wiped out her sexual history with Damian.

Damian, however, could care less about any of that. "I wasn't your first before," he whispered in her ear. "But I am your first now. And I want to be your last."

Ruby sighed with pleasure. That moment of pain had already subsided. All she could feel right now was Damian's pulsing cock.

Damian himself was groaning. He had his face in Ruby's neck and his shoulders were shaking. He couldn't hold himself on his arms, so he collapsed on her body. He squished Ruby's chest with his own.

Ruby held him there, just like she held his hips with her legs, making sure to encase him completely. Her eyes rolled back in her head. She could feel something warm seeping out of her folds. She must have been incredibly wet, making it easy for Damian to start thrusting.

"Stars!" Damian grunted. "How have I lived without this for so long?"

Ruby wasn't sure. She was just chasing that pounding below her hips, so she matched each of Damian's movements. It felt so incredible. For a few moments, Ruby forgot where she was and who she was. All she could see were colors. Sweat trickled down her face. Her temperature skyrocketed and the pulsing down there got worse.

When Damian started rolling his hips to grind the hell out of her vagina, Ruby climaxed. She clutched Damian's back, nails in his skin, as all that tension seeped out of her. She sighed. She closed her eyes and smiled as those waves of pleasure hit her one after the other. Damian kept them alive with every thrust he delivered, but he couldn't hold it for long—he exploded.

Damian kept her hips up against his as he ejaculated. He looked like a madman with his eyes wide open like that. He took deep breaths as all that pleasure wracked through his body and destroyed him from the inside out.

Eventually, Damian tucked his head beneath her chin and didn't say a word. Ruby held him like a big baby. Their hips were still pasted together, and there was quite the mess on the comforter, but Ruby would clean it in the morning.

"I thought I had lost you," Damian whispered in her ear. "Twice. I realize now that I never did. Not when you went into hibernation . . . and not when you lost your memories. I only wish to stay by your side for all of eternity. I don't want to die."

Ruby was going to make sure that didn't happen. He just didn't know it yet.

"I want to make love to you again." Damian finally got up on his elbows. He looked down at her. "Until you're all I see, hear, and feel, darling."

Ruby smiled.

Damian leaned down and kissed her lips. He started a slow, sensual trail to her chest.

Ruby wanted him to suck on her breasts. She guided his head there, and just as he flicked her nipple with his tongue, there was a scream from outside.

Damian jumped. He glanced at Ruby, startled, and then reacted like he should have: he grabbed his boxers from the floor and noticed Ilan's gun on the nightstand.

He looked at Ruby, who didn't move anywhere near as quickly. Her nipples were incredibly sensitive now that Damian hadn't finished fondling them. Nonetheless, Ruby sat up as Damian rushed out to see what was going on.

The screaming was coming from the hallway outside. Faye was at the door, ready to investigate, but Damian stopped her.

"Stay back!" he commanded. "Don't go outside." He checked the camera and looked at what was going on in the hall. There were a number of officers running past their door. A few maids were looking out of their rooms to see what all the commotion was about.

Ruby was back in her shirt and underwear. She made some tea as Faye finally slipped out into the hall. Damian stayed by the door, although he must have surmised they were in no danger if he was lowering the gun.

At last, he joined Ruby in the kitchen. He crossed his arms. "Is there something you'd like to tell me, darling?"

"I'm not sure there's anything to say." Ruby sipped her chamomile. Damian's lavender and honey was a lot better.

Faye said it all. She ran back in and croaked, "Ray is dead! And whoever killed him wrote 'I'm a rapist pig' above his head!"

CHAPTER 17

Elysium

Ruby and Damian couldn't leave Faye's quarters to see Elysium scramble to figure out who the hell had killed a hybrid. For the next few days, they couldn't even stay in their room—they had to stay in the underground tunnel because security was in and out searching for the culprit. The most difficult part for investigators was lack of a suspect. Plus, there was nothing on anyone's camera.

Ruby said nothing to Damian as she spent her days writing poems in her journal in perpetual darkness. But Damian wasn't mad. Actually, he couldn't stop staring at her. He looked wondrous, as if he couldn't believe Ruby had pulled a kill like that. Of course, he had warned her not to do anything hasty, but he couldn't yell at her when she had eliminated scum from the planet.

There was, however, a potential risk for them. Investigators took Ray's body to the lab for an autopsy and a cause of death. Scientists were bound to figure out what had killed him. Concentrated Slainium worked like a charm, but it was also never supposed to fall into the hands of unauthorized personnel.

While Damian didn't chastise Ruby for the death, Faye did.

"How could you?" Faye croaked. This was at night after a long day of security raiding everyone's quarters. Ruby and Damian had come up to eat. "How, Sage? You know we're skating on mighty thin ice here!"

"He was knocking on the door," Ruby said matter-of-factly. She had yet to tell Faye that she knew the whole palace's layout by heart now, but it was obvious that she and Damian had been sneaking out at night. "And I wasn't going to let him rape you again. Not in front of me."

"Stars!" Faye held her face. She fell into her chair and just sobbed. "They think it's me!"

"They don't have proof."

"IT DOESN'T MATTER!" she roared. "Don't you get it? *Someone* has to pay for this! All of his stupid friends knew that he liked to pick on me, and he just so happens to show up dead a few doors down from my room?"

"I'm sorry," Ruby said sincerely. "But I'm not sorry."

Damian said nothing.

Ruby supposed they were lucky that no investigator ever pinpointed who had killed Ray. There was absolutely no proof or evidence that Faye had been out of her quarters at night, especially when she hadn't even answered the door. Plus, where had she gotten all that concentrated Slainium from? Other hybrids became the prime suspects in the investigation since it was no surprise Ray had racked up quite the number of enemies.

As for Faye, she stopped crying about the incident and focused on her mission. A whole month later, when Diamond City was supposed to be in the month of Love, Faye was finally ready with their new identities.

"All right," Faye said, looking at Damian across the dining table. "Your name is Chad Livingston and you are the youngest son of the Livingstons, who live in the Ground District. They are the wealthy owners of Surgium Incorporated, dedicating their whole lives to perfecting the energy source that Elysium uses."

The Ground District was the lowest tier in Elysium society,

Ruby learned. There was Ground, Sky, Space, and Heavens, where the palace was.

"And you, Sage," said Faye, "are Adele, a noble warrior from the Allard household. You aspire to be like a hybrid, but your physical limitations are a problem. You know you don't stand a chance against genetically enhanced freaks, so you train in secret. You were homeschooled and taught everything there is to know about Elysium. You just recently scored a job here as a palace maid. Your wish is to grow closer to the hybrids."

"And you know these families?" Ruby asked.

"I do. All the humans are pretty close since we survived together. My great grandmother, for example, was friends with Allard ancestors."

"So . . . that's it? We're in?"

"Indeed." Faye smiled. "You are officially hired and you are invited to register as an employee at the front office tomorrow morning."

Ruby froze. That's because she recognized this was the first step to an opportunity to achieve what they had come here to do. She snuck a glance at Damian, whose face remained neutral. Perhaps he was thinking about potential tactics. Faye didn't say what she recommended one way or another—she had done her part in getting them in.

"Tomorrow, you will be escorted to your rooms and introduced to our wardrobe." Faye indicated what she was wearing: a white jumpsuit, similar to what the hybrids wore, but with one black cuff around her right arm instead of two. One, Ruby learned, represented Faye's status here in Elysium. She was at the bottom of the totem pole, beneath any hybrid walking these halls.

"That's fucked up," Ruby blurted out.

Faye shrugged. "It's true, isn't it? Hybrids are certainly stronger."

"And what does Rhett wear? All white?"

Faye chuckled wryly. "You'd think, but no. The Prime is quite the ostentatious one with his wear."

Wardrobe aside, Ruby recognized this would be her final night with Damian. That made her more anxious than any silly symbol of status. She longed to communicate how much she'd miss him, but it'd be highly inappropriate when their number-one concern was survival. This was one of the last times they'd see each other until that tournament Samson had mentioned. No phones or secret letters here, unfortunately... Worse, they were implanted with trackers. Faye showed them the tiny scar on her forearm.

"We must come up with a plan," Damian said to Ruby after dinner. He was washing the dishes since Ruby had cooked filet mignon. Elysium's greenhouses were nearly as big as Diamond City. Ruby had been doing some research on them since arriving here. "Once we receive the tracker, it'll be even more difficult to go anywhere."

"What do you propose?" Ruby asked.

They had already snuck out plenty of times at night to do their share of surveying. Faye had layouts for the other floors, but that wouldn't do them much good until they learned their specific assignments the next morning. The only valuable bit of information that Faye relayed was that there were ten maids per floor and two had recently retired to enjoy old age. It was good to know no one was dying around here, although Ruby couldn't say rape was any consolation.

As she spent her final night holding Damian in her arms, she thought about Hayes and his warning. It crept up out of the blue and for good reason.

What if the Prime recognized her as Wren's sister?

It was foolish to worry about it now, when any chance of seeing Rhett was still so minuscule, but Ruby spent a great deal of energy wondering how she'd pass as a housemaid. In her head, everyone she walked by the next morning on her way to the registrar knew who she was. While Faye was worried about being seen with two strangers inside the private halls of the palace, Ruby worried that someone would point and shout, "Wren!"

But there wasn't anyone wandering the halls this early in the morning. Aside from a few maids who were trained to keep their heads down and noses in their own business, security was scarce. Hybrids had busy day schedules to follow, so there wasn't one in sight.

It was a relief to Ruby until they reached the front of the palace. For the first time since entering Elysium, they were among a true crowd. The palace's processing center was full of potential employees, from first interviews to tracker implantations. Regardless of status and species, of course, everyone was in the white uniform with the black bands.

"Are we allowed to modify our wardrobe?" Damian muttered. He was making faces at everyone. "Perhaps something slight and subtle? I've never understood black and white."

"Those are Elysium's colors," Ruby said. They were standing in line for trackers now. They had already taken care of their paperwork and registration.

"And they're quite dreadful," Damian drawled. "Could you imagine if life were like that? No in-betweens? And before you open your mouth, I am not talking about my love for you—that is as extreme as it can get. Very extreme."

Ruby smiled. "Then what are you talking about?"

"Everything else, *Adele*." Damian kissed her nose.

"I understand, *Chad*." Ruby kissed his nose, too. "Of course you'd have an exception."

"There are always exceptions."

Ruby wished there'd be an exception here. As they got closer to the office for their trackers, she realized she'd be parting ways with Damian soon. Inside, people branched off based on last name. "A" and "L" were so far apart.

Ruby gazed at Damian longingly.

Damian kissed her hand. "I will find you anywhere, darling. No matter where they assign you."

And so, Ruby entered her designated area. There were a handful of humans seated politely in chairs, reading through magazines. A large screen flashed with the latest news: Elysium's Center for Hybrid Development was having their annual hybrid tournament at the end of the year. Apparently, ECHD was among everyone's topic of conversation at all times of the day. Based on how calm people seemed to be around here, it's what they depended on for peace. So long as ECHD was fully functional and producing hybrids, what did anyone have to worry about?

"And let's take a look at the school's graduating class this summer solstice!" announced the reporter excitedly as cameras focused on the handsome young men and women standing in front of their school. They were all in the white-and-black uniforms, but because they were hybrids, they had two bands.

Pigs for slaughter. That's all Ruby saw as the cameras got a good look at the faces. Hybrids just like her, but trained to fight. To kill. There were no couples holding hands or making googly eyes at each other.

Ruby's eyes drifted to a painting right next to the TV. While the palace halls were littered with palace paintings in all filters, this one was of a building shaped like a pentagon.

Elysium Laboratory.

"So you're Adele Allard, are you?" said the lady at the front desk. Ruby could tell she was a hybrid because of her amber eyes. This was a characteristic that Enhanced shared as well.

"Yes," Ruby said.

"And you were interviewed and hired by Faye Sabine?"

"That's right."

"I can definitely see all the information here." The hybrid scrolled through the computer. Ruby wondered if Faye knew this hybrid at an intimate level, too. Just how had she managed to process all that fake information into Elysium's system? "All right, have a seat."

No questions.

Ruby sat down in the chair next to the desk. She had to slip her arm through a ring and brace herself for the tracker. It was quick, but excruciating. It felt like a wasp had just needled its way into her.

"Step to the back for your ID and uniform as well as room assignment," said the hybrid stoically.

The uniform was exactly like Faye's. It was easy to slip on and zip up. There was an entire line of them against the wall. There were a few stalls on the other side for changing in private. The only other couple in the room were donning the same uniform, although from the weapons clipped onto their belts, they looked like they had just graduated to top-notch security at the palace.

When Ruby was ready, she left the locker room and retrieved her ID from the front desk. The hybrid took one good look at her, making Ruby's stomach flip-flop, but said nothing else.

Exhaling a bit in relief, Ruby took the elevator up to the hundredth floor of the palace. She had guards escorting her the whole time, although they didn't provide her with any valuable insight into the job. Ruby was the only new maid on this floor and everyone expected her to know her way around. There were no helpful hints or pieces of advice from the silent duo in the corner of the elevator.

She had a communicator similar to Samson's, too, that displayed her schedule starting tomorrow. She and a trio of women were sweeping through all the hybrid rooms on this floor. Cleaning carts were in the storage closets.

1009 was her room number. It was already late afternoon by the time Ruby arrived. Although she hadn't done much this morning, the entire process was exhausting as hell. She was still nervous, too, wondering who had stayed in this room before her and what experiences they'd had here. Were they raped by hybrids often?

She met a dreary silence. It was also dark inside. Ruby felt for the lights and some dim ones came on in the corner. A horrible chill shot down her spine as she looked up and around at the plain-as-day walls. Like Faye's quarters downstairs, she had a kitchen, living area, and two bedrooms. The furniture looked small and uncomfortable, but that's probably because everything looked wrong to Ruby right now.

She missed Damian.

Ruby looked out her balcony. Whereas Faye's had a breathtaking view of a waterfall, up here she could see all of Elysium. There were blinking lights all over the place, but they were perfectly spaced from each other, orderly . . . like a grid. Perfect geometrics. No accidents . . . no incidents.

In Diamond City, it'd be hard to tell if the lights were coming from a building or a passing vehicle. There were some nights when it'd be pitch dark. Sometimes, there were districts that were hardly lit up at all. It didn't always used to be like that, though . . .

Ruby remembered the old Diamond City. Not the one she saw from the palace with Louis. She remembered another sight from a different balcony. It was the one from the complex she had stayed at with Candice and Olivia. The Starlight Complex.

The Silver Gears concert. That's *right*.

A pair of warm arms wrapped around her waist. Ruby didn't jump because she had already heard Damian sneak up behind her. She let her head rest on his chest with a small sigh.

"That paint looked ridiculous on me, didn't it?" Ruby said.

"It did not, darling." Damian pressed his face into her neck. He kissed her shoulder. "You looked spectacular, especially when you disarmed that security guard with your blade."

"Geoffrey was infected with Red Fever," Ruby said.

"Yes, but Nova cured him."

Right. The little scientist from Winterfeld who was loyal to Damian. She had stayed with Louis in Diamond City all these years, and Ruby had a feeling that Damian had arranged that purposefully.

"Damian, how are you here?" Ruby turned in his embrace. She tried not to laugh at his uniform. He must have been in a rush to find her. "Can't they see that you're not in your room?"

"I took the tracker out," Damian said with a lazy smile. He might have admitted he had just pranked his best friend.

"How the hell did you do that?"

"I used a blade. It wasn't the prettiest hack job I've ever done, but I took advantage of my fast regeneration to ensure that my skin looks beautiful." He showed her his forearm. Clean and smooth. He kissed it, making Ruby laugh.

"You're so crazy."

Damian pushed a few strands of hair away from her face. "And then I looked out my balcony and sensed you were outside. I scaled the building from my floor until I got to you."

It was all flat steel. At least the palace at Heart had convenient grooves and cracks here and there, as minuscule as they were. Damian's acrobatics aside, Ruby caught onto a certain detail.

"You 'sensed' I was out here?" she said, arching a brow.

"Yes, darling." Damian continued taming her hair. "I can sense where you are."

"But you've never been able to 'sense' me before. Do you know how many times I saw you from the top of Heart's palace?"

"Pathetic, isn't it? I never noticed you. It was Castor and Pollux who saw you first."

Ruby lowered her head, smile fading. "I feel so ashamed, Damian."

"Why?"

"Because I ran away from them like a fool." Ruby's lip trembled. "I should have never run away."

"You didn't know any better." Damian let his fingers trace her face now.

Ruby touched his wrist. The Soulmate Bracelet. "I asked you to marry me," she said to him. "I think we were in the Carat District. I fixed that bracelet myself."

Damian kissed her forehead.

"I wrote you another poem," Ruby said, smile returning. Little butterflies fluttered in her stomach. "Would you like to read it?"

Damian chuckled. "No, darling."

"It's not that bad!"

Damian snorted. "Stick to pizza."

Ruby crossed her arms and glared at him. "Like your poems are any better."

"Tons better. Don't you remember the songs I'd sing to you while you were in your cocoon?"

"You're such a cheater!" Ruby exclaimed. "Those were Silver Gears songs!"

Damian's eyes widened. "You remember?"

"Snippets." Ruby shook her head. "Definitely nothing crazy, though."

"And that's fine. Don't strain yourself."

"I try not to. Although I am thankful that I do remember some things."

"I've realized it doesn't matter," Damian said. A soft wind blew all the beautiful hair from his shoulders. "You are still the same Sage I know. Who else has the balls to cut off someone's penis?"

Ruby scowled. "He deserved it."

"It turned me on."

"You were turned on by someone losing their penis?"

Damian chuckled. "No. I was turned on by you. You're so high-risk, darling. No penis is safe, it seems."

Ruby shrugged. "Only if those penises misbehave."

"Mine can be a bit rebellious."

"Then you'll have to train it."

"I don't think it's capable of learning."

"Then I think you're in trouble, aren't you?"

Suddenly, Damian burst out laughing. His eyes were bright and his cheeks were round. He had nice teeth as well, which Ruby only rarely saw.

"But I have faith in you, darling," Damian said huskily, thumb brushing over her lip. "I think you'll be a great teacher." He seemed to be picturing exactly how that tight mouth would fit around his shaft. "And I'm ready for my first lesson."

"That's not romantic." Ruby stepped past him. They were out in the open, and if her neighbor stepped out, they'd be exposed. Damian wasn't supposed to be on this side of the palace.

And then Ruby froze when she saw the bouquet of flowers on the table. She whipped around to Damian, who leaned against the sliding glass door and crossed his arms. "When did you get those?"

"At the shop downstairs," Damian said smoothly. "When you

went in for your tracker. I had to wait forever for mine, so I took a stroll until they called my number."

Ruby was speechless. *That* was definitely romantic. She got angry, though, for not going out of her way to get him something. "You get me something like that and all I have is a dumb poem?"

"It's not dumb. It's just really bad."

"Wow." Ruby rolled her eyes. "I don't know what to say."

Damian shrugged, but he couldn't help the smirk that spread on his face. "There is nothing to be said."

The worst part about this was Ruby's cheeks. They were on fire. If she didn't leave this room, she was going to die of embarrassment. She cleared her throat and announced she was going to fix herself something to eat. She watched Damian unbutton his jacket and take a seat on the couch at last. He reached for the remote and turned on the TV.

"Tonight is the last episode of *Ask*," Damian said.

How could Ruby have forgotten? It had become their go-to show at Elysium the past few weeks, a comfy rom-com that made her laugh and brought out a side of Damian that was emotionally intelligent. He seemed to know who liked who, even when Ruby disagreed, and which couples had ideal chemistry, even if they weren't together. The main character, Erica, had her eye on a guy that she wasn't very confident with. On this episode, they were going on a date and—of course—the grand finale was the sex.

Wonderful. Ruby would rather not watch, but Damian was fascinated.

"He is a horrible seducer," Damian noted. "He just takes off her pants and thrusts into her without any foreplay. That's like playing a fastball game without warming up."

"Are you a sex expert, too?" Ruby finished her frozen pizza. Whoever had fixed up her room had stocked her refrigerator with provisions in case she got hungry. This was her second box. Damian was still trudging through his first slice.

"Very much so," Damian purred. "Look at her face, darling. Does she look like she's enjoying it?"

Ruby shrugged. "I don't know—she's moaning."

"That doesn't mean a damn thing. You never moaned and you always enjoyed our sex."

"How do you know what I enjoy or not?" Ruby's face was blazing now. Was it healthy for her temperature to be this high? Thank God she had the pizza to look at.

"I could tell." Damian smirked. "And you'd always climax hard. You'd squeeze the hell out of my cock and nearly cut off my blood flow."

Ruby smacked him with a pillow. "You're *so* dramatic. I'm trying to eat without choking on my food, Mr. Expert."

Damian laughed. "There's nothing to be ashamed of, darling. Sex is an art. Do you see how he's just thrusting into her? He doesn't care about his partner's pleasure. Sex shouldn't be all about you—it should be about the other person. It's an experiment. To touch secret places and rub certain parts." He scooted closer to Ruby. "And I know what you like."

Then Erica screamed. Her boyfriend sighed.

"There is nothing better," Damian purred to Ruby, who was over trying to eat anything tonight, "than passing my tongue over your wet snatch, especially after I've made you climax—"

"Give me the remote." Ruby made for it on the table, but Damian grabbed it first and kept it out of reach.

"You haven't forgotten, have you, darling?" Damian cooed. "How I'd describe exactly what I'd see in between your legs and how each lick would make you quiver—"

"No, but you're way too excited right now." Ruby swiped at his hand. "Give me the remote!"

"I can't help it," Damian said deeply. "Especially when you're rubbing up against me like that."

"If you give me the remote, then I won't have to rub up against you."

"But I want you to rub up against me."

"Why? Is it because you have a problem?"

"A very *big* problem," Damian breathed, eyes wide and intense.

"Which is why I need a powerful woman to tame me." He laid back on the couch. Naturally, Ruby moved to straddle him and finally pry that fucking remote from his hand.

Damian closed his eyes and arched his back. He held Ruby's hips to keep her there. He no longer cared about the remote because the sex scene was over. Right now, it was all about Ruby and what she'd do next.

There wasn't much to think about or consider. The number of times Ruby had thought about this was outstanding. The longing for his touch every night was close to driving her insane. Sometimes, their kissing went a bit far, but Damian never pushed for more, not since that night they had finally done it.

Tonight, however, was an exception. Not even the Lolligo themselves could pry Damian away from Ruby. He wrapped his arms around her back, hands gliding up to her shoulders, and brought her right down onto his mouth.

Ruby kissed him.

Hard. Slow. Deep.

Ruby had had plenty of his mouth in the past, so she didn't spend much time on it now. She grew bolder in her ministrations, both because Damian had done this to her before and because it felt so natural to move on to other parts. Why wouldn't she want to kiss his sharp jaw or his powerful throat? Ruby used her hands to part his jacket and push up his shirt to touch his abdomen, all the hard muscle there. She made sure to rub his chest, too, especially his nipples, and that's when she felt something wet in his groin.

Ruby sat up, confused for a moment. Damian was groaning and holding his face.

"Stars, darling!" he panted. "Why are you so damn *hot?*"

Ruby didn't mean to laugh, but she found his premature orgasm funny. She surmised it didn't take a lot to make him climax, although maybe it was the way she had handled his nipples.

"They're sensitive, darling," Damian breathed, touching them beneath his jacket. "And if you want me to hold out, you're going to have to control yourself."

"How sensitive can they be?"

"I don't know what you do, but you do it every time." Damian flared his nostrils. "Would you like me to give you a taste of what it feels like?"

Ruby stopped laughing.

Damian sat up and pushed her onto her back on the other side of the couch. He made sure to wrap one of her legs around his hip to keep the pressure between their groins tight. Damian was already hard again, and Ruby had that familiar pounding in her abdomen.

Damian tore off her jacket and made quick work of her shirt and bra. Ruby's breasts were rather small, but it wasn't size Damian was after. He wasted no time clamping his lips around one of her nipples. He sucked on them like his life depended on it, making colors explode in Ruby's vision. His tongue was relentless and his hand squeezed her other breast like putty.

Ruby grunted with pleasure. She held Damian's head as she bent her back and rubbed up against his hips. She closed her eyes and got lost in a world she didn't visit often. Sex wasn't something she chased or craved, and that's probably because it wouldn't be anywhere near this good with someone else. It was the pounding that was driving her insane, and it didn't help that Damian slid his other hand into her pants.

"Damian," Ruby breathed, opening her eyes.

"That's right, darling," Damian said with his mouth still hanging all over her breast. "Moan."

No. Ruby didn't want to get loud and obnoxious, but she couldn't push him away.

"You are going to climax for me," Damian said, sitting up as he continued to fondle her. "Whether you like it or not."

Ruby didn't have any shoes, so it was easy for Damian to shed her pants and underwear. She couldn't help the heat that crept up her body, and that had nothing to do with pleasure.

"Are you embarrassed?" Damian asked her.

"Of course I am!" Ruby sputtered.

Damian was staring at her *there*. Naked. At least when they had

had sex the first time, it was in the dark. Now they were under those dim lights that seemed ten times brighter than before. The TV was still going on in the background, too.

Damian chuckled at her. "Why?"

"Just because you're a sex god doesn't mean I am!"

Damian laughed loudly. "That might be, but you don't have to be a 'sex god' to enjoy this. There is nothing to be ashamed of, Sage. You are so very beautiful."

"It's a vagina," Ruby said flatly. "How beautiful can it be?"

"Oh, you have no idea." Damian hooked her legs over his shoulders. "So many magical moments in that tight little snatch. It excites the hell out of me." And then he dove right into her "snatch"—Stars, his tongue was right there, licking up her folds slowly, and then it was inside her.

Ruby was pretty sure her whole body was about to explode. She didn't have anything to clutch but the couch beneath her. When she moaned, it sounded like a grunt because she was trying to hold it in. Even if she was no longer ashamed, she was in control. That was something Damian had to work on because he obviously had little resistance. Ruby, however, came when she wanted it and it frustrated the blazes out of Damian.

The man was relentless, though. He didn't stop thrusting into her with his tongue. It was as if he was making out with her vagina. He was pulling out all the stops to make her crumble, and then Ruby gave it to him.

Ruby's head and heart were both pounding in rhythm. Her legs were shaking and her belly was pudding. She felt all the wetness Damian was eagerly lapping up like a dog and she didn't understand how he could be so... thorough. As if he were eating ice cream. Ruby thought it was gross, but Damian was enjoying himself. That's because the only thing that mattered to him was her.

Ruby understood that now.

"Damian," Ruby breathed, looking down at him. A few thick strands of his hair were tickling her ribs. Ruby held his head with her hands, another wave of heat creeping up her body. This time it was neither because of the sex nor embarrassment. She knew what it was.

Love.

Love for this man, who gave his heart and soul to her, worshiped her every step, and did everything only after thinking of how it would affect her. If that wasn't love, then Ruby didn't know what was.

She brought her legs down one at a time. She wanted him on top of her, so she hauled him up her body with her arms. Then she initiated the kissing session of a lifetime. She worked on his shirt, which she nearly ripped, and then undid his pants, which Damian helped her with.

He still had his boots on, but he didn't bother taking them off. It was too much work, and right now he was searching for the perfect way to enter her. The tip of his penis kept nudging her in different spots along her folds.

"Take them off," Ruby breathed against his lips. Hers were so swollen, full of saliva. Damian didn't stop kissing her, so he probably hadn't heard her.

"Damian." Ruby squeezed his ass cheeks with her hands. It was like trying to mold hard clay. "Please take them off."

"Why?" Damian's voice was raspy. "Are they in the way? All that matters right now is my penis." He held it to her hips, but he didn't enter her. He was still teasing.

"Because I want you completely naked." Ruby had to push him off if she wanted him to cooperate.

Damian fell indeed, nearly hitting the floor with his knees because his pants were around his ankles. Ruby had never seen anyone unstrap boots as quickly as he did in that moment. With an erection like that, he had to be in pain.

They had done this before, but Ruby still braced herself. She clutched his shoulders as he climbed back onto her body. More kissing helped her relax, but then it was time. Ruby looked up at him.

"I won't ever hurt you," Damian whispered to her. "Ever, my Star."

He used his hands to spread her legs further apart. And then, in just seconds, he sunk right into her.

They fit together like a puzzle piece. Ruby's legs wound around his hips. Her eyes rolled back in her head as pleasure surged through her veins. She held onto him as he did her, hands on his shoulders. She groaned as he started to thrust, and this time, she didn't hold it in.

Ruby couldn't. Even if she wanted to, she was in Damian's mercy. Her nails dug their way into his skin because she was clutching him for dear life. She already knew that he was vital to her very existence. Whether she was Sage or Ruby, she had always been drawn to him. Having found him again, she couldn't imagine ever living her life with someone else. It was as if Ruby didn't have a choice. She had never been more sure of something in her life than at this moment with Damian.

By the time Damian climaxed, he was all out panting. He was groaning into Ruby's neck and still pumping his hips because it felt so good to do so.

And it did. It felt incredible. But Ruby wasn't sure how she was going to get up from here. She didn't know if her legs would ever work again. She was completely spent and burning up with a fever.

"You look so incredibly sexy like that," Damian whispered against her throat, licking her skin.

"I look like hell," Ruby admitted.

"Despite how long it's been, I've never forgotten just how incredibly ... *wet* our sex can be."

"You're the messy one."

"No, darling," Damian chuckled. "It's not all me. We are a team."

And it was only bound to get messier. Damian and Ruby never left the couch. They went at it four more times in the same position, sometimes with sleep in between. Only toward the final hours of night did Damian turn them over so he was on his back and Ruby was on his chest.

Damian drew circles on her shoulders. Ruby gazed at the sage leaves on his forearm. Whoever did the tattoo had done fabulously with the little details. Sage leaves had a lot of veins.

"I still say it would have been easier to use the bed," Ruby mumbled in her sleep.

"Emergencies happen," Damian said.

Ruby was too exhausted to move. Sex aside, yesterday's trials had really drained her. Her duties weren't what worried her, though—it was the turnout of this whole mission, the tournament in the summer, and what would become of Rhett.

"You can always take the day," Damian said to her softly, caressing her cheek now. "And I will stay with you."

"Then that will really make us look suspicious," Ruby mumbled. "We can't afford that kind of attention. We just have to hold out for a bit longer..."

Ruby fell asleep. The next time she woke up, she was alone on the couch with a blanket draped over her body. A pillow had replaced Damian's chest. Damian was cooking something in the kitchen because Ruby could hear the sizzling, but he was also ... singing?

"When the stars are visible at night
I know my days with you will be bright
Let's stay together, love
Hold my hand and look up above."

It was low and to himself, so it definitely wasn't intended for Ruby to hear. She listened to him for a few minutes longer before sitting up. She winced at the soreness between her legs. She brushed her hair with her fingers, frowning at the unruly tangles. Damian's hands had completely destroyed her yesterday. The way he had held her head to suck the soul out through her mouth had Ruby in a trance. She stared out the window, at the balcony they had been standing in last night, but she didn't really see the sky. She didn't even register it was morning.

"Stars," Ruby breathed, wondering if there was something

wrong with her. She leaned on the coffee table (the remote was on there) and stood up at last. Damian must have picked up all their clothes because they weren't on the floor. Ruby's uniform was hanging in the back of the bathroom door.

After her shower, Ruby dressed and fixed her hair. She tied it into a bun, wondering how her first day on the job would be. She had never worked for anyone else before . . .

Damian didn't seem very worried. He was in boxers that were a bit too tight around the groin and prancing around the kitchen like a ballerina on tippy toes. He whistled as he set the table, the peppiest mood Ruby had yet to see him in. She was so taken aback that she stood there and watched him. When he noticed her, his whistling turned low and sensual.

"Good morning, darling."

Ruby laughed. "Good morning, Damian."

Breakfast looked mighty impressive. With the roses as a centerpiece, this looked like dining meant for royalty. They were the exact same food items Damian prepared for Faye, yet they looked fancier now. Those eggs were scrambled and seasoned just right because they were shiny; the waffles were crisp and golden; and the toast was perfection. Ruby wasn't one for coffee and even that was spectacular.

"Wow, you went all out." Ruby took a seat. "I didn't know there was so much food in the refrigerator."

"Indeed." Damian served her some orange juice. "This place is well stocked."

"It is." Ruby stared at his crotch.

Damian snickered. "See something you like, darling?"

"Yes," Ruby said. "But I'm not going to tell you what it is."

"Let me guess: it starts with a 'p' and ends with an 's'."

"Your pecs? Those are pretty fabulous."

Damian stared at her.

"What?" Ruby scowled at him. She sipped her juice. "You thought I didn't remember that stupid trick? Not falling for that twice."

Damian smiled. It quickly turned into a grin. His eyes got bigger and brighter, too, as if the soul stuck behind them had found freedom at last.

"Damian, we're on a mission," Ruby said patiently. "Shouldn't we be focusing on something other than your genitals?"

"We are," Damian said. "Trust me—I am raring to get the fuck out of here. We finish this Squid at the ball they're holding right before the hybrid tournament and we'll finally be done. But before that happens . . ." He took the last steps to reach her.

Damian leaned down and kissed her deeply.

Ruby swooned.

"We enjoy every minute we have together," he said against her lips. "Whether we're here or at home. Nothing else matters to me. I am through sacrificing you for others."

Ruby couldn't argue. She also couldn't stop her cheeks from burning. Again. She was completely and utterly under his spell. They spent so much time rubbing noses and licking each other's faces that Ruby forgot about the time. She took a leaf out of Damian's book, though, because she didn't care. She could kiss him forever. It was Damian who told her to eat.

"Not me, darling," Damian purred. "Your food."

It was so hard to let him go. Although Ruby was looking at her breakfast, she made sure to keep an eye on him as he withdrew to the kitchen. He was still rummaging around the cabinets for more utensils and plates.

This was what Ruby imagined it would be like to live with Damian. She'd get up in the morning, go to work at her restaurant or place of employment, and return home to spend the rest of her evening with him.

At Elysium's palace, Ruby didn't see Damian at all during the day. He was on the seventieth floor, so by the time Ruby finished her rounds, it was time to retire. Somehow, Damian always made it back to her room first, tracker removed.

"Did anyone say anything about the tracker?" Ruby asked as Damian mashed some potatoes in a bowl.

"Of course not," he said. His hair was in these intricate braids today, perfect for labor. How the hell had he done that pattern, though? "Who's going to notice? Just like no one noticed I sprayed my cuffs red and silver."

Ruby gasped. Damian had taken off his jacket, but he had painted the lines on his pants, too. Those red and silver stripes stuck out like a sore thumb. Damian was probably the most colorful maid in the palace.

"Damian!" Ruby hissed. "You can get in trouble!"

Damian shrugged. "The uniform is terribly bland."

While it did look good on him, Ruby wondered why those colors.

"They are Ruby City's colors," he said happily. "Are they not?"

Wow. Ruby had completely forgotten about her own damn city. She was so confident that her sons and the rest of the Emerald City military were doing well that she hadn't given them much thought at all the past couple of months.

"Damian, I appreciate your loyalty," Ruby said sincerely. "But what if someone sees you and gets you in trouble?"

"And who is going to do that exactly?"

Ruby sighed. "Who knows. But can you please just be careful?"

"You need to be even more careful than me." Damian turned serious. "There is much gossip among the maids. There have been many assaults on the women. You haven't heard anything?"

Actually, all the women here were too scared to talk. Besides, Ruby wasn't too focused on anyone else when she was still trying to get the hang of her new job. Cleaning rooms, doing laundry, and scrubbing toilets definitely wasn't on her list of favorite careers. She had seen other maids in the hall, but she hadn't made any eye contact with them. It looked like the maids were going out of their way not to draw too much attention to themselves.

By the end of their third month at Elysium, Ruby had mapped out the entire hundredth floor. She knew which hybrid stayed in which room and what they were like based on what they chose for decor. Sex magazines (for both men and women), walls full of weapons, and wardrobes featuring an array of uniforms and training gear were common, but family portraits were not. Of course, hybrids came from test tubes . . . not wombs.

Without contact, however, it was impossible to tell which hybrids would make suitable allies. Ruby, unfortunately, was seriously lacking in that department. She wasn't even sure the two maids she had managed to befriend were trustworthy. Isadora and Lilian were just as reserved and timid as she was.

"I'm still working on learning more," Ruby said to Damian one night. "So I don't have anything else yet."

"What you do have is quite impressive," Damian said. "And the fact you've been able to survive for this long without raising suspicion is even more impressive."

Ruby supposed it was. She was putting out feelers for whom she might be able to depend on come the Tournament Ball in the summer. Other than that, though, there was nothing special about cleaning and tending to hybrids all day long. What she looked forward to most every single night was Damian.

She jumped on him whenever she saw him. Sometimes he surprised her by slipping in through the front door or magically appearing in the living room. They spent the whole night together, either watching shows, baking cookies, or playing card games. The people of Elysium were really into *Squared*, which was a geometrical take on standard cards. Instead of kings, queens, and jacks, there were circles, triangles, and squares. The more sides a shape had, the more powerful it was as a card.

One time, Ruby had filled her hand with icosagons and annihilated Damian. She couldn't stop laughing for hours. The best part? Damian was a sore loser.

"You cheated, darling," he growled as Ruby threw a fit on the floor. She was clutching her stomach. "You're not supposed to have more than three of the same card."

"Who says?" Ruby drooled. "Just admit it, Damian—you lost."

Damian didn't admit it—he just stayed mad about it. That was, of course, until Ruby hopped on his back and kissed his cheek and neck. Affection always turned him into pudding, and that's how she won him over every time.

Of course, they didn't always play cards. Damian loved to draw and he spent whole nights sketching in his little notepad. Sometimes, he made Ruby pose. Once in a while, he made her strip.

When that happened, Damian couldn't take his eyes off her for long. Even his drawing wasn't enough to entertain him when he had the real Ruby right in front of him. He'd stand up, yank off his clothes, then draw her into his arms in an embrace they didn't break until morning.

"I don't remember many days like this," Ruby said softly, drawing her finger up and down his forearm. He was spooned behind her with one of his arms beneath her body. His other was on her hip. His rings felt so cool on her skin.

"That's because we didn't have many," Damian said.

Ruby could imagine there had been a number of challenges in her previous life. It was sad, though, that they hadn't had a whole lot of time together. It was a little life that was easy to get used to. Ruby didn't ever want it to end. She had grown attached to him and their routine here at the palace.

Entire seasons had passed without notice. It was mostly because Elysium didn't celebrate the same holidays that Diamond City did. There was only one event everyone here looked forward to and that was the Tournament Ball in the month of Light. The summer solstice would be upon them and the games between the hybrid academy's top notch warriors would begin.

Or so ... that's what was supposed to happen. Ruby and Damian had to kill Rhett.

But after that day ... what would become of Ruby and her little life with Damian?

"I will never leave your side," Damian whispered to her every night. "Whatever trials arise, we will face them together. We will go home ... and put all this drama behind us."

Ruby smiled. She believed it. And that's what made her the happiest woman on earth.

CHAPTER 18

Black Market Cells

All the maids had to dress their absolute best for the Tournament Ball. For that night only, they could ditch the black-and-white uniform that Damian hated (and had modified extensively since; Ruby wondered how security hadn't arrested him yet) and wear something formal. That meant it was time to go shopping. The streets were absolutely packed in downtown Elysium as citizens prepared for the long-awaited event not too far in the future.

The maids didn't have or need an escort, so Ruby and Damian went together. They met by the processing center at the front of the palace, which was reviewing applicants and implanting trackers like usual. Ruby thought so very little of the apprehensive faces around her when she found Damian strutting right up to her. He made her laugh because he was the only fool with red and silver on his uniform. To the crowd, he might have been someone of importance. Everyone stared at him, but Damian only had eyes for Ruby.

"Let us go, darling," Damian sang to her, wrapping an arm around her waist and taking her right out of the palace.

They were off to see the city for the first time in their lives. Ruby had to fight not to hold his hand or look at him instead of the tall towers before her. This was the chance of a lifetime—what so many preachers in the Clarity District dreamed about—but Ruby's mind was focused on one thing. Her cheeks burned and a smile crossed her lips.

"What are you thinking about?" Damian asked her huskily as they crossed the bridge to the driveway. There were buses and limos picking up palace residents. "Would you like to try a new position tonight?"

"It's not always about the sex," Ruby muttered.

"Ninety percent of the time it is, yes."

Ruby rolled her eyes.

Damian reached out with his hand. His fingers touched hers. Then they wound together like a braid. He didn't seem to care that they were in public and drawing attention. Actually, there weren't a whole lot of people looking at them to begin with, even if Damian stuck out among the black and white.

Ruby raised his hand to her lips and kissed his knuckles. Damian did the same to her. Then they stared at each other for an obviously long time.

"My heart is beating so fast right now," Damian whispered, eyes devouring her. "I'm not sure I'm well."

Ruby froze. She grew worried for a second, wondering if Damian was having some sort of attack, but then she realized that Damian wasn't in danger. He was flushed just like she was, and it was Ruby's heart that started a fierce pounding next.

Ruby was relieved. Regardless, she had acquired the vials of Reinforcement from Ilan a while ago. It hadn't taken him very long to snag a few after his medical appointment one afternoon. This was before Ruby had started her new position on the hundredth floor, so the vials were still in her trunk in the guest bedroom of Faye's quarters. Now it was up to Ruby to tell Damian about them, but she still hadn't mustered up the courage to do so. She wasn't sure how he'd react and she never wanted to dampen their light-hearted interactions. Right now, Ruby couldn't dream of destroying the love blazing in his soul.

"I want to kiss you," Damian said deeply.

"We can't in public," Ruby said.

"I'm not sure it's a sin in Elysium to love someone, is it?"

"We can kiss tonight. In private."

Damian wasn't taking no for an answer. He led Ruby right to the bus, bulldozed his way to the back, and found a perfect spot in the corner to make out in. Just as he wrapped an arm around her and brought her in against his chest, someone exclaimed, "Hey, Adele! You're here!"

Ruby looked up. Isadora was bumbling onto the bus and she quickly darted to the seat in front of Ruby. She was with her friend, Lilian, who stared at Damian as she sat down.

"Hey, there, Isa," Ruby said happily. "Glad you could join us."

"Is that Chad?" Isadora asked innocently. If her eyes had teeth, she would have gobbled him up seconds ago. "Wow . . . he's so good-looking."

Ruby huffed. "Don't inflate his ego."

Damian looked annoyed at the company, but he was intrigued by the sort of friends Ruby was making on the hundredth floor. Moreover, the sort of things she was telling them and the kinds of conversations they were having inside storage closets. "They know me?"

"But of course!" Isadora said happily. "Adele talks about you all the time! I just didn't know you were this—"

"Beautiful," Lilian breathed.

Damian smirked. Definitely not good for his ego. "Did she tell you I was a good kisser, too?"

"That, she omitted."

Damian touched up his lips with gloss. Cherry was Ruby's favorite, too. "Let me demonstrate."

"Can you please calm down?" Ruby snapped at him, avoiding his lips. "Or they're going to think there's something wrong with you."

Perhaps it wasn't such a bad thing, the two women seemed to be saying in their heads. They were blushing, too, as Damian managed a kiss to Ruby's jaw and then neck. There was something really wrong with Damian this morning, so Ruby and Isadora switched seats. Ruby climbed into Isadora's and Isadora didn't really think twice about crawling into Ruby's. Her face was so red it was the exact same shade as a tomato.

Now, Ruby could actually enjoy the trip to Elysium. The bus levitated to the sky then took off to downtown. Ruby peered out the window at the skyscraper made out of cubes that looked like they were stacked one on top of the other. Another looked like a double helix. There didn't seem to be any rhyme or reason to the shapes, other than innovative and stand-offish engineers. The speed trains here were much higher up than those in Diamond City, too, weaving through buildings like roller coasters. Hover cars zipped by so quickly that it'd be impossible for anyone inside to read all the billboards. That's why those were mostly lights, colors, and logos with a clear, distinct name. It seemed that the Cupid's Arrow equivalent of alcohol in Elysium was something called Magic Hat. It was a special drink served in a top hat that sent people into comas for days.

Ruby knew it was Surgium that gave Elysium residents an edge over the rest of Abloudor. Limitless, clean power made projects like the *Hovering Amusement Park* possible. Ruby wondered if she'd ever get to see it. How did anyone make a gigantic attraction hover in midair?

The ride to downtown Elysium was no more than twenty minutes from the palace, so they arrived quickly. Ruby was so excited that she was one of the first people off the bus. She flashed her ID to the driver, got her tracker scanned in the parking lot where all the other buses were landing, and was ready to see this foreign world.

Ruby wound her arms around Isadora and Lilian. Together, with Damian as their shadow, they headed out to Main Street for a full-blown shopping spree. While their goal was to buy a dress for the Tournament Ball in a few weeks, they couldn't help but stop at every store they passed. There was so much to look at and daydream about. There were expensive gadgets like Prism Cubes for interior designing and air purifiers that mimicked any scent in the world, including rotten garbage or fermenting vegetables. "Perfect for any occasion!" it said.

But, alas, Ruby didn't have anywhere near the amount of money she needed to afford any of that. Her allowance for today was five hundred Units, awarded to her by the Prime for her services to the palace. It looked like Ruby and company would have to settle for finding the right clothes.

They stopped at Top Wares. There was a men's, women's, and unisex section. Ruby was perfectly happy with a simple white dress, so long as the skirt wasn't too long. She liked showing her legs. She despised heels because they destroyed her feet, but little ones were bearable.

"Oh, that looks perfect, Adele," Isadora commented. "Did you see what Chad is trying on?"

Damian didn't go for dresses, but he did pick something that was pretty close. It had a low neckline with frilly sleeves, a tight belt, poofy pants, and knee-high boots. It was dark blue with gold accents, reminding Ruby of a sexy pirate aboard his ship looking for treasure. Damian was clearly in his own element, looking at himself in the mirror and fixing his hair, as if gauging what style would look best with these clothes.

"What do you think, darling?" Damian called to Ruby. "Come here."

Ruby stepped over. She was still in her own simple dress, so she got to see what she looked like by Damian's side. And ... wow. She was so plain and boring compared to him.

"A blue belt." Damian found one in the accessory carousel. "With some boots. We'll be matching."

They would be. Isadora didn't want to miss out, so Damian helped her pick something similar. As the two drifted off toward the men's section for some jacket alternatives, since Isadora was always cold, Ruby wondered where Lilian had gone off to.

Ruby looked for her everywhere in the store, but Lilian definitely wasn't here. She picked up a faint trace and realized that Lilian had stepped out.

Concerned, Ruby took off her dress and changed back into her clothes. She left it on top of Damian's fancy getup to indicate she was taking it and rushed out of the store after Lilian.

Crowds streamed up and down the street. Most of them were humans, excited to see yet another tournament play out. There was nothing more entertaining than watching a bunch of hybrids kill each other on the battlefield and fight for the ultimate honor of becoming a Prime Warrior. It seemed that, in all the commotion, no one really noticed that hidden room tucked in the corner of a random alley, behind a garbage dump of all places. The containers were airtight so Ruby didn't lose track of Lilian's scent.

Ruby stood before that elusive door. There was no indication of what could be behind it, but she guessed it was a closet of sorts. When she pressed her ear against it, she heard voices from within. There wasn't much of an echo, either. Unfortunately, she couldn't tell what they were saying.

Ruby definitely didn't want to be caught out here, so she took the staircase to the balcony overlooking the door. From above, she waited for Lilian to emerge. When minutes turned into an hour, she grew worried, wondering if Lilian had been kidnapped or bribed. She didn't detect any fighting inside. Not too long after that, at long last, Lilian emerged fixing her shirt and clutching her purse.

That's when Ruby knew Lilian had just had sex.

It was a bit conspicuous to climb onto the roof, but Ruby wanted to make sure she made it back to the store before Lilian did. Her heart was racing now and her adrenaline was soaring. She returned to Top Wares in record time and found Damian by their pile of clothes on the bench.

"There you are, darling," Damian said happily. "What do you think of Isadora's wear?"

It looked incredible, actually. Isadora was still examining herself in the mirror, marveling at how that jacket looked atop her tight cocktail dress. The jacket offered more chest, shoulders, and arms, giving her body much more frame. Maids at the palace were fragile, skinny creatures. Even the attendants marching through the store looked a bit on the feeble side, stoic because they were trained to behave like robots. Or was this a human tendency amidst hybrids and Lolligo that ruled over them?

"Wow," Ruby said. Then again, Damian was a fashion expert. He was just as good at detecting when Ruby got herself into trouble, too. He gave her a hard look that said, *Explain.*

"Lilian's not here," Ruby said out loud. "She stepped out and I don't know to where."

"Maybe to another store across the street," Isadora said to her reflection in the mirror.

Ruby grabbed Damian's wrist and pulled him into a safe corner. As Isadora continued to gape at herself, Ruby said, "She had sex with someone. I know she did."

Damian arched a brow. "She had sex in public? What's wrong with that, darling—"

"She went to this weird place a few blocks from here—I followed her!" Ruby cut him off. When Damian saw she wasn't bullshitting, he turned serious, too. "It was isolated behind a dump. When she came out, she was clutching her purse." Ruby's face fell. Horror entered her veins. "Do you think she sold her body for money?"

"Was it for money? Or was it forced?"

Ruby didn't know, but she let Damian be the judge when Lilian came back. Isadora got to her first.

"Hey, where did you run off to? We were all wondering where you were."

"Sorry," Lilian said nonchalantly. "I wanted to see something across the street. Did you guys find something here?"

"We sure did! Now, come on—let's pick something for you!"

Ruby knew that she couldn't get involved in other people's sexual affairs, but something didn't feel quite right. While Lilian didn't appear to be in any imminent danger, Ruby was starting to get a bad feeling about what was truly going on in Elysium's darkest street corners. Such a pretty city on the outside . . . but what kind of black markets were lurking in the shadows?

"Darling, it's best not to get involved," Damian said to her, watching Isadora rummage through some shawls in the basket. "We don't know details, and unless the girl is offering them, we can't go investigating right now. The worst case scenario is rape, but we cannot take it upon ourselves to kill whoever is manipulating her. Not now, in plain daylight, when we can be caught. This isn't the palace where we can sneak around—these are streets we are not familiar with and a society that has everyone on a short leash. Plus, if Elysium suspects there are intruders in their midst, which they already do, they can call off the ball and then we'd be stuck."

Damian touched Ruby's chin and forced her to look at him. "Understand?"

Yes. But that didn't stop Ruby from wondering what the hell was going on the entire way back to the palace or deciding to go see Lilian when she had the chance. She left Damian a note on the counter so he wouldn't worry when he came to see her later that night. Just a little bit hesitant, Ruby knocked on Lilian's door on the other side of the hundredth floor.

Ruby held her breath. She closed her eyes and waited for a response.

There was nothing.

Ruby wiped her face. Her uniform felt so damn tight around her neck, wrists, and ankles. She knocked again, but she wasn't expecting different results. Lilian wasn't here. Or, it seemed, Ruby hadn't heard the low growling the first time.

"Lilian?" Ruby knocked harder. There was obviously something very wrong on the other side of the door, but she couldn't break the steel or get past the eye scanner by force. If she tried, she'd really draw attention to herself.

Ruby tapped on her watch and called emergency. She managed to get through to the other line when a roar echoed in Lilian's room and an enormous *bang!* shook the hall. Whatever was in there had just dented the door, and one more hit had the steel split sideways.

There was a *monster* in there.

A big fucking monster with a huge body and large bat wings,

except it wasn't gray and skeletal—it was fleshy and squirmy, as if it was still configuring itself and getting used to its own shape.

Ruby screamed. She rushed down the hallway and the monster lashed out with a vicious blade, nearly decapitating her. Ruby crashed to her knees and scrambled for cover. The monster braced itself for another attack, preparing a second blade to finish off its prey, and Ruby had to roll if she didn't want to be skewered.

That's when security finally arrived and took over. Five guards rushed to the scene—all hybrids—equipped with those small guns that would shoot down a monster of any size. It was weird how composed they were, as if they were used to these types of incidents. Ruby, however, was too startled to stick around.

She finally made it to her feet and took off. She couldn't open the door to 1009 fast enough, and then she slammed right into Damian's hard body.

"Damian!" Ruby cried, clutching his shoulders.

"Darling, what's wrong?" Damian held her face, checking for wounds, but Ruby was unscathed.

It was all thanks to her sharp reflexes, or she would have been cut into pieces. She cried at the thought of it, just as she cried at the thought of Lilian turning into that monster.

"I-I don't know what she did, but she turned into a monster, Damian!" Ruby croaked. "A-and I don't understand how that happened!"

It was taking Ruby an awfully long time to process this whole incident, but Damian seemed to be figuring it out just fine. He leaned by the front door to listen to the commotion on the other side of the building. Security guards were making their way to every room, knocking on doors, and asking everyone to remain inside until they gave the all clear.

"What's going on?" Ruby croaked.

"You said you saw a monster," Damian said softly, turning to her.

"Yes!"

"Strange. A similar incident happened near my quarters as

well. Guards rang in our scanners and told us to stay inside. We just didn't know why."

"What?" Ruby breathed. "How long ago did this happen?"

"Weeks," Damian said. "I didn't think much of it. Neither did anyone else, apparently, because no one spoke about it afterward. It's scary to think that perhaps they did know what it was all about ... but chose not to say anything. Or maybe the incident wasn't important enough to warrant any attention."

"So you think people are turning into monsters? I-I don't understand—how?"

"I'm not sure. But if I had to guess, I'd say that hybrids who don't fit in to palace life are a bit bored in the city and love experimenting with their blood. Any living being that hosts too many Cells are not human." Damian sighed. "It's possible that Lilian went to see a hybrid this morning. It's also possible that humans want more out of life, so they find ways to seek things that are not necessarily theirs. Understand?"

Ruby wiped her eyes. Her knees grew too weak to hold her body weight, so she took a seat at the table. "Did she have sex with a hybrid?" she asked out loud. "In exchange for ... blood? But Wren's blood didn't turn people into monsters."

"No," Damian said. "But enough of it did turn Kilstrong into a monster. And we don't exactly know what sort of blood Lilian received in exchange for her services. Perhaps it was contaminated blood. Or perhaps it wasn't truly blood at all."

And that's what Ruby was afraid of. She just didn't trust anything any hybrid gave her here. That's why those vials of Reinforcement were still in her trunk, locked away until she could verify that they would indeed save Damian's life. What on earth would she do if she gave him poison instead?

"Be strong," Damian said to her. He took a seat next to her and held her hand. "We are here on a mission. We need to focus on that."

Ruby nodded. "I know."

CHAPTER 19

The Tournament Ball

Damian was right: there wasn't a single mention of last night's incident anywhere in the palace the next morning. Ruby certainly didn't hear any of the other maids talk about it in passing, and when she met up with Isadora at the end of her shift, Isadora didn't have much to say on it, either.

"How can you be so nonchalant about this?" Ruby said incredibly. "This was your *friend*, Isa."

"And what am I supposed to do about it, Adele?" Isadora said sincerely. There was a strained look on her face. "Security arrested her and took her away for a reason. I always knew she wanted to be an Enhanced, so maybe she was into some shady dealings after some hybrid promised her it was possible. I talked to her until my face turned blue, and that didn't seem to do me any good, did it?"

Ruby's mouth dropped a little bit. "Are you serious? That's all you have to say?"

"What more do you want me to say?" Isadora snapped. "Look, I really don't want to talk about it. I need to focus on my duties and get ready for that ball. Not all of us are meant to be big and powerful. I wish Lilian would have understood that."

Ruby told Damian about Isadora's comments. Damian wasn't surprised by them, either. It seemed the people of Elysium were more brainwashed than Ruby had ever thought. When high-ranking women like Faye were nearly accepting of rape every other night, it wasn't a wonder that other humans behaved in similar aloof fashions. Not necessarily because they were slaves . . . but because their places in society were far below hybrids. Their voices were puny, non-important.

Ground status.

Damian was always there to ensure Ruby's thoughts didn't get out of control. He'd hold her at night and soothe her to sleep, which helped Ruby's sanity tremendously. But nothing was more comforting than the time Damian spent with her when her period struck in the month of Purity.

Ruby had experienced her first menstrual cycle at this time last year, right before her final weeks of the spring semester at Royal Academy, but she certainly didn't remember the pain, nausea, or cramps quite like this. She had already been feeling the tingles in her abdomen days prior, but when the blood gushed out in the middle of the work day, she nearly passed out. She was ready with a tampon, but that did nothing for her fever, chills, and fatigue. By some miracle she finished her shift and then passed out on her bed, where Damian found her later that evening.

"Darling?" he croaked, rushing to her immediately.

"Oh my God, Damian . . ." Ruby groaned. "I'm really envying that penis now!"

And she meant it. Ruby was completely out of commission for the next twelve hours straight. In between bouts of unconsciousness, she found Damian bathing her, changing her tampon, and force-feeding her soup. He stayed with her like he always did all night, except he didn't get any sleep.

"Before you became pregnant, you told me how bad these were," Damian said to Ruby, who shivered against his body. "But I didn't think it was *this* bad."

"Did I get this bad with the pregnancy?" Ruby asked quietly.

"Not like this."

And it wasn't a 5-7-day period like human and Enhanced women endured—this was a whole month. Ruby only found a bit of relief when she hit her second week.

"Seriously," Damian breathed as he helped her with the tampon. Ruby didn't fight him at this point. "How do you shed this much blood?"

Sometimes it felt like Ruby was shedding her whole uterus. Maybe that's what was happening, but she didn't know because she had never been to a doctor. The thought of them sent chills down her spine.

All Ruby knew was that this was one of her body's natural processes. Damian urged her to stay in her room and rest, but Ruby fought through the symptoms to make sure she showed up to work every day. Sometimes, the dizzy spells were so bad she'd wobble on her feet when she walked. She never told Damian how terrible she truly felt, but he could probably sense it. He was probably thinking better this . . . than another pregnancy.

That's why they had stopped all sexual intercourse weeks in advance. Oral sex, however, was and always would be on the table. Which meant Ruby to Damian, because there was no way she was allowing his mouth anywhere near her nasty period. Damian understood, of course, but he didn't push her to do anything. Most of the time, it was just kissing. Ruby would be too tired for anything else and then she'd fall asleep.

Inconveniently, the Tournament Ball was here. Despite her intense period, this was Ruby's chance to kill Rhett and end his reign in Elysium.

Ruby couldn't bring any weapons, but she could bring jewelry. Thanks to Samson, she knew how to solidify Slainium and weave it into a bracelet. It wound around her arm three times. She remembered she used to wear these a lot in her prior life.

As Ruby put on the dress she had purchased from Top Wares, she thought about Lilian. It was sad that these humans felt stuck in their roles as servants and lessers of society with no way out.

Ruby wished there was a way to alleviate the pressure, to make living a bit more bearable. Once in a while, she thought about Elias and Johanna. More often than not, those gunshots echoed in Ruby's head.

Damian came by that afternoon to fix her makeup. He applied all sorts of foundations, powders, and blushes to her face. Ruby just kept her eyes closed and her expression relaxed. Her favorite part was when he snuck a kiss to her lips. Sometimes, it turned into a neck nuzzle.

"Are you trying to seduce me or get me ready for a party?" Ruby asked.

"Both," he whispered huskily against her skin. "I got you something. I ordered it from the Elysium catalogue."

Ruby sat up a bit more, curious. She watched Damian reach into his pocket and pull out a ring. It was all silver, encrusted with diamonds. Wait—where on earth had he gotten that expensive piece of jewelry?

"Damian!" Ruby croaked. "Where did you get this?"

"I bought it," Damian said, sliding the ring onto her right finger. He knew it was her dominant side, so perhaps he thought it'd offer luck in battle.

"With what money?"

"Let's just say I know a few people, too." Damian touched her hair and then her face. "I've made some friends. And through them, I was able to strike a deal with the Prime."

Ruby's eyes widened. "*What?*"

"Indeed. I'd rather not talk about what I owe that ugly Squid if all goes south today, so let's ensure we get it right."

"What on earth are you talking about?" Ruby sputtered. "God, Damian, you're so fucking infuriating sometimes—what the fuck do you mean you 'struck a deal with the Prime'? You never told me you met him!"

"That's because I haven't," Damian said calmly despite Ruby's escalating heart rate. "I've only communicated my interests through one of his loyal advisors, whom I happened to meet after my shift a few days ago. I wanted to know how it was possible to better myself in order to climb the ranks of society. His advisor told me he had never seen anyone quite as strong as me, and that the Prime would be very interested in meeting me. And so, he gave me the money I needed to buy this ring from the catalogue. I now owe the Prime my skills, whatever that might be."

Ruby's heart was pounding at the speed of light. "So you're a prostitute now?"

"Absolutely not," Damian said quickly. "This isn't about sex. The Prime could care less about my penis—he wants to test my abilities. Not against him, though—against humans. His advisor described a private tournament of sorts, bloody battles between humans for the Prime's exclusive entertainment behind closed doors. I don't intend on participating, darling—I just thought this was the best way to ensure he dies. He doesn't know I'm a hybrid, so it'll catch him off guard. To ensure I am victorious, I will need that bracelet around your wrist. The ring does look beautiful, though—"

Ruby took it off and shoved it right back into his chest. "I don't want it. Tell the Prime's advisor that you've changed your mind— that you value yourself far more than some piece of jewelry."

"I value *you*, darling—"

"I DON'T NEED A FANCY RING!" Ruby exclaimed. "What on earth is wrong with you, Damian?"

"I don't want you to fight," Damian said flatly. "You can't fight in that condition, so I have no choice but to participate in whatever sick battles the Prime conducts in his quarters. Not only is attacking him in the middle of a ball suicide with all the security he has around, but this will ensure the least amount of collateral damage as possible."

"So I have to depend on you now?"

Damian sighed. "I'm asking you to trust me. I'm doing this because it's the best way."

"There has to be another way."

"There isn't. I've thought so extensively about this that I just can't see another way."

"Well, forget it!" Ruby spat. "You're not 'selling your skills'! You're not his bitch!"

"Rhett is going to die anyway." Damian sounded so incredibly detached that it was driving Ruby mad. "So what does it matter?"

"There aren't any guarantees, you idiot! You're the first one to tell me that you're in failing health!"

"I am telling you he will die. And shortly after he does, I will have to take his blood. It is the only way I will be able to live."

Ruby held her breath. "What do you mean?"

"The blood of a Lolligo can make us stronger," Damian said. "It's what all these hybrids here use for even more strength. Samson did it with you a few times as well."

"How do you know this, Damian?"

"I don't. I'm just guessing at this point."

"I don't like this." Ruby shook her head. "At all. It's crazy because you'd have to take Rhett's blood *before* you poison it, not after. How on earth are you planning on doing that?"

"I plan on battling him, darling."

"Without any weapons?"

That was kind of a dumb question because Damian knew how to shape-shift very well. He could grow two blades from his arms as easily as drawing a sword.

"We can ask Samson for his blood!" Ruby sputtered. "Why does it have to be Rhett's?"

"Because there is a chance we might never see Samson again," Damian said, with that shit look on his face. "And there is a chance he might not want to help us. I have set up my meeting with Rhett and I know what I have to do."

"YOU'RE SICK!" Ruby yelled. She pictured Damian tearing a helpless human to pieces. She pictured him slaughtering a few more innocents before turning on Rhett to do the same to him.

No mercy. No remorse.

Ruby started hyperventilating, and nothing Damian did or said calmed her down. There was no way they were going to the ball all hyped up like this, so Damian had to wait for her to clear her head.

"Trust me, darling." Damian ran his hands down her back. Then he wrapped his arms around her waist and laid his head on her shoulder.

"Give me the ring," Ruby demanded quietly. "And if something happens to you, I'm throwing it away."

Damian agreed. He was too calm for Ruby's sake, but maybe this was how he won battles.

Especially the difficult ones.

Ruby knew that she and Damian made a dashing couple. They got the entire room's attention when they entered through those double golden doors on the south side of the palace. They had taken a tram through a chute to reach this coveted space not everyone was privileged enough to see.

The majority of humans and hybrids could only dream of what this grand ballroom looked like, with a ceiling as high as the sky and pillars that must have been taller than some of the skyscrapers in the city. Despite the dangerous crowd, Ruby found the whole set-up quite dreamy. She marveled at the architecture as well as the decor: there were paintings of Elysium from different angles on the wall and there were blood-red carpets on the floor that led up to the dais on the far-end of the room. There, Ruby noticed the only Lolligo in their presence.

Rhett.

Indeed, the ginormous Squid was mingling with his circle of advisors. He towered above them like the oppressive being he was. His box-like clothes gave him a color and flare that was hardly necessary—it was like calling attention to a pile of shit. While that was a style Ruby had never seen on anyone before, she concluded it was the most outrageous thing a Lolligo could wear.

Despite that, there were many hybrids that were trying to get into his circle. But there was only one person Rhett truly cared about, and that was Damian as he entered the room with Ruby in his arm.

Ruby couldn't help a glare. For an instant, the amber eyes met hers, but Damian was good about steering her away from that vicious gaze and making it focus on him instead. How couldn't he? He was the handsome maid that dressed in red and silver and promised levels of pain and misery unknown to man.

Isadora wasn't too far behind them, although the table of expensive wines caught her attention. She didn't care that she was in the presence of the most powerful Lolligo in existence. Ruby would have been in the same boat had that fucking Squid not been eyeballing *her* husband.

"No," Ruby said to Damian, who found a table for them in the back corner. It was right next to a pillar so it'd offer the most privacy. Not that Rhett would forget Damian was in the room any time soon. "I'm not letting you do anything with that freak. Fuck that. You're not his entertainment and you're not going to taint your soul by killing innocent people."

Damian chuckled, but this was no laughing matter. Ruby flared her nostrils at him. "Calm down, darling," he said to her. "I know what I have to do. But you must have patience."

Fuck that. This was stupid. Ruby didn't have to put up with this. Damian had her bracelet, but all that Ruby needed to do was take down that son of a bitch on his throne, the same one that had kicked out Samson and planted himself as the head of all these robots who posed as people. Pathetic.

"You two made it!" Faye found their way to them next. She looked quite beautiful, even if age was starting to show on her face. Although Ruby quickly realized it wasn't the accumulation of years that bogged her down—it was this place. This set-up. The pressure.

Ruby would have loved a conversation with Faye, but she needed a moment for herself. Not only was her freaking period driving her mad, tumbling around in her uterus as if someone was washing dishes in there, but her anxiety was starting to overwhelm her focus. She had to take a seat and tune out her surroundings completely. Perhaps Faye was asking her a question, but Ruby wasn't anywhere near listening.

Weapon. Attack. Kill.

As soon as Ruby dropped her eyes to her plate, she saw the knife. It wasn't sharp, but it could cause some damage. All she had to do was get this into Rhett's fucking eye and she'd be home free. Damian could use her bracelet then, scratch him with it—plunge it into his heart—and free everyone here from his oppressive ass.

"May I have this dance?"

Ruby looked up and her heart dropped.

No, it free-fell.

Fucking Ilan was here! How the hell had Ruby forgotten about him? He could recognize her now, snitch on her to everyone here! Holy hell, what was she supposed to do now?

But Ilan looked quite serious. He was looking straight into her eyes with his hand extended. The mole on his chin was unscathed, although Ruby's desire to rip it out wasn't as strong now.

"I don't dance with rapists," Ruby hissed. Her abdomen squirmed in agreement.

Ilan closed his eyes, taking in the insult. He must have been expecting it. Then he opened his eyes and said in a composed manner, "I'm not a rapist. But there's something I have to talk to you about, so might you please take me up on my offer?"

The next worry was that Ilan was about to reveal the Reinforcement was fake and ineffective. Thank the Forefathers Ruby hadn't given it to Damian, after all.

Yet, that wasn't what Ilan had in mind, either.

Ruby stood up. She had forgotten that Damian was right next to her and that he didn't have any clue who this jackass taking his wife to the dance floor was.

"Excuse me," Damian said to Ilan roughly. "But might I help you, sir?"

Ilan looked confused.

"That there is my wife you're asking to dance."

Ilan gasped. "Forgive me, sir—I had no idea! While the lady is stunning this evening, I only wish to dance with her and nothing more."

"Hands off," Damian spat. "Before I cut them off and shove them down my garbage disposal."

"It's fine, Dami—Chad," Ruby corrected herself. She nodded her head at him, indicating with the seriousness in her gaze that this was important. And that, like him, she had made her fair share of acquaintances without telling him about them.

Asshole.

Damian didn't have any clue who Ilan was, but he couldn't do anything about him now. Worry that Ruby had been trying her hand with other hybrids crept into his face, but he quickly dismissed the thoughts. He visibly composed himself and cleared his throat. He trusted Ruby, so he didn't let his imagination get the better of him and said nothing as Ilan took her to the dance floor.

A DJ was playing electronic music that was easy to dance to, with pitches that weren't too high and melodies that were just the right tempo for a relaxing sway. Ruby was glad she wouldn't have to execute any complicated moves now—she could hardly stand straight. A sharp pain attacked her left ovary.

"Goddamn," Ilan breathed, as he very gingerly—and carefully—laid a hand on Ruby's waist. He was looking at Damian. Ruby took a peek herself.

Damian looked ready to annihilate someone. His face was turning red.

"Will he kill me?" Ilan croaked.

"Possibly," Ruby said coolly. "If you don't behave yourself. Now what the fuck do you want?"

"I should be asking you that. You're not human, are you?"

"And when did you figure that out? Before or after I was about to cut off your penis and feed it to you?"

"Like you did Ray?"

Ruby kept a straight face. "Exactly like that. I don't know who the fuck you people think you are here, but you're sick—all of you. Has the power gone to your head?"

Ilan sighed. "I would say so, yes. But there is much more to it than that."

"I doubt it."

"Look, we don't have much time together," Ilan said, lowering his head to Ruby's ear. "But I know you're not human and you're not here by coincidence. Are you perhaps a spy? Or are you here for something bigger and better?"

Ruby furrowed her brows. "Like what?"

"You tell me. But I just wanted you to know that we're on your side." Ilan lowered his voice so much it was hard to hear him. Ruby had to strain her ears to catch what he said next: "We want Rhett dead, too."

Holy shit.

Ruby wasn't too sure who the "we" was, but she didn't have time to ask questions. She had to prioritize, and right now what was most important was Damian's safety.

"The Reinforcement," Ruby said. "You swear to me it's the real one?"

Ilan might have forgotten all about it. Perhaps he had, and he was under the impression that Ruby had already consumed it for herself. If he didn't look shocked that she was still alive, then the Reinforcement he had given her had to be legitimate.

"Yes, it's real," Ilan said sincerely. "I wasn't lying to you." He had to press his lips to her ear. It looked like he was nuzzling her, but he didn't want to look suspicious. Too much whispering was sure to alert Rhett, who was actually too busy staring at Damian to notice the treasonous couple dancing right in front of him. "I thought you wanted it because you were here to kill Rhett."

Ruby held her breath.

"I thought that's what you were after—?"

Ilan didn't get to finish. Damian swooped down on them like an overgrown bat in fabulous clothes and yanked Ilan right off of her.

Everyone turned to watch.

"You wanted to dance?" Damian sneered at him. "Or burrow the fuck out of her neck like a goddamn chipmunk in his goddamn tree? Know your place, dipshit."

If Ruby weren't trying to decipher what Ilan had just told her,

301

she would have been burning with embarrassment. Her head was spinning like crazy, spurred on by the horrible cramps in her abdomen, and only Damian could bring her back to reality.

He smelled so incredibly good. His hair was swept to the side, knotted in the most intricate pattern Ruby had ever seen. The tips fluttered with every step he took, certain strands dancing around his shoulders. His shirt was so beautiful, the neckline plunging all the way to his abdomen, and all Ruby could stare at were his pecs.

Reality? Ruby's head was in the clouds. Her body was pressed up against his, too, and it was hard to ignore his crotch, even if they had multiple layers of clothes between them. Ruby's skirts were big enough to shield her, but she felt every inch of him. The final blow was when Damian leaned down and kissed her.

It was a show. A warning. A call to attention so there was no doubt among the sea of hybrids that Ruby was his. The kiss was more aggressive than usual, too. While it was Ruby who usually turned up the heat, Damian's lips were like a vacuum cleaner. He destroyed her and her concentration as he ravaged every inch of her mouth at every angle possible. He tilted her chin up so he could suck on her lower lip like a lollipop.

The only reason Ruby didn't collapse was because she met Rhett's eyes.

And he was delighted.

Perhaps he had not been expecting Damian to be compromised. Or maybe he hadn't been expecting to watch him suck the soul out of Ruby's body through her mouth. The look on Rhett's face shifted to pure and utter happiness.

His soon-to-be fighter had a *love* interest? The stakes would be sky high.

A strange, powerful energy radiated from Rhett's entire seven-foot form. All the stripes on his colorful, boxy getup seemed to be glowing.

Ruby was a bit taken aback by that look. She had never seen, nor could she have imagined, a Lolligo who was so... twisted. Whereas Lolligo like Samson and Jamie shied away from deceitful dangerous beings, Rhett found pleasure in turning them against each other.

His prized possessions were standing behind him. Those hybrids were all hand-chosen to be his best fighters, to take part in vicious tournaments, go to war, and conquer in his name. Perhaps there were a couple of hybrids who loved the attention, but it was clear that the majority of them were sick of it.

As Damian held her closer to his body, Ruby looked at every face over his shoulder. From their expressions, she could read exactly what they were feeling.

Ilan wasn't kidding.

"I love you, darling," Damian whispered to Ruby.

Wait . . . was this a goodbye kiss?

Damian let her go. With a tender look on his face, he turned from her and faced Rhett. It was his turn to go up there and take his place next to those hybrids. Or maybe it wasn't supposed to be so obvious—this was in a ballroom, after all—but Ruby should have never underestimated Rhett and his sick ways. She had heard of it from so many of the maids who "went missing" or showed up with missing limbs, internal bleeding, and burned skin. Ruby didn't want to imagine the sort of fights they engaged in to stay alive, but the thought was enough to grab Damian and push him to the floor.

Fuck the plan. Fuck Damian. Ruby was *not* allowing Damian anywhere near Rhett, not a foot in any fucking arena or yard.

Ruby pointed her steak knife at Rhett. This was the craziest stunt she had pulled yet. The DJ went completely quiet. The silence was louder than any gunfire as what looked like a young human girl pointed a utensil at the strongest Lolligo on earth.

No regrets. Reckless as hell—Ruby acknowledged that—but she couldn't wait for any plan to unfold when Damian's wellbeing was on the line. Plus, they had a good half of the hybrids in the room ready to spring into battle on their side.

"And who . . ." started Rhett in Lolligo, "are you?"

Everyone in Elysium spoke Lolligo, so Rhett was expecting Ruby to be fluent, even though she was clearly an intruder. No human had the balls to brandish a steak knife in his face, nor could they ever glare him down like Ruby was now.

Ruby didn't speak, though. It wasn't in her best interest to entertain him or anyone with words. She was riding momentum like she would a horse, knowing she had to keep going now that she was already squeezing the hell out of the saddle. Face-to-face with an opponent like this, Ruby could either attack or stall. She knew that the hybrids wouldn't get in the way and even some of Rhett's most loyal ones would stand aside just to see the drama unfold.

It was hard to gauge just how popular or well-liked Rhett was. It was clear everyone respected and feared him, but would they stick out their own necks for justice? If pricks like Ilan were willing to plot coups to overthrow him, then perhaps everyone else was in the same boat. Ruby had to have hope.

Nonetheless, this was dangerous and crazy, as Damian indicated by grabbing her wrist and pulling her back. But his plan was dangerous and crazy, too, and Ruby didn't appreciate him making decisions like that behind her back.

Then you should have given him the Reinforcement, said a voice in her head.

So true. If Ruby had given it to him earlier, maybe he wouldn't have been acting like a martyr now. This was her fault. Then again, how could she have trusted someone as sleazy as Ilan?

Ruby quickly realized she was putting way too much energy into the past when it no longer mattered nor was it relevant to what was about to happen next. She pushed Damian aside—again—and braced herself to combat the sickest fuck she had ever laid eyes on.

Rhett clicked his razor-sharp teeth. He had twice as many as Samson.

And he was going to put them all to use when he tore the skin off her very bones.

Rhett was going to annihilate her here and now.

CHAPTER 20

Exchange

All the Lolligo had telekinesis. Some were more developed than others. Samson had never really used it against her in training because he focused on physical strength. Any practice Ruby had had with it had been on her own. She could wield it a bit, but nothing like Rhett, who crushed every single bone in her body with a look alone.

Stupid. So stupid. Ruby had hesitated to attack and now she was crumbling on the floor like a cookie. She couldn't stand on her own two legs as pain like she had never felt before shot through her every limb. She didn't even think about her period.

"SAGE!" Damian cried out, rushing to her side immediately. He held up a hand to Rhett—about to ask him to stop—but Ruby stabbed him through the palm instead.

"Put . . ." she panted into his face, "your fucking hand down." Blood dribbled down her nose. She coughed a bit. Thankfully, it didn't take her long for her body to heal. The only reason Rhett didn't follow up and attack was because he found the interaction entertaining.

"You don't *ever* bow down to anyone!" Ruby barked at Damian's stricken face. "You don't ever become someone else's *bitch* for me! There are ways to defeat our enemies without showing them your ass."

Ruby got to her feet again. This time, she had no weapons. Her steak knife was now in Damian's possession. Fortunately, she didn't need any to attack the amused Rhett.

She flashed forward. It was fast. She threw all her energy into crossing the short distance between her and Rhett. With that energy, she created an illusion, so she was able to hold his attention while her physical body swerved around his line of sight and struck him from the side. She slammed into him hard, and she swore it was like ramming into steel. A few more bones broke in her shoulder and arm because fire erupted from those spots and consumed her.

Rhett retaliated quickly, seizing her other arm and flinging her across the ballroom. He threw her so hard that Ruby crashed through the stained glass on the back wall and plummeted to the depths below.

Ruby already knew why it was taking so fucking long to regain her composure, but if she didn't do it, she was going to fall to her death. She barely got her head up to see Rhett floating in the air above her, unleashing a shower of spikes upon her.

With a burst of energy, Ruby swerved around one of the spikes and grabbed onto it. She rode it down to that deep, dark abyss, with Elysium's great palace growing smaller up above. Ruby knew that she wasn't going to survive a fall like this, so she swung from spike to spike until she was close enough to the edge of a cliff. Like a spider, she jumped and grabbed onto the wall, fingers and toes curling in as much as possible.

Blood trickled down her face from unfelt scratches. Despite the tampon, it felt like it was running down her thighs, too. Her dress was ripped along the left side. It reminded her of Damian, who was doing God-knew-what in that ballroom right now. Ruby feared for his life like she never had before. The only way to save him was to climb, and that's what Ruby did. She had never been afraid of heights before, but she couldn't help a glance or two at what waited below.

"How pathetic."

Ruby froze.

It wasn't the words in Lolligo that gave him away—it was the presence behind her. The energy that spilled out of him was dark and dirty, like oil contaminating an ocean.

Slowly, Ruby looked over her shoulder at him.

Somehow, Rhett was hovering in midair. He looked like an alien that had just descended from space, encased in an ethereal glow with boxy robes flapping in the wind. The amber eyes pierced hers like knives, teeth clicking a lot like Samson's would.

"Who the *fuck* are you?" he spat.

Ruby lowered her head. Her fingers and feet were on fire. "You don't even recognize her . . . do you?"

Rhett flared his nostrils. "Who?"

It didn't seem that Rhett had any idea what Wren looked like. He probably only saw her as a tool, another lump in a test tube that was good at providing whatever sample scientists needed. Samson and the other Lolligo had never been ones for aesthetics or beauty, either, unless it was in designing a five-course meal, weapon, ship, or building.

Ruby jumped at Rhett. She used the energy around his body as a platform of sorts and sprang up. She wasn't going to cover even half the distance she had dropped, but her fingers wouldn't have lasted on the edge of that cliff a second longer. Besides, with some momentum on her side, she used her arm as a lasso and grabbed onto one of the ballroom's pillars above. She would have made it were it not for Rhett, who unleashed another wave of spikes and skewered her to the wall.

Ruby lost consciousness. She had a spike through her chest, side, and right hand. Her legs were dangling beneath her. She had lost this fight the moment she had charged at Rhett in the ballroom. She should have taken a more strategic approach that didn't involve a steak knife, but she couldn't help it when Damian was in trouble. Tears welled in her eyes.

Ruby didn't die because someone came plummeting from above. Perhaps Rhett had been caught off guard by it, too, because Damian managed to latch onto his body and tie Ruby's carefully-woven bracelet right around his neck.

Hard.

Was it anyone else, they would have lost their head. But this was a Lolligo whose resistance was near god status.

Rhett gurgled. Damian pulled enough to choke him and draw blood, but Rhett wasn't weak enough to allow anything more than that. He swiped the bracelet right out of Damian's hands, just as Damian swung around and jumped onto the wall behind Ruby. He used a few of the spikes as an anchor, although Ruby swore she could feel wings on his back.

"Forgive me, darling," Damian said in her ear. Ruby already knew that pain more intense than those fucking cramps was coming, and she cried out as Damian pulled the spikes from her body.

Rhett was roaring like a lion. It was crazy that he was still able to levitate like he did despite the Slainium in his blood. The energy got thicker and stronger, burning all of Damian's back and Ruby's exposed arms.

"D-Damian," Ruby croaked.

Damian freed the last of her limbs then he wrapped his arms around her waist. He leaned right back and plunged into the abyss with Ruby cradled against his chest, just as Rhett struck where they had been moments ago.

With Damian embracing her, it didn't feel like Ruby was falling. If she didn't see the blurs of the cliffside around her, she would have thought she was in bed. She was tired enough to sleep, but nowhere near drowsy enough to lose her focus.

Eventually, Damian stopped their fall. He did indeed have huge, fleshy, skeletal wings that he used to propel them back into the air. All Ruby could think about as he flew up was how many Cells this was costing him. They passed the ballroom where there was some sort of commotion—a scuffle had broken out between a few of the hybrids—and landed on the roof. Damian laid Ruby down on that sleek even steel, kneeling by her side and checking her wounds to make sure they were healing.

"HOW DARE YOU!" Rhett was back in the air above them. He was heaving like a bull, veins squirming beneath his pink skin. His eyes were bulging and his teeth were larger. There was a nasty abrasion around his neck from where Damian had choked him. It was easy to see that the concentrated Slainium was working. "HOW DID YOU TWO PESTS GET IN HERE?!"

No weapons. Ruby had nothing, and Rhett had what he needed to end them. He was clutching the bracelet with all his might, toying with the idea of strangling both Damian and Ruby to death at once. He was too aggravated to grow excited at the moment.

"How we got in here is none of your concern," Damian said. "What matters is that we're here to stop whatever plans you have of taking over Abloudor."

"Did Samson put you up to this?" Rhett breathed. "You half-wits don't even realize that he's using you! It's what he does to everyone he meets!" He turned to Ruby. "I know you now. You're the fabled twin everyone's been talking about. Samson lied about the true 'Sage'—that's you, isn't it?"

Ruby got to her feet. For the first time in her new existence, she acknowledged and embraced it whole-heartedly. "Yes," she said.

She noticed her leg was bleeding. There was a shard of glass wedged in there. Damian was staring at it, too.

"I can't believe he put you up to this!" Rhett sputtered. "A couple of arrogant hybrids in *my* palace. I don't know how long you've been here, but it's a damn shame you continue to resist."

Ruby dug her fingers into her wound and yanked out the glass.

"Sage!" Damian took a step toward her, but Ruby stopped him from coming closer.

Ruby took the glass and clutched it in her hand. In the face of this Lolligo, she was going to get annihilated. She was seeing double and her whole body was falling to pieces. The horrid flow of blood between her legs never ceased. At the same time, she had to hope there was a way to live because Damian's life depended on it.

His wings disappeared. A horrible paleness struck his features as he lost the strength he needed to fight. He coughed up blood because his back was still bleeding heavily from those burns.

Ruby couldn't let his weakness distract her. So long as she fought and defeated Rhett, she'd be able to save his life. That's what mattered now.

This time, with a shard instead of a steak knife as a weapon, Ruby attacked. Rhett exploded with tentacles to swat at her—Ruby dodged every one until she got up and personal. She had the shard that she thrust into his chest and then pushed up, cutting him wide open.

A gash was nothing for a Lolligo, but there was a significant amount of Slainium in Rhett's body. He jumped back, needing the break, and froze in midair like a giant octopus. He used his tentacles to latch onto his surroundings and suspend himself right above the abyss below.

Ruby clutched the shard again, knowing that momentum was on her side. If she could get one more hit on him, she might be able to win this.

She didn't get cocky, though—she stayed focused.

Ruby flew forward, dodging tentacles as they swiped at her. She ran on them, jumped from them, until she reached Rhett's face again.

He was having a hard time concentrating with all that poison in his blood and it showed: his eyes were extremely dilated and his panting got worse.

"DAMN IT, GIRL!" he sputtered.

From up here, Rhett could see that it was chaos inside the ballroom. Or, rather, that the rebel hybrids had completely overtaken the loyal ones. A lot of them had stopped fighting to watch Ruby do what no one had ever dreamed of doing.

Ruby jumped over Rhett's face and landed on his back, right behind his head. She was ready with the shard, but she had completely missed the pair of tentacles holding her bracelet nearby. Using the same maneuver Damian had on him, he seized Ruby around the neck and yanked her back.

It took everything and more not to lose her grip. Ruby squeezed the fuck out of Rhett's sides with her hands and knees just to hold on. It cost her her hyoid, but it was worth it if she got two more hits with the glass.

Damian was screaming. He grew two huge blades from his arms and rammed them into Rhett's face. Ruby had already gotten the hit to the base of his skull, but she had that chain pulling back on her throat. Eventually, Rhett's grip slackened and Ruby fell backward.

"SAGE!" Damian jumped over Rhett's head and grabbed her before she fell.

Rhett was withdrawing, but he wasn't done yet. He kept a tight hold on the cliff behind him, clothes all destroyed and body twitching as it morphed back into its humanoid form.

Using his wings, Damian brought Ruby back to the roof of the ballroom. He set her on her feet, checking the gash around her neck. It wasn't the blood that made him start wheezing—it was the Slainium that was in it.

"S-Stars!" Damian choked. "N-no, darling!"

"It's fine," Ruby panted, holding onto his shoulders. "I-it wasn't that much . . ."

But who was she kidding? The dark stains were spreading up her neck and down her chest. It didn't help that her heart was beating frantically now, either.

"Here." Damian tore a slit in his wrist. "Drink my blood—"

"Damian, I'm fine," Ruby insisted. "Please . . ."

There was no way Ruby was taking any of his blood. God, Damian needed all the help he could get. She had to keep it together to convince him of that. She had Rhett in her line of sight and all she had to do was deliver the finishing blow. The problem was she had no weapons and her shape-shifting would take too much energy.

Just as Ruby looked around for a makeshift weapon, there was an explosion from below that caught her off guard. It sounded like the hybrids were still battling one another for dominance.

Damian wrapped an arm around her waist. "We need to retreat," he said.

"Faye's room," Ruby said at once. She could still see Rhett beyond the smoke, but Damian became her priority now. "Can you take me back to Faye's room?"

Damian didn't hesitate—he flew off the roof of the ballroom and zoomed past the chute to the palace. The whole area was in disarray, but Damian didn't need to bypass security when he was an expert at finding his way around all those spires by now. He found Faye's balcony on the first floor and broke through the glass.

Ruby was half conscious by now. That Slainium was eating her up alive. Her whole body was throbbing like a drum, and she wanted to throw up. Ruby didn't have any idea how she was going to make it out of this, but she and Damian both knew that she wasn't without getting her blood pumped. There was only one person who could do that readily, and he was nearly a hundred miles away. Damian had every intention of flying through that tunnel to make it to Samson, though—

"Wait, Damian," Ruby panted. She clutched the shirt on his chest with her hand. She gazed into his eyes earnestly as she said, "Lower me ... please."

"Sage, we don't have time for this!" Damian yelled at her. "We have to go now!"

Ruby was already climbing out of his arms. She stumbled across Faye's room. She ignored the bed as much as she could on her way to the closet. She found the case full of syringes in one of the shoe cubbies, exactly where she had left it. Risky, perhaps, but there was something about that brother-and-sister photograph in the corner that soothed her. Although she had never told Faye about the Reinforcement syringes she had bribed out of Ilan, she felt good in that little crevice. In fact, when she saw the picture of the man, she wanted to cry.

"Lolligo Cells," Ruby croaked, hands fumbling as she tried to open the case. She was trying not to look at the face of the man smirking at her. "T-these are for you, Damian."

"ARE YOU FUCKING KIDDING ME?!" Damian exclaimed. It was hard to tell if he was outraged by her having this or by her thinking this was their priority right now.

Ruby didn't care about Damian's yelling—she prepared a syringe anyway. She went to inject him, but Damian seized her wrist and pried it from her fingers. Ruby wasn't sure what happened next because she swayed on her feet and crumbled to the floor. Damian held her, injected her with the Reinforcement instead, and whispered in her ear, "You need it more than I do, darling. I . . . I-I honestly don't know what I need."

"But . . ." Ruby rasped. "Your . . . condition . . ."

"I'm fine, darling." Damian nuzzled her neck. "And you know . . . I will find you wherever you go."

The palace was groaning. Something was wrong—something was happening. It sounded like more than just security was raiding the halls and tearing the place apart.

There was a vicious knocking on the door. Someone was about to bulldoze into Faye's room, as if they suspected that's exactly how the two intruders had wormed their way inside. Damian didn't have anything but the laser gun Ruby had stolen from Ilan that day. He kissed her forehead and took off.

"Damian . . ." Ruby croaked. "Wait . . ."

But she couldn't keep her eyes open for a moment longer. She collapsed.

"Psst . . . Sage."

Ruby grimaced. Her body felt like it was on fire. Her breaths were shallow. Her mind was hazy from lack of oxygen, but her hearing was just fine. Someone was calling her.

"*Psst, Sage!*"

That was definitely Samson. Ruby heard him in her dreams sometimes, but this was real life.

"Is she there?" asked another voice, an equally familiar one. This one belonged to Hayes.

"Yes," Samson said. "I see her, but no one else."

"Is she conscious?" Jamie asked next.

"*Sage!*"

All Ruby managed was a groan. That was enough to fish Samson out of the tunnel and into Faye's closet. He crawled over to her like a humongous child trying to stay low and out of a bully's line of sight. He was quick about making it to her side and bringing her into his arms.

"Sage!" Samson croaked.

He must have seen the dark Slainium stains on her skin. Jamie must have seen the box of Reinforcements behind the photograph because he took a look at them. He figured out what it was instantly. Hayes started an obvious panic.

"Is she dying?" Hayes rasped. "L-look at all the blood!"

Samson took a knife and slit Ruby's wrist. He let her bleed out like crazy. She was already doing that from in between her legs, but this blood was directly from her vein. The bloodletting was supposed to clear her body of all toxins, but it was going to take a hell of a long time. At least there was Lolligo Cells to spare now.

Those were supposed to be for Damian, Ruby thought to herself weakly.

She drifted in and out of consciousness. At the same time, she was aware of Samson moving her to Faye's bed and peeling off the scraps of her dress. Hayes couldn't pry his eyes away. Samson didn't care about nudity, but he knew that young human boys were horny as hell.

"Want to see her pussy?" Samson sneered at him. "It's full of blood, but some guys like that."

Hayes turned a beet-red and shook his head. He faded into the corner as Jamie came around to the other side of the bed and continued to deliver doses of Reinforcement to Ruby's vein.

"He's ... dying ..." Ruby whispered. Tears welled in her eyes.

"What?" Samson was cutting another slit in her wrist. He had a bowl to gather her contaminated blood.

"Damian's ... dying ..."

"What the hell do you mean he's dying?"

"His Cells..."

Jamie looked concerned. "His Cells are deteriorating?"

"I don't know what's wrong," Ruby croaked. "A-and I'm so scared..."

There was a scuffling at the front door. Jamie froze, and Samson snapped, "Send the human to go see who it is."

"Why me?!" Hayes exclaimed.

"If he screams, get ready to run," Samson said to Jamie, who nodded.

Hayes started hyperventilating, but he really didn't have a choice in the matter. He had his own laser gun in his hands, but that wasn't going to do much against the Lolligo. At this point, he already knew that obeying commands was his only option. Pure white in the face, he edged into the hall just in time to see who came bursting through the door.

There was a scream. Ruby recognized Faye.

"S-stop!" Hayes said bravely, pointing his weapon. "Put your hands up!"

"Please don't shoot!" Faye cried. "I live here!"

Samson identified the intruder immediately, too. He flew from Ruby's side to meet up with his number-one spy. Apparently, there was more to it than just camaraderie.

Sobs tore from Faye's throat. Ruby sat up because the burst of emotion from the palace's head maid was powerful. It called to Ruby, who couldn't miss the exchange she had been waiting to see for six months now. She stumbled and tripped on her way to the bedroom door, Jamie at her heels. It was well worth it because Ruby witnessed this next scene with her very eyes.

Faye kissed Samson in the mouth.

Ruby forgot all about her poisoning and period. She gawked at the display of affection between Lolligo and human, breathless. Hayes and Jamie were in a similar state.

Faye was so small compared to Samson. Samson lifted her so effortlessly. At the same time, he could crush her like an eggshell if

315

he wanted. His chest and arms were three times the size of hers, but that didn't seem to get in the way of their embrace at all.

"Are you hurt?" Samson asked her in Lolligo.

"N-no." Faye dabbed at her eyes. Samson put her down, and she quickly composed herself. It was difficult, though. She had just witnessed two fights in the ballroom: one between the Prime and two palace maids and another between the hybrids themselves. She sported a few rips in her dress and gashes on her skin from her journey back to her quarters. "I-I'm fine, Samson." Faye's eyes found Ruby. They widened instantly.

"Damian!" Ruby sputtered. "H-have you seen him?"

"No," Faye said. "Not since the two of you charged at Rhett. I-I don't know what's going on, but there are monsters *everywhere*. They've killed so many people! S-Samson—we have to get out of here—"

"No!" Ruby said at once. "Not without Damian!"

There was no way for Samson to know how bad the situation was until he saw it for himself. But he did know that regardless of what was happening, Ruby was in no shape to fight. He had her sword at his hip, but he didn't even think about giving it to her.

Ruby did something crazy instead: she swiped it from his belt while he was busy with Faye and charged down the hall until she reached the front door. She had every intention of scouring this place despite how weak she was. Jamie had injected enough doses of Reinforcement to keep her moving and the tampon between her legs was big and clean enough to offer a few moments of comfort while she got down and dirty with her sword upstairs. She only had a shirt, underwear, and socks on, but Ruby wasn't here to win any beauty pageants.

"DAMN IT!" Samson exclaimed. "GET BACK HERE, SAGE!"

It was Samson who had to go stomping after her. He had clearly underestimated her ability to move when Damian was in danger, so he didn't catch her in time to stop her from attacking one of the monsters that Faye had been crying about outside.

Ruby had seen this monster before. Not only had she seen one burst from Lilian's room, but she remembered the one she had fought at the Junkyard near Wolfeld. The one her sister had created.

"Taz," Ruby breathed to herself. She remembered now.

A monster. No—a severely mutated human with too many Cells.

The *Mutatio* roared in Ruby's face. Ruby prepared her sword and cut him down. She just barely dodged the swipes from those gigantic forearms. All it took to secure the win was a single pierce from her blade. It was all thanks to Slainium.

"SAGE!" Samson cried after her.

No time to talk. Ruby was determined to make it back to the ballroom where she suspected Damian had gone in search of Rhett. She was sure to find a hybrid or two along the way or even a clue as to what had happened in the palace while she was unconscious. There were more Mutatio littered throughout the halls. Ruby wondered where they had come from. When she got to the tram, she saw a nest of them hovering in the sky like locusts.

Ruby looked out at the horizon. The sun had freshly set, indicating an entire day and night had passed since the ballroom incident. But she was looking at the building they circled around, the one in the shape of a pentagon.

Ruby had never seen it in person, only in posters. But she recognized what it was.

The laboratory.

There was a clear fight going on there. While the winged monsters Ruby had cut down were large, the one she saw now had muscle packed into every inch of its body. It had a snout with teeth, pointed talons from the tips of its fingers, a long slender torso, and legs that could bring down buildings on their own. Ruby had never seen a monster like that before. So tight, so perfect, as if that was its natural state. Its aura indicated it was male. A dominant one, too.

The Mutatio flying around him paled in comparison, were unable to take command. The Slender One overwhelmed them each and every time. He had more than just physical strength at his disposal, too—like Lolligo, he could utilize telekinesis. To beat Rhett, he had to.

At first, Ruby didn't recognize the Prime, either. This Rhett looked like a bodybuilder on steroids with the grace of a track star. His shape-shifting was equally impressive, weaving between weapons as easily as flexing his fingers. He clashed with the Slender One over and over again. The impact was so powerful that it produced shockwaves that tore down anything in its vicinity, including the Mutatio flying around it.

"ARE YOU INSANE?!" Samson roared at her from behind. He had caught up to her at last. From the blood specks on his face, he had cut down his share of monsters to get here. "You're weak, injured, and possibly dying! What the *fuck* do you think you're doing?!"

Samson noticed the fight, too. He instantly recognized Rhett, but his eyes lingered on the Slender One even more. "What the hell is *that*?!"

"I-I need to find Damian!" Ruby croaked to him. "P-please help me find him, Samson!"

"How the hell do you even know that he's here?!"

Where else would he be? was Ruby's question. She wasn't sure where that Slender One had come from, but Damian had to be down there somewhere.

"Sage—"

"I'm not leaving without him!" Ruby exclaimed angrily. She was ready to do something dumb—like jump off the platform and race the rest of the way to Elysium's laboratory—but Samson grabbed her.

"Come on," he said gently, although he was still staring at the two fighting in the sky.

Ruby climbed onto Samson's shoulder. She glimpsed a few hybrids standing atop the destroyed ballroom, watching the ongoing battle as well. A few noticed her, but they didn't wave or call her attention. They seemed paralyzed in the face of monsters they had never seen before, too. Hybrids were trained to fight other hybrids and humans, not Mutatio.

Samson held onto one of Ruby's legs to keep her steady then jumped. For someone with such a big body, he landed quite gracefully in the grass below. He took off across the fields toward the only part of Elysium that Ruby had yet to visit. His powerful thighs propelled them like a rocket.

The force of the winds made Ruby slump onto Samson's back. She wrapped her arms around his neck from behind, hands clutching her sword. For some weird, fucking reason, her eyes stung with tears. Little sobs escaped her throat.

"Are you kidding me?!" Samson hissed at her. "Are you crying? *Again*? At a time like this?"

Ruby was so scared. She kept looking down at all the bodies they passed, fearing that one of them would be Damian's. If hybrids had been slaughtered just as easily as humans, what's to say that Damian hadn't met the same fate? Ruby had a hard time communicating that because it would take too much energy.

Samson picked up on it anyway, so he stopped berating her. He wore a solemn expression as he lowered her to the ground just a few miles away from where Rhett was fighting that slender monster.

"I hit him with the Slainium you gave me," Ruby said quietly. She wiped her eyes. "I don't understand how he's still alive."

"It wasn't enough." Samson eyed her sword. "You're going to have to pierce him with that. I'm just concerned about Rhett's opponent. There's something wrong."

It sure did feel wrong. Ruby wasn't sure what it was about that monster that was so familiar to her. The way he moved, flipped, ducked, and attacked all pointed to Damian.

She had sparred so many times with him. Perhaps not as Ruby, but in the past, as Sage, they had spent quite a bit of time swinging swords at each other. She had practically memorized each of his moves, including the ones he used to throw her or his opponents off. But that wasn't Damian up there . . . it couldn't be.

"Focus, Sage!" Samson snapped his fingers in her face. He was looking at the horde of Mutatio now. "All you need is one hit on Rhett. Find an opportunity and do it. I'll hold off any other distractions, but you're going to have to finish him."

Ruby tightened her grip on her sword. Samson wrapped a

319

tentacle around her waist and, like a fastball player, swung her around and launched her across the palace yard and into the air.

Rhett didn't notice her, but the Slender One did. The distraction got him a blade straight through the chest. Rhett must have touched his heart because he didn't pull back—he sneered.

"Useless, isn't it?" Rhett snarled at the Slender One. "For we are near invincible. But that doesn't mean I can't slow you down."

Rhett ripped out the monster's heart. He cast it aside like trash, and that's when he noticed Ruby flying right at him. It was too late to move out of the way, though—Ruby pierced him with her sword, straight through the neck.

And that's when she remembered where she had seen the Slender One before.

The painting at the Art Carnival. The one from year 100 in the Cut District. The one Ruby had gone to with Louis. The painter—Melancholy—had told her that the Slender One was the Warlord's true from. He had caught glimpse of it somehow.

David. That was the painter's real name.

Ruby remembered. She remembered *everything*.

CHAPTER 21

Sage Arpine

Sage landed on the cobblestones below. She ran over to the still-beating heart on the ground, blood splattering all over the place. She grabbed it without hesitation, as if she were picking peaches, and reached the Slender One sprawled on his back a few feet away.

Still alive. The monster was already climbing onto his elbows, but he wasn't moving as quickly. Sage tucked his heart right back into the gap in his ribcage.

The amber eyes poured into her soul. The sharp teeth clicked as he growled. But the long talons came up and caressed her cheek just like his fingers did every day.

"Y-you!" Rhett gurgled at Sage from above, pulling the sword out through his back. "HOW DARE YOU!" He smashed into the ground before her, blade in his hand. "HOW DARE YOU!" He swung the blade like a madman, with every intent to slice her to pieces. His reckless moves made him unpredictable, but easy to trip up when Sage had the opportunity to.

Sage jumped back. She ignored the fighting going on above her between Samson and the Mutatio, and evaded more of Rhett's crazy slashes. It wasn't long before fatigue set in and the after-effects of the poison in her blood intensified. Rhett grabbed her face, Sage dipped fast, knowing the blade was coming, but she couldn't evade the full strike.

Rhett got her right in the arm.

Sage fell back on her ass. So did Rhett, who couldn't stand on his feet any longer. He crumbled to his knees and hunched over as the Slainium continued wreaking havoc on his body. He wheezed as if someone were sucking the air out of him.

"S-Sage..." Rhett snarled.

Sage grabbed her sword. Despite the blood spurting out of the wound on her arm, she got on her feet and raised it. She swore she was going to die, but before she did, she had to ensure Damian's safety. That was all that mattered.

"That's you!" Rhett sputtered. "The one Samson hid from us!"

"How do you know that?" Sage said.

Rhett wheezed with laughter. "My beloved told me... everything about you, Queen of Diamonds."

Only one person used to call Sage that. Long before Jared had. The only problem was Sage had a hard time associating that person with Rhett's "beloved". Then again, if Rhett had a long line of hybrids visiting him in bed every night, then perhaps "beloved" wasn't too far from the truth. Wren wasn't only a test subject—she was a sex slave.

At least, that's what Sage thought. How horribly mistaken she was.

"What on earth is all that racket?"

Sage looked up just as a huge explosion of energy decimated the fields. It was as if someone had dropped a nuclear bomb right in the center of all the green grass, scattering debris and dust in every direction. Sage flew back a good distance before someone captured her in their arms.

It was Damian, who cushioned her fall. His body felt different in this monstrous form, yet familiar at the same time. Sage could see blue and green veins all over his skin like a spider's web. His muscles were bigger and much more defined, as hard as steel, but so easy to lean back on.

"Rhett!" whined Wren's familiar voice—Sage still couldn't see her through all the smoke. "I want *him*! Give me *him*!"

Rhett grunted in acknowledgment. The Lolligo was about to keel over, but he seemed compelled to grant Wren's wish. He threw back his shoulders and puffed up his chest, ready to fly through whatever obstacle was in his way to get to Wren's object of desire.

Damian.

Lasers started blasting out of nowhere. Sage whipped around to find Samson had finished off the small fry and had turned his full attention to his nemesis. Laser gun in hand, he aimed right for Rhett.

This was Sage's chance.

Sage nudged Damian's cheek with her nose. She indicated there was no time to think but that she loved him regardless of what the hell had happened to him. Then she dislodged herself from his arms. She used the last bits of her strength to close in on Rhett and drive her sword straight through his heart.

Rhett's body slumped forward. Sage crumbled. She hit the ground with her bare knees, scraping her skin. Her socks were full of holes, but they had done their job protecting her feet.

Sage had done it. But this time it wasn't Damian who caught her. An invisible force closed in around her, freezing her in place.

"Not so fast, sister!" Wren shrieked. "You just don't die, do you?!"

Sage couldn't see her, but she could see the horrified looks on Samson and Damian's faces. They were looking right at her, unsure of how to save her without getting cut into pieces first.

A tall sensuous body came up behind Sage. White pale arms snaked around her torso as one of those hands held a blade to her neck. Cool breaths fanned Sage's neck and then came a laugh.

"Oh my God . . ." Wren chortled. "It's been so long, sister! Where have you been the past thirty years? You haven't come to see me once!"

Fuck, fuck, fuck! Sage thought crazily in her head, wondering how the hell she was going to get out of this hold. She squeezed her eyes and gritted her teeth, but that was all she could do. She wasn't dumb enough to expend the little energy she had to free herself because it would only get her killed. It was going to take more than wriggling out of her sister's arms to survive—she was going to have to dodge blades, teeth, and bullets without keeling over from exhaustion.

"SAGE!" Damian roared in his monster voice. Samson kept shooting him these side-eyes, but he was more horrified by Wren and the second wave of Mutatio poised atop the laboratory. This was like Taz multiplied by ten. Just what sort of liberties had Rhett given this woman?

"Sage, Sage, Sage," Wren snarled. "It's always about my sister, isn't it? *She's* the special one because she spends all day making pizzas. Well, I've had just about enough of that!" She tightened her hold on Sage, blade to neck, but kept her eyes on Damian. "Handsome man, there isn't a whole lot of time to negotiate. I can feel my sister slipping away, so if you don't act fast, she's a goner." She cleared her throat and announced,

"I want you in exchange for her."

No! No, no, no, no, no!

FUCK NO.

"Please . . ." Slowly, Damian reverted back to his human form. It was crazy how his wings withdrew, his body shrunk, his hair grew back, and the ripped clothing around his body dangled like scraps. Sage had never seen anyone transform so seamlessly before, and she didn't want to begin to imagine how Damian had learned to do that. "Don't hurt her."

Damian was fucking doing it again! Sage already recognized that pussy-ass tone all too well, ready to negotiate with the enemy in order to save her.

"She is already dying," Wren reminded him. "Right now it's a matter of her chance to live."

Sage couldn't believe that she was in her sister's clutches *now* of all times. Just when she thought her sister had been sliced into pieces on a cold hard slab, she comes out in a beautiful frilly dress with skin as clean as porcelain. Wren might have been used to create hybrids, and possibly all those Mutatio up in the air, but she had been treated like a princess.

Rhett's princess.

Rhett was dead, but Wren was no stranger to battle strategy or her blade, especially when it was to get what she wanted.

Think! Sage screamed at herself. She was in the arms of her sister—who couldn't possibly be that fucking strong—with poison flooding her body and her period destroying her uterus. Rhett's carcass was just inches away with her sword still protruding out of its back. There was no chance Sage would be getting that unless she could worm her way out of her sister's grasp. If only she had a distraction, someone who could smack Wren over the head so she could move.

Damian was already the center of attention. Samson was the only one who could potentially do something, but he was retreating.

The coward—where the hell was he going? Why wasn't he doing anything? Was he truly that scared?

Darkness crept into Sage's vision.

"Come now, pretty boy," Wren cooed to Damian. "Take your wench and come with me."

Damian, no... Sage shook her head as Wren tightened her hold on Sage's neck. The blade dug into her skin, drawing blood. It was a regular blade, though. It paled in comparison to the sword that had torn her bicep wide open.

Oh, God—how was Sage going to get out of this one? She'd rather die than allow Damian to become Wren's slave. He'd be another Taz: mindless, power-hungry, and bloodthirsty. But then again, Damian wasn't like that, so Wren would torture him, rape him, and possibly cut him into pieces.

"Wren..." Sage choked. She clutched Wren's wrists as she said again, "Wren... Diamond City... your Cells are in Diamond City..."

Wren giggled. "My Cells?"

"Y-yes . . . isn't that what you wanted?"

"Oh, sister! Don't you see that my Cells have practically created Elysium? All of these wonderful creatures are because of me!"

"Yes, like Taz."

"*Just* like Taz," Wren emphasized. "That's what happens when you flood a human's body with my blood! They're like super Enhanced!"

"But what about the Enhanced who don't deserve you?" Sage rasped. "You never did finish your mission, did you?"

Wren's grip slackened ever so slightly. "I haven't had the chance, Sage. I've become the queen of Elysium and created all these wonderful babies. Artificially, but they're mine all the same, all approved by *me*. Rhett loved me, sister, and you killed him—"

"I know," Sage said quickly before Wren's anger could spike. "But the Enhanced in Diamond City never deserved your blood. You didn't choose them like you did Taz. They were all chosen for you when you were held prisoner in that laboratory. You didn't have any say."

Damian looked horrified that Sage was spurring Wren on like that. Making her go after innocent Enhanced was crazy, but Sage didn't have anything else and she knew her sister all too well now.

Decimating Diamond City had been the plan all along anyway.

"Don't worry," Wren sneered in Sage's ear, although Damian and Samson could probably hear her, too. The Mutatio were as still as statues above them. "That's exactly what I intend to do, sister. Didn't I tell you from the beginning that this world is ours? Isn't that why we were created? Rhett told me *everything*. We came from Emerald City, you and I. We were twins among many other sisters, sent to the Cut District together. We were meant to take over."

As Wren spoke, Sage relaxed, so naturally, Wren's grip did, too. Sage had the perfect opportunity for one final burst of energy to escape that hold, and she would have done it regardless of the aircraft that zoomed over them out of nowhere.

"What?" Wren looked up as two huge Lolligo came flying right at them.

Sage ducked, rolled on the ground, grabbed her sword from Rhett's body, and braced herself for the attack that would end Wren's life. All she needed was one thrust, preferably through Wren's heart. Unfortunately, Sage didn't come close to delivering it.

The two Lolligo landed with a *bang!* Debris flew everywhere as their heavy boots touched ground. Wren jumped back into her nest of Mutatio, which came to life in one violent burst of energy.

"SAGE!" Damian cried.

Sage whipped around to him. She reached out a hand and noticed the torrent of blood coming down her left side like a waterfall. Her knees buckled. She hit the ground, but one of the two Lolligo wrapped an arm around her waist to support her.

Sage recognized that Lolligo as Tyrus. The first time she had met him and Herman was in their previous forms, right after returning to Winterfeld with her cocoon babies strapped to her chest. They had rescued her then, too, but had died shortly after. Louis had raised the eggs and become their mentor throughout the years. The two were loyal to him, so that's whom they were going to return to. That was Louis up there in the aircraft, after all.

But then Tyrus and Herman saw Samson. Perhaps the two were loyal to Louis, but Lolligo shared a bond they couldn't easily ignore. That's why they froze.

"GO!" Samson barked at them. "TAKE HER!"

"NO!" Damian shrieked, launching across the grounds to reach Sage, but he wasn't fast enough.

Tyrus jumped over a thousand feet into the air. He made it into the aircraft with ease, delivering Sage to a circle of people that weren't her friends.

This wasn't Emerald City. These were all Diamond City officers, who didn't care about the Mutatio in the distance. Their mission had never been to fight opposition—it was to rescue Sage. Herman lingered on the grounds below because he had to stop Damian from tearing down the ship. All this while Wren rallied her Mutatio to go after them.

"Ruby!" Louis cried.

But Sage was no Ruby. She was no fucking pushover.

She drew her sword as the military raised their guns. Foolish, because they wouldn't dare shoot her.

"My name is not Ruby," Sage said to Louis. She was holding the sword with her right hand. Her left was dangling uselessly at her side, completely black thanks to Slainium. Sage didn't care, though. All she needed to finish off this asshole was one hand.

"My name is Sage," Sage spat at him. "And you have a fucking load of explaining to do, you little shit."

Perhaps not now, though. The pilots drew their attention to the surge of black specks that shot into the sky like bats.

Mutatio. A hive of them. Perhaps over a million.

CHAPTER 22

Back Home

It was Louis' job to get them the hell out of there, so that's what he called for. His pilots turned them the fuck around and back toward the Roaring Mountains, toward Diamond City. Sage would have screamed because Damian, Samson, Jamie, Faye, and even Isadora were still down there, in immediate danger, but she had hope they'd make it out alive. Herman was among them and he was strong enough to help them out of that hellhole.

Right now, Sage had to focus on herself. It was she who was surrounded by the military with a useless arm at her side and a period that wouldn't let up. At least her tampon hadn't started leaking yet.

"Please..." Louis said softly, his hands up in surrender. "Please, Ruby—Sage—"

"That's right," Sage said quietly. "It's Sage now that I've regained my memories and am no longer your fucking puppet. You sick piece of fuck, is that how you treat me after everything we've been through? As a goddamn commodity?"

"I don't want to talk about this right now—not when you're in ill health."

Louis was staring at her left arm, which was all black. The Slain-ium was spreading slowly, but it had taken a great deal from her body already. Sage couldn't feel her left arm anymore, so she did the only thing that made sense in her head: she grabbed it with her right and tore it right off.

Louis and all the soldiers cried out. The only reason Sage didn't pass out was because she hadn't felt a thing. Blood spurted out of her shoulder, but the poison had already destroyed her nerves. It was working its way into her chest now, although at a slow rate.

"S-SAGE!" Louis croaked. "OH MY GOD! Y-YOU'RE ARM—?"

There was a bang as something crashed into the side of the ship.

"S-sir!" cried one of the pilots. "We've got something on our wing!"

Impossible. Those Mutatio hadn't been close enough, nor were they fast enough, to reach them. There was only one other person with enough drive and conviction to pull a crazy stunt like this one, crawling to the door and tearing through it with the most monstrous set of talons Sage had ever seen.

Damian was here. The ship blew up with emergency sirens as the cabin depressurized and powerful winds swept inside. The crash was the least of their worries because Damian was here to slaughter them before they even touched ground.

When he roared, his snout seemed to grow bigger. His teeth were long and sharp. Veins pulsed throughout his body, muscles contorting as the Cells inside him multiplied and expanded. Sage still had no idea what the hell had happened to Damian, but she knew she had to stop him from killing these people.

Sage didn't hesitate: with sword in right hand, she rushed him, slammed into his body, and pushed him out of the ship.

"SAGE!" Louis screamed after her, peering out of the destroyed door to watch them free-fall. He was holding onto the frame by the skin of his teeth, but he made sure to bark to his pilots, "FOLLOW THEM!"

Sage was in midair. Blood trailed out of her left shoulder. Her right hand lost its grip on her sword, but Damian was there to catch it and her body. He reeled her into his chest and used his wings to soften their landing.

Sage . . . Damian said in her mind.

Sage lost consciousness. She didn't know where Damian was going, but he flew with purpose. Sage liked that because she could rest in the meantime.

It was only when he landed at the base of the Roaring Mountains that Sage realized they were at Samson's ship now. Bruce and the Lolligo egg, Vince, were waiting for them there. Apparently, Samson, Jamie, Hayes, and Herman still hadn't made it back.

"HELP!" Damian roared. He kept a tight hold on Sage's body, wings fully extended. "She needs help!"

That's right. The Lolligo could cure her. Damian had said he didn't trust them, but he must have thought they were the preferable option over Louis.

This time, he was wrong.

Bruce was ever the silent giant, except for right now when he held a gun up and nearly blasted Damian and Sage from existence. Sage couldn't believe what she was seeing, but Bruce was actually attacking them?

Damian threw them to the ground, nearly crushing Sage but sparing her from the laser. The explosion shook the very air out of Sage's lungs and brewed all sorts of questions and doubts in Sage's head. It got messy quickly, like a hive of wasps that had been disturbed.

Just how involved was Samson in all this, for one? Had he truly planned to kill Sage and Damian on their return? If Bruce was doing just that, what's to say he hadn't been ordered to by Samson? Why would he take it upon himself to kill her otherwise? These Lolligo didn't act without the consent from their Prime.

Damian flew through the mountains as quickly as he could. He was weaving between and around valleys and sometimes taking cover in the woods to assess his surroundings. Amazingly, Louis' aircraft was still making rounds, too, searching high and low for them.

While Damian seemed capable of expending great amounts of energy, Sage was at the end of her rope. There was no medical help anywhere around here, so Damian did the only thing that could save her life.

Sage felt him land. His feet slammed into the ground as his wings kept him balanced. He shifted back into his human form as he laid her on the ground. He sobbed because he must have seen her missing arm. There wasn't a lot of blood, but Sage wasn't regenerating.

"Darling..." Damian croaked. He sounded so miserable that it broke Sage's heart.

"Damian," Sage said softly, to assure him she was conscious.

Damian tore a gash into his wrist and made her drink his blood. Sage suspected that it was no longer like that of a hybrid's. Damian had clearly done something to himself or else he wouldn't have been able to transform into that Mutatio form. It reminded Sage of the time Blackburn had injected himself with those modified Cells... Damian had been about to do it, too, then... but had he done it recently?

Had he taken something?

Now that Sage had had her fill of blood, Damian ripped open what was left of her shirt and checked her wounds. He whimpered but composed himself enough to bandage them with the scraps of clothes he had left. He drew his finger-talon up her chest to her neck. He must have been following the trails of poison.

"You'll clean it out," Damian reassured her. There was a time Sage thought he'd make an excellent nurse. Now she realized he was way too queasy and unsure of himself to offer any hope.

Damian pulled down her underwear and took out her tampon, too. That menstruation was going to need extra padding, which Damian provided as well. He stacked strips of his torn getup in her underwear, lined it just right, and pulled it back up to her hips. Then he wrapped up her body in what was left of his jacket, leaving him naked.

Once Damian secured Sage, he reeled her back into his chest. It was absolutely freezing out here, so he found a small cave to camp out in for the night. He leaned Sage against the wall then went out to find firewood.

Sage glanced at the sword on the ground. Samson still had the sheath somewhere. He had come to rescue her... or so Sage had thought... now she wasn't sure...

"SAGE!"

Sage must have fallen asleep because she sprang awake. Damian dropped all the wood he had gathered and rushed over to her. He touched her face, her cheek, and gawked at his hand.

Blood... and hair?

"Damian..." Sage mumbled. She winced. "Do you have to be so loud?"

Damian kissed her forehead. He gave a small sob. "Don't worry, darling... I'll get us back to Emerald City... Kevin will take care of you."

"Damian... there's no way you can fly all the way out there."

"Tomorrow morning, we'll head out. I'll do anything it takes to get you to safety."

Sage managed a weak smile. Her eyes were about to drift closed again, but Damian didn't let her fall asleep. He offered her more blood just in case she was on the brink of death.

Sage didn't think she was about to die. She could feel every throb and burst of pain in her body, particularly in her womb and shoulder. While the first was going to take a while to settle down, the second wasn't healing. Regeneration seemed to be fighting against the poison in her blood. At the moment, perhaps, it was a tie. The Slainium had stopped coursing through her body.

"Thank you," Sage whispered to Damian.

Damian kissed her lips. It was soft and reserved in case he sucked the last bits of life out of her. When Sage kissed him back, his shoulders eased up and a smile crossed his face. Sage felt it against her lips. It made her bolder, but not too much more. She was incredibly weak. Then again, kissing Damian always sucked the energy right out of her. He knew how to wrap her around his finger, how to make her swoon as if he had possessed her soul.

Damian had so much explaining to do . . . but Sage would be sure to scold him later.

Damian picked up her body and held her against him the whole night. It was freezing, but his skin was so warm. Still, Sage didn't really sleep because she was in so much pain. Instead, she listened to Damian talk about his life the past thirty years. He told stories of their boys, Candice, Olivia, Geoffrey, and Micah, who—apparently—was a troublemaker?

Sage arched a brow. "Troublemaker? I didn't get that vibe at all."

"Definitely," Damian muttered. "He's made Candice cry. The biggest incident of all happened in ninth grade when he pranked a girl who had dumped him. He got her expelled from the cheerleading team."

Sage raised her head. This, she would have never guessed. Micah was so well-mannered and polite.

"I threatened to take him with me to Emerald City if he didn't speak to the principal and admit what he had done. Castor spoke some sense into him and Pollux had some stories of his own to share."

Sage chuckled weakly. "Did you really make Castor copy the scriptures?"

Damian snorted. "The little shit thought that he was so high and mighty. He definitely got that from you."

"Oh, please. I didn't make people carry me around in a palanquin."

Damian laughed. "I was hoping you would have forgotten about that."

Sage shook her head with a smile. "Never."

"I suppose I should be honored that you still love me regardless."

"It would be impossible for me to stop loving you, Damian," Sage said.

Their kisses were soft and short all the way until morning. This must have been a record for longest kiss in the world. It wasn't a kiss-kiss, but it was a kiss because their lips touched in rhythm. It took very little energy. It assured Damian that Sage was still alive and it allowed Sage to indulge in something other than pain. Damian's lips were a bit chapped and bloody, but that was fine. They were still soft and inspired the same familiar warmth in her belly.

When morning rose, Sage did feel better. She was too weak to walk, though, so Damian had to lift her. When the wind hit her body, the cold seeped into her bones. Her hair had stopped falling out, but it was thin and frail.

"You're doing so well, darling," Damian said. He had already given her more of his blood. "Let's go."

Sage curled into his chest. "Don't push yourself..."

Damian grew his wings and took off into the sky. He didn't have any clothes on, but the cold didn't seem to bother him. He didn't waste any time flying south, into a horizon that didn't show any buildings or signs of civilization. They must have been terribly far from Diamond City... Sage had underestimated just how far Samson had flown. They must have covered hundreds of miles to make it to Elysium.

Damian flew without a hitch. He made a descent when the sun started to come down. They were in the middle of a forest now. There weren't any convenient caves nearby, but Damian set up a makeshift camp between a couple of trees. It had been a whole day since they ate anything, so he went out to hunt after starting up a fire.

Sage remained curled up against a tree. Her shoulder was pounding like crazy. The cramps in her abdomen had subsided for now. She was more awake, too, and tuned in to her surroundings. That's how she was able to hear an incoming ship from miles away.

She froze. This wasn't the first time a ship had gotten awfully close, but she was still terrified. That meant either Samson or Louis were on the prowl, and she wasn't sure which one she trusted.

There's no way they can find me here, Sage said in her head, looking up at the dark sky. Sure enough, a speck flew through the stars.

She might have missed it had she been human. But as a hybrid, she knew better, just like she knew her luck was bound to run out. There was no way she and Damian were going to make it back to Emerald City without resistance.

The ship started its descent. Sage clambered to her feet and grabbed her sword with her right hand. She knew it was Louis and she didn't hesitate to get the hell out of there—

Herman crash-landed right in front of her, stopping her escape. Sage raised her sword, heart rate out of control. She braced herself, unsure if she was going to attack or defend in the face of someone who was maybe an enemy, but Damian made the decision for her.

His hand shot straight through Herman's chest. Blood splattered down Herman's front. This was a Lolligo who could regenerate at the speed of light, but there was a reason Bruce had opened fire on Damian. Damian threw the four-hundred pound body aside with ease.

He found Sage and ran to her just as Louis came down with his soldiers. Damian reeled her into his side, about to soar back into the air, when Louis raised his hands and yelled, "STOP, STOP!"

It was hard to tell if he was commanding his soldiers or asking Damian to hold it. A few of his soldiers did fire, and that was the distraction Herman needed to compose himself. It was also Damian's chance to get the hell out of there—

"STOP!" Louis shouted again. His face was bloody red. "YOU OWE ME, DAMARIS!"

"I 'owe you'?" Damian had a wave of concentrated energy gathered in the palm of his hand. He was ready to blow all these fools to kingdom come. "I OWE YOU NOTHING!" he barked.

"I SAVED YOUR LIFE!"

"AND ENDANGERED SO MANY OTHERS!"

"STOP BEING SO DAMN STUBBORN!" Louis cried. "LET ME TAKE YOU AND HER BACK TO THE CITY!"

Sage rested a gentle hand on Damian's forearm because she sensed Damian was going to annihilate everyone standing around them regardless of how pleading Louis was. She looked into his eyes and asked him to reconsider that reckless decision he was about to make because there was no way he could get them to Emerald City in one piece. On top of that, Sage was awfully curious to know what sort of role Louis had played in this mess.

"Just come with me!" Louis tried again. "I promise—nothing sneaky—Sage needs help!"

Damian roared. He rattled the very grounds and trees with the power of his lungs. With Sage glued to his side, he was about to leap forward, but Sage stopped him again. She dug her heels into the ground.

"Damian, no."

"HE DESERVES TO DIE!" Damian bellowed. "HE TRIED TO KILL ME THAT DAY!"

Sage already knew the story. She had put two and two together very quickly. Damian had suffered a heart attack and nearly died—sure—but how was that Louis' fault? There must have been a reason Louis was still alive right now—why Damian hadn't torn him to shreds yet—and Sage figured that out, too.

Louis had indeed saved Damian's life . . . in order to save his own.

Sage didn't know the details behind that deal yet. Louis must have been up to something at the lab, fiddling around with Cells and concoctions. Damian might have put a stop to all those experiments in Emerald City, but he hadn't had any say-so over what Louis was doing in secret. It was scary when Sage thought of it, especially when there were serums that could turn hybrids into full-fledged monsters. There was no way that could have been Louis' intentions, though—something must have gone wrong if Damian now had the power to transform into a Mutatio.

Just what else did Louis have in his arsenal? And what sort of role had he played in bringing Jared and Venus to power?

Unfortunately, this wasn't the time to answer those questions. At the very least, Sage could rest easy knowing that Jared, Venus, and their gang of Enhanced were dead.

But she remained skeptical of Louis, and so did Damian, who didn't think returning to Diamond City was a good idea at all.

"Can I please just explain?" Louis said desperately. He looked close to crying now. "And can we please get Sage some help?"

"Like fucking hell I'm going to allow her anywhere near your doctors, you fucking piece of shit!" Damian exclaimed.

"If I wanted to use her, I would have done so already!" Louis yelled. "And you know that, Damaris! That year that she was—"

Ruby.

"—I could have extracted her blood and sold it, but I didn't! I hate you and how you get in the way of everything, but I would never do anything to harm her."

"You already did!" Damian hissed. "You kept her from me, you fool! Her husband! Her children, damn it!"

Sage raised a hand again. She didn't know if this was a bad idea or not, but she didn't like the alternative any better. Having Damian fly for thousands of miles could exhaust him and it could also spell danger for her. She looked into his eyes and said tenderly in her mind,

Damian . . . it's all right. Please let's go to Diamond City.

Sage didn't know if this was telepathy or how the hell she was even doing it, but she suspected it was the blood—his Cells inside her. Damian picked up on her words and responded.

No, darling—you don't understand. This piece of shit is not who he says he is.

Sage sighed. *I know. But he owes me an explanation and we can't leave Diamond City by itself. Not if my sister is still out there.*

No answer from Damian said that he agreed. That didn't mean, however, that he was going to allow Louis to take her in his aircraft. Damian took charge of Sage's transportation. Without another word to anyone, he blasted into the air and barreled right to Diamond City.

Sage wrapped her arm around Damian's neck. She kept her face there so that the wind wouldn't cut her eyes. She closed them, wondering what on earth Louis had fed Damian . . . She asked him in her mind, but he didn't respond to her.

It was a bittersweet moment to see Diamond City again. Sage

338

would never mistake the tall spirals of the palace or the Ferris wheel from the Royal Amusement Park. Memories of her time at Royal Academy made her long for the days when her biggest worries were her final exam and finding a way to get onto the fastball team.

Sage was, of course, being selfish. That would mean ignoring Damian and any other responsibility she had to her family.

Damian must have sensed her thoughts somehow. He came to land on the very spire that Sage had become so good at scaling. He stood at the peak, where he had seen her for the first time exactly one year ago. He held her in his arms as he said, *I will do whatever you tell me to.*

Sage looked at him.

Damian's face was long with exhaustion. His eyes carried the heavy burden and experiences of their time in Elysium.

If you wish to disappear, then I will make it so, Damian said to her.

Sage curled back into his chest. She closed her eyes and listened to the slow thumping of his heart.

I saw so much when I left the capital that night, Sage said. *Things in Diamond City . . . are really bad. I'm not sure I can turn around and ignore it all.*

Damian floated down the spire until he reached her bedroom window. He must have forced Louis to show him where he had been keeping Sage in the palace if he knew where it was.

Inside, all was where Sage had left it last. Her *Defenders Unite!* posters were on the wall, her stack of fastball cards were on the table, her history textbooks were still on the bed, and her shoes were, of course, all over the floor.

Damian carried her right into the bathroom. He started the shower then stripped her of all her scraps-for-clothes. Her T-shirt, underwear, and socks had definitely seen better days. Sage realized she had fought Rhett in Faye's house garbs. How ridiculous had she looked?

Damian was gentle around her shoulder. He gasped when he saw how much it had healed.

Some. There were no longer torn or dangling ligaments. There was a tiny stump there now. Sage's hair had stopped falling out, but it was still thin. It wouldn't be growing back in a while.

"You are doing so well, darling," Damian whispered happily.

Even her period had stopped some, although the ripped pieces of his getup were drenched in blood.

Nonetheless, the Tournament Ball was far behind them. All that mattered to Damian was Sage's recovery. He helped her into the shower and stepped in after her so he could clean every smear of blood and dirt off her body.

At some point, Sage fell asleep in his arms. She felt him when he dried her and then when he carried her into bed, but she didn't stir.

"I will watch over you," Damian said to her.

Sage smiled at him. God, he was beautiful. And now that he was clean? She raised a hand to caress his cheek. He still looked like the Damian she had first met. Dark eyes, sharp nose, perfect cheeks, and defined chin. Maybe a little older—more age here and there—but he was still the sexiest man alive.

Sage was pretty sure she was the luckiest woman in existence.

Damian took her hand and kissed it. Then he rubbed his cheek against her arm, right over her tattoo of his name.

That's when Sage fell asleep again.

CHAPTER 23

True Feelings

"I don't want you anywhere near her. Not you nor those fools you call palace security."

"I want to talk to her."

"Not until she wakes up. My doctor will be here shortly to evaluate her, and then we'll see if you're worthy enough to even breathe the same air as her."

When Sage opened her eyes, she found herself in her room. She was tucked into bed, lying on her back, and looking up at the ceiling she had decorated with glow-in-the-dark stickers. They always helped her sleep at night, sent her mind on a journey to some faraway place and time. At the moment, the small lamp on her nightstand was on. Her right arm was over her stomach with three IVs in her veins.

One bag, Sage saw, had blood. It was thick and red, possibly Damian's. Another had saline solution. And the other was loaded with pure vitamins.

Sage took a deep breath. She relaxed her whole body, knowing that Damian had been her bodyguard and probably set these IVs himself. Perhaps she was being a bit paranoid, but she was hard-pressed to trust anything that Louis said or did. Now that she knew the whole truth about him, she feared what he might be planning next. There was no way he was going to let her escape . . . was there?

The door to her bedroom opened. Sage sat up a bit, but she exhaled in relief when she saw Damian.

For someone who had flown hundreds of miles, he looked incredibly well. His hair was long and shiny, combed to the side, his skin was pale and flawless, and his clothes were neat and pressed. He had a simple blouse with buttons, tight pants, and boots. All he needed was a jacket and he was ready to attend the next ball

He didn't come into the room alone—a few servants stepped forward with a tray of food. This was for Sage when she woke up, and Damian looked absolutely delighted he had caught her on time.

"Darling." Damian practically ran. He couldn't get to her fast enough, just in case Sage decided to fly out the window. When he reached her bedside, he got down to his knees, took her hand, and kissed it. He rubbed it as he peered into her eyes and smiled. "How are you feeling?"

"Clean," Sage admitted. Clean clothes and sheets were a nice change of pace from the past couple of days. So was the dryness in her uterus. Thank God the bleeding had stopped for now . . . the cramps were still there, though.

Damian chuckled. "I concur. Life just isn't the same if you don't smell good."

The servants set the tray on Sage's nightstand. Damian shooed them away then took the lid off each of the three platters himself.

There was chicken soup, sweet potato mash, and a bowl of boiled eggs. Damian knew that was Sage's favorite.

"Come now, darling." Damian picked up the chicken soup. "Let's eat, shall we?"

Sage was definitely starving. She sat up some more, although she could do without Damian feeding her. She let him because she couldn't hold the bowl and the spoon at the same time.

"Did you rest?" Damian asked her, bringing the spoon to her mouth.

"I did." Sage sipped the broth.

"It's safe," he assured her. "I watched the chefs myself."

Sage looked at him. She pictured Damian breathing down the necks of everyone in the kitchen. "For real?"

"Of course. Do you think I trust any of these fools after what they did to me?"

Sage decided not to ask about any of that until after she finished eating. By the time she consumed her three boiled eggs, which Damian had cut into pieces and fed to her in small bites, Louis had already heard that she was awake. He hovered by the door, perhaps a bit scared that Damian would tear him into pieces, but he was hopeful he'd get his two cents in.

"Sage?"

Sage looked at Damian, whose face contorted. She rested her hand on his forearm.

"Let him come in," Sage said softly. "I want to hear him out. Please, Damian."

"You're not leaving my sight," he said.

"Then you can stand in the corner of the room. Louis won't mind."

Looking like he had just swallowed olive oil, Damian got up. He tore open the door and snarled, "She wants to talk to you. But you *better* not lay a fucking hand on her."

Louis raised his hands in surrender. He inched into the room, giving Damian a wide girth, and made his way toward Sage.

Unlike Damian, Louis looked a bit disheveled. While he had showered, he must have dismissed the servants in charge of his hair. His eyes were big and intense, shining with all the guilt and regret he felt within his soul. Clearly, there was a lot he wished to unload now that Sage was awake and aware. He wasn't allowed to sit on her bed, so he pulled up a chair. He scanned her from head to foot, taking his time in assessing her state. He sighed a bit, shoulders deflating, and clutched the edges of his seat. When that didn't suffice, he folded his hands on his lap.

"Sage," he said quietly.

"Not 'Ruby' anymore, I guess?" Sage said tightly.

Louis sighed again. He didn't have to glance over his shoulder to know that Damian was in the shadows, watching them like a vampire.

"No," he said softly. "Not anymore."

"You took me from my home," Sage said. "You pulled me out of that cocoon and kept me from everyone."

Louis shook his head. "I didn't 'pull' you out. You had already hatched. You crawled out of that cocoon, and I must admit . . ." He swallowed thickly. His eyes filled with tears. "You looked absolutely beautiful."

Damian made a low guttural sound, but he didn't take a step. Sage could see his fingers flexing by his hips, itching to wrap themselves around Louis' throat.

"Your hair was long like a doll's," Louis whispered, the tears slipping down his cheeks. "And when you looked at me . . . it was without sorrow. Without pain. Without worry. I couldn't bear to taint something so pure with the evils of this world. And that, of course, includes your very own husband."

Damian drew his gun. It wasn't any of the ones they had picked up in Elysium, though—it was his pistol. Sage didn't have a clue where he had been keeping that all this time, but she did know the history behind it. Over a hundred years ago, Damian had killed his father with that gun. Today, Louis was its next victim.

A look from Sage ensured that didn't happen.

"Is that because you thought Damian brought me pain?" Sage asked Louis calmly.

"Of course he does!" Louis swiped at his eyes. "Of course he does, Sage! From the very moment you met him, he's done nothing but torment you! You've never truly been able to trust him and you spent the last few years of your previous life worrying over whether that bastard was being faithful or not. How do we truly know that he didn't use you to birth his sons, who have practically taken over Emerald City—"

"HOW DARE YOU!" Damian exclaimed. "Motherfucker—"

"Damian," Sage cut him off. "Please."

It was equally painful for her to hear Louis speak this way. But she wouldn't be able to rest in peace until she heard the rest.

"I wanted you to live a new life, Sage," Louis croaked to her. "Away from the turmoil and guilt. Away from people who want to hurt you."

"That's why you had Bram killed," Sage said.

Louis hesitated. He looked a bit caught off guard that Sage would bring up such skeletons from the past. He nodded, though. "Yes. I think you and I both agree that that traitor deserved it."

"What about all the people who died in Diamond City because of you and your shitty leadership?" Sage asked quietly. "Did they deserve it, too?"

Louis wiped his face. He gave half a sob. "I'm nowhere near the ruler Damaris is."

"I'm not talking about that. I'm talking about Jared and Venus." Sage frowned. "The deal you struck with them. What happened to this city as a result of it."

"I didn't strike any deals," Louis snapped. "I didn't authorize *anyone* to move Venus out of the Carat District. There was a bloody massacre there, a revolt of sorts as her street gangs overrode my security. You can ask Damaris—I called him for help immediately. That's why he came."

"How on earth did they create so many Enhanced?"

"Jared must have been sharing his blood. B-but I didn't have any clue! I even had the military stationed there—Geoffrey was in charge of operations there."

"I told you to execute him," Damian spat.

Louis sighed, sounding frustrated that he had to admit this next part. "And perhaps you were right. I should have. But I felt so horribly for Jared that I couldn't bring myself to do it."

"What about Jared's babies?" Sage asked. "What happened to them?"

"Sage ... they died. Many years ago. Not too long after you went into hibernation."

"How?"

"I don't know," Louis said. "But we found them at that warehouse in the Carat District, dead. They had hatched, but Damaris' doctor had determined that they weren't fed the proper nutrients. In other words ... Venus hadn't given them her blood like you had given blood to your twins."

"Did you use them, Jared, and Venus for your experiments?" Sage asked.

"Yes," Louis replied. "As well as Tyrus and Herman."

"What happened to Damian?"

"He had a heart attack after you escaped from the capital," Louis said, voice losing power. "He got so mad that he nearly brought the palace down. Gertrude told me that he had already been suffering from a debilitating disease or condition of sorts. Truthfully, a lot of the Enhanced have been, too. I know I have."

If Sage hadn't already been sitting up fully in her bed, she was now. This was the first time she had heard Louis speak of this, although he was always drinking his "vitamins".

"A disease?" Sage said. "Or aging?"

"Yes," Louis said. "Humans age and die, and so do Enhanced. The Cells we took from your sister eventually wither and dissipate, aging us significantly and making us prone to diseases. For that reason, I had Nova experiment a bit with a way to 'reinforce' those Cells. While she hasn't come up with anything definitive, there were a few prototypes we were willing to use on Damaris to save his life."

Sage's eyes swerved to Damian. "So ... it worked?"

"Not exactly. The prototypes we had were for Enhanced Cells, which are different from that of a hybrid's. Well, not too much different—it's just that Damaris was suffering from something else. Aging isn't the only problem in his case."

"The hybrids at Elysium all used some kind of reinforcement for their bodies," Sage said.

"Yes, but that's them," Louis said. "For us—Enhanced—we had to go with what worked, so we used something called Cell X. It was one of Nova's many creations. It's supposed to prompt the Cells to continue replicating at a healthy rate."

That would explain how Damian had been able to transform into a Mutatio. Other than that, Sage wasn't picking up on any of the downsides to whatever this "Cell X" was. She kept oscillating between Damian and Louis, searching for drawbacks, but the both of them had rather straight faces. Upon closer inspection, Sage saw Louis grimace. Then she noticed Damian look away.

"Cell X is a mutagen," Louis explained quietly. "Which means that it changes your genetic makeup—"

"I know what a mutagen is," Sage snapped, not liking how morose the conversation was getting. "Is Damian cured from the debilitating disease he had?"

"From his weakness? It would seem so, but Cell X has caused certain changes in his DNA. While his Cells are replicating like they're supposed to, there are abnormalities in his blood as well." Louis hesitated. "He can become a Mutatio now . . . seemingly at will." He gave a side glance to Damian for this one, seeking confirmation.

"Yes," Damian said uncomfortably. He crossed his arms. "For now."

"Wait," Sage said, "are you implying that this Cell X can turn him into a monster? Permanently?"

Louis and Damian looked surprised she had caught on so quickly. Sage seemed to have guessed the situation pretty well, because Damian turning into a monster was a definite possibility. If his Cells were replicating at abnormal rates, it was only a matter of time before they went haywire.

"Well." Sage clung on to hope. "Can't Nova do something about it? Fix it?"

"If only it were that simple," Louis murmured. "It's an experimental drug, so I don't know—"

"Cut the bullshit," Sage spat. "She can figure it the fuck out—she's a scientist and she knows what the hell she's doing. If, for whatever reason, this is rocket science to her, then maybe Damian's boyfriend can figure it out or maybe even—"

Sage wanted to say Samson, but she didn't. She still didn't know where Samson's loyalties dwelled, so she had to hold her tongue and ignore the tears in her eyes. It was hard to tear out the image of Bruce opening fire on them from her mind.

Damian was smiling, though. Either Sage's outburst entertained him greatly, or he was relieved to see her spunky self. Louis looked depressed by it.

"I suppose we should give it time," Louis conceded softly. "The situation with Damaris, that is. As for Wren—"

"Not now," Damian snapped at him. "Sage isn't going to be making any decisions concerning her sister while she is confined to a bed. You will let me handle that, fool."

Louis pursed his lips. If he could, he'd fling Sage's empty food tray at Damian's face. But he was trying to be civil and he was already in hot water for his behavior, so he kept quiet.

"How are you feeling?" he asked her. "Damaris doesn't let any of my medical staff in here."

"Of course not," Damian sneered. "You are not to be trusted. I don't care how well you took care of her or how many toys you bought her when she was in your custody—you are a sneaky son of a bitch who has no regard for other people's memories or feelings. You know what she means to me, and what I . . ." He didn't like to impose, but he saw the fervent look on Sage's face and said, "mean to her."

Louis said nothing. He stood up without ever looking away from Sage. His eyes were that dark blue, a sign that he was under a great amount of stress and grief. He touched her right hand with his and leaned down to kiss her forehead. "I'll see you in the morning," he said to her. "Please rest."

Sage watched him leave. She was a bit numb to everything right now, so she wasn't sure how to feel about Louis. While she wanted to thank him for offering her a fresh start in life without the trials from her old one ... it wasn't fair to Damian.

After a few servants collected the empty food tray, Damian closed the door to the room.

"Why didn't you tell me?" Sage asked him quietly. "About Cell X or whatever the hell it's called?"

"I didn't want you to worry about me, darling," Damian said earnestly.

"You led me to believe you were dying. I threatened to cut off Ilan's dick for those Reinforcement shots."

Damian chuckled. It was wry, though, with nowhere near the same amount of amusement as usual. "Forgive me. But even I don't truly know what will happen to me. I feel so very powerful, but at the same time, I feel like I'm losing all sense of self. In that form, I can't think rationally."

"But you can still control it?" Sage said.

"Yes," Damian said. "I have the capacity to transform ... but I find it difficult to retain my human form sometimes."

"Have you been to see Nova?"

"No. I have refused to leave your side."

"Tomorrow morning, then," Sage said. "Please go and see her."

Damian bowed to her. "I will, darling."

He stepped into the bathroom to get ready for bed.

Sage took out her IVs since they were done anyway. She made room for Damian, who joined her in bed. He wasn't wearing anything but his boxers, so Sage could see his skin and check him for injuries. While there were no visible bruises, she noticed he was much more vascular and tense than normal.

"We'll figure it out, Damian," Sage said to him.

"That's my line," he said to her.

"I've kept the ring." Sage showed him her finger. She felt a bit silly because Damian had probably already seen it. Nonetheless, she felt the need to flaunt because the ring was gorgeous and that horrible incident with Rhett was behind them.

"It looks beautiful on you, darling."

"Whatever happened to my wedding band?"

Damian sighed. "I'm not sure. You had it on your finger when you hibernated . . . but then it must have disintegrated."

Sage frowned. "Oh."

"But that one is so much better." Damian took her hand and kissed it. He rubbed her knuckles. "Look at how it glitters." He looked up at her. A smirk curled on his lips. "Do you want to know what's even more beautiful?"

"My vagina?"

Damian laughed. When it was deep and robust like that, Sage knew it was genuine. "You do indeed have beautiful genitals, darling, but I'm talking about your arm." He touched her left shoulder gingerly, where the stump was growing into something more. "It's regenerating."

"Yes," Sage said softly. "I'm sure it is."

"Your hair seems thicker, too. It looks like we've filtered out most of the poison, although I am still concerned there will be permanent damage. My 'boyfriend' will be here in the morning." Damian laughed again.

Sage scoffed. "Why are you laughing? Isn't it true?"

"Whatever you say, darling." Damian kissed her nose.

"So you're allowed to make fun of my boyfriends, but I can't do the same to yours?"

Damian arched a brow. "Other than Wyatt, August, Gregory, and Hayes, is there someone else I should know about?"

"Stars!" Sage exclaimed angrily. "Wyatt wasn't my boyfriend! And Hayes—are you kidding me?"

"Yes," Damian said happily. He kissed her nose again. "I am totally kidding you."

They started their kissing competition again. This time, it was more than just a soft pressing of lips—it went a lot deeper. Not too much tongue, but sometimes Damian got a bit bold or Sage wanted a bit more. They didn't stop, even when Damian spoke.

"You were so wild in Elysium," he said against her mouth. "You actually attacked Rhett head on like that . . ."

"Of course," Sage said. "I didn't want to let you fight him on your own. I didn't want you anywhere near him, you in your pretty dress."

"I'd like to think that more than just my dress is pretty."

"Everything about you is pretty."

Damian purred. "Details, darling."

"Inferencing is necessary to survival."

"All right ... so what can you infer by the way I'm kissing you right now?"

"That you really love me," Sage said. "And I can infer by your hard-ass erection that you want sex."

"I do," Damian admitted, kissing her lips again. "But now is not a good time."

"I guess there are ways to remedy that, aren't there?"

"No, darling. Not right now. Just ... rest."

His resistance was pretty astounding. At least, it was for the first fifteen minutes, and then it became obvious that Damian was in quite a bit of discomfort. He stopped the kissing just to use the bathroom, but Sage didn't let him go.

She took care of him like she always did. She didn't have her left arm, so she straddled him for a better angle and reached into his boxers with her right hand. She kept her lips to his, her body low, and satisfied him with a few hard pumps.

Damian, of course, didn't want to lose his reputation as the number-one lover in the world. After his orgasm that seemed to last for hours, he brought Sage down onto her back, kissed her lips, and trailed his hand down her body until it slipped into her shorts.

"Damian," Sage rasped. "My period!"

"It's all right, darling."

"There's blood." Sage made a face as Damian went in.

"And?" Damian said, eyes lidded. "There is nothing wrong with that. So long as you're not dying, I don't care. You are still beautiful."

His fingers were all stained now. They were uncomfortably wet with a fluid that wasn't ideal during sex, but Damian pressed on.

Sage was sore as fuck, and she in no way needed this, but she didn't fight him. She relaxed on the bed, battled Damian's lips, clutched his shoulder with her right hand, and felt his fingers moving inside her. Pretty soon, Sage couldn't concentrate on the kiss. In fact, she couldn't do much at all. She closed her eyes and hung on to every bit of delicious pleasure that Damian was giving her.

She had a feeling it wasn't going to last.

"I love you, Damian," Sage mumbled against his chest. Damian had reeled her back into his arms. "I love you . . . no matter what."

"I know," he said softly into her hair. "And I love you no matter what, too, darling."

CHAPTER 24

Evacuation

"Psst . . . Sage."

Sage swore she heard someone calling her. It didn't sound like Damian because it was in Lolligo. She thought she was hearing things in her head, so she went back to sleep until she heard the voice again.

"*Sage!*"

There was a short, curt tap on the window.

Sage looked up. She hated to peel herself from Damian's warm chest, but she wanted to know who was out there. She peeked over her shoulder at the window.

The curtains were drawn, but not all the way. A thin sliver allowed the person standing on her balcony to peer inside the room. Sure enough, that was Samson's ugly face pressed to the glass.

Fucking creep was Sage's first thought, but then she remembered Bruce. The bastard had nearly blasted her to smithereens.

Samson must have read the distress in her eyes because he shook his head, as if indicating that had been a mistake. He didn't make any moves to enter, though. He stepped back in hopes that Sage would come to him.

Perhaps Sage hesitated at first, but she was too attached to Samson to ignore him. Plus, she was dying to know what had become of Faye, Isadora, and the other hybrids in Elysium. Had that prick, Ilan, made it out alive?

The next problem was slipping out of Damian's arms without waking him. They were wound tightly around her body, as if he had been holding his teddy bear all through the night.

Sage glanced at her left shoulder and noticed a raw arm hanging limply by her side. She freaked out a bit because it looked horrendous. Nonetheless, she kept it against her body as she kissed Damian's chin and whispered that she had to get up for a second.

"Bathroom . . . ?" Damian grumbled with his eyes closed.

Sage didn't want to lie. "There's someone outside the window. Damian, it's Samson."

Damian sprung wide awake. He clambered to a sitting position on the bed, and Sage followed.

"Relax," she said to him. "Please. I didn't want to startle you. Can we just hear him out?"

"He wants to kill us!" Damian hissed.

"We don't know that for sure. Just because Bruce fired at us doesn't mean that Samson is going to. Please, Damian, let me do the talking. If he attacks me, then you have my permission to kill."

Damian was breathing like a bull. Sage wasn't going to move until he calmed down. It was only when Damian finally relaxed some five minutes later that Sage got up. That must have been enough time to prove that the Lolligo weren't going to burst in here and zap them to death when they were half naked.

"Put on your shirt!" Damian snapped.

"Yes, sir," Sage grumbled. "I think I know that my tits are hanging out."

"They're not hanging, darling—they're perky as hell."

"Shut up." Sage picked up her shirt from the floor. "Plus, Samson's seen me naked before."

"But has the whole fucking crew seen you naked, too?"

That included, of course, Jamie, Bruce, and Hayes. The answer was actually yes, but Damian wasn't having it tonight.

"I didn't know you were so modest," Sage quipped. "I want to know who hasn't seen your package."

Damian chuckled. "Take a survey. Only a select number of people have been lucky enough to meet my package. I don't just show it to anyone or else where's the suspense? It's how I keep people on their toes."

"I'm sure." Sage was done with this conversation. She was ready to confront Samson, but Damian held out some shorts for her.

Sage snatched them from him and put those on, too. Now that she was ready, minus her pillow hair, she opened the curtain a smidge more and unlocked the sliding glass doors.

Samson was standing there with the *Luse* hovering behind him. How the hell he had flown this thing without alerting security, Sage could only guess. She spoke too soon, though, because Louis' forces were starting to make their rounds and were lingering a bit too close to the palace. Samson didn't seem to care about annoying pests.

"They're coming," was all he said.

Sage's eyes scanned the horizon. The sun's first few rays weren't even visible yet.

"Wren and her monsters, Sage. We need to get the hell out of here."

"Samson," Sage said slowly. The thought of a full-scale invasion scared the shit out of her, yes. An evacuation even more so. Moving all these people would take days, maybe even weeks, and there just wasn't enough time to secure them. But all of that paled in comparison to Sage's true concern.

Samson: friend or foe?

Involuntarily, Sage reached for her sword. It wasn't on her body, though—it was in the room somewhere. She could feel Damian standing right behind her.

"I don't understand," Sage said.

She understood Wren one hundred percent. What she was having a hard time grasping was Bruce's betrayal. He wasn't part of the
crew hanging out of the airship, although Tyrus was. It looked like
he had hitched a ride out of Elysium with his old friends.

Samson's eyes settled on Sage's arm. "Did he do that to you?" he
asked quietly.

"No." Sage held her arm close to her chest. "This was Rhett. I
had to tear it off or else the infection was going to spread."

"You need help."

"I do."

"I'm sorry he attacked you!" Samson sputtered. "And by 'he', I
mean Bruce—I'm sorry! But you have to understand it wasn't me
by any means, Sage! Either way, we really don't have any time for
this—I know the Warlord is wary of me—but you trust me, don't
you?"

Sage's lip quivered. She figured that if Samson truly wanted to
kill her, he would have done so right then and there. Then again, he
did need her to defeat Wren and her forces . . . right?

"Yes," Sage said with as much conviction as she could muster.
"I do trust you."

"Then you need to alert the Warlord and Louis. Please . . . do it
fast. Oh." Samson reached for something on his belt. Sage stiffened
for a second, but then she recognized her sword's sheath.

"Thanks." Sage took it.

Samson had nothing else to say, so he withdrew. Sage looked
up at Hayes, who looked like a peanut next to the large Lolligo. He
must have directed Samson to Sage's room. Only he would know
where it was in the palace.

When Sage went back inside, she felt as heavy as ever. Damian
had already heard everything, so Sage didn't have to talk. She did,
however, sink into his body, using it as an anchor for her own.

She buried her face in his shoulder and closed her eyes. She
dropped the sheath on the floor.

Damian lifted her and walked her back to bed. He laid her down and told her not to worry. He caressed her regenerating arm and ran a few fingers through her hair.

"Allow me," Damian said to her. "Just rest, darling."

"I can't let you do this by yourself," Sage said softly.

"How can you expect to expend any amount of energy in your state? Despite the trials on our hands, I want you to recover. I will speak to Louis and coordinate an immediate evacuation of Diamond City."

It was crazy that Sage could fall asleep so quickly after learning about their emergency, but she did.

The next time Sage woke up, she was alone in her bedroom. She got a horrible feeling in her gut, as if someone had punched her. It had nothing to do with her period, either. She cradled her stomach as she sat up, looking at her window for any indication of what time it was.

Morning. It didn't look like a whole lot of time had passed since meeting Samson outside.

Samson.

And then Sage heard the booms.

She sprang to her feet immediately. Her sword was in its sheath in the corner of the room. She hardly noticed her new arm by her side: thin and useless, but nearly regenerated. She moved around a bit easier, too, but she wasn't anywhere near ready to fight.

That's what Dr. X would say, surely, if he were able to examine her. He was supposed to be here by now. Sage didn't hear anyone in the hall, so she wondered if Damian was by the runway, intercepting ships coming in from Emerald City.

Regardless, Sage couldn't hang back when there was a clear commotion going on outside. Without even donning any shoes (although she did have socks), she stepped out onto the balcony with her sword and saw exactly what was incoming.

From out here, it looked like a nest of locusts. Thick, black dots with wings were slowly making their way toward the palace. That meant they had already infiltrated the Color District.

Sage's heart dropped. She wondered if Damian had already evacuated everyone.

There were some Diamond City airships in the sky attempting to deter the onslaught of Mutatio, but they were more of a distraction than an actual force. Their blasts shook the air and everything beneath it. Debris fell off of some of the buildings.

Despite Diamond City's efforts, however, the Mutatio didn't let up. They barreled through some of those ships like torpedos and flew right for Heart. A few groups had already spread out to neighboring districts.

Sage unsheathed her sword. She climbed onto the railing, balancing herself on her soles.

"SAGE!"

Damian was calling her. In fact, he was by the fields, in the very same place he had spotted her just last year. There was an Emerald City ship carrying a few familiar faces from Mousafeld.

Dr. X was one of them, that creepy-looking guy with the poofy hair and thick glasses. It was hard to tell if he had aged or not. He was certainly bolder than before, standing amidst a swarm of approaching Mutatio instead of hiding in the ship. Perhaps he was salivating to finally get his hands on Sage. Wasn't it Gertrude who had said Sage was the only female hybrid they knew?

Bile churned in Sage's gut.

Sage heard roars, but she didn't hear screams. There weren't any people beneath her feet scurrying around or searching for cover. The evacuation must have already taken place. Damian must have been waiting for Dr. X to arrive while keeping a close eye on Sage's window from below. He must have anticipated she'd be rail-walking and doing something crazy like facing more enemies in another comfy T-shirt, shorts, and wooly socks.

Damian didn't waste any time taking off into the air, but the Mutatio were faster. One had already launched itself at Sage with a handful of talons.

Sage was thin enough to be underestimated, especially with a handicapped arm tucked beneath her ribs, but she was no fucking pushover. Sage only needed one hand to slice right through that thick torso, and it was the greatest feeling in the world when she did.

It was a bit of a miscalculated move on her part, because Sage had nowhere to land but hundreds of feet below. Thankfully, she didn't free-fall for long—there were enough Mutatio there to break her fall, just like there were plenty to swarm Damian, who did have his weapons to fend off attacks this time.

Dr. X had to retreat. It looked like Damian was searching for an opportunity to reel Sage into the ship with him, but that became difficult when so many Mutatio got in their way.

Sage fought off her fair share of them until she started to lose momentum. She was fast, jumping from back to back, but it was only a matter of time before she slipped up and got a claw to the face. The strike made colors explode in her vision and threw off her focus completely. She was easy pickings in midair, and one of the Mutatio slammed right into her.

The Mutatio impaled her, driving her miles across Heart with its talon straight through her belly. They were flying so fast that the wind felt like whips on Sage's back. She looked right into the amber eyes in front of her and made sure to keep a tight hold on her sword. That, she never let go of, no matter how much blood she coughed up. The Mutatio roared in her face and started its descent with every intention of breaking her body in half.

Sage swore she could hear her sister laughing from somewhere, clapping on the Mutatio as they rained havoc on an empty city. That was Sage's only saving grace at this point: whatever happened, no innocent people were going to die.

Sage raised her sword and brought it down on the Mutatio's arm. She hacked away at it like a mad woman. The Slainium took effect almost instantly, making the monster screech like a banshee.

It stopped its descent just to shake her off. Sage hung on for dear life, driving the talon further into her body. She coughed up blood, but she never let go. She needed this monster as a cushion or else she was going to die. There was no way she'd be surviving a fall this long with a five-hundred-pound monster on top of her. That's why Sage turned them around so she was on top when they finally hit the ground.

The talon was all the way in. The pain, blood, and stars were a small price to pay for her life. Sage fought for consciousness as she got to her feet and pulled the damn spike out of her stomach at last. The Mutatio's arm slunk to the ground.

Sage collapsed on the grass. She panted like crazy and vomited all over the place. She rolled onto her side and noticed a house just down the street.

She and the Mutatio had landed in a neighborhood . . . somewhere. Wherever it was, it was pretty far from the capital because Sage could hardly hear the booms, shouts, and roars from the battle between the Mutatio and the Diamond City military. They quickly became white noise as she focused on the line of houses in front of her.

They were pretty far apart from each other, and there was something traditional about them. Unlike the sleek silver buildings in the city, there was something old school about the way these had been built. Old-fashioned cement blocks and drywall were still holding up many years later. There was one house in particular that was especially peaceful and warm.

Clutching her wound, Sage went for cover. It wasn't until she broke a window and tumbled inside that she realized this was . . .

Holy shit.

Aurora's house.

Sage's safe haven.

Indeed, she was *home*. The living room was the same from so many years ago, the furniture well kept. Sage's family photos were still on the wall, with a few new editions featuring Candice, Olivia, Geoffrey, and Micah. They were all Aurora's descendants. Of course, Sage was part of the tree as well, so she, Damian, and the twins had a few frames on there, too.

Sage swallowed thickly. It smelled like vanilla. The floorboards hadn't been swept in a while thanks to all the fighting, but the dust wasn't too bad.

Cleanliness was of no concern to Sage at the moment, though—it was fear. She didn't want to look into her old room, but she did.

Sage stopped by the doorway. She gazed at the human-sized cocoon, split down the middle as if a large butterfly really had hatched from there.

Sage dropped her sword. She crumbled to her knees. She hung her head and cried.

"SAGE!"

It never failed: Damian popped out of nowhere. Somehow, he had sniffed her out like roses in a field of sunflowers. He crashed into the house through another window and stumbled over a table until he found her.

"Darling!" Damian exclaimed. He swept her into his arms and checked her new battle wound. It was even more horrifying than her sickly arm. That, at the very least, was regenerating.

Sage wanted to embrace him, but she couldn't lift her arms. She curled into his chest instead, crying for him ... for them.

"I'm sorry," she croaked.

"For what, darling?" Damian croaked back. "For nearly giving me a heart attack? What on earth were you thinking, standing on the balcony like that? In your goddamn pajamas, no less! Seriously—are you insane?"

Sage sniffed. "Maybe a little ... but that's what you love about me ... right?"

Damian wasn't in a playful mood, so his chuckle was a wry one. He was furious—Sage could tell by his breaths and how tense he was.

"Come, darling." Damian picked her up and took her to the bathroom, where he took off her clothes, cleaned off the blood, and checked her wounds.

"You should totally be a nurse ..." Sage murmured, clutching his shirt as he sat her on the counter and applied antibiotics to the nasty gash in her abdomen.

"That's only because you want to see me in scrubs." Damian chuckled again, this time lighter. "I'm sorry to disappoint you, but scrubs are the one thing I will never wear."

"Why?"

"So plain. It doesn't suit me. Unless, of course, you're suggesting I wear a pretty dress. That, I will do."

Sage wrapped her arms around his neck. At last, she got her skinny arm around him, too. She slumped against his shoulder and whispered, "I'm sorry."

"For what, darling?"

"It ... must have been so miserable." Tears welled in Sage's eyes again. She hid them by pressing her head against his sleeve. How was it that he still smelled like teakwood and lavender even when he was covered in blood? "For you ... to see me like that ... i-in that cocoon ..."

Damian stiffened in her embrace. Sage thought she could feel every emotion coursing through his body at that moment like tiny electric currents. He gave off vibes of horror, fear, grief, and pain. So much pain. Countless nights spent wondering if he'd ever truly see her again.

"I'm sorry," Sage rasped. "You didn't deserve that, darling ... everything you went through on your own, raising our boys, leading a city ..."

Damian held her chin. He tilted her head up so he could look at her. "And I would do it again," he whispered. "If it meant I'd get to spend another day with you. I know now that I live and breathe only for you. You are all that matters to me ... and I will always be by your side, even if I no longer look the same."

"We'll find a way to take care of it." Sage kissed his neck. "I promise. Samson is here." She raised her head again. "Wait ... where is everyone?"

"Ruby City," Damian said.

Sage's eyes widened. "Really?"

"It was the closest place to move everyone to on such short

notice. It was also the only place that has Surgium, which Samson swears he can use to defeat the Mutatio."

"How is Surgium going to defeat a bunch of monsters?"

"He said something about powering weapons that fire concentrated Slainium." Damian shook his head. "But I'm not entirely sure."

"Is there anyone left in Diamond City?" Sage asked.

"No. I know you're exhausted, but it would probably be a good idea to leave as soon as possible. We don't want to get caught up in a storm of those monsters."

Sage touched his cheek. "Are you all right, Damian?"

Damian kissed her nose. "I'm fine now that you're not falling off the top of the palace. You sure do like climbing it, don't you?"

"I've gotten good at it." Sage puffed up her chest.

Damian chuckled. He helped her put on a bra and panties then dressed her in some clean clothes he plucked from the closet. Sage wondered who the clothes belonged to.

"Candice and Olivia came to see you a lot more often than I did," Damian said. "Sometimes, they'd stay the night with you. Micah, too."

Sage nodded. Right.

Damian buttoned her jacket. He picked up her sword and handed it to her. Sage strapped it around her chest. Then Damian took her hand and led her out of the house.

Back outside, Sage didn't realize a storm had blown into Diamond City. It was wet and cold, even if they were in the middle of the month of Purity. These kinds of weather conditions had never bothered her in the past, but she felt so weak and minuscule now.

"Come." Damian wrapped his arms around her. Without warning, he took off into the air. Soon, he was flying over the Circular Forest.

Sage wanted to say that this was convenient, and she was already thinking of ways to get Damian to fly her to places, but she got distracted with the sight below. She got to see all the distance she had covered in the Scarfaces' van, when Hamilton's dying body had slumped onto her lap. She wondered how her canine companion was doing...

There was really nothing to see, though. There were hardly any visible roads leading south to Ruby City. In fact, there was nothing around for miles. It was a miracle any Diamond City runaway had found them...

"I would have come for you," Damian said.

It took Sage a few minutes to figure out what he was talking about. She didn't forget that while she had been visiting Two for Pizza for the first time since waking up, Damian had been sick in bed, dying after having that heart attack.

"I know you would have," Sage said softly. She tightened her hold around his neck. It was so cozy against his chest. "And I'm sorry that I ran from you."

"Did you run from me because you were scared of me?"

"No. Well, yes. I didn't know you were my husband or that you wouldn't arrest me for climbing the palace. I didn't want to be discovered. I think I was more startled than scared, though."

"It was the strongest pain I've ever felt in my body," Damian went on dismally. "After I nearly beat Louis to a pulp, there was a thick, drowning pressure in my chest. As a hybrid, I would have never dreamed to feel such a thing. I couldn't feel parts of my body. I soon lost consciousness, and when I woke up, Nova was at my side. She and Louis offered that Cell X serum, and despite the consequences and side-effects, I consented."

"Why do you sound so guilty?" Sage said.

Damian didn't respond. He could have given an excuse—the wind cut in loudly at that moment—but he kept quiet.

"Damian," Sage said.

When Damian said nothing, Sage turned around and noticed that they were nearly upon Ruby City. They were flying over the plains where Sage had battled the Scarfaces after training with Samson for so many months. Jared had cackled like a maniac at her and what had happened to Damian. Unlike that time, however, there were loads of vehicles and airships parked there. Many Diamond City residents were still coming down the ramps and beholding their new home for the first time.

Red and silver were the colors. Flags were perched at every check-in. The insignia—a ruby with two crossed swords—was front and center for everyone to see.

"Ruby?" Randall was one of the many officers keeping order. He was in his white battle armor with a gun in his hands, ready to shoot at the first foreigner he spotted. Damian's flying form must have been a shock, but then he saw Sage and his face lightened up.

Damian landed and carefully set Sage on her feet.

Sage didn't stray far from his body because her knees were still wobbly. Her arm was pounding, too, curled up against her chest as it finished its regeneration. When she turned to look at Damian, she noticed he wasn't well, either.

His breathing was a bit erratic and his skin was a strange milky color. His vascularity looked even more pronounced than last night. Sage already knew those were all after-effects from Cell X as well as the fighting and endless fighting, but still.

Sage had every intention of getting him to a room, but she didn't want to be rude to Randall and the other officers who came out to see her. She bowed her head.

"Hello, Randall."

Word that Sage had arrived spread fast. In minutes, she had a sea of people come out of everywhere to see her, a lot of which she didn't know or recognize. There were hushed whispers of the "Optimum" among them, and that name only grew stronger as more of the crowd realized who she was.

It was Randall who made some room for her. He could sense that Sage and Damian were in desperate need of privacy, so he pushed everyone aside.

Sage appreciated the gesture, but she wasn't making it to her room any time soon. Crystal Light was so far away from here, and there were so many more people to intercept on the way. Family and friends scrambled to find them, and one of the first to pop up was Micah.

"You need a hospital," Micah said at once.

Sage could look into the boy's face and finally recognize this as the son of Candice and Geoffrey. A small ball of warmth manifested in her chest and spread throughout her body. It made her extremely nervous, especially when she thought about the nieces and sons she had yet to see after so many years, and she wanted to cry.

"We just need a room," Sage said, keeping herself together. The last thing she wanted was to deal with a bunch of doctors. God only knew where Dr. X was among this city exploding with new residents. She didn't have the strength for it, and Damian knew that, so he didn't fight her decision. Except that wasn't entirely why he kept quiet about it, though.

"Fuck," Damian cursed.

Sage turned to him. Her heart stopped beating when she saw the veins on his face.

He was clutching his head with fingers in the shape of talons, but he didn't linger to become a spectacle in the middle of this crowded street. He sprouted his wings and took off into the air so quickly that no one else had noticed there was anything wrong with him. Other than the fact he could fly, a feat neither Sage nor Samson had accomplished.

"DAMIAN!" Sage cried, and she took off, too. She didn't care who she trampled over as she raced to stop her husband from doing something reckless, like run away from the only people who could help him. Sage didn't want to use her sword to hurt him, so she kept that in its sheath and grabbed a knife from a nearby restaurant. She had never been to Vacation Spot, but they had tables set up outside with umbrellas and menus. It looked like today's special was the French Onion Soup.

Sage knew she was going to have to get to higher ground in order to catch Damian. Her balance was all fucked up because of her arm, so the closer the shot, the higher the chance it'd hit its mark.

She scaled the side of a skyscraper and flung the steak knife right at Damian's face.

She got him in the eye. The injury was minuscule compared to what was happening to the rest of his body, but it was enough to make him stumble. He dipped, and Sage took this chance to jump, grab him around the neck, and drag him right back down to street level.

By now, everyone in Ruby City knew that Sage was here. That's why Pollux, Castor, Candice, and Olivia were waiting for them below, gathered around Sage and Damian as they slammed into the ground with a rumble that made people scream.

"Dad?" Pollux croaked. He couldn't help staring at his mother, too, but it was Damian who was in clear distress here.

The only way to silence him was to knock him out completely. As Damian struggled to tear the steak knife out of his eye, Castor leapt out of the crowd and locked his arms around Damian's neck. Although he looked just like Pollux, Sage knew that the twin with the drawn brows, intense gaze, and hard jawline was Castor.

The scary part was they looked just like Damian. Their faces were exact replicas and their hair had the exact same shades. Their styles were different, though, and reflected their personalities well: Castor's hair was combed back, slick and neat, while Pollux's was long and swept to the side. They looked just like they had last year.

With a city to run and people to command, it didn't look like the twins had had a lot of time to experiment with looks. Their Emerald City uniforms were as plain as day.

Sage took a step back as she witnessed Castor wrestle Damian to the ground. She found Candice and Olivia in the crowd and met their eyes.

Her heart was doing very painful things in her chest at the moment. Thirty years later, Candice and Olivia were no longer teenagers—they were grown-ass women that Sage no longer recognized.

Candice was tall, hair blow-dried and styled professionally, with mature, smooth features. The hard looks and pouty lips whenever she didn't get what she wanted were gone. Shockingly, Olivia was even taller than her sister with a bust that turned heads and legs that were more toned than Sage's.

Holy hell . . . Olivia had boobs.

And ass.

A nude model.

Right.

Damn.

Sage dropped to her knees as her emotions overcame her. If those two were unrecognizable, then what the hell did Sage look like to them? Nearly bald with thinning hair, a mangled-up arm, and period stains in her pants?

Candice and Olivia were crying. They had never forgotten their unbeatable aunt, though, and they never would. How could they? Sage's impact on their lives would last an eternity. They each had a necklace with a small vial of blood. Sage remembered giving that to them years ago.

"Mom?"

Sage looked up as Pollux scrambled over to her. He wrapped a protective arm around her body and drew her into his chest like Damian would. He held her head close to his, kissed her temple, and breathed in her scent.

Sage didn't remember ever feeling this way in her life. Heavy, but not just with the woes of fighting, extreme fatigue, and desperation toward Damian's condition—with love and grief all at once. Love for her family, but grief for the thirty years of life she had missed out on.

"Back, boy!" cried a familiar voice.

Sage looked up as Castor obeyed and spun off the writhing Damian. It was Samson with his laser gun, and he didn't mind blasting off one of Damian's arms to keep him quiet. Then Jamie sprang forward with a sedative to knock him out completely.

Sage stood. Pollux never loosened his hold, as if he were guiding a dying woman to her feet. It didn't matter that Sage was an indestructible bitch who had spent the past year taking down Scarfaces, dethroning Lolligo, and infiltrating Elysium—to Pollux and

Castor, who rushed to her other side in case she shattered, she was a delicate tea cup.

Castor got one good look at her. The glittery dark eyes were Damian's without a doubt. But the look on his face was all Sage. Sage knew because she was asking herself the same questions.

Was Damian going to live? Were Samson and Jamie capable of helping him with his condition?

They were about to find out.

CHAPTER 25

Reunion and Separation

"**W**e've got him, Sage," Samson called to her, amber eyes as intense as ever.

Sage stared at him, but she wasn't sure she was registering his words. There was a terrible ringing in her ears and an aggressive trembling in her body. She felt so fucking helpless and useless. Her limbs were frail and her grip slackened, so she was unable to hold anything in her hands.

Castor and Pollux were holding her tightly. Between the two of them, they kept her on her feet.

Sage's eyes flooded with tears as more misery crashed over her. This time, had it not been for her boys, she would have been bawling on the ground.

"Aunt Sage?" Candice whispered worriedly.

Sage stood there without moving or responding to anyone. She looked like hell, needed a hospital immediately, and fought to remain conscious, but didn't engage with the people who stepped closer to her.

"Please give her space," Castor commanded, before Sage ran out of air to breathe.

It was a bit eerie, but her boys seemed to know exactly what she wanted. They didn't take her to her complex, nor did they carry her to Samson's ship on the south side of the city—they took her to a nice little square with a fountain and bench. The shops here had yet to open, but with all the Diamond City residents coming in, it wouldn't be long before discount banners went up and music started playing in the corners. Right now, the solitude did wonders for her. Castor and Pollux sat her down.

"Mom?" Pollux said softly. He got to his knees in front of her.

Castor sat down next to her. He still had an arm around her shoulders. He kept her head against his chest and his nose in her hair, as if he was inhaling her scent and taking her all in like Pollux had.

Sage closed her eyes. She looked like she was sleeping, but it was more like meditation. She eased her thoughts as well as her body. It helped calm her raging emotions and any throbs of pain from her injuries. With time, those slowly healed, too. Her left arm was growing nicely. Her cramps had lessened.

Castor and Pollux seemed to be in the same trance. Castor had his head on Sage's while Pollux was curled up at her feet, his cheek on her knee. They didn't speak, but they knew so much.

That was the feeling that Sage got. As she sat there in that meditative state, distinct memories entered her mind and they weren't her own. They were strange ones, too. She knew she was in a cocoon—somewhere nice and warm—but she could see things and hear voices. Her very first memory was of someone crying. It wasn't her, either—it was Damian. Why on earth could she hear Damian crying? He was cooing at her. Or rather, he was cooing at Castor and Pollux. He was talking to them like living beings.

"They haven't even hatched yet," Sage said.

"So?" Damian countered. "They are part of the party, too. Trust me—they'll remember this."

Sage remembered that party near Centerfeld. Apparently, Castor and Pollux did, too. They remembered her fight with Blackburn, how she constantly fended for them. They remembered those months they had spent with her at Tyrus and Herman's camp. Just like they remembered when they had hatched for the first time since birth, opening their eyes to the world around them and seeing her front and center.

Sage held them tightly. She could see herself fighting X@me. She could see Damian kissing all over them and acting stupid. She remembered their trip to the Royal Amusement Park in Heart. That had been one of the best days of Sage's life ... and theirs, as well, even if they had been so young ... And then she saw herself lying in bed, wilting away before their very eyes. She was about to enter hibernation.

It was surreal, but Castor and Pollux hadn't forgotten her, either. All through their lives, they had kept her memory in their hearts. They each had a Diamond City insignia tattoo on one wrist ... with a Star Raider insignia on the other. Pollux was the artsy one, so he had Sage's hand-written letter tattooed on his back. The only problem was it wasn't finished. Sage had never gotten to finish that letter.

"... Is so very proud of you," Sage whispered.

Pollux raised his head. Castor did, too.

"Your mother is so very proud of you," Sage said again. "That's what I wanted to write."

Pollux took her hand and kissed it. Castor kissed her temple and cheek.

Sage smiled. She could sit between these two handsome fuckers all day. She wasn't in any hurry to interrupt the peace, no matter how badly she wanted to talk to Candice and Olivia.

"If only you knew," Castor murmured. "How Pollux almost burned the kitchen down at the restaurant."

Pollux kicked Castor in the shin. "I didn't know how much fuel I needed to add to the oven! That was Candice's fault."

"As long as you don't fuck up the pizza," Sage murmured back. "That's all that matters to the customer ..."

"Well, I didn't," Pollux said defensively. "I just miscalculated on the fuel, is all. Castor needs to tell you about how he almost got into a fight with one of the customers because he hadn't gone by the table in minutes."

"I refuse to deal with people who are not respectful," Castor said majestically. "As Claritians, they were incredibly rude to Olivia for her choice of career. And so I feel my mannerisms toward them are well justified."

"Did you ever have to deal with Claritians at the restaurant?" Pollux asked Sage.

"Not too often," she replied. "Although I did get into a fight with one when I visited the Clarity District. I was doing research on the Lolligo curse. I told them it was a bunch of bullshit."

"Oh, the *curse*," Pollux breathed. "Like why it's always raining in Diamond City."

"There is a scientific explanation," Castor said. "Since Nuclear Devastation, our climate has become considerably warmer in parts where there are significant amounts of radiation. Because warm air tends to hold more moisture than cool air, the chances of rain are much more probable."

"All right, genius, then why is everything else around it nearly frozen over?"

"Did you not hear my explanation? Radiation is significantly higher in some places than others. Diamond City, in particular, has higher radiation levels. That's why humans are more prone to becoming sick and dying. It makes diseases like Red Fever more prone to spreading as well."

"I still say it could be a Lolligo thing," Pollux muttered as he rolled his eyes. "I mean, we found a bunch of their corpses here in the Science of Tomorrow. Maybe they did want to punish us and set off the higher radiation on purpose."

Castor glared at him. "That does not seem likely. Radiation isn't good for them, either."

"But it could have been their counterattack. Had they died or lost the war, they could have set off more radiation. Perhaps it was their way of weeding out the weak."

"Maybe Samson knows," Sage said.

"He doesn't want to talk to us," Pollux said. "He tells us that we're annoying brats."

"Speak for yourself," Castor said. "But I managed to hold a decent conversation with him about Diamond City."

Sage raised her head. "Diamond City?"

"We really don't mean to trouble you with this burden right now, Mother, but we've detected some Mutatio in the vicinity the past few weeks."

"We think it might be Wren," Pollux said. "She's looking for you."

"Is she a danger to anyone?" Sage asked, growing concerned.

"No. We've been keeping an eye on any and all activity in those parts, and so far, there don't seem to be any major threats."

"We believe the Mutatio are neurologically connected to her," Castor said. "Although you, Wren, and Father have the ability to turn others into Enhanced, we must remember that an overabundance of those Cells can destabilize the subject. It can lead to mutations of epic proportions, as we've seen in the Mutatio. We're not sure if this makes it easier to combat them or not, but we don't let anyone leave the city until Samson tells us it's safe."

Sage's stomach was somewhere on the floor. She feared the answer to her next question. "So Wren's coming?"

"At some point, yes," Castor said. "Although we are hopeful Samson will have a means of defeating the Mutatio easily by then."

"The Mutatio have Cells like we do," Pollux said softly. He laid his head back on Sage's lap. "So a weapon with Slainium should do the trick. While I'm looking forward to ending her for good, I'm a little bit worried about Dad."

Sage would have given anything to have Wren as her only problem right now. She should have known that Damian's condition was much more dire than she had anticipated. That's why she was completely caught off guard when she heard a roar and then an explosion in the distance.

Sage stood up; Castor and Pollux were there to steady her. They should have suggested she lie low and seek shelter, but they didn't bother. They sensed her intentions and accepted that she wasn't going to walk away from her husband's distress call. As weak as Sage was at the moment, she wasn't about to ignore whatever the hell was happening.

Without words, Castor and Pollux reacted: Castor picked up Sage while Pollux stuck close by. They jumped toward the smoke, which they already knew was coming from Samson's ship. Just what the fuck was going on?

Damian, Damian, Damian.

His name rang in Sage's head like a bell. The echo was devastating on her eardrums as true fear and panic burrowed its way into her body and ate her up from the inside. Her mind conjured up all sorts of scenarios, and they all included death.

What if Samson was dead, torn to bloody pieces by the monster even he couldn't contain on his ship? That indicated Damian was out of control, and there was simply no hope of getting him back at this point.

Sage was semi relieved when she found a fuming Samson standing outside the *Luse*. Jamie was there as well, looking out into the distance. Most infuriating of all, Bruce and that egg were standing there as if the fucker had never tried to destroy Sage with his own gun. All was calm, but it was crazy how quickly the whole situation escalated.

Castor placed Sage on her feet then joined his brother in the most brutal and well-coordinated attack Sage had ever seen. The two of them indeed moved like ninjas, working their speed, skill, and weapons to pummel Bruce right in front of everyone's eyes. Their attacks were fast but powerful, and between the two of them, Bruce stood no chance. In just minutes, Bruce's huge body was on the ground with Castor and Pollux holding a dagger to his neck and chest. They had cut the egg from its strap around his torso.

"What the fuck?!" Samson exclaimed; Jamie stumbled back. "WHAT ARE YOU DOING?!"

Sage already knew. Castor and Pollux must have seen her memories when they had been bonding earlier. They must have known or detected that Bruce had opened fire on Sage and Damian, nearly killing them.

"Go ahead," Bruce said in Lolligo. "Do it."

To everyone's shock, the twins understood and spoke Lolligo perfectly.

"You tried to kill her," Castor said in Lolligo, as fluent as his Lucidum. Damian must have taught them both when they were younger. "And that is inexcusable."

"STOP THIS NOW!" Samson barked, stomping over to them and waving his huge arms.

"Tell him," Castor said to Bruce. "Tell him what you nearly did to Mother."

Samson was hyperventilating, but he had stopped throwing his fit. At last, he was listening to the words coming out of Castor's mouth. Perhaps he already knew that Bruce had nearly killed Sage after escaping from Louis, but he certainly hadn't done anything about it.

"I-I know!" Samson sputtered, eyes oscillating between the twins and the felled Lolligo on the ground. "I know what he did and I already apologized to Sage!"

"An apology is not enough."

"It was a misunderstanding!"

"But he nearly shot me with a goddamn laser when Damian and I went looking for you at the safe house," Sage spat. "So my boys have every right to be cautious."

Samson looked devastated to hear that Sage was green-lighting attacks on Lolligo, but he understood the justification because he didn't bicker. Castor and Pollux weren't going to act rashly without purpose, knowing that a Lolligo as an ally was detrimental to their success. Bruce's actions, however, were unacceptable and someone had to dish out punishment. It should have been Samson, but the twins certainly didn't mind getting their hands dirty.

As for Sage, she didn't stick around to ask questions. She knew exactly where Samson kept the scooters and grabbed one. Before any of the Lolligo could protest, she hopped on and took off after Damian, who was her priority right now. She knew that Castor and Pollux would be right behind her, and she was glad for this small reprieve from her sons because she burst into tears.

"DAMIAN!" Sage called into nothingness.

Night had fallen. It was so dark that Sage only knew where she was because of the moon and its very faint light. She used it as a beacon to help her navigate these empty lands. For some reason, the farther south she went, the harder it was to breathe. She didn't know if it was the radiation levels, or maybe it was just her body that couldn't take so much heat, but she felt sick. The wind was roaring in her ears and it never stopped, even when she came to a skidding halt before the aggressive Damian in the middle of nowhere.

He looked like he was throwing a tantrum. He clutched his head as his body continued to swell, probably from a proliferation of cells, and he morphed into the ugliest monster Sage had ever seen. With a double snout, multiple eyes, torn-up wings, and limbs growing out of everywhere, this was the biggest mess of Cells she had come across since her journey through Cell Land.

"NO!" Damian roared in a voice that wasn't his. "NO!"

Sage ran straight to him. She didn't care about the flailing tentacles or the talons that pierced her as he continued to morph. The Damian she knew was gone, but that didn't stop her from wrapping her arms around his body. She squeezed her eyes closed as she clung to him for dear life. She held her sobs in and opened her mind.

Sage communicated so many things to him at that moment. She showed him a series of memories that they had shared in the past, from when she had first seen him on that palanquin, met him at Mousafeld, and joined him on their first campaign, to when they had fallen in love, fought in so many battles together, and married in the Carat District.

Damian did stop fidgeting. He did settle down some, body relaxing despite how it kept mutating.

"No matter what, darling . . ." Sage whispered against his head. It was in the shape of a rod now, full of squirming veins, but this was her beautiful Damianos . . . and she was never letting him go. "I will always love you. And you are still the most beautiful man on the planet."

Damian stopped whining. Sage never let him go. Even when he

was ten times her size and in the shape of a large mass of Cells, Sage didn't loosen her grip. Tears streamed down her eyes, but that was her only outlet.

"Mother?!" Castor exclaimed from behind her.

He and Pollux were here. Samson and Jamie were, too, both on one of those scooters that was way too small for their bodies. Nonetheless, they pulled up at the site.

More tentacles grew out of Damian's body. They sprouted like roots, weaving into the ground. Damian's skin hardened into what felt like a shell. A thin layer of mucus burned anything that came into contact with it.

"Mom!" Pollux grabbed her and plucked her right off his father's body. Castor checked her for any wounds, but the mucus wasn't too deadly. Not yet at least.

"What's happening?" Pollux croaked at the sight of his father. "What the fuck's going on?!"

Castor turned to Samson, who stood there, looking quite dumbfounded. Not as much as when he had heard Bruce had intentionally shot at Sage, though.

"His Cells were expanding and replicating," Samson said softly. "And there was no way for me to fix it. I didn't have time."

"What's going to happen to him?!" Pollux cried.

Samson shook his head. "I don't know. I have yet to truly analyze the serum that Nova gave him, but my guess is that it mutated his Cells rather than preserved them. To be frank, I wasn't even able to draw blood before the sedative I administered became obsolete."

"So now what?" Pollux croaked, hyperventilating. "You can fix him, right?"

Silence from the Lolligo said they couldn't make any promises. From the looks on their ugly squid faces, they had dabbled very little in the sort of mutations a hybrid could go through when exposed to potentially harmful treatments. Perhaps Samson hadn't allowed for that sort of experimentation in Elysium. Damian had been quick to shut them down in Emerald City. Louis was the only fucker of the group that had taken liberties.

As for Sage, she quickly lost all the strength in her legs. Her body was wrecked, and fatigue was finally catching up to her. Emotionally, the last of her control shattered. Her love for Damian was about to burst out of her chest, and it didn't help that she was witness to a mass of flesh and limbs that would never be a person again.

Sage leaned against one of Damian's sides, noting how his skin was no longer smooth and soft—it felt hard and rough like a cocoon. Memories of her sons in cocoons and then the picture of what she had left behind post hibernation made her shiver. She started shaking violently as realization tore through her and grief finally found its place in her heart.

Damian was gone. There was no way this was hibernation. To this second, his body was still growing, morphing out of control. Roots covered the ground like a net, even sprung up like thick tree trunks. He was shifting into a form there was no coming back from, and that's what hit Sage the hardest.

"We need to get her out of there," Samson said at once. "Sage—we—can be devoured."

And Sage would love nothing more. She would die the happiest woman alive so long as it was with Damian. She, however, couldn't be selfish. She had a city to run and a family to defend, and so she let Castor and Pollux sweep her into their arms.

Sage just shook some more. She wrapped her arms around Castor's neck and buried her face in his shoulder where it was nice and warm. She held back her sobs, but the tears flowed freely.

"Get her back to the city," Samson said to the boys. "I'll stay here with the Warlord and see what I can do."

I can't leave him," Sage whispered to Castor. "Please don't take me away . . ."

So Castor and Pollux set up a camp here. They had those portable homes that made the middle of nowhere an ideal place to stay. This one was the size of a single family home, equipped with a living room, kitchen, two bedrooms, and a bathroom.

For Sage, it reminded her of the first time she had made love to Damian. August had died and Wren had been kicking through Wolfeld's junkyard. Those had been such uncertain times. Sage had had no idea if she would ever get back into Diamond City. Somehow, she and Damian had been able to gather enough forces to make it possible, although Sage would have never thought Bram would sell his own daughters to the council.

The memories were painful to relive, but Sage still found solace in the comfort of her bedroom. She had Castor and Pollux with her at all times, keeping an eye out on the Lolligo and their father. When Sage had the strength, she got up to see his body through the window of her home. She could see his large outline in the distance, and it brought tears to her eyes every time.

Castor and Pollux seemed to know how to distract her so she didn't fall into a horrible depression. Pollux loved to tell stories a lot like Damian did, and that's how Sage caught up with a lot of what she had missed the past thirty years. Castor liked to play boardgames and he proved from very early on that Sage wasn't going to stand a chance against him.

Candice and Olivia came by to see her as well. While it destroyed the little control Sage had over her emotions, she couldn't be happier to see that her nieces were alive and so . . . mature. Beautiful.

And then there was Geoffrey, of course.

He no longer had his small afro. He was completely bald now, but his head was shaped nicely and his features were fine and easy on the eyes. He looked a lot like Wyatt, which always made Sage smile. Thirty years later, Geoffrey was an Enhanced who hadn't aged much, but he had a lot more muscle since joining the military. Sage could see it through his uniform. All soldiers wore black cuffs.

"Always wanted to be like you," Geoffrey said to Sage proudly. "Even if it meant giving up engineering."

Candice raised her hand. "And I'm a writer now, Aunt Sage. I found out I really liked it in school. It helped me escape a lot of life's problems. Now that Micah's managing the restaurant, I was able to get a job at a local news station."

"I am so happy to see that you girls moved on with your lives," Sage said. She was curled up in an armchair, sipping on the hot chocolate Castor had made for her. "Truly."

"It hurt us," Olivia admitted quietly. Her quads were so thick they took nearly half the couch. "At first, it was hard for us to move on. Damian was the most devastated one of all, but he kept it together so well. Dr. X gave us all hope, and so long as you were alive, we kept our heads up."

Sage made a face. "Did that creep seriously examine me while I was in a cocoon?"

Pollux laughed. He was sitting on the floor, legs crossed. "I'm glad I'm not the only one who thinks he's a creep! He asks me about you every time he sees me in Ruby City, and I can't fucking look him in those googly eyes of his. I just say that you're on a mission to help Dad and that you don't want to see his strange ass."

Geoffrey laughed. "That's harsh."

"It's true, though. I just want to respect Mom's wishes."

Sage smiled lovingly at her son. The last thing she wanted to see was Dr. X at her doorstep.

"Shouldn't you have Dr. X examine you, Aunt Sage?" Olivia asked. She was fully aware that Sage was supposed to look like a twenty-year-old, not a fifty-year-old.

"Fuck me, Olivia," Sage spat. "I'm not that desperate. Although Damian clearly was." She had muttered that last part, but Pollux heard her loud and clear.

He roared with laughter. "I always wonder what Dad sees in him, too. *Still* sees in him, because he trusts him with his life."

"Well, Sage has Samson, doesn't she?" Geoffrey said, amused. "I'd say the Squid—"

"SHH!" Everyone hushed him. Samson was in the kitchen, making dinner. Sage laughed this time.

"Oh!" Geoffrey covered his mouth. "Sorry—the *Lolligo*'s been doing a good job with her. Sage still has a bit of recovering to do, but she's improved a lot since she's moved back here, hasn't she?"

"Samson is not a doctor," Castor said, dropping more marshmallows into Sage's cup. "And neither is Jamie. The Lolligo love experimenting with human anatomies, but they are far from experts. Dr. X, on the other hand—whom you all seem to enjoy ridiculing— is an excellent doctor. And so everyone in Emerald City trusts him. When it came to Mother's cocoon and Father's condition, there was no one else to turn to."

Pollux snorted. He flipped his hair back. "And look at what fucking good that did us. He tells us to leave Mom's cocoon alone for fear something would rupture, then Pretty-Boy Louis comes along and what does he do? Kidnaps Mom from the fucking cocoon like Dr. X told us not to. And let's not even get started on Dad—Dr. X never found a cure for him." He shrugged. "I think Dr. X is all talk. Just because he studied every Enhanced in Mousafeld doesn't make him a god. I say he did it more to see people naked than because he cares about their wellbeing—"

Sage dribbled hot chocolate all over her lap. She laughed loudly. Pollux joined in again. The only one who didn't look amused by all this was Castor.

"No worries, bro." Pollux clapped Castor's shoulder. "We all know you like it when you get your penis examined. I mean, I like it, too, but not when Googly Eyes does it—"

"*Shut*," Castor hissed at him, "*up*."

"Oh, God." Sage's stomach churned. It didn't help that she had a vivid image of Dr. X touching her son's genitals, but according to Castor, Pollux was the one acting like a dick.

"He's done no such thing, Mother." Castor glared at Pollux, who was dying on the floor. "Nothing that goes beyond a doctor's duty in ensuring their patient is healthy. Or else Father would have had him executed."

"True." Pollux cleared his throat. He composed himself and sat back up again. "Dad was always there to ensure no one took advantage of us. Even Gertrude and the others are never safe, no matter how friendly they are."

"What did Dr. X do to me in the cocoon?" Sage asked, still worried. She didn't care what reassurances anyone else gave—that guy was still a creep.

"Well," Candice said, still chuckling at Pollux, "he couldn't really do much. There was no way to break the cocoon without hurting you. The most we could do was scan the cocoon to see what was inside, and for the first ten years, there was nothing."

Sage furrowed her brows. "What?"

"It's as if your body disappeared," Olivia said. "But you were still alive because there was movement in there. We weren't sure what it was, but your body was reconstructing itself. It's as if you were being born again, Aunt Sage."

Castor had pictures to show her. While Pollux protested exposing Sage to such images, Castor smacked his brother's hand away and hissed.

"She has the right to know!"

Sage's hands shook as she scrolled through the images on Castor's phone. She was mesmerized by the messy strings of flesh and squirming mounds of . . . something.

"Do you remember anything?" Olivia asked curiously.

Sage shook her head. "Only snippets . . . voices. Nothing crazy, though. Sometimes it felt like I was dreaming."

"This is all so crazy, isn't it?" Geoffrey leaned forward on his knees. "How you died and came back to life like that? While it wasn't a death-death, essentially you went through what Squids— Lolligo—go through."

"Does it happen to all hybrids?" Olivia asked.

She was implying if it could happen to Castor and Pollux, who shook their heads.

"We don't have the same abilities as a hybrid," Castor said.

Sage arched a brow.

"We can't create Enhanced," Pollux explained. "Not with our blood. It's not quite as potent as yours or Dad's."

"We are, however, just as strong as hybrids," Castor said, puffing up his chest a bit..

"My point is Venus hibernated just like Aunt Sage," Olivia said, ignoring the arrogance. "But did Jared hibernate? If Damian's going through some debilitation—which has nothing to do with Cell X— then why didn't Jared?"

"Who's to say Jared didn't go through something similar?" Sage said. "He was pretty weak when I fought him."

"I think that Louis' remedy made him worse." Pollux shook his head with a grimace. "That was all bullshit, and we should have never given him that shot to begin with!"

"What would the alternative have been?" Castor asked, sounding bored with it all. "We were out of options, and if we didn't act fast, he would have died."

"So then now what?"

"Well . . . Samson is out there. And I believe Nova and a few other medical professionals are going to analyze his condition."

"Don't trust them," Pollux said, sipping on the last of his hot chocolate.

"We don't have a choice," Castor said patiently. "They're on their way here now, actually, and I think Micah is tagging along with them."

"Say, where is Micah?" Sage asked.

Geoffrey snorted. "With his new girlfriend."

Sage didn't quite catch on to the implications of "girlfriend" until Micah walked into the house with Kendra at his side. It took Sage a long while to register what the two holding hands meant. She was horribly behind in all the Ruby City drama and gossip, so she gasped when it finally hit her.

They were *together*. And all Sage could say to that was thank God because Hayes was an asshole. Kendra must have finally seen the light, or perhaps she had detoxed from all those bad flings she'd had, because she looked so much happier now. She always had her hair done, but she actually smiled and acted like a human being (not a robot). Even so, she still paid her reverence to Sage. To think Kendra had known who Ruby really was all along.

But if there was anyone who was bursting with happiness at the sight of Sage it was Hamilton. That dog raced into the living room and dove right into Sage's chest, knocking her and the armchair over backward.

"Hamilton!" Sage laughed. She wrapped her arms around his beautiful, sleek body. His coat was groomed and shiny. His tongue was huge and it passed over every inch of her face.

"He's been a good dog," Kendra said happily. "Always guards Crystal Light with his life . . . and sleeps by your door, Sage."

"That's because he misses me!" Sage held Hamilton's face. She got panting and slobber all over her, but that was fine. Hamilton was her partner, and she loved him so much. She carried him in her arms as she fixed her chair and set him on her lap, even if he was way too big to lounge on anyone's legs. The cutest part was when Hamilton rolled onto his back and exposed his belly. Now he looked like a big baby.

"Why does he only do that with you?" Micah grumbled. "I've tried so hard to cuddle with him, but he just steps away."

"I guess he just likes me more," Sage said happily.

"And how are you doing, Aunt Sage?"

The grief of Damian's condition was obvious, but it was her frail body and thin hair that really drew attention. While most of Sage's hair had grown back, she had cut it for an even look. It was in a bob style now. She wondered what Damian would say if he saw her like this . . . He used to love to braid her hair . . .

"I think she's been recuperating," Pollux said happily. He reached for Sage's hand and rubbed it with a smile on his face. Hamilton sniffed his wrist. "And I think a little bit more time is all that she needs."

The question was, of course, if Damian would recover. Like Sage, Samson never strayed far from Damian's body, but he did seem helplessly lost on how to fix him. He came by every evening to check up on her, which included updating her on Damian's condition and making sure she was getting enough food into her body.

He hadn't even mentioned the word "train" because Sage didn't move around too much.

It was hard to do anything without Damian.

One evening in the month of Innocence, exactly three months after Sage had returned to Ruby City, she and Samson were in the kitchen all by themselves. Castor and Pollux were in the office, delegating leadership roles to Gertrude, L, and Tai, and formulating strategies to combat Wren in Diamond City. Hamilton was curled up by the table, waiting for scraps.

"His body has greatly mutated," Samson said quietly. He was standing over the stove, doing what he did best: pork stew. He was making the broth extra spicy since it was positively freezing outside. Fall was upon them, but not without a vicious drop in temperature. "And while it's stopped growing so quickly, it doesn't stop completely. His body is the size of a small shopping center now."

Sage said nothing. She was staring at her blank little notebook, at a complete loss for poems. She hadn't been able to write a single thing since Damian had mutated.

"I'm still trying to figure it out, of course," Samson said quickly. "Jamie and I. Just like we've been looking over Cell Land and the goop left behind from Venus' transformation. Completely different cases, but it brings me that much closer to understanding how Cells work."

"Louis killed him," Sage said quietly.

Samson looked at her over his shoulder. The great sigh that left his chest said that he couldn't refute that. Directly, perhaps, Louis wasn't at fault. It was Nova, after all, who had administered the faulty treatment. Still, Sage couldn't see how that changed anything. Damian was as good as dead. He had changed into the very monster he didn't want to become.

"Just give me more time," Samson said. "Faye told me everything that you did for her in Elysium, how you decimated those hybrids." Samson cracked a smile. He was trying to make light of an otherwise serious situation, but Sage wasn't buying it. "You saved her from being raped."

"Is that what this is now?" Sage said. She kept staring at the blank page in front of her. "A favor for a favor?"

"No," Samson replied strictly. "This is a brother and sister who will do anything for each other. And that's what I vow to do, Sage."

"Like the sister you used to have when you were human?"

Samson's large frame visibly froze.

"I saw the photograph in Faye's closet," Sage muttered. "I figured it was you. Although I will admit I prefer you as a Lolligo."

Samson swallowed thickly. He said nothing, though. Either he didn't remember his past life . . . or he didn't want to talk about it. What would be the point? Emotionally, Lolligo were rocks. They didn't care if it didn't affect the way they lived.

Regardless of Samson's reasons, it was nice to know that he was on Sage's side.

Sort of.

"Why did he attack me, Samson?" Sage said.

Samson took a deep breath. "I think you know the answer to that. You and Damian spooked him."

"We're supposed to be allies."

"I know. I explained that to him."

"What the fuck is wrong with him?" Sage spat. "I risked my life to kill Rhett and that's how he repays me?"

"He's been punished," Samson said quietly. "I assure you. I know he deserves death, but I'm looking at the bigger picture here. There are only a few Lolligo left . . . and I can't find it in me to kill him."

Sage supposed she understood that part. Were it any other person, she would have severed Bruce's fucking head from his shoulders and crushed that goddamn egg for opening fire on her and Damian. But she needed Samson right now . . . She wouldn't have had any kind of hope otherwise.

The twins were fighting for control over Diamond City, but whatever strategies they were employing never reached her ears. It was clear they were making an effort to keep her out of any wars or trouble.

As the new year approached, Sage didn't see many improvements in her mental or physical health. While all the Slainium was out of her system by now, she hadn't picked up a sword at all. How on earth had Damian found the will to fight while Sage had been asleep? Mustering the strength to do anything but lounge around the house all day was so difficult . . .

Sage knew it was wrong because there was so much of life to enjoy, but guilt trips didn't make it any easier to get up and move. She preferred to stay away from family and friends so no one would have to see her mope. There were so many amazing people to talk to in Ruby City—Paige and Pedro asked about her all the time, according to Micah—but she didn't want to bring anyone down.

Instead, Sage wanted to spend all the time she could with Damian. So she'd get up in the middle of the night, step out onto the snow through her window, and quickly and quietly sneak away from the house so Castor and Pollux wouldn't hear her. Hamilton sensed all her movements, but he didn't intervene when he knew where she was going.

With fierce winds blowing in her face, Sage trudged across the Outskirts and into the forest. It wasn't exactly made up of trees, though—there were trunks of thick flesh with bloody string and tissue hanging everywhere. It was a scene taken straight out of a horror film, but Sage didn't feel scared. In fact, she grew wondrous as she stepped into the red abyss, looking at all the squirming pieces of muscle and tendons. She rested her hand on some. The ring on her right hand glinted beneath the moonlight. She closed her eyes and smiled because she remembered the party in Centerfeld.

Green and silver. Sage had always said that Damian was a sexy fairy man wandering through the woods. She could smell him, too, the teakwood and lavender that was so prevalent on his skin. It was from his favorite cologne, which Sage had asked Micah and Kendra to purchase on her behalf.

"When you get better, I know you'll be using it," Sage said to Damian. She placed the gift on the ground, its cute little bow shimmering. She smiled at the mess above her. "I know you'll take a shower and want to smell good. This time, can I blow-dry your hair?"

"But of course, darling." Damian chuckled. "All you had to do was ask."

Sage shook her head. "I don't know how to use that roller brush."

"Evidently."

"You're such an asshole."

"But that's what you love about me."

Sage snorted. There was no way she was going to admit to that. She was feeling a bit weak, so she took a seat on the ground.

"Why don't you rest, darling?" Damian asked.

Perhaps she would. Sage leaned her head back against a trunk and quickly dozed off. She woke up to the call of her name and then a rough shake of her shoulders.

"Mom?!"

Sage jumped a bit. Pollux quickly picked her up from the ground.

"Mom, what are you doing here?" Pollux panted in her face. "Were you here the whole damn night?"

It was morning. It was just hard to tell with all the gray clouds up above them.

"I had to give the cologne to your father," Sage muttered, rubbing her eyes.

Pollux turned his head. Castor, who was standing right behind him, did the same.

"What cologne?" Pollux said, confused. "I don't see anything."

Sage confirmed the cologne was no longer on the ground where she had left it. Or where she believed she had left it . . .

Castor and Pollux brought her back to the house immediately.

Like a worried mother, Samson was standing outside the door, waiting for them to return with his huge arms crossed. He was nervous as hell, and it wasn't only over Sage's whereabouts and mental state.

"The Mutatio from Diamond City are coming this way," Samson said, more to Sage than the twins, who already knew what the situation was. "It seems your sister is making a move. The bitch is here."

CHAPTER 26

Ruby Red

"**B**odies" and "Mutatio" were the two words that registered in Sage's head. Once they did, her immediate question was what everyone was doing about it.

Castor cleared his throat. He looked a bit irritated that Samson had blurted that out. They might have secretly agreed to keep Sage out of the loop while she was in a delicate state, but Samson wasn't going to bank his chances of survival on anyone else. If only he knew she had just wandered into Damian's nest and spoken to herself.

But wait. Sage hadn't spoken to herself. She had spoken to Damian for sure . . .

"The Mutatio," Sage said slowly. "What do you mean they're here?"

"Exactly that," Samson said stoically. "They've found us. We have those fucking bats in the Outskirts that are looking for us. I don't have any doubt that they are under Wren's control. They've become her tools and are extremely dangerous. I never dreamed they'd find us all the way out here so quickly . . ."

"We've had to quarantine everyone," Castor said. "And it's creating quite the panic."

"But the weapons have come along," Pollux said with hope in his tone. He was looking at Samson. "Right?"

Samson had stayed to take care of Damian, but apparently Jamie and Bruce were in the middle of working on weapons that rivaled the Scarfaces'. Most of all, they were powered by Surgium. They were supposed to give Diamond City a fighting chance against those monsters. Word was there were a few prototypes in the hands of Ruby City's security force, but what good were a few measly half-ass guns going to do against a horde of Mutatio?

"Yes," Samson answered Pollux slowly. "But that's still going to take some time. What we're doing right now is good enough: Emerald City forces are on standby, and when we're ready, we'll fight back. Unfortunately, there isn't much we can do about Ruby City. It's too late to evacuate."

"What do you mean it's too late to evacuate?" Sage said, blinking hard. Was Samson seriously implying that the Mutatio were here already? "What the fuck are you talking about—?"

"We can't move all those goddamn people, Sage! We've instructed them to hide and that's the best we can do." Samson oscillated between Sage and her sons. Then he glanced at the walls of their house. "We'll need to move or we'll be caught out here—"

"I'm not moving," Sage said at once. "Not only do those people need our help, but what about Candice and Olivia? What about Damian?"

"Mother." Castor took her hands and got on his knees. This was a sign of submission—of respect—to Sage. He kneaded her knuckles as he said, "Father will be fine. Because Father is . . . not a body anymore."

"I'm not leaving," Sage said.

"You are in danger here. It will only be a matter of time before those Mutatio find us—find *you*."

"Then why the fuck haven't you dealt with them yet?"

"Because there are *thousands*, Sage," Samson spat. "And we don't exactly have the man or firepower to get rid of them all, understand?"

Sage glanced at her sword in the corner of the room. She said so much with that little gesture without having to utter a single syllable. All three caught on right away.

"There is no warrior out there who can cut down all those mutants with just one sword," Pollux tried to reason with her. "There is a more strategic way of doing this: we have to wait until the Lolligo are finished with the weapons. Because the Mutatio have Cells like we do, Slainium will affect them greatly."

"I see," Sage said quietly. She certainly didn't like the looks she was getting from these three. Not that she felt threatened or like she was in any kind of danger, but there was no chance on earth that they were going to let her stay and fight. Samson had a ton of powerful sedatives at his disposal and he wasn't afraid to use them if it meant saving Sage's life. "So we're supposed to let Ruby City suffer? We have to turn around and run away like cowards?"

"This is strategy," Samson said flatly. "Not retreat."

"When do you plan on leaving?" Sage asked.

"Tonight," Samson said, watching her closely. "I don't anticipate the guns taking much longer. Plus, as Castor said, this is about saving you. The people in Ruby City are in lockdown, ready to deal with the Mutatio, and I don't think anything will happen to Damian all the way out here."

Bullshit.

Bullshit, bullshit, bullshit.

The people in Ruby City were in lockdown and they were "ready to deal with the Mutatio"? That was a fucking lie. And Damian was still in a nest, immobile, and nothing would happen to him if a swarm of Mutatio decided to feast on his flesh?

Samson, Castor, and Pollux already knew that Damian was a lost cause. He was dead to them, completely deformed now that Louis had fucked him up. Castor and Pollux might have had iron

hearts around Sage, but they had already done their share of grieving in private. They had accepted their father's fate and were ready
to turn around and run.

Fucking cowards. What sons of Sage were they?

True, unbridled fear struck Sage in the heart. It felt like a lightning bolt and it knocked the fucking wind out of her. She got so
dizzy that she had to excuse herself for the bathroom.

She threw up violently. She made sure the shower was running
so that no one could hear her. After she finished, she collapsed on
the bathroom floor.

She kept an ear out for movement in the hallway, but there was
nothing.

Actually, Hamilton was sitting right outside her door. He was
whining. But it wasn't loud enough to draw attention. He was in
clear distress, but he trusted Sage's decision to fight.

Sage was expecting to hear Castor and Pollux talking shit about
her, but they were quiet. They seemed to be in her room, packing
her things. There weren't any words exchanged between them at
all. Perhaps there was nothing else to discuss since they had already
made up their minds.

Damian. Sage closed her eyes. She thought very hard about him,
as if her thoughts could make his physical body manifest in front
of her. *I won't give up on you, darling. I know you're going to be fine . . .
just like I was fine . . .*

It was so fucking futile, and Sage was convincing no one, but
she clung to every bit of hope that she could. That's the only way
she was able to get on her feet, take a shower, and throw on some
clothes. As she zipped up her coat and tied her boots, she kept an
ear out for the trio in the house. Silence said the trio still wasn't
talking to each other, but the rummaging suggested that the three
were shoving what they could into luggage to get the hell out of
here.

Sage took a deep breath in and out. She had to steel her will,
just like every single time she stepped onto the battlefield, and man
the fuck up. As an eighteen-year-old, she had grabbed a sword and

fought for her district. As a 118-year-old, she had sought out the Warlord to save her city. And now, as a 152-year-old, she had to go back to Ruby City and defeat the Mutatio for good.

"Hey, Mom," Pollux said, meeting her in the hallway. "Feeling better?"

"A little," Sage replied. She walked right by him without much eye contact. She petted Hamilton's head as he bumbled up next to her. She was searching for her sword, which was still in the corner next to the front door. Castor was in the living room, communicating with people in Ruby City. Samson had her breakfast like always. He was serving it on the kitchen counter.

"All right, Sage," he said with his back to her. "I've got you your eggs, hash browns, and bacon—extra crispy, just the way you like it—"

Shleck.

Sage did it quickly and quietly. She thrust the sword straight into Samson's back and pulled it right back out again. She had missed his heart, but a strike like this with this much Slainium incapacitated him quickly, so Castor and Pollux were going to have to get him to Jamie right away.

Or else the brains behind their weapon-making would be dead.

No one could have done it better than Sage, but Castor and Pollux could detect blood in the air like vampires. Plus, Samson's large body hit the floor with a thud.

"Mom?" Pollux was the first to find her. He was pretty fast, too, dashing into the kitchen as if he had just teleported through dimensions. His eyes widened at Sage and then at Samson's body on the floor. Hamilton remained sitting by the table, looking serious. He already knew this was not the time to ask for scraps. "Mom—w-what did you do?!"

"You two must think I'm fucking stupid, right?" Sage said. She picked up her breakfast and started forking some eggs into her mouth. She leaned back against the counter and crossed her feet at the ankle. "Like I was born yesterday? I don't know what kind of lies the Lolligo and everyone else in Emerald City have been feeding you, but giving up is not how we do things around here. You 'don't have the man or firepower to get rid of them all'? Are you crazy? You have two goddamn armies full of capable people. Fight, damn it—people are depending on you—your *family* is depending on you."

"But it's true!" Pollux started. "There are nearly a *thousand* of those things, Mom!"

"If you don't stop them," Sage said quietly, "then an entire city will die. Your father will die. Is this what Samson convinced you to do? Is this what he wants? To finish off Damian, the last threat to the Lolligo?"

"Of course not," Castor said calmly. "But there is nothing we can do for Father now, Mother. Samson told us there was no coming back from that state—his Cells have mutated beyond repair."

"It's not what any of us want to hear, but it's true!" Pollux croaked. At long last, the feeble dam he had used to keep his emotions at bay came tumbling down. For the first time in six months, since Damian had entered that unstable state, Pollux cried in front of her.

But Sage wasn't sympathetic. She finished her eggs and moved on to the hash browns.

"Right now, your life is more important," Castor said, ignoring his brother's breakdown. "And so we decided—"

"*You* decided," Sage said. "Not 'we'. Why? Is it because I look like shit or because the two of you promoted yourselves to my official babysitters?"

"Mother, that's not it at all. Given the circumstances, this is our best option—"

"Says who?" Sage said. "Says *you*? Without even consulting me?" She grabbed her dagger—Kendra's dagger—and flung it across the room. She hit Castor right in the forehead, knocking him clean off his feet.

Pollux cried out. He shuffled back, tripped over the garbage can, and fell on his ass.

"If you want to retreat, then so be it," Sage hissed at them both.

"But I would have never believed that your father raised you to be a pair of cowards. You are hybrids, far stronger than the rest of the warriors in Ruby City, and it is your duty to *fight*. You fight, damn it, and you certainly never give up on your father, who sacrificed so much to raise you.

"Family comes first." Sage crossed the kitchen. Pollux scooted back from her, cowering. Sage grabbed him by the shirt and hauled him up. She slammed him into the wall. "Get off your ass," she hissed at him, "and get Samson the help he deserves. Then be a good little bitch and go hide in his ship, will you?"

Sage shoved him again. Eyes burning, possibly an amber color, she glared down at him. "Pathetic."

Without another look at the mess in the kitchen, Sage stepped out of the house, Hamilton on her heels. She was grateful that Candice and Olivia hadn't been there to witness this shit-show. She wondered whose side they would have taken, knowing her and her crazy stunts whenever someone she loved was in danger. Right now, their safety took center stage. Sage had no idea what the Mutatio's intentions were, but she prayed that no one had died.

Sage took one of Samson's scooters and didn't waste any time starting her race across the Outskirts toward Ruby City. She didn't look back and she also didn't stop to think if her recklessness would truly get her killed. She supposed, at the moment, she didn't really care. If no one stopped these Mutatio, they were going to take over, kill everyone she loved, and reach Damian's nest eventually.

There were strategic ways to go about this, though. Sage knew about this tunnel entrance because she had explored the hell out of Ruby City before it became populated. It took some time to get to that elusive trapdoor under inches of dirt and grass, but she found it eventually.

Hamilton whined.

"Stay here and keep look-out," Sage said to him. "I'll be fine."

Sage lowered herself into the tunnel. She thought of Damian as she did, how he had held her on the way down and then supported her as they trudged through the darkness. Samson's tunnel to Elysium was a lot bigger than this one—Sage couldn't stand at all. She had to crawl on her hands and knees.

So she started. The tunnel wasn't polished by any means. There was still mud and muck dripping from the ceiling and walls. Sage was already soaked to the bone. She tried not to let it deter her focus and kept her eyes ahead at the never-ending darkness. She was already used to these tight, cramped spaces, but not without Damian.

There was no Damian to push her on or remind her to eat and drink water. There was no warm body to hold or soothing words to inspire confidence in what Sage was doing. Slithering through these tunnels was nuts, and every time Sage came out on the other side, she had horror to face.

At Elysium, it was Ray raping Faye. Now, it was a pitch-black room that was musky as hell.

Sage threw back the trapdoor and took a much-needed breath. She pulled herself up and over the threshold until she was on the floor, on all fours. She curled up for a moment, truly terrified of how dark it was in this storage room, and listened for movement above her loud breathing.

Nothing. All was still.

Not even the clothes hanging on the rack fluttered. The boxes in the corners were stacked neatly.

Indeed, Sage had been in this room before. She and Paige would eat kale chips and talk about life. The Ruby City insignia was on the wall. But nothing about it felt familiar when it was this stuffy.

Gathering her resolve, Sage climbed to her feet. Her knees shook. She nearly fell over as she took those first steps across the room and toward the ajar door. The coppery smell hit her instantly, burning her nostrils on its way up to her brain.

Sage held her mouth. She knew what was coming.

Bodies.

Paige, Pedro, and their children.

The four of them were dismembered. They had been left on the floor like dirt.

Sage found a garbage can to throw up in. She heaved like she never had before. She didn't remember this much bile and this much pain, even when she had beheld the palace in Heart for the first time after Wren's attack. All the death she had witnessed that night—Wren holding Gregory's head—had smashed her over the head. But at least Louis had cleaned up the place. Here—*this*—was raw.

This was hell.

"NO!" Sage wailed into the garbage can. She screamed at the massacre right in front of her eyes. "NO!"

Stupid, stupid, stupid—the Mutatio would hear her for sure! But no matter what Sage did, she couldn't keep it in—she screamed until her throat tore in two.

Crazy thoughts—random thoughts—Sage could bring them back!—If she used her mind, she'd put the bodies together and they'd live—Hell, she could use *her* blood and take care of them immediately—Yes, they'd become Enhanced—it was a brilliant idea!

Sage cut her arm and sprinkled her blood all over the piles of limbs. She ignored the glassy stares from the wide-open eyes and stepped over the tiny hands that used to belong to the children. She wheezed as she continued to let her blood flow like a waterfall, then slipped and fell on the floor again.

She looked up at the body mirror in between the racks of clothes. She gazed straight into her face.

There was blood everywhere.

Sage crawled over to the mirror. She clutched the frame in her hands. She gazed into her reflection.

She wasn't used to short hair. She didn't recognize how thin her face was, either, gaunt as if someone had drained her of blood. Her frame was skinny, too, tender. But why was there so much blood on her?

Sage slammed her head into the mirror. She cracked the glass and her skin. The sting struck her like lightning, but she liked it— she hit the mirror again.

"MOM!"

A pair of hands grabbed her shoulders and yanked her back

against a warm chest. Those arms were as loving as Damian's and held her tightly, to stop her from squirming and finding more dangerous items to break. The sobs from the throat behind her were deep and heart-wrenching. That was true misery right there.

"Here." Castor kneeled on the floor next to them. He had gauze and bandages in his knapsack, which he used to clean Sage's cut and cover any remnants of it. Thankfully, it healed quickly ... but what didn't dissipate was the trauma.

Sage remained in the arms of her son, staring out at the racks of clothes. She saw a leather jacket that she thought Damian would like. She really wanted to buy it for him.

"How much do you think that jacket is?" Sage asked Pollux, looking up at him. "We should ask Paige."

"Mom ..." Pollux croaked. "They're dead."

"We can't stay here." Castor was looking out the window. There weren't any sounds coming from the street, but some undesirable was bound to walk by at some point.

"We can't exactly parade out there, either," Pollux said to him. "Why don't you take a look around and see what's going on?"

Castor complied. Ruby City was way too quiet for their liking. They had Diamond City's entire population here, so where had everyone gone?

"How much is the jacket?" Sage asked Pollux.

"Shh, Mom." Pollux cradled her head and kissed her temple. He picked her up to step away from the bodies. He gazed sadly at the pile in the middle of the floor. Only a Mutatio could have performed such clean slices. There were no guns at play here—this was all shape-shifting.

They waited for Castor to return, but there were no signs of him, even an hour later. Pollux poked his head out through the door, still holding Sage in his arms.

The street lights flickered. There were bodies everywhere.

"Pollux," Sage whispered against his chest. "Take me to them ... I have to give them my blood."

"Mom, they're dead. They can't turn into Enhanced anymore."

"Please, take me."

Pollux wasn't going to listen. Sage could do very little to fight him because she felt so weak. Perhaps he didn't believe that her blood could do any good in a bunch of dead people. Sage used a piece of glass stuck on her sleeve to open another cut in her palm. Pollux didn't notice until they were already down the street and she was letting it drip all over the corpses.

"Mom!" he hissed at her. "Are you for real?"

"I can save them," Sage said.

Something came flying at them out of nowhere. Sage recognized the silhouette way before the Mutatio was in her face—the talons that the thing brandished could cut her whole body into pieces.

Pollux jumped out of the way and Sage jumped out of his arms. She grabbed her sword and flashed forward without hesitation. She would have been an open target, but she was fast, thrusting her sword right through the Mutatio's belly.

The Mutatio looked her straight in the face. Its eyes were big and blank, yellow and glittery. They bore into her soul without a single speck of recognition in them. Whoever this man used to be was long gone. Wren had made sure of that.

It didn't make ending his life any easier, though. Sage had to be quick about slicing his head off and then moving out of the way as his comrades whipped around to attack her next.

Sage jumped again, landed on the Mutatio on the right, and shoved her sword straight through its mouth. Pollux got the one on the left. It looked like his blade was made of Slainium as well. Courtesy of Samson, probably. The three of them had become fast friends in this scheme.

"Damn it!" Pollux panted. "Where the hell is Castor?"

He wasn't anywhere in sight. Sage wondered if he had gone to check on their family at Crystal Light. She was tempted to head there next, but then Pollux pointed to the horizon and said, "Look!"

A scene from her worst nightmares: a swarm of Mutatio rushed through the street like oversized mosquitoes. Ruby City residents were dead all over the place, sprawled on the sidewalks or against cars. Just what kind of quarantine had Castor and Pollux initiated here? Then again, they couldn't stop the Mutatio from crashing through windows and hauling out victims.

Sage had to kill if she wanted to get to Candice and Olivia. Pollux hesitated at first, but he jumped in after his mother to help her slay the monsters. Thankfully, it didn't take much to cut one down when they had Slainium at their disposal. It seemed a bit too easy, but maybe that was because the Mutatio weren't in their right minds thanks to so many Cells—they didn't seem to have a whole lot of coordination. Some were more dead than alive.

Sage couldn't do anything about the humans those Mutatio used to be in Elysium, but she could save the Ruby City residents. There was hope—even for the corpses on the street—so Sage opened another cut and trickled her blood right over them. If Venus and Wren could do it, why couldn't she?

"Mother?!"

Castor.

Sage looked up and saw him burst out of Crystal Light.

"Mother, come!" Castor waved her over frantically.

Sage dashed inside with Pollux right behind her. There were more bodies on the lobby floor, but Sage was ready to feed them her blood. Pollux grabbed her and steered her right out of there, but not before Sage made sure she dripped as much red over their eyes and mouths as possible.

They followed Castor into the hall. There were signs of struggle here, too, and Sage could picture some of it in her head: Mutatio slamming against the doors and tearing them down; anyone in the way had scrambled for cover, scurrying behind whatever bookcase they could find or into whatever closet was open. Not everyone had been lucky, though, and the proof was on the floor.

More bodies. Sage tried to tell Pollux to stop, but Castor was taking them to the basement.

Candice, Olivia, Micah, and Kendra were among a group of survivors. Someone must have thrown them all down here when the Mutatio had invaded. Sage pictured Geoffrey as one of the ones who had taken the initiative, maybe along some of Ruby City's defenders like Randall. Where on earth were they?

"Ruby!" Travis croaked, popping out of a shadowy corner.

"Save us!" Jasmine cried, hands on her head.

"What's going on out there?!" someone else cried.

"Where's Geoffrey?" Sage said; Candice and Olivia went bumbling over to her.

"A-Aunt Sage?" Candice croaked when she saw all the blood on Sage's face.

"Dead..." Micah murmured from the floor. He and Kendra were both up against the wall. "We were... dead. We're supposed to be... dead."

Sage didn't know what they were talking about because Candice and Olivia didn't let her focus on them for too long.

"You can't fight!" Olivia exclaimed. But this was the Optimum, who was supposed to be indestructible, so Candice stepped forward despite her aunt's feeble condition and said, "Geoffrey—Geoffrey went off to fight!"

There was a boom outside, making everyone in the basement scream. Sage ran off, followed by her sons, to see what was happening so close to the complex.

Just more Mutatio. *Everywhere.* Bodies, blood, and death. Perhaps a good chunk of the population had managed to find cover and stay hidden, but what about the ones who hadn't been so lucky? All the ones lying facedown on the street or cut into pieces because Wren wanted to cause as much misery as possible? Jo's Yo-Go employees were sprawled outside, throats slit.

"Blood..." Sage whispered. "My... blood."

Castor and Pollux kept pulling her along, though. It became a tug-of-war with the two of them, because Sage didn't want to give up on all these people. She knew her blood was magical and it could do so many great things, like turn humans into Enhanced, and she was sure it could do something now, even if all these poor people were dead.

Sage choked on a sob, but she didn't have much time to cry. Castor and Pollux carried her down the street, one under each of her arms, and planted her right in front of that wretched building with the dead Lolligo and heaps of radiation.

Science of Tomorrow.

The Lolligo had cleaned it up, of course. Samson knew how to contain the radiation and Jamie used it to create Surgium. They had taken the corpses and analyzed them, but they had never told Sage their findings. As for the rest of the building, Samson, Jamie, and Bruce had had a field day going through all the Old World research and trinkets.

Sadly, none of it mattered when Mutatio were standing on the building like gargoyles. Unlike last time, the Mutatio looked . . . messier. As if someone had thrown bucketfuls of acid all over them. Their skin was bubbling and these massive warts were releasing pus.

Just like Taz, Sage told herself. *That's what these monsters are. Too many Cells.*

Now, the Mutatio were moaning. Their faces were distorted, eyeballs looking like they were going to explode from their sockets. Their mouths opened and closed, but they couldn't speak. The sounds coming from their throats were indecipherable. Some of them flailed while others twitched. There was no purpose to their movements. They weren't even trying to escape their hell, probably because they didn't know they were in hell to begin with. They were just following orders, whatever words Wren was delivering into their minds.

Sage closed her eyes. She clutched her sword as tightly as she ever had in her life. She had been doing this for so long, since she and August had become lovers in school and practiced fighting together. Her first training session was the night after she'd had sex for the first time, when August convinced her to help the coalition get rid of the corrupt Overseer in the Cut District.

"*We need you, Star,*" August had said to her. "*Who else can help us fight?*"

That's right. Sage had to fight. Clearly, there was no one else here to do it. Samson was too selfish to risk Sage without high enough probabilities of victory. Castor and Pollux didn't know what else to do, either. It always came down to Sage, and she accepted that. She wasn't mad about it. It's what she had been bred to do, after all.

"Forgive me," Sage said. She was talking to the groaning Mutatio, but she was also talking to God. She had to kill. She closed her eyes. Maybe if she didn't see it, it'd be better. "But I can't let you live on like this."

Sage lunged. She never saw what she was doing, but she felt everything—how the blade cut into flesh, severed cartilage, bones, and tendons. She heard everything, too—how the blade *slurped* through soft tissue and malfunctioning organs. Most of all, she smelled everything—how gases escaped the corpses and shot up her nose, and how that thick coppery stench of blood attacked her brain and never left.

"Ow . . ."

Someone was groaning.

"Ow . . . ."

Sage wasn't sure how many Mutatio she had cut down by now. She couldn't feel the sun on her face and shoulders anymore, so maybe dusk was approaching.

"OW!"

Sage didn't stop. She couldn't stop. She heard some screams in the distance from Mutatio that were more awake and she sensed them ready to flee Ruby City. She couldn't let them get away, so she leapt into the air, as swift as an acrobat, and cut them down in their places. What kind of Mutatio were these? Children? Women? Young men like Charles with their whole lives ahead of them?

"OW!"

Sage never wavered because she couldn't. Her job wasn't done yet. She had more Mutatio to maim, to ensure that no one in Ruby City got hurt. She turned around and jumped right back into the heart of her city.

"OW!"

More bodies, more groans.

"OW!"

The sun was coming up again—Sage could feel it behind her eyelids—

"Mom!"

"Mother!"

Two presences came up behind her. Friendlies, of course—those were her sons who laid their hands on her shoulders. They got her to settle down because Sage had already done her job. She had decimated every living Mutatio in between these buildings. It had taken her a whole night and day, but she had done it. And now she was looking up at a true monster.

The one she had seen at Elysium's palace that day she had gone shopping with Damian at Top Wares. The one Lilian had transformed into. The one Lilian had given everything to achieve, including her body.

It was every human's dream. Who didn't want power and glory after so many years of crawling in the lower classes? Now was Lilian's chance to prove herself and show her master that she could conquer Ruby City. Rhett was dead, but Wren was very much alive, lounging in her throne in Diamond City somewhere.

She was probably laughing her head off.

This was hilarious.

CHAPTER 27

Puppets

Lilian's body wasn't like the other Mutatio's. It was in the middle of morphing, Cells replicating and taking shape. It seemed Wren's Cells affected everyone in different ways. Lilian looked bigger and sturdier than the rest of the beasts standing around her. Sage wondered if Wren had given Lilian a special concoction, something stronger, to make her stick out above the others. Lilian must have given the sob story of her life, promising to fulfill whatever wishes necessary so long as she had power. How many times had she been raped by hybrids? Or had boredom blown out her senses?

Wait—had that had been Wren in the back room that day?

Whatever the case, Lilian was a well-developed Mutatio now. She seemed cohesive enough to think and rationalize and know that the young man in her arms was of dire importance to Sage.

Sadly, it no longer mattered that Lilian used to be a friend. All that mattered was that fucking *thing* was holding Geoffrey in between her claws, his head poised and ready for crushing. Lilian used to be so pretty, but all Sage could see was a demented, fucked-up psychopath who had way too much power in her hands and way too much of her sister's influence.

It was the gleam in Lilian's eyes: pure Wren.

Sage didn't move. Not if she wanted to save Geoffrey and assess the best way to tear him out of Lilian's hold.

"*The Optimum...*" It wasn't Lilian's mouth that was moving. In fact, there wasn't any sound coming from her at all. The words were in the air, a projection of sorts. "*Queen of Diamonds. You never stop fighting, do you?*"

Sage pointed her sword at the monster in front of her. Now that she had opened her eyes and could see again, her panting escalated. Her eyes burned with tears. Misery filled her belly and spread throughout her whole body.

Castor and Pollux kept her grounded. Their hands became heavier and heavier on her shoulders. They each had a sword, stained with blood. They were ready to kill again. They were ready to join their mother's crusade. They weren't cowards.

"SAGE!"

Gertrude.

Sage looked up at the aircraft hovering close by. Gertrude and her crew were here. They must have come for her as soon as they had learned her location. From their sweaty, bloody faces, they had been fighting, too.

But her friends weren't the focus at the moment. Sage's eyes went right back to the amber ones peering at her from atop that gigantic mouth spread in a grin.

Hilarious.

Suddenly, there was an earthquake. The ground shook, cracked, debris toppled off buildings, and another horde of Mutatio found them. Actually, there were only about a dozen, but still.

This was insane. More of them? How was this living hell a reality?

"*We...*" said Lilian's voice once more, without the use of vocal cords, "*are hybrids. And we... are the new species.*"

"Perhaps so!" exclaimed Paul, making Sage look up again. To her, he would always be Preacher. That's what he did best.

He answered the powerful Lilian without a speck of fear in

his eyes. He always had something to say at the right moment. He kept his head together in the roughest of times. He helped Damian through so much misery and he offered words of wisdom to Sage when she needed it most. God only knew how many times he had drilled some discipline into the twins, too.

"Perhaps hybrids are the new species," Preacher said. "But they are in no way gods. They are merely tools to be used by both Lolligo and the humans. That's what the term 'hybrid' implies, my lady."

Lilian roared. The power of it made the ground rumble some more—Sage kept close to the ground.

"*Do you not understand?!*" Lilian spewed. "*Hybrids are even more powerful than Lolligo because our Cells are compatible with that of humans! We can take humans, change them, control them, and even bring them back to life, and that's exactly what I've done!*"

There was barking from afar.

Hamilton!

Sage wanted to run and help out her companion with whatever was happening, but she couldn't move a muscle when Geoffrey was still in this bitch's hold.

"*Come over here and I'll let him go,*" Lilian said coolly. "*But it's time for you to die.*"

"You're not going to let him go," Sage said quietly. "First of all, you're not Lilian—you're my fucking sister's puppet. It's obvious you take great pleasure in striking down people like cattle. How is my family any different? As soon as I'm gone, you'll do them, too. Even if I sent them off on a ship, you'd still delight in tracking them down and slaughtering them like animals."

Lilian looked impressed. Sage had faced far too many fucked-up adversaries to not know how to play this game already.

"You have to live, Sage!" Geoffrey croaked from Lilian's talons. He might have been trained—an Enhanced himself—but Wren's elite line of puppets was powerful, too. Sage still had a hard time believing that Rhett had been behind creating this sea of ugly creatures, as fancily as he used to prance around the palace in those

411

weird-ass robes. "Your blood can bring them back, don't you see? YOUR BLOOD SAVED MY BOY WHEN HE WAS DEAD!"

Sage blinked. She wasn't too sure what Geoffrey was talking about.

A few of the new Mutatio tried their hands at the Optimum and they leapt forward.

Sage threw up her sword. She met their attacks head on, clashing with all those claws every time they swiped at her. She grit her teeth as the little strength she had started to wane after so many hours of fighting. She was so utterly exhausted, but she wasn't alone.

Castor and Pollux jumped in. Like a tag team, they took over the fighting on their mother's behalf. They knew their way around a sword as if they had learned how to wield one before even picking up a pencil. Sage pictured Damian thrusting one into each of their hands before they could utter, "Poppa." Not only could they intuit each of the Mutatio's moves, but they knew each other, too: Castor struck one in the face and then Pollux ducked from behind the other to evade Castor's blade. While Sage would have been thoroughly impressed, she was thinking the same thing Damian's crew was.

"They're so strong!" Tate croaked, clutching his gun to his chest.

"Don't you get it?" Lilian sneered. *"My Cells!"*

While it was obvious that the Mutatio would be a cut above the average human, it wasn't likely they'd be able to best Castor and Pollux, who were both hybrids. Like Sage, they had decimated waves of these monsters, too. That's how Sage knew these dozen Mutatio in particular were something special. Wren must have been experimenting . . . Sage didn't know if it was the rapid multiplication of those mutated Cells, but something was very different with these twelve. She didn't like how confidently those Mutatio, who were supposed to be a lesser breed, danced around the trained Castor and Pollux or how—just with their fists—they shattered sternums and incapacitated them both.

Sage jumped in. She didn't even think twice—with her sons on the ground, gasping for air, she let out a furious yell of her own and stabbed that fucking Mutatio that wouldn't die in the chest.

"Is that the answer?" Lilian cooed. *"Killing them? Are you going to kill the rest of my precious babies, too?"*

Only if they attacked her first. Sage was running on fumes, but she didn't let it show. She brandished her sword in the face of the other eleven, ready to take them on, too. Or so she pretended to be.

These Mutatio took the bait: they didn't move a muscle.

"What did you do to them?!" Pollux exclaimed at Lilian.

"Cells are power," Lilian said, looking a bit sour now. *"But they can be so much more."*

It didn't matter. Ultimately, Sage had to kill Lilian. She had to stop the rest of the Mutatio, too, but it was Lilian who was Wren's most prized possession now. That sick, twisted bitch thought there was no better feeling in the world than to use one of Sage's friends against her.

But Lilian was no longer Lilian and she had chosen this. Sage had to stop her. She had to eliminate her.

Sage braced herself to do just that. She was ready to drive her sword straight through that humongous mouth and silence that fucking voice. She tried not to listen, but she realized those words were not taunts. Those were threats.

"If you move," Lilian snarled, *"then I will kill your friend here."*

"SAGE!" Gertrude cried again.

"JUST KILL HER!" Geoffrey yelled.

End her. Sage's hands shook around her sword. *End her now!*

"Not so fast, Queen of Diamonds!" Lilian waved one of her many arms around. *"As I said ... I will let him go if you comply."*

"What do you want?" Sage asked quietly.

"Your Cells, of course!"

Neither Castor or Pollux protested because this was Sage's conversation. Gertrude and the others kept quiet, too, breaths held at how Sage was going to respond to that.

"I want your Cells," Lilian said again. *"And the Warlord's. He had a glorious amount of power last time we fought. He can turn into a Mutatio, too?"*

Sage clenched her fists. "He's not exactly awake at the moment."

Lilian actually hesitated. "*What do you mean?*"

"He's . . ." Sage fought for control of her thoughts and her body. If she allowed images of Damian to overcome her, she was going to cry. If she let fatigue settle in, she was going to crumble to the ground. Already she felt like disappearing, like nestling into Damian's nest, but she had to keep her head up if she was going to make it out alive. "He's incapacitated. His Cells have grown and expanded out of control. Kind of like what's happening to all your puppets, Wren."

Sage lowered her head. She clutched her sword. "He's dead."

Lilian paused once again. "*How can this be?*" she breathed.

Sage wasn't about to waste her precious energy explaining it to someone like Lilian. Her focus was on herself and the sacrifice she was about to make. Then again, what sort of sacrifice would it be? In giving herself over to Lilian, she'd die and her enemy would become stronger. She closed her eyes and fought the hot wave of tears building up behind her lids.

"I'll take you to him," she choked.

Blasphemy.

The twins' eyes widened, and Gertrude and the others gasped from their aircraft. Tate nearly fell off. Sage had cut down all these monsters to save Damian, not feed him to Lilian. Sage wouldn't dream of betraying Damian to anyone, but what choice did she have now if she wanted to lure these Mutatio away from the city?

"Stop this," Sage croaked to Lilian. "Stop this right now."

Lilian still didn't move. It was a miracle Geoffrey hadn't peed his pants yet, but the look on his face said he was ready to die for the right cause. "*I don't believe you'll take me anywhere. You first, Queen.*"

Sage pointed her sword. "Fuck you, bitch. I'm not stupid enough to give myself or Damian over to you without a guarantee that you're going to save lives. If my crew can't confirm that you've told your cronies to back off, I'm not doing shit."

Mom! Pollux seemed to say with his quivering eyes. *What are you doing?!*

Buying myself and you guys time, Sage said in her mind. She wasn't sure if her sons could hear her, but those were the signals she sent out as she stood there and contemplated her actions.

Lilian took an awful long time to process the request. Even the Mutatio were stock-still on the ground. Not that they were going to attack Sage anyway—not when their companion was still twitching on the floor in all his blood.

"I'LL TAKE YOU TO HIM!" Sage roared when Lilian didn't respond.

Sage panted loudly. She closed her eyes, and this time the tears really did fall. She choked on a sob.

Forgive me, darling, she said in her mind. *I won't let anything happen to you, but I'm hoping to buy us time.*

But what Sage pictured in her head was not what happened in real life. She thought she and Lilian would be taking a leisurely stroll through the Outskirts until they reached Damian's nest. She never imagined that Hayes, Jamie, and Bruce would rush into the city with a pair of those laser guns that the Lolligo had been working on. They were prototypes, weren't they?

"Don't do anything, Sage!" Hayes called to her. "We've got these sons of bitches! Trust me—we've won."

"*Oh?*" Lilian' lips curled into a sneer. "*You've won, have you, boy? When half of your city lies in ruin?*"

"That's what you think."

One of the Mutatio lunged at them.

To everyone's awe, Hayes rolled to the right, dodging those talons like a pro. His first shot was surprisingly accurate, which was why he caught the Mutatio off guard. Then he had to focus on defense because he was just a human. Well, that's why he had the Lolligo as back-up, so the scuffle ended in a draw. Even the Mutatio didn't seem very keen on attacking seven-foot Squids with huge biceps and an equally intimidating laser gun.

Lilian looked annoyed.

"We've got this, Sage," Hayes said. He took a quick glance at her. "*You've* got this."

Sage still didn't quite understand what was happening. She

wouldn't, either, until she saw a cluster of half-naked, bloody people stream into the street. Some of them were carrying laser guns. Only a handful had those prototype ones Samson had passed around.

"Don't do it, Optimum!" one of them cried. "You're our only hope of bringing them back!"

"What the fuck?" Pollux breathed from behind Sage. No one but Hayes seemed to know where the disheveled mob had come from.

"You stay right there, Sage." Geoffrey smiled at her. Lilian must have forgotten about him. "And you defend this city just like you were born to do. Don't—"

There was a splatter of blood. For a second, Sage thought Lilian had finally decapitated Geoffrey, so she screamed. But then she realized it was Lilian's head that was missing. Hayes and the Lolligo didn't hesitate—they took this chance to gun down the other startled Mutatio.

It happened so quickly that by the time Sage blinked, it was over. Geoffrey was on his knees, helped up by the half-naked mob, with Lilian's headless body falling back on the street.

Sage looked up and found Louis standing on the roof of a nearby building.

He had a gun in his hand. Tyrus and Herman were ready to shoot if any more of Wren's puppets came out.

"Sage?" Louis called. "Are you all right?"

No. No, Sage wasn't all right—she wasn't fucking all right! Lilian had decimated so many people here and it was because of Louis that Damian was dead!

"You killed him," Sage whispered. Tears welled in her eyes. Her fists shook. Her nails cut into her palms. "You killed him . . ."

"Mom!" Pollux exclaimed as Sage raised her sword.

She pointed it at Louis, who didn't make any faces. The son of a bitch was too damn calm in the heart of this storm, as if he had been expecting Sage to react this way. Worst of all, he was still parading around in his white-and-gold uniform, as if he was the fucking All-seer around here.

"Mom, please listen," Pollux urged her. "Louis might be an ass-

416

hole, but if he hadn't given Dad that serum, Dad would have died at the palace. He would have never seen you again. He would have never spent the time that he did with you."

"YOU IDIOT!" Sage shrieked at him. "Don't you get it?! Louis fucked up the serum on purpose so that Damian would eventually die! Nova is no pushover—she never has been—and there was no way on earth she'd give him a serum that was faulty! This was Louis' fault—LOUIS' FAULT—AND I HAVE TO KILL HIM!"

"Mom—"

Lilian screamed. She had a fresh new head, but the regeneration had cost her because she looked like she was going haywire. She actually took off into the air, destroying a good portion of the street, and shot through the night sky.

No! Sage panted as she gazed up at that monstrous, bumbling form beneath the moon. She knew exactly where Lilian was going. *Not like this!*

There was so much force behind Lilian's wings that she knocked Gertrude and the others back. Castor and Pollux moved to cushion the landing of the aircraft and whipped around in search of Sage as they did.

"MOTHER!"

"Keep them safe!" Sage cried as she ran for her scooter in the Outskirts.

No, not Damian—NOT DAMIAN!

Sage didn't know how on earth she found her scooter in the middle of nowhere, right next to the trapdoor that led to the underground tunnel, but she did. It helped that Hamilton was nearby, waving tentacles around to get her attention. He was barking in place, confused by the mass flying overhead, but he stuck by Sage's side.

Sage straddled the seat, revved the engine, and exploded across the Outskirts. There was no way she was letting that thing up there anywhere near Damian—no fucking way—she had to do something—but what?

What was Sage going to do? How was she supposed to beat

Lilian and all her flailing limbs with just a measly sword? Even Lilian knew that Sage didn't stand a chance—she—*Wren*—was cackling the entire way to Damian's nest.

DO SOMETHING!

Sage could scream at herself all she wanted, but she wasn't getting any immediate solutions. She had a sword on her belt, but how was that supposed to cut down that monster? How was she supposed to stop people from dying while protecting her husband?

Sage screamed.

Then, from behind, she saw Hamilton's tentacles grow. They were massive now, propelling him into the air like a torpedo. He latched onto one of Lilian's appendages and held on like a pro. With a monstrous roar of his own, Hamilton ripped a chunk of Lilian's flesh right off her body.

It was so futile that it looked pathetic. Lilian didn't even bother to look for what the hell was nibbling at her ankles.

"Please!" Sage croaked to God. She knew that no matter what she did, people were going to die. If she allowed Lilian near Damian, people were going to die. If she allowed Lilian to eat her, people were going to die. If she killed Lilian, Wren was going to send more of those demos and people were going to die. That never stopped—it wasn't going to!

So Sage did what she always did in these impossible situations: she let her instincts take over. Once her mind was set, there was no going back. It generated the best possible scenario based on the circumstances Sage was in, so she knew what to do and how to do it. She was under the belly of the beast and she was going to have to stop it.

Single-handedly.

Sage stood atop the scooter's seat. She clutched her sword, then looked up. She prepared to jump and skewer that bitch in midair.

But wait . . . she didn't have to do this single-handedly.

Hamilton roared into the sky. The moon was shining brilliantly—it was a Full Corn Moon because farmers had to harvest the crops they had spent so much time and energy planting. Sage had to do the same, and so did Hamilton, who had to protect his city full of people who petted, fed, and played with him. To do that, Hamilton had to pull out all the stops.

Hamilton was no longer a dog.

He was a monster as big as Lilian. He had wings, too, so he looked like a griffin without any hair. His paws were more like claws now and his snout housed more teeth than it could hold. Hamilton gave another roar and tore into Lilian's body, stopping her in midair.

It was Sage's turn now: she jumped, sword up, and sliced right across Lilian's belly. Acid and stomach juices gushed out all over her, burning her skin, but the attack seemed to stall Lilian a great deal. Sage threw out an arm, grabbed one of Lilian's appendages nearby, and swung onto her back.

Lilian took a nosedive.

Sage jumped off and Hamilton caught her in his mouth before she hit the ground. The skin on her face, chest, and shoulders was hissing, but Sage ignored the pain when Lilian was still a threat below. Instead, she settled on Hamilton's tongue, belly down, and pointed her sword again, both hands around the hilt.

Hamilton knew what to do: he dived. His lips kept a slight pressure around Sage's body, keeping her in place.

Sage kept her blade up, wind whipping her face as she flew right toward Lilian's large head and skewered her to the ground.

Hamilton let Sage go and pulled up before he crashed, but he wasn't done yet. As Sage jumped out of the way, sword in hand, Hamilton circled back around and tore off Lilian' head, teeth sinking into her skull.

"SAGE!" Gertrude cried from afar—she and her crew were here, already opening fire on Lilian, as Preacher asked the dead Forefathers in heaven for their protection against the evils on earth. Castor and Pollux must have hitched a ride with them because they jumped out of the aircraft. "Look out!"

Sage was too close to Lilian to evade those blasts, so Castor and

Pollux grabbed her. They carried her to safety as a blinding light engulfed what was left of Lilian' body, courtesy of Damian's faithful rebels.

Sage cried. She clung onto her boys and bawled. Not so much for her injuries . . . or the horrible pain she was in . . . but for Ruby City.

So much pain and misery. The people hadn't deserved it.

And Diamond City, where her sister dwelled. Where the Mutatio were probably twice as monstrous. Where Sage would never be able to step foot in again. Where her pizzeria remained closed to the public.

Sage dropped the sword. As if her body weighed over ten tons, she hit her knees. To her, it didn't matter that she had brought so many people back to life when the one person she truly loved . . . the one she knew she couldn't live without . . . was gone.

Sage screamed. Castor and Pollux cradled her between them, but nothing helped.

Nothing worked.

Nothing would.

CHAPTER 28

A Bitter Camaraderie

nd Sage couldn't do anything about it. There weren't any medics on board Gertrude's ship, and Sage needed more than just a few bandages. Castor and Pollux fed her their blood. Sage didn't remember anything beyond that. Maybe a few faces and startled cries as they carried her away from Lilian's body . . . but that was it.

"Darling." Damian caressed her face.

"Damian." Sage smiled. She opened her eyes and her heart fluttered.

God, he was beautiful. He was gloriously naked, too, in the middle of this enchanted forest. His long silky hair curtained his sharp features and his muscles were chiseled to delicious perfection. Sage wanted to reach out and touch him, but Damian told her not to.

"No, darling . . . you can't afford to move."

Right. The burns. They had destroyed all the tendons in her arms. Oddly enough, Sage could still see her tattoo there. *Damianos Damaris*. That was intact.

"You'll heal," Damian said.

Maybe so. Sage must have looked horrific, but Damian continued gazing at her lovingly, as if he was admiring a fine piece of art.

His fingers were long and slender, gliding down the skin of her face. He touched some strands of her hair and pushed them back from her eyes. He tucked them behind her ear.

"The bob cut looks good on you, darling."

"How can you say that?" Sage whispered. Honestly, her hair was the least of her worries. She must have looked like an ugly piece of meat with pus leaking out of her gashes.

"Because it's true," Damian said happily.

"My looks . . . aren't what matter now." Sage's eyes burned with tears. She convinced herself it wasn't her deformities that were important to her at the moment, but perhaps to some extent they were. When she was looking at Damian, she remembered what she had lost . . . and could never get back.

"You will never lose me," Damian said to her, still brushing hair from her face. "I will always find you."

"I can't be selfish . . ." Sage shook her head back and forth. "I can't be selfish . . . not anymore . . ."

"In what way, exactly, are you being selfish? Because you want something for yourself?"

"I want you . . . so badly . . . a-and I want to live, but . . . I . . ." Sage squeezed her eyes closed. She gave a dry, wheezy sob. "Look at what Wren did," she croaked. "Look at how many people . . . have died . . ."

"Perhaps," Damian said softly. "But you brought them back to life, didn't you?"

Sage sobbed. "Did I?"

"What happened to them is not your fault."

"I-I feel like it is."

"Would there have been another way to stop her, Sage?" Damian sat on the grass next to her. He held her to his chest as he rubbed his nose against her temple. His skin was smooth, soft, and warm. "What other way was there, darling?"

Sage didn't know. She was losing consciousness pretty quickly. It was nice because the reprieve was just on the other side, but it was painful because there was a cold hard truth she had to acknowledge.

Hybrids were devastating. First, it was Venus . . . and now it was Wren.

Who was still alive and cackling in Diamond City.

Sage's city.

"It's good to see she's actually sleeping," someone said from above.

Gertrude.

When Sage opened her eyes, she saw the freckled face and coppery hair. Tate was standing right next to her, half her size.

Sage would have never thought to see the day these two would become an official couple, much less a married one. There was a softness to Tate's features that made him much more human than he used to be. How the hell had Gertrude done it? Tate had been nothing short of a beast who used to spit insults and bully women like they were scraps of meat. Sage was happy to see he had changed for the better.

Behind Tate were branches of . . . flesh. Not actual trees. Sage quickly realized that she wasn't sitting in a forest with Damian. That wasn't his chest she was leaning against—this was his nest.

Gertrude and the rest of the crew looked a bit uneasy. They kept glancing at the appendages hanging around them, as if expecting them to attack or lash out. Despite their creepy setting, no one was in any danger. Even Hamilton was curled up by Sage's feet, taking a bit of a break from all the fighting.

"How are you feeling?" Sonia asked her.

Sage wasn't sure. She couldn't feel much right now. She took a glance at her arm, at all the boils on her skin. She noticed thin tendrils embedded in her veins like an IV. There must have been over twenty of them. It was a bit jarring, but Sage didn't feel any pain or danger from being connected to this . . . nest. She only wondered how Gertrude had managed it.

Gertrude shook her head. "We didn't know where else to take

you. The nest was the closest place. Ruby City is currently under reconstruction."

"What do you mean 'reconstruction'?" Sage murmured.

"We have to fix stuff and clean up," Tate said, as if he was explaining this to a toddler. "I'm not complaining, though—things could have been so much worse. Can you believe we actually managed to hold off the horde?"

"Where are Castor and Pollux?"

"They went to survey the city," Gertrude said.

"Is everyone all right?" Sage croaked. "D-did people die—?"

"We don't know the numbers yet. Let's wait for an update. The only thing we can confirm is that Lilian is dead and the rest of the Mutatio are, too. Only a handful managed to escape."

Perhaps there was some relief in hearing that, but it was short-lived. When Candice, Olivia, Geoffrey, and Micah popped into Sage's head, she knew she couldn't rest. She had to get up from here—

"Hold it." Gertrude pushed her down. Sword Devil was holding Sage's sword. "You are in no condition to go anywhere. Sage . . . we thought you were dead."

"What?" Sage croaked. Why did she sound like a goddamn frog?

"For a while there, you didn't have a pulse." Tate cleared his throat. The rest of the crew looked horrified at the idea of Sage dying. "Castor and Pollux were desperate. Hamilton started howling. We didn't know where else to take you but here. No matter how much blood the twins fed you, or how many times we attempted to resuscitate you, there was nothing."

Nothing . . . There was nothing . . .

"Was I dead?" Sage said.

From the looks everyone gave each other, it seemed she had been.

"So we brought you here," Gertrude went on, looking disturbed. "And as soon as we did . . . the nest seemed to come to life. Well, it did come to life." She indicated the spindly vines embedded in her arm.

"Once you were stable, the twins left to see how things are in Ruby City," Tate said.

Sage couldn't hear anything. No one was crying.

"So . . . I was dreaming?" Sage mumbled. "I saw . . . Damian . . ."

"We haven't seen him," Sonia said sadly. She clutched her elbows. "We were sort of hoping he'd be here, actually. We still don't know what this nest is, but—"

"Did you really throw a *dagger* at Castor?" Tate sputtered, as if it was a question he had been dying to ask. "*And* stab Samson?"

Sage rubbed her head. "I did."

"Holy *shit*. You're the toughest fucking woman I've ever met. I mean, you haven't even met your kids and you're already throwing blades at them?"

"It was a kitchen knife."

Tate shook his head at Gertrude, who turned a bit pale, and it had nothing to do with Damian's nest.

"What?" Sage said.

"We have a kid." Tate smiled. "You remember, right? His name is Conor."

"Yes, you told me." Sage allowed herself to smile a bit. She was a bit ashamed she hadn't taken the time to catch up with her friends. "And congrats."

"He's a handful," Tate said quickly, implying, *There's nothing to congratulate here. We sort of regret having a kid, actually.* "And we've been going crazy trying to find ways to parent him effectively. We asked the Warlord for advice, but you know how he is with kids— he spoils them like fucking crazy when they're not his own."

Sage looked up at Gertrude, who nodded to confirm that.

"So . . . you need a disciplinarian?" Sage mused.

Tate got on his knees and crawled over to her. He put his hands together in prayer. "Castor and Pollux practically kiss your ass. Those boys will do *anything* for you. We can see it. They practically worship you and they've only known you for six months out of their thirty-plus years of existence. How do you do it?"

Sage snorted. "You don't take bullshit. Period."

"I don't take bullshit—you know me! We've given Conor over to Margaret for help in the archives—nothing—we've given him over to Sonia and L but they're never home—nothing—we've given him to Tai and Sword Devil for training—nothing—we've had him stay with Ramon and Eric, and you know what dicks they can be—nothing—we've had him stay a few days with Cecilia, Bernard, and Shane, but those three are terrible at parenting—so no."

Sage chuckled weakly. "Have you tried giving him over to Preacher?"

Tate rolled his eyes and Gertrude pursed her lips.

Preacher raised his hands. "I have advised a thorough blessing and one-on-one time with the Lolligo in prayer and worship of their great deeds, but the male and female parent will not relent."

Tate groaned. He sounded more frustrated than exasperated now. "I'm sorry, but I don't believe in any of that stuff and I don't want Conor turning into some religious freak—no offense, Paul, but seriously! I'm *Tate*—I'm the badass from Mousafeld—and Conor should be respecting *me*, but he doesn't!"

"I think Tate is being a bit of a pussy, to be honest," Gertrude huffed. She grinned at Sage. "But when you come to Emerald City with us, you'll see what we mean."

Sage smiled at that thought. It was nice to think of a future in which she'd go to Emerald City and live a normal life. She'd like to start a pizzeria there . . .

But before those happy thoughts could take root and manifest into a possible reality, Sage shifted her focus to the hell that awaited her in Diamond City. She had no idea how they were going to win now that Samson was out of commission. She meant to ask about him, but to her great frustration, she fell right back asleep.

When she woke up some days later, there was no one standing around her. Sage could feel a few presences outside the nest. Castor and Pollux sounded like they were in a bit of a panic.

"I don't want to send anyone to that hellhole," Pollux said. "We can't risk our best fighters. As much as we want to save Diamond City, we're going to have to wait."

"Well, we can't exactly twiddle our thumbs here, can we?" Tate said bitterly. "That fucking bitch really knows how to manipulate people. She's pure chaos. How much longer until she sends more of those winged freaks to Ruby City?"

"She wants you, my lady."

Sage looked up. She found Preacher sitting by another chunk of fleshy appendages. His robes were surprisingly clean despite the amount of time he had spent near slime and mucus. The look on his face was more serious than it usually was.

"And she won't stop until she gets you," Preacher said.

"How many are dead?" Sage asked quietly.

"I don't know, but the casualties are low. In fact . . . I'm not sure there are any. We are very blessed you offered your blood to those who needed it in Ruby City."

"Where is Samson?"

"The Lolligo Prophet, it seems, is still incapacitated."

Sage held her face with her dirty hands. She fought down a sob.

"I'm not sure this is your fault, exactly," Preacher said carefully. "But you have quite a bit to think about, my lady. It seems it will soon be your turn to perform the Ultimate Sacrifice. Wren is not going to stop, nor are we going to be able to defeat her on our own."

Sage was slowly starting to come to that conclusion. She didn't acknowledge Preacher in any way, though. She gently caressed the tendrils from Damian's nest that were still embedded in her skin. Her beautiful diamond ring sparkled.

"I have to live," Sage said quietly. "I have to kill my sister."

"The Warlord performed the Ultimate Sacrifice and he survived," Preacher said. "I'm sure you will find a way to do the same."

"How do I look?"

"A little more rejuvenated, my lady. But you still look like you're in need of a vacation."

"I think I need to isolate myself in your church," Sage mused.

"Those Lolligo scriptures are sounding pretty fascinating right about now."

Preacher smiled. "I would very much enjoy that. I will make sure to document the wise words of the Optimum."

Sage didn't feel like she could delay any further, so she got up. She didn't like learning that Samson was still unconscious, possibly close to dying. It was the absolute worst of her nightmares, and she had already experienced so many in such a short amount of time. Sage had wounded him... so now she had to fix him. She steadied herself on her legs and watched as Damian's tendrils withdrew from her arm. She took a deep breath.

Where are you, darling? Sage said in her mind, but there was no response. For a moment, she thought she was rather foolish for expecting one. Damian hadn't been seen in months. This was all that was left of him.

Hamilton came bumbling up to her from nowhere. He sniffed around her feet.

Someone had changed Sage into clean clothes. As baggy as they were on her body, at least she had a jacket and pants. She had lost so much muscle. Despite how easily she'd gain them again with a few training sessions, it was still so devastating.

A few more steps, and Sage made it out of the nest. She found her sons and friends arguing with one another about how to proceed.

"She's only getting *stronger*," L tried to reason with Pollux, who wasn't having any of their strategies to act recklessly. "We're going to have to go in there and take care of her ourselves."

"How exactly?" Pollux said coolly. "You show your faces, and she'll arrest you so quickly you won't have time to state your claims."

"I was thinking Sword Devil could go in there—"

"No one is going," Sage said, stepping forward. "Not yet."

They all gasped, whipped around, and stared at her. It was taking them quite some time to process her words. Castor and Pollux looked ready to argue, but they waited for her to explain what she had in mind.

The truth was... Sage had no plan. She had no clue what the

situation was in Diamond City and if there was a way to defeat Wren's influence without any casualties. Sage grew heavy at the thought of it, but there was no other way forward than to get those guns from Samson. "Standby" plans didn't sit well with Damian's rebels, though—they had barely managed to survive the first onslaught of Mutatio.

"We can have another wave of Mutatio at our doorstep," Ramon argued at once. "And we cannot afford to fight them again. We also have nowhere to move all these people."

Right. That's why the twins had planned on leaving them all behind. Sage was still incensed by that horrendous decision, but Pollux and Castor were looking at this from a strategic point, not an emotional one. It was obvious that Sage was their best chance of taking Diamond City back, so it was her life over everyone else's. It was fucked up, but it was survival. Something told her those two had taken a leaf out of Samson's book.

"The Mutatio won't be back," Sage said, wondering what sort of ideas Samson had planted in their heads behind closed doors. She was going to have to beat it out of them. "My sister might be desperate to beat me, but she isn't going to act recklessly. She's going to bide her time and possibly count her blessings in Diamond City. Ultimately, that's what she wanted. Ruby would have been an extra prop. Her failure has been a shock to her system and she won't try again if it means losing more of her pets."

"So now what?" Tate said. "We twiddle our thumbs and pray that she doesn't attack us again?"

That didn't sound like the Sage any of them knew. They all stared at her, waiting for her to say more.

But Sage had nothing . . . other than her sword, which she took back from Sword Devil. And Kendra's dagger, too. "I want to see Samson."

Castor gave her his jacket. Pollux tied a scarf around her neck. They looked at her, and she looked back.

Mother, Castor said with his eyes. *We need to give Samson some time.*

I want to see him, Sage said again.

Castor and Pollux glanced at each other. They both sighed. Sage's heart dropped.

"Oh, great," Tate sneered. "They can communicate telepathically. Now we all know what they're saying. Perfect."

"I'll go on ahead, then," Sage said to them all, ignoring Tate. "Meet me back at the house."

"Sage, the Lolligo don't want visitors!"

"I don't give a fuck what they want."

They weren't going to let her wander around alone, so they followed her all through the Outskirts until they reached the *Luse*.

Because the Lolligo had been performing experiments with Damian's nest, they weren't too far away. Nonetheless, Castor and Pollux supported her to the very front steps. Gertrude and the rest of the crew stayed a safe distance away. Perhaps Jamie and Bruce had their own way of warding off pests.

Yet, when it was Sage, Jamie peeked through the door and exhaled in relief. He didn't dare point any guns at her. That seemed to be Bruce's job.

"Get that motherfucker out of my face," Sage spat at Jamie, sensing Bruce in the background. "Or I'll cut him down like I did Samson."

Jamie raised his hands. "We mean no harm."

"No," Sage snarled. "Only when I need help and you decide to betray me. Then I have to be careful around you, don't I?"

Castor and Pollux said nothing because they agreed. In fact, they were quite tense, as if they were ready to tackle the Lolligo the moment Sage gave the signal.

"Samson," Sage said to Jamie when she climbed the ramp.

There was light sobbing coming from deep within the ship. Sage stepped inside with the twins right on her tail. She reached the laboratory that served as a medical space every once in a while. That was the case now: Samson was on that cold, hard table Sage knew so well.

There was a machine hooked up to his arm. It was pumping the

Slainium out of his blood and providing him with a fresh batch. That was because Sage had stabbed him through the chest.

Faye was on his chest, crying over him. She sat up as soon as she saw the trio at the door.

"S-Sage?" she croaked.

"Is he all right?" Sage asked.

And then, as if Wren herself was possessing her, Faye's face contorted. It was as if a curtain had descended upon her features. A new soul took control, throwing away the kind, welcoming Faye that Sage had spent so much time with in Elysium. A hellcat emerged.

"You BITCH!" Faye shrieked. "*YOU* did this to him?! You stabbed your own ally—your own *brother*—because of some suicide mission in the Outskirts?!"

Sage didn't even have the chance to respond—Faye wasn't done.

"HE SACRIFICED EVERYTHING FOR YOU!" Faye went on. "AND THIS IS WHAT YOU DO TO HIM?!"

"Please stop yelling," Castor said to Faye. "It isn't helping anyone."

"SAMSON IS GOING TO DIE BECAUSE OF YOU!" Faye bellowed at Sage, face red.

Sage took a meek step back, but Faye had more to say to her.

"You are dangerous!" she hissed, spitting like a cat with rabies. "And you and your lot have to die—!"

"Hey!" Pollux exclaimed. "Shut the fuck up! You're not God to decide who lives and dies around here—if it weren't for my mother, you'd be dead! From what I can tell, Samson's still alive! My mother always puts her life on the line for other people, and that is not the sort of treatment she deserves from bitches like you!"

Castor was already tugging Sage out of the ship. Before Faye said any more hateful words, it was best for Sage to leave here with some dignity. At the very least, she was able to walk then run as far away from Faye as possible.

Head still spinning, Sage wasn't sure where she was going next. The wind was piercing and cold. Every breath felt like tiny razors cutting up her lungs. She shivered in Castor's arms, hiding her face in his chest because she didn't want to see anyone else. There were people calling out for her, and Jamie was one of them.

"Optimum!" he cried. "Forgive her! She is just very distressed—you know how humans are!"

Right. Humans were emotional. Lolligo were not. They were willing to sacrifice an entire city of people all to keep one person safe.

Insane.

"Please be patient," Jamie said. "We will continue to work on the guns."

Right. Guns. Fighting.

"I understand why you did it, Sage."

Bruce gasped audibly from inside the ship. Jamie's brow was set, though.

"You care about the humans," he said. "And that is what makes you commendable. I hear you saved everyone's life in Ruby City, including the ones who were already dead. You've helped us and we will help you. Please be patient with us Lolligo—we can be rough around the edges."

Castor stepped forward cautiously. He made sure to keep a tight grip on Sage's body in case she got any ideas of taking off and never looking back.

Perhaps, if Castor hadn't been holding her, she would have. She contemplated it every single day for the next six months.

CHAPTER 29

The Promise

"Sage! *Hello!*" Paige waved her hand in front of Sage's face. "Are you listening to anything that I'm saying?"

"What?" Sage looked up. She peered into the large eyes above her. "Oh, no." She rubbed her face. "Sorry."

"You're daydreaming again, aren't you?"

"Well, a little."

Paige grinned. "You have to admit you look beautiful."

Sage was standing in front of the mirror. She was being fitted for some nice clothes today. Why should she have to wear rags when Paige and Pedro had an incredible selection of fabrics? For the summer, Sage wanted a nice blouse, some snug jeans, and comfortable shoes. No boots or flats—just a nice pair of shoes for walking.

"I think you look incredible," Paige said with that happy smile on her face. As giddy as she was, she still looked more like a man than Travis did. Her sharp features, coarse hair, and squarish body rivaled any macho man's walking down the street. And Pedro? Sage was lucky if he said "good morning" to her. "And this is exactly the sort of style you need to just take it easy for a bit," Paige went on.

"You've been working so hard the past few months, helping us re-build and all."

Indeed. With Jamie, Bruce, Louis, Hayes, and her sons by her side, Sage had toured all of Ruby City to survey damages, attend security meetings, and talk to the people she had brought back to life with her blood. Who would have thought? Maybe only Samson, who hadn't left his ship.

Her blood was magical... sure... but it sure as hell couldn't bring Damian back.

"Don't lose faith." Paige patted Sage's shoulder. "The nest is still there, after all. And you told me you talked to him?"

"I'm not sure," Sage said, fiddling with the ring on her finger. "I think it was a dream."

"Well, just wait. If he comes back, he'll love that jacket you bought him."

It was folded on the chair. Sage saw it every time she walked into this shop, but buying it had hurt too much until now. For the past six months, she had been hanging around friends and family every day and she allowed them to fill her with that god-awful word.

Hope.

Sage shook her head.

Pedro was bent over the table, taking measurements of a dress he needed to have ready for this afternoon. There were a lot of people in Ruby City now. Business must have really been booming. He even had his kids helping him with inventory in between online classes.

Sage lamented the whole Mutatio attack. While no one had died thanks to her blood, the quarantine her sons had initiated, and her early intervention against the monsters, she had nightmares of bodies piled up in corners. Despite the fortunate outcome, no one should have had to experience that hell. Sage had already yelled at her sons for sacrificing the city like they did, but that didn't appease any of the turmoil inside her. The attack had *still happened* and that bugged the hell out of her.

"You look beautiful," Paige said happily. She brushed some of Sage's hair back. It was still in a bob cut, although it was starting to get long again. "And things will be all right. You'll see. We may not have Diamond City, but we do have each other here. We have Emerald City for defense. Most of all: we have you."

Sage turned to Paige, who was way too optimistic for her taste. Nonetheless, she forced a smile. "I guess you're right."

"Are you going to the fastball tournament tonight? My money's on Tai."

Sage's smile got a little bigger. "I bet on Sword Devil. I never underestimate her."

Everyone had urged her to enter the tournament, but Sage hadn't played fastball in ages. The last time she picked up a ball was at Royal Academy. She had daydreamed of the day she'd go pro, when she still hadn't realized that that dream would never come true. Candice was hopeful, but Olivia was honest.

"Pizza's your thing!" she'd say with a small pump of her fist.

"She can still learn, can't she?" Micah said. "I mean, she is 'young.'"

"The Optimum can do anything," Kendra said honestly.

Yes, and turning an entire city into Enhanced was one of them. Sage had saved a lot of people from death, but she had also given her blood to the rest of the population. The very thing that the Kilstrongs had dreaded . . . that Damian had fought so hard to achieve . . . happened.

Sage supposed she felt good about herself. She knew older people like Travis and Jasmine were going to live longer, better lives. Despite the fact they were all exiled in Ruby City, people here still made it work.

Diamond City citizens had united and built another powerful high-functioning city. There were schools, colleges, offices, sports, restaurants, shops, theater productions, concerts, and art festivals. Those were Sage's favorite. It was crazy to see that David, Damian's former lover, was still part of the crew.

His paintings were a bit different now, though. Instead of the monstrous Damian he had depicted over thirty years ago, he drew a beautiful man with long silky hair and angel wings. Behind the angelic Damian was an entire city of nurtured people. Emerald City, perhaps.

Sage had bought the painting and hung it in her room at the complex. Sometimes, she'd stare at it for hours. She'd write her cheesy poems, too. Not much, because she'd start crying knowing that Damian would never read them, but then Castor and Pollux gave her an idea.

"Why don't you read them out loud to him?"

So the twins took her to the nest every night after dinner. With her little book in her shaking hands, Sage would read the poems out loud. She wasn't sure if Damian could hear her, but she'd hear the nest rustle. Or was that her imagination?

"Darling dear, I miss you so
I take walks through the night and feel you around
Without you, my spirits are low
Until the day you come back, maybe I'll be found."

Pollux cleared his throat loudly. Castor elbowed him and hissed, "Shut it."

Castor wrapped a protective arm around Sage and glared at his brother anew.

"What?" Sage said.

"Nothing, Mother," Castor said defensively. "Pollux is just being an asshole."

"I didn't say anything!" Pollux exclaimed.

"Mother wrote those poems for Father and all you can do is make faces! Grow up, will you?"

Sage knew her poetry was bad, but she certainly didn't mean to instigate fighting between her sons. Then again, she had already learned that it didn't take much for those two to start bickering.

The height of their adversity came that night of the fastball tournament. There was an arena on the east side of the city, and all of Diamond City's best players stepped onto the court. There were thirty players in total. There were players from the Porcupines there—from all four districts, actually—but Sage's money was still on Sword Devil. Castor had bet on her, too, but Pollux swore that Tai was going to bring this home.

At long last, it was time to start the matches. The referee called for the first two players, and then the game began.

Sage had to admit that she immediately forgot about most of her problems. When the adrenaline rose inside her, driving her to sit up straight in her seat as the players below started a crazy volley, she dreamed of a happy future. She wasn't sure why, but she believed that she'd be a professional on the court with Damian and her twins cheering her on from the sidelines. It wasn't likely at all, but she could dream and pretend, and perhaps that was all she needed to taste just a little bit of happiness.

As expected, Tai and Sword Devil were able to beat all of their opponents, including the ones from their own city. Emerald had some talented players, too, but they paled in comparison to those two beasts.

Finally, it was time to see who came out on top.

After a few close shots and some heart-pounding dives, it was tied at game point and—

Tai.

Pollux's mistake was boasting he had won to Castor's face. The two started fist-fighting right in their seats. Candice had to step in and separate them.

"I swear you're worse than children!" she shrieked.

Micah laughed. "God, she gives me the same spiel."

"He's an asshole!" Castor exclaimed, spit flying from his mouth. His face was red. Pollux was no longer laughing now that he had a bloody nose.

"That might be, but you're the bigger fool for throwing the first punch, aren't you?" Candice spat. "Where is all that self-control you practiced?"

"Trust me, Aunt Candice—it's hard around that stupid fuck!"

Sage laughed. This was so not appropriate right now—and she was the mother here—but she pictured Damian disciplining these two. Of course, Pollux wouldn't have dared to instigate his brother in the presence of his father—so this brawl would have never happened—but if it had, everyone knew Damian would have taken the twins aside and cut off their tongues. According to Olivia, it was one of Damian's favorite punishments.

Sage's eyes widened. "What?"

"Pollux was twelve and said the f-word," Olivia said as the crowd around them roared with applause. The referee was congratulating Tai down in the arena. Candice was still scolding Castor and Pollux, going on about "acting like adults when their mother needed them most."

"I would have cut off his tongue, too," Sage agreed. "No cursing until adulthood."

Olivia giggled. "Right."

Despite Castor and Pollux fighting and losing a ton of money to each other, it was one of the best nights of Sage's life. There were after-parties all over the city. Even some of the Clarity District priests joined in on the celebrations, which the Lolligo and the Optimum had allowed them to partake in.

Samson, Jamie, and Bruce were in their ship, though. Sage tried to stay away from them after what Faye had said to her. Besides, she was perfectly happy at Gary and Tiana's club.

This was a space for dancing and drinking. Here, Sage was surrounded by hope and not thoughts of tomorrow. All these people were depending on her. Perhaps Paige was right and everyone was happy living here, but surely they missed home . . . even if Louis had proven to be a lousy Allseer.

Sage wondered if Louis would still be Allseer after all this. Then again, he was a Kilstrong, and that family didn't let go of power easily. They clung to it like vampires on a human's neck.

Sage smiled as she caressed Hamilton's head. He rested it on her lap, amber eyes peering up at her. He couldn't talk, but he could definitely sense her thoughts. Hamilton's expression was serious and unrelenting. He gazed at her much like Damian would when she was about to do something dangerous.

"Hey there, Sage."

Hamilton looked up at his old master. As if he had nothing to say to him, he trotted off to hang out with Micah and Kendra.

For the first time in months, Hayes was grinning. It had been so long since Sage saw this happy peppy side of Hayes that she often wondered if she had dreamed it up in the past. Those times they had spent on campus testing each other for their midterms and dreaming of what they'd be doing in the future felt so . . . long ago.

"How are you holding up?" Hayes asked her casually. Although he was grinning, he was in no way being cynical. His face softened as he regarded her. Sage wasn't used to this genuine, good-natured Hayes.

"I think I'm fine," Sage said softly. She gazed at her glass of cherry soda. "I'm happy that everyone's together and enjoying life as much as possible."

"Me, too. We've certainly come a long way." Hayes waved a server over. He asked for some soda, too.

"Who would have thought you'd become the Lolligo's best friend?" Sage mused.

"That's just the thing." Hayes sat forward. His grin got bigger. "Jamie says I've gotten to be very valuable. When all this is over, he, Bruce, and the newborn Lolligo—Vince—are all going to explore the Outskirts. I want to go with them."

Sage arched a brow. "On an expedition?"

"Wouldn't that be incredible?"

"It does sound pretty cool."

"You're invited, you know," Hayes said. "I know it's always been your dream to travel."

"Ruby's dream," Sage corrected him gently. She looked down. "Sage's dream . . . is a little different. I have family and people I love to look after."

"Yeah." Hayes nodded at her. "I know. Ever since we left Diamond City, you've been fighting so hard. Nonstop. And so I wanted to apologize, Sage: I tried to yank you away from your life and family. I was a real, royal dick for what I did, how I banged Kendra just to spite you." He sighed. "I look back at it now and I want to punch myself. Maybe you can do me the honors? Just please don't knock out any of my teeth. I spent weeks whitening them."

Sage chuckled. "I won't punch you."

"I think your husband already taught me a lesson that day he stabbed me." Hayes shivered. "Well deserved, too, even if I wanted to kill him with all my might. I thought he was the most dangerous man on the planet. I told Samson, you know, about him. He agreed that hybrids were dangerous."

Hayes gasped. He feared he had said too much, but Sage didn't react one way or another. Not when everything he had just said was true.

"We've caused much misery from the moment we were born," Sage agreed. She watched Micah and Kendra get up from a table to dance. Candice, Olivia, and Geoffrey were laughing about something in the corner. They kept looking around the room for her, as if in hopes they'd see her approaching their group, but they didn't want to interrupt her conversation with Hayes. "We were supposed to unite the districts in Diamond City . . . save the Lolligo . . . and kill the corrupt Overseers."

"Which *you* did," Hayes emphasized.

"Maybe," Sage said softly. She swirled the last bits of soda in her glass. It was flat by now. "But my sister turned a lot of people into Enhanced. Thanks to her power, humans had something to fight for again. Kilstrong wanted it all for himself. Then there was boredom among the hybrids in the Carat District, too. So many innocent women died in Smallfeld thanks to those reproductive experiments. And then all this catastrophe with my sister, all because of hybrids."

"But it was thanks to a hybrid," Hayes said, "that we managed to win and survive." He took her hand and kissed it. "It was thanks to you, Sage, that I became an Enhanced, too. And for that, I am forever humbled."

"Do you remember ... when you wanted to give me a new life?" Sage asked him quietly.

Suddenly, there was a vicious uproar. Travis was getting down and dirty on the dance floor with Jasmine. That old man could swing his pelvis a lot better now that he was an Enhanced.

Sage didn't think it was amusing at the moment. She stood up, still holding Hayes' hand, and took him outside where it was much more quiet.

All the shops had closed already. The night lights were dim and cozy. There was a fresh breeze now that the sun wasn't blaring down on them. To think it had been two years since they had arrived in Ruby City. Sage hardly recognized these streets anymore.

Sage turned to Hayes. She looked him straight in the eyes. "Do you remember, Hayes?"

"I do." Hayes took a deep breath. "But Sage ... that's obviously in the past. And that was my teenage-boy fantasy: to sweep you away and show you the world. But Damian—"

"I love him with all my heart and soul," Sage croaked. It was hard to keep a straight face when she knew she'd never see him again. His smiles, his expressions, his comments, and his drawings. She still had the little notebook he had given her tucked away in her coat's pocket. She knew she had to give it to Castor and Pollux soon. "And every day that passes ... is another day of misery for me." She dabbed at her eyes.

"I know I have to be strong," Sage went on despite the tears. "And this isn't about me. This is about what's good for the people. All of this fighting—despite my heroics—happened because of hybrids. My sister is still in Diamond City, and I know I have to get rid of her. But once this is over, I want you to give me a new life, Hayes."

Hayes' breathing was super tight right now. He knew damn well that the "new life" Sage was talking about was not the one with him in the Outskirts. Sage had no intention of exploring new lands and encountering hidden civilizations of people. She had every intention of ending her journey on earth very soon.

"I want you to kill me, Hayes," Sage said. "And you can ... with that gun."

Hayes slapped Sage's hand out of his grip. He choked on his own disbelief. "Are you fucking kidding me, Sage?"

"No," she said seriously. "I'm not."

"You can't possibly ask me to kill you—that's not fair! What the hell's wrong with you?!"

"There is nothing wrong with me. This is what I have to do—I know it now. Don't you see that so long as hybrids exist, there will always be wars, fighting, and power grabs?"

"Sage." Hayes grabbed her shoulders. He shook her a bit, peering crazily into her eyes. "So long as *humanity* exists, there will always be wars, fighting, and power grabs. This has nothing to do with what you are. You blame hybrids, but your sons are hybrids, too—are you going to kill them?"

"My sons are old enough to defend themselves and stave off corruption," Sage said steadily. She knew in her heart that was true. That was the only reason she felt comfortable saying it. "But me ... I've lived a long life, Hayes. And once I've killed my sister, I want to put it behind me."

"G-God!" Hayes croaked. "Are you serious, Sage? You don't really want to die, do you?"

"I'm done," Sage said. "I don't want to do this anymore or see anyone else get hurt. I've given you all a gift, left you with the tools you need to succeed, and all I want to do is go to sleep. Forever."

"But why *me*, damn it? Why, Sage? Why did you ask *me*—why didn't you ask Samson or your nieces?!"

Sage shook her head. "They wouldn't be able to kill me. Samson talks a lot of shit, and maybe he thought about ending me at one point, but he can't go through with it."

"AND WHAT MAKES YOU THINK *I* CAN?!" Hayes roared. "THAT'S NOT FAIR!"

"You wanted me to have a new life."

"Have you lost it?! A new life doesn't mean I want to kill you!"

"But that's what you're doing," Sage said patiently, "by ending my current life. Don't you see yet, Hayes?"

"What if I refuse?" Hayes spat. "Will you take your own life?"

"I'd rather not." Sage touched the place where her sword would be. "But if I have to . . . then I will. I was only hoping you'd give me an honorable death, Hayes."

Hayes' eyes were red and watery. His lip shook. He opened his mouth to protest, but Candice burst outside.

"Hey." She looked at them. Her eyes oscillated between Hayes and Sage. "Everything all right out here?"

"Yeah." Hayes couldn't get away from Sage fast enough. He slipped back into the club, dipping beneath Candice's arm.

"Aunt Sage?" Candice said gently. It had been thirty years, but she knew her dear aunt scarily well. As an Enhanced, she was that more attuned to her vibes and energy as well. "Are you . . . all right?"

"Sorry," Sage said, crossing her arms. "It was just getting a bit loud in there. I think I'm ready to retire for the night. I'm going to see Damian."

"Do you want me to get the twins?"

"No. I'll go by myself."

"Aunt Sage." Candice let the club door click closed behind her. She was tall, beautiful, and so mature now. Her face was sharp and angular, and her eyes held a light that only people who had lived a long time had.

Sage had missed so much of Candice's transition into adulthood that it broke her heart in two. Tears welled in her eyes.

"I know what you're thinking," Candice went on, looking a bit disturbed by how emotional Sage was. That was never a good sign. "You want to do all this by yourself, don't you?"

"I'd rather not," Sage replied uncomfortably, wondering if Candice had overheard her conversation with Hayes. There was no way, though—the music blasting behind them was the perfect barrier for eavesdroppers. "But if it means saving people, then I'm willing to do what it takes."

"You've done an incredible thing," Candice said to her. "You've helped so many people here. And soon, we'll all be moving back to Diamond City. Samson's almost done producing those weapons that'll give us a fighting chance. I know you've already been through so much war, but I guess what I'm trying to say is: hold on. We're almost there." Candice stepped closer to her. With a smile, she took Sage's hand. "No one knows this yet . . . but I wanted to tell you that I'm pregnant."

Sage gasped. "Really?"

"I took a pregnancy test this morning. Yes—I know." Candice rolled her eyes. "Geoffrey couldn't keep his hands off me since we got here. We've finally been able to spend some time together and live the life we envisioned. In Diamond City, he was always on missions in the Carat District or kissing Louis' ass in political meetings. Here, though, where Louis doesn't have too much say-so and the twins are in charge, things have been more normal in our relationship. I've been taking contraceptives, but those things aren't foolproof, are they?"

"Wow," Sage croaked. She was about to burst with happiness, and—embarrassingly—it came in the form of more tears. She hated crying so damn much, but she couldn't stop the fresh flood, no matter how hard she fought it.

"Geoffrey and I decided that if it's a boy, we'll name him Damian." Candice grinned. "And if it's a girl, well . . . we're going to name her Sage."

Sage hid her face in her hands. She sobbed.

"Aunt Sage?" Candice said, concerned.

"I-I'm sorry!" Sage rasped. She sounded like someone had punched her in the stomach. "But this is such wonderful news . . . Candice, I'm so happy for you."

"You'll be there this time, right?" Candice asked hopefully. "For the birth. You'll hold my hand and tell me to 'push that fucker out'?"

Sage laughed. Face shiny with tears and snot, she said, "You've always got to push those fuckers out."

"And you noticed, right?"

Sage wiped her eyes. "Noticed what?"

"Aunt Sage—*Olivia*! She's been getting close to that girl from Elysium. I saw them holding hands at the tournament, and they were dancing awfully close to each other now."

Sage arched a brow. "Are you talking about Isadora?"

"Yes!" Candice grinned. "That's her. I think it's kind of cute, actually, and I'm so happy for Olivia. She had the heartbreak of a lifetime a few years ago. Did she tell you about her agent?"

Agent? What agent?

Sage shook her head. "No."

"Well, she fell in love with her agent," Candice explained. She looked so excited, as if she hadn't gossiped about family in a long time. Perhaps Damian truly had run a tight ship when it came to honesty and talking about people to their faces. No shit-talking. Surprising, really. "Which was the wrong thing to do. That's like falling in love with your boss. Damian warned her not to mix business with pleasure, but you know how hormones are and when you're taking nude shots all day and posing in all kinds of positions, things are bound to happen. So they got it on, but then she found out that the guy was having sex with every client he had. Olivia showed Damian the proof, and let's just say that we haven't seen him since."

"Wow," Sage breathed. What on earth had Damian done to the guy? "I didn't know."

"Olivia's been heartbroken since," Candice said. "She's taken a break from dating, but still—it didn't look good for her mental health for many years. I thought she was never going to get over that guy." Candice smiled. "Well, maybe things will be different now. And with you here, Olivia's as hopeful as ever. We're all so happy we can be a family again—you can run the pizzeria with Micah or maybe even start a new one in Emerald City! Micah's looking into going to college, so a change of scenery would be amazing for him."

"I agree."

"The twins are going to need you, too, Aunt Sage. Now that

445

Damian's resting, they're putting the next Allseer in power. Those two don't want to rule, but Damian's closest advisor, Josiah, will. But still—they're going to look to you for guidance. I feel like an idiot sounding like the mother here, but I know it's been awkward for you after so many years of hibernation."

Candice took both of Sage's hands now. She kneaded her knuckles. "Aunt Sage, no one blames you," she said sincerely. "We know it wasn't your fault . . . but now that you're awake, we want you to live a life with us."

Sage's lip trembled.

"Mom?"

"Mother?"

Castor and Pollux arrived in their car. After the tournament, they had taken off to see Samson. It looked like they had stopped fighting over that stupid bet because they were smiling now. They came over in their leather jackets and boots. Castor had his hair slicked back, showing off his beautiful features, and Pollux had a fresh buzz cut on the side of his head. The rest of his strands were long and shiny, genetics that he and his brother had inherited from their father. Definitely two of the most handsome men Sage had ever seen.

"I think she's done partying for the night." Candice nodded at them. "Aunt Sage, we'll talk later." She kissed Sage's hands and returned to the party.

Alone with her sons, Sage cleared her throat. She was thankful her tears had dried by now so there was no evidence of her crying. She looked up at her sons, mighty curious all of a sudden. "So, any relationships I should know about?"

Castor and Pollux glanced at each other.

"I just got the scoop from Candice about Olivia's love life and I just realized I don't know anything about yours. You boys seem well disciplined and respectful, but I haven't forgotten who your father is."

"Oh." Pollux turned an ugly red.

Castor just stood there, undeterred. "Sex and sexual dalliances don't interest me," he said blandly.

"There's something wrong with him," Pollux admitted, more crimson than a cardinal now. Maybe he was embarrassed to admit the sort of experiments he had partaken in, so he focused all his energy on Castor. "Like, I know he has a penis and testicles because I've seen them—kinda small, but you use what you're given—know what I mean—but anyway—"

Castor seized Pollux by the shirt, about to punch him, but Pollux ducked just in time.

"What?!" Pollux exclaimed. "It's true, asshole!"

"There is nothing 'wrong' with me," Castor growled. "I just don't like sex. I prefer to spend my time and energy reading books on piloting or perfecting my skills as a fastball player. You, on the other hand, are a complete nutcase." He turned to Sage. "I honestly don't know how Father hasn't castrated him yet. Pollux likes them in all shapes and sizes, Mother."

"I-I just like to experiment," Pollux sputtered.

"A bit too much." Castor smiled. He was losing the battle against his amusement. It seemed hard for him not to laugh.

"No!" Pollux exclaimed, waving his hands. "Don't tell her!"

"Tell me what?" Sage mused, wondering just how good Castor was on the fastball court.

"Pollux has always been well behaved," Castor explained. "So I will give him that much. When he hit puberty, he started to take an interest in one of our palace maids. Father strictly forbade him from taking advantage of a helpless girl who was just there to earn a paycheck. Besides, the maid was way too old for him at the time. So Pollux moved on from his first crush to practically everyone in the sixth grade."

"Not true," Pollux grumbled. "I dated a lot, but not *everyone*. And when I got to high school, I was very well behaved."

"Then college happened," Castor said. "He and I went to a military academy in the capital where we honed our skills as warriors and learned how to intuit battlefields. It was a boarding school, and Father thought it'd be a perfect opportunity for us to fully mature without his constant influence. That was, until he heard Pollux was getting a little too friendly with all our classmates. You see, Pollux was there to have a good time, not learn—"

"Not true!" Pollux sputtered. "And I'm friendly with everyone—why is that bad?"

"Yes," Castor hissed, "it's bad when you flirt and sleep with everything that breathes! Let's just say that the academy's rankings dropped across the board that year." He huffed at Sage. "No one had any clue why because our classmates kept this asshole a secret. So, to see what was going on, guess what Father did?"

Sage laughed, picturing all this in her head. "What?"

"He hid in Pollux's dormitory one night. It was a random night, too—right in the middle of the semester—and no one suspected a thing. To this day, I still don't know how he got in undetected. There are always students everywhere and rumors spread like wildfire."

"I swear I didn't see him!" Pollux choked.

"He was sitting in the corner between the shadows," Castor said to Sage. "Pollux and his companions were so horny that they didn't see him, either. So the eight of them crawled into bed—"

"Eight?" Sage choked.

"I'm sorry, Ma!" Pollux wailed. "It's just I was experimenting as I said—"

"And Pollux said that Father was actually *talking* through the whole thing." Castor cracked up with laughter. "Oh my Stars."

Sage was horrified. " 'Talking'?"

"Making sex sounds and everything!" Pollux cried in horror. "Egging us on and shit! I thought it was one of the guys and it turned me on even more! He told me who to stroke, who to suck, and who to fondle as I got the banging of a lifetime. And then, just as I climaxed, I saw him in the corner of my vision.

"I think I had a heart attack." Pollux clutched his chest. He was panting, as if he was reliving that moment over again in vivid detail. How could anyone forget something like that? "Literally, my entire world stopped. Father was just sitting there, staring at me as if he were a corpse. It was the most unnerving thing ever. He even asked me, in front of everyone, if I was going to finish sucking the dick I had in front of me. Or maybe I wanted to finish the pussy waiting for me on the pillow."

Pollux sighed. "I was so embarrassed, Mom... and utterly ashamed. Dad literally grabbed me by the back of my neck like a dog, hauled me up from the bed, and had me apologize to my partners about what a disgrace I was to the throne. 'I couldn't control my sexual urges, and therefore, I just got you all expelled from the academy.'" Pollux lowered his head. "Myself included."

Castor snorted. "Rightfully so."

"Wow," Sage said softly. Inside, her heart yearned for Damian so much that it hurt. She knew why Damian was so hard on Pollux... because he'd had orgies as Warlord of Mousafeld himself. He always described his shame and regret. They were actions he could never take back. Pollux had been way too young to be involved in shit like that. Plus, he had been ruining the school and distracting other students.

"At first, I didn't understand what the big deal was," Pollux said. "Everyone in my group had consented. No one was being raped or forced to do it. But then I realized it wasn't about the sex—it was about honor, about upholding your dignity and focusing on what was important. I wasn't at that school to have sex—I was at that school to learn.

"I gave a speech to my class before I stepped down. I would have been expelled, of course, but I wanted to do right by everyone. I apologized to the school, and then Dad took me back to the palace."

"So where did you finish your studies?" Sage asked.

"I took classes online," Pollux said. "I had to because I spent the next four years traveling the city. I worked in all kinds of stores, took charge of community projects, and visited every impoverished sector I could. It wasn't until I started working at the homeless shelters that I learned the true meaning of life.

"I was so ashamed by what I had done that I apologized to Dad and the entire city. This time, I meant it. I really wanted to get into the military like Castor, but no one wanted me after that scandal. I was a disgrace. It wasn't until Castor became a general that he recruited me, and I've been his spymaster ever since."

Sage smiled at Castor. "That was very noble of you."

"I know he needed a chance," Castor said. "Besides, Pollux has settled down now. I don't think he's partaken in another orgy since."

"No way." Pollux started coughing. "Or else I'll see Dad in that chair again and I won't be able to climax." He turned to Sage with puppy dog eyes. "Are you ashamed of me, Ma?"

"Of course not," Sage said. "We all have to get a kick in the ass once in a while."

"Have you ever done something shameful?"

"You mean like an orgy? No."

"You've never done anything bad?" Pollux breathed.

"Of course," Sage mused, surprised that Damian hadn't tried to throw her under the bus. Then again, the fucker didn't have any negative stories about her because Sage had been (and was) a goody-two-shoes. Damian was an expert asshole, but he never made up stuff about anyone. He found falsehoods too destructive and unfair. "Just not to the point of taking eight people to bed and disrespecting academy rules."

Pollux sighed, but Sage wasn't going to beat him up.

"Oh!" Sage grinned. "I stole some kid's lunch money once."

Pollux blinked at her. "That's it?"

Castor snorted. "Be honest, Mother: the kid deserved it, so your 'sin' was justified."

"He did deserve it," Sage said. "But it's still stealing."

"Perhaps, but the reason is justified."

Pollux waved his hand. "Not helping."

"How about we cease talking about Pollux's indulgences and trying to find fault in Mother's past?" Castor suggested. "And play a game of fastball instead?"

Sage's heart stopped. "Fastball?"

"Certainly. The court is empty now, and I've been longing to play for some time. I also know that you enjoy this sport as well."

It was Sage's turn to blush. God, she was terrible . . .

"Come on." Castor took her hand. "We can rest later."

"I think Castor just wants to prove he's better than you," Pollux said from behind, keeping up with them. "He's a dick, you see?"

Sage laughed. "I think he's a very genuine person."

"You're right: that's why he's always a dick."

Castor glared at him, but he wouldn't dare start another brawl in front of Sage. He did well ignoring his brother's insults, which did get a bit out of hand when Pollux said, "I swear he's the biggest asshole."

"You can shut the fuck up now," Sage spat.

Pollux quieted down instantly.

Castor kissed Sage's cheek.

The fastball court was empty. This was Sage's chance to shine. Her imagination took off, throwing her right back into that finals match between Royal Academy and Cut University. She grinned as she looked up and around the stadium, wondering what it would be like to have people cheering for her.

"I haven't played fastball in years," Sage said quietly. "Since Little Man's death . . ."

Not that Castor and Pollux would know who Little Man was. Or maybe they did.

"Dad told us," Pollux said, flipping his hair back. "But that's in the past. We have to look forward to tomorrow, don't we?"

Sage smiled. Tears welled in her eyes again. "Yes."

"And after we take back Diamond City, Castor and I want to show you Emerald. Hey—we can take a tour! That way you can see everything, Ma. You've never been to Emerald City, have you?"

"No," Sage said quietly.

"Well, what do you say?" Pollux bumbled up next to her. "We'll take a mini vacation, just the three of us, and enjoy ourselves! I promise no more orgies for me. Maybe a dalliance or two with a hot chick, but I curtain the windows and lock the doors."

"Father spared your penis," Castor murmured, "but I don't think Mother will. She'll cut it off in front of everyone."

Sage laughed. "That's my specialty."

Pollux cleared his throat. "So we've heard."

"That sounds amazing," Sage concurred. "Not the penis part—the vacation."

"So is that a promise?" Pollux said hopefully.

Sage's lip trembled. She, of course, couldn't say no to her beautiful boys. Hope got the better of her once again, and she nodded.

"Promise."

CHAPTER 30

The Fight for the Future

It was a fastball game for the ages.

It took Sage a little while to get comfortable on the court again, but she found a rhythm by midnight. She could meet each one of Castor's hits with ease. She could tell that he was going soft on her, though, and it infuriated her. Regardless, she didn't complain because she was just warming up. Pretty soon, Castor had to up his game when Sage got a bit more aggressive with her hits. Their best volley was nearly twenty minutes long, and Castor only slipped up because Pollux let out a piercing whistle.

"Damn! Mom's a pretty bad bitch!"

"Are you for real?!" Castor yelled at him after missing that shot by miles. "You're going to make me go deaf!"

Soft clapping made them all look up. To their amusement, Tai and Sword Devil had just stepped into the stadium.

"If I had known there was a fastball after-party, I would have stayed," Tai said happily.

"The champ is here!" Pollux exclaimed, waving his hands like a cheerleader. "Castor is about to get his ass kicked—*again*!"

"We saw your moves," Sword Devil said to Sage, bowing her head. "You are very good."

If Sword Devil was talking, then that was a huge compliment. She wouldn't have been wasting her energy otherwise.

"I want to play the Optimum," Tai said, stepping onto the court.

"And then I want to fight her," Sword Devil said. "With swords."

Sage didn't want to fight any of them, actually, because she knew she was going to get her ass whipped. She grew anxious at the thought of losing, but it'd be worse if she pussied out and walked away. She had to take up the challenge, so she did.

If she expected to lose, then she wouldn't be disappointed when it happened. And if it didn't happen, well, she'd be pleasantly surprised.

Sage *was* able to keep up, after all. Tai didn't take it easy on her like Castor did, but this was life or death for Sage, who didn't want to look like a fool. She gave it all she had, even if she had to tumble on the concrete and scrape up her elbows and knees. She lost a few volleys, but she also won a couple against *the* grandmaster Tai. When it was game point, Sage came back twice, and just when she thought she was going to win, she couldn't get to that corner shot in time.

"Wow!" Tai clapped from his side of the court. "Nice try there, Optimum! Truly!"

Fine, Sage had lost . . . but at least she wasn't humiliated. Castor and Pollux pulled her to her feet. Sword Devil wasn't going to bed tonight until she had her match against Sage.

"Here you go." Pollux gave Sage her sword. He was always carrying it around for her. Like everyone else in Ruby City, he was expecting an attack at any moment.

Sage hadn't fought in such a long time . . . but that didn't matter. Swinging her sword wasn't something she could ever forget how to do. Perhaps her body was a bit out of shape and wasted thanks to all the blood she had given, but she could still put opponents in the ground. Sword Devil was no exception. Of course, Sage had studied that battle between Sword Devil and Damian so many times at Royal Academy, so she knew exactly what she was up against, but she was by no means afraid.

In fact, Sage was confident. This was going to be quick.

To take down Sword Devil, Sage had to play quite a bit. "Play" meant to entertain each of Sword Devil's strikes. She had to dodge every swipe, roll, jump, and run, and *not* ever retaliate herself. It looked like a match that was pretty uneven, and, for the most part, it was, because Sage never got a hit on Sword Devil.

Sword Devil had two swords. Evading her was quite the challenge. But her excellent handling and skill were worthless if Sage was fast. Sword Devil was going to have to win on pure stamina, but unfortunately for her, she was bound to tire out eventually.

Sage was pretty tired, too, but she knew how to conserve energy and use it at the right time. That's what Damian had done in his match and that's what Sage had to do here. So when Sword Devil's moves got sloppy, and they weren't quite as precise as they had been at the beginning of the battle, Sage got her finishing blows in.

Hard.

One to Sword Devil's face, breaking her nose, and the other to her exposed belly, breaking her sternum. Sword Devil flew back, lost her grip on both her swords, and hit the ground, unmoving.

"Whoa . . ." Pollux breathed.

Castor looked impressed.

Tai was gawking.

Sage sheathed her sword and gave it back to Pollux. She could say that she was done for the day.

"Optimum." Tai bowed. "I am truly humbled by your fight today. Forget fastball—would you duel me instead? When you have recovered, of course."

Sage smiled. "Sure." She looked at the comatose Sword Devil next to the fastball net. "Is she going to be all right?"

"My lady, I'm sure of it." Tai checked his companion for a pulse. "She is definitely still alive."

"I'll call a medic," Pollux said, screwing up his face in an effort not to laugh.

Castor led Sage out of the stadium. He held her hand gently like Damian would. He kissed it, too.

"Thanks for playing with me tonight," Sage said to him with a smile. "I truly appreciate it."

"But of course, Mother. I know you enjoy fastball greatly. Aunt Olivia always told us how terrible you were at it, but I honestly thought you were rather adept."

"I think you took it easy on me, but I still had fun."

"Indeed. Perhaps we can play again tomorrow."

Castor's phone went off. Sage had already learned from Damian that that was never a good sign. Castor and Pollux were in charge here, so of course they'd be primary contacts, and calls at this time of night were definitely a cause for concern. Sage held her breath as Castor answered it.

"It's Randall," Castor said to Sage. "He says he spotted movement north of Ruby City. Looks like we've got some visitors."

Sage imagined that the only visitors they'd be getting were Wren and her Mutatio. There was no one else out there, but Sage was guessing at this point. There was always the possibility of stragglers.

Castor didn't hesitate: he picked up Sage and dashed through the city until they reached its northernmost point. These were the same plains Sage had fought Jared in. She had also come across many Diamond City stragglers here as well. This time, there was only one scooter and a very shaken Ilan on top of it.

Ilan?

Castor landed right in front of him, Sage in his arms. He put her down. "Who are you?"

Ilan stared at Castor. From his crazy hair, unkept beard, and shaggy clothes, he had been on the run for some time. His panting said that his pursuers were no pushovers and that he was lucky to be alive. He slowly turned his head to look at Sage. "A-Adele?"

"It's Sage." Sage studied him, too. God, she had sworn he was dead. Samson hadn't seen him leave Elysium at all. None of the hybrids had jumped aboard his ship in their frantic escape from that place. "Ilan, where the hell have you been?"

"Do you know him, Mother?" Castor asked, but he could catch on pretty quickly. The answer was evident when their tones were this casual.

"Diamond City." Ilan stepped fully off of his scooter. He looked from Sage to Castor again, as if searching for Damian between the two. Perhaps, for a second, he had confused Castor for Damian, which wouldn't be accurate if Castor was referring to Sage as "Mother".

"This is my son, Castor," Sage said.

Ilan blinked rapidly. *You have a son?* he seemed to say with the tightness of his lips.

"Mother, who the hell is this?" Castor asked again, because now he was getting different vibes. It was obvious that Ilan was thinking of more than just friendship.

"He's a hybrid from Elysium," Sage said, taking a step forward. "He actually helped me defeat the Prime."

"Y-yes." Ilan bowed his head. For someone who had escaped from Elysium and had perhaps been hiding in Diamond City, he didn't look too banged up. "And I've finally found an opportunity to travel to the esteemed Ruby City."

Sage drew her sword, making Ilan jump. "What the fuck do you want?" she asked again.

"Please," he whimpered, hands in the air. "I'm not here to cause trouble! I actually escaped from Diamond City to come find you when no one was looking." Ilan exhaled. Now that there was a less likely chance Sage was going to lop off his head, he could explain.

"There's nothing but Mutatio and hybrids in Diamond City," Ilan said. "And, as you know, security to get into the city is very tight. There are only a handful of us hybrids there, and I just managed to escape."

At last, Sage noticed the bloodstains on Ilan's clothes. He must have killed a Mutatio or two to make it here. From the distress glimmering in his eyes, a few of his buddies were gone.

"So she's holding you prisoner there?" Sage said.

"She's not letting anyone escape." Ilan wiped his face. "Obviously, she doesn't want anyone contacting you. By now, I'm sure she knows that someone's escaped . . ." He looked over his shoulder.

Sage looked up, too.

In the distance, flapping their wings in the air, were what looked like birds. But Sage already knew that those were the Mutatio. She could hear their roars. Castor touched his temple.

"They know what I've done!" Ilan croaked. "And they've probably slaughtered everyone!"

"Perhaps not everyone," Castor said softly. "If they were smart enough to hide."

"I'm sorry, but what the hell are you all waiting for?!"

Sage blinked. Ilan gritted his teeth.

"Why are you just standing there, allowing that *bitch* to take over?!" Ilan yelled.

Castor threw the first punch. His fist blasted Ilan right in the middle of the face, knocking him on his ass. Castor seized his shirt, hauled him up, and held a blade to his throat. " 'Allowing'?" he said dangerously. "Is that what you think we're doing? 'Allowing' this to happen? You have no idea everything that we've been through the past six months fighting those demons that nearly wiped out our entire city."

Castor threw Ilan to the ground.

"Fine," Ilan choked. The mole on his jaw was intact. It was hard to believe it had survived all these ordeals better than they had. "Fair enough. But what about now? What are you planning?"

"As if we would tell you."

Pollux and Tai finally made it to the scene. Gertrude, Tate, Sonia, L, and the others probably already knew they had visitors and were awaiting updates. Right now, there weren't any to give.

Sage's intentions had never been to allow her sister to take over

Diamond City. She knew that she had to get stronger if she was going to stand a chance of defeating her and all those monsters. Samson was still working on the guns, but Sage knew she had to work on herself, too.

And so, that's what she did the next few months.

It took Sage a while to recuperate her strength and stamina, but she trained as hard as she ever had in her life. She started with Castor and Pollux, who were excellent sparring partners, and then recruited Tai and Sword Devil to give her hell. Eventually, it turned into a routine: breakfast, training, dinner, poetry, and sleep.

On the weekends, Sage visited Damian's nest. She'd sit next to one of those masses of flesh, stroke it, kiss it, and recite all her horrible poetry out loud. Sometimes, Castor and Pollux went with her. Others, they knew she needed her time with Damian alone. Other than her poetry, Sage wouldn't really say much to him. She felt that any words of hope were meaningless. It's not like Damian could hear her anyway.

Although Sage got the impression that he could. When she spoke to him, she'd feel shifts in the air. Little tendrils would come out and weave around her arms in a very gentle manner. It'd feel like someone was stitching a wooly sweater right on her skin.

"I love you, darling," Sage whispered to the air one of those times she had come to visit. "And our sons do, too. They respect you so much."

No response. Sage felt a thick warmth in her chest, though, as if a flower were blooming inside her. She hugged that feeling to her body as tightly as she could. When she fell asleep, she had dreams of Damian. They weren't memories, either—they were random moments of her and Damian watching *The Rainbow in Me* on the couch, taking professional nude photos (Sage would never do that), or walking through the city at night when they could see all the colors. Pinks, purples, and blues were always flashing about in the Cut District.

Her home.

"I'm going to take it back," Sage promised him. "That's my city, Damian. I've given my life for it so many times and I'm not going to let it go."

That promise kept her motivated. Sage didn't let Hayes forget what his mission was afterward, but she didn't think too much of it herself. In her head, she was going to Emerald City to be with her sons and take that much needed vacation. She'd be holding Candice's hand during childbirth and maybe watching Olivia get married.

It was nice to see a happy Olivia for once. Not that the girl wasn't always bumbling around, but she exuded a certain peace now that she and Isadora were going steady. At least, that's what Sage heard through family gossip. She saw them together, too, during one of her training sessions with Castor at the fastball stadium. The rest of the Diamond City military were using the fields outside for drills.

"Adele—*Sage*—is definitely incredible," Isadora agreed. She was munching on popcorn with her feet up. In Elysium, she had never been so relaxed or sported such classy clothes. Paige and Pedro were working hard to make sure everyone had a fashion statement. Isadora even had red highlights in her hair, which Pollux had done himself. He was surprisingly good with hair. In fact, he had given Sage a cut last weekend. "You should have seen her in Elysium during the ball. I've never seen anyone stand up to the Prime the way she did that day.."

"My aunt is fearless," Olivia said happily.

Perhaps that's what it looked like on the outside. On the inside, Sage was just as terrified as all of them. Fighting and training were ways for her to shove those insecurities down. That's why she basked in this battle against Castor, whose moves were becoming sloppy and giving Sage plenty of opportunities to pull off an easy win.

"Wow . . ." Pollux breathed from the sidelines. "And I thought Dad was intense."

"You're trying to overpower me," Sage said to the panting Castor, blocking another one of his strikes, "but that's not how you're going to win. You need to come up with a strategy that exploits any slip-ups I make. You're so concentrated on what *you* can do that you don't even pay attention to me. I haven't seen you observe me or follow any of my movements yet."

Castor dropped his sword. He crumbled to the ground and lowered his head. "It matters not. Even if I observe you, it wouldn't make much of a difference."

Pollux snorted. "It wouldn't."

Tai and Sword Devil could both attest to that.

"It does make a difference," Sage said to Castor. "You just have to know what to look for and you have to start seeing patterns. Everyone has a weakness."

"Except for you," Castor mumbled.

Sage laughed, but then she saw Samson.

Her face fell.

"Trust me," Samson said out loud, striding into the stadium. "*Especially* her."

Preacher gasped. He along with his friends from the Clarity District, who made a big block of white in the corner of the arena, stood and bowed to the Lolligo in their presence. Then they raised their hands and praised the dead Forefathers in the skies for sending Samson, the Lolligo Prophet, to them in times of need.

Sage wasn't having any of it. The only thing she was grateful for right now was her break. She was tired and hungry. She let Castor and Pollux handle Samson and made her leave. This time, unfortunately, escaping wouldn't be that easy.

"Hold it, Sage." Samson stepped forward. "I've come to see how you're coming along. Rumor has it that you're kicking everyone's ass, so it's about time someone put you in your place." He cracked his knuckles. "What say you we spar and see what you're really made of?"

"Don't know," Sage said coolly. "Would your lovestruck bitch approve of that?"

Samson blinked.

Castor and Pollux, who had clearly never spoken to Samson about Sage's run-in with Faye, looked away. The rest of the arena, preachers included, was stock-still.

"What?" Samson said.

"You know exactly what, you fucking Squid," Sage spat. "First that motherfucker you call an ally nearly shoots me and my husband down, then you try to kill my husband by allowing monsters to raid the city, and then when I stop you all your bitch can tell me is that my 'lot' and I need to die. Does that include my sons, too? And every other fucking hybrid that's helping you fight for some semblance of freedom?"

Samson was turning pale. It was hard to tell because he didn't have any skin, but his fleshy muscles were a very milky pink now.

"We're sorry, Samson." Castor was the only one brave enough to speak. "But Mother still doesn't trust us after what happened with the Mutatio. She feels greatly offended that we didn't believe in her to defeat the forces that endangered this city as well as my father's life. She expected us to perform better."

It was hard to believe that Castor and Pollux hadn't already talked to Samson about this, but maybe they didn't want to stir any trouble. Ruby City was doing so well, and the last thing they needed was animosity between their strongest fighters.

Even so, it had been almost a whole fucking year since the Mutatio attack, and Samson had never bothered to wonder why Sage was avoiding him? Perhaps he hadn't. He had been so busy with his mass production of weapons—and Lolligo were in no way emotional beings—so maybe it had completely slipped his mind.

No—bullshit. Samson wasn't stupid. He had been giving Sage space and time on purpose, banking on her "getting over it" eventually. Clearly, she still hadn't, and now Castor was explaining to Samson yet again why Sage was taking her sword and getting the fuck out of there.

"Fine, and I get that," Samson said loud enough for her to hear, "but what's all this about my 'love-struck bitch'? SAGE!" He thundered across the stadium to reach her, but Sage drew her sword.

"Let's get something very fucking clear here, Samson," Sage snarled. "I am too goddamn old and I've been through too goddamn much to put up with your prejudiced bullshit. I don't know what you and your girlfriend are hiding, but you're going to have to kill a lot of fucking people to accomplish your goal."

"WHAT THE FUCK ARE YOU TALKING ABOUT, SAGE?!"

Suddenly, it dawned on Sage: if she died, then who on earth was supposed to defend all these Enhanced against the Lolligo? The three Squids already had the weapons to decimate anyone with Cells, so why not wipe out the entire city from existence, too? Samson and his Lolligo would be the true saviors of humanity then.

Sage couldn't die. Not yet. Not until she killed the Lolligo first.

Until she killed Samson.

"What 'goal'?!" Samson continued to yell. "Can you speak so we can all understand what's going on in your fucked-up head?"

"I'm the one who's 'fucked up', am I?" Sage said. "You're right: I am fucked up. I've always put my trust in you, but now it's obvious what your plans are, and I want everyone here to know it." Sage raised her voice in hopes that even the people standing outside the stadium could hear her.

"The Lolligo want to wipe us out!" Sage exclaimed. "All of us! They're only using us now to get back into Diamond City, but once we defeat Wren and the Mutatio, they'll come after our heads next! Every hybrid and Enhanced will die!"

"HOLD IT!" Samson cried. "Where on earth are you getting this from?! We're here busting our asses to help you!"

"Excuse me, sir," Castor said politely. "But it's true what Mother says. It was Faye—your love interest—who planted doubt in all of us as far as the Lolligo's true intentions. My brother and I heard her ourselves: she wishes to destroy the hybrids because she sees them as a threat. What makes us think you won't follow through with her claims when we're done taking over Diamond City?"

"This is crazy!" Samson sputtered. "All because Faye said some stupid shit while I was goddamn unconscious? Are these the sort of games we're going to play here, Sage, when we've known each other for so long? If I wanted to kill you, I could have!"

"I know that," Sage said icily. "And you don't have to keep reminding me. But you weren't going to kill me when it was in your best interest to keep me alive and fighting in your wars. That's what all this has been about: using me to fight no matter how 'fucked up' I am."

This time, Samson hesitated. Sage's glare got more intense.

"Deny it, Squid."

"We've helped each other," Samson said quietly. "Have we not?"

"Maybe we have, but I'm not going to take any chances when it comes to your loyalties. These people depend on me, and I won't be caught off guard because I think you're my brother. You would have killed Damian if I hadn't stabbed you, and so I'm going to make myself clear."

Sage looked at Castor and Pollux, whose faces were turning pale, too. They wouldn't dare defy her, though.

"I want you to exterminate the Lolligo once my sister is dead," Sage said to them. "You don't let a single one survive."

"Sage..." Samson croaked. Actual tears welled in his eyes. "I don't understand—"

"I'M DONE WITH YOU, SAMSON!" Sage roared. "I'M FUCKING TIRED OF THESE GAMES I KEEP PLAYING WITH YOU! I always believed in you, even when Damian told me you had ulterior motives, but it's become so obvious to me now that your end goal is to kill me and anyone with Cells in their body! Bruce nearly blasted my head off when I was down, and you jumped at the chance to let the Mutatio consume Damian!"

"No..." Samson took a sharp breath. "I would have *never* let him die—"

"BULLSHIT!" Sage sputtered. She threw her sword at Samson's feet. "Bullshit! That's *fucking* bullshit—BULLSHIT!"

Sage turned around and walked away. She heard a thump as

Samson fell to his knees. He didn't seem capable of standing. Castor joined Sage's side immediately. Pollux bumbled down from the stands to reach them.

"Please give me another weapon," Sage said to them. "A regular sword this time. No Slainium. No metal that a fucking Squid has touched."

"Yes, Mother," Castor said.

"Yes, Mom," Pollux said.

The next morning, Sage had breakfast at Jo's Yo-Go. She felt calm. She was at peace. Her hands didn't shake as she wrote another poem for Damian in her little booklet. She was enjoying some freshly-squeezed orange juice (those indoor farms were truly incredible) and killer raspberry danishes. Hamilton was having his usual Berry Goji Getaway.

The strangest part was everyone else was calm, too. Nobody approached her, gave her funny looks, or asked her about the Lolligo incident at the fastball stadium last night.

That's because anyone who had witnessed that fight, worse than any of the ones they were about to wage against Wren, had kept it to themselves. Perhaps if they stayed quiet about it, they could pretend it never happened. They could ignore Sage's threat to the Lolligo and just move on with their merry lives. If they didn't speak about it, they wouldn't give it life, wouldn't allow it to spread and become reality . . .

Sage had no regrets. Perhaps there were inklings of doubt here and there, which were fueled by grief over Damian's state, but then she quickly realized that wasn't it at all. It had nothing to do with her emotions and everything to do with evidence.

That, she wasn't making up. The Lolligo wanted to exterminate hybrids and Enhanced, and they were looking for any opportunity to do so. That's what Bruce had proven . . . right?

"Allseer Louis."

Everyone in the shop stood up. Everyone but Sage, who was

busy writing in her book. She was nearly done with it, too—the last page. Pretty soon, she'd give this to Damian. Then she'd leave for war in Diamond City.

"Thank you, but there's no need for that," Louis said politely. "I'm here for some breakfast."

And Sage, of course. He didn't hesitate to order his eggs and bacon then take his tray and sit down right in front of her.

Sage looked up. There was the beautiful Allseer Louis in all his white-and-gold glory. His blond curls were soft and bouncy. His plain shirt and pants fit him perfectly. He might have gone up in size or two because he was a lot more muscular than he had ever been in his life. He smiled.

"How are you, Sage?"

"I'm fine," Sage said curtly. "For now."

"I hear you've been training hard. It's nice to see you're back to the Sage we all know and love. Not that we don't love you when you're not fighting, but you know we look up to you."

Sage continued to write her poetry. Louis got a bit uncomfortable because his prompt to get her to speak had failed. He was going to have to say something else.

"I heard we were getting ready to infiltrate Diamond City," Louis said. "What are your thoughts?"

"You want to know what my thoughts are?" Sage didn't stop writing. "All right, I'll tell you. Louis... when we return to Diamond City, I want you to step down from the throne."

Louis stared. Steam was blowing into his face from his eggs and bacon.

Sage had to meet his eyes so she could communicate how serious she was. "You asked me a long time ago what you had to do to be a worthy Allseer. Well, you're a shitty one. Because of you, I watched a couple commit suicide after the motel manager kicked them out of their room. You hated Damian so much—were so fucking prideful—that you never asked for help. Instead, you let your own people die and starve. People in Diamond City were miserable because of you, and don't tell me otherwise because I saw it with my own eyes. So when you get back to Diamond City, you and the council are going to hold an election. The districts will each pick a candidate they feel is worthy enough for the throne. You are going to step down and allow someone else to take over."

"I can't control everything," Louis said quietly.

"Bullshit," Sage spat. "You can fucking help people as much as you can. But your head was in the goddamn clouds searching for ways to get me into your bed. That is unforgivable."

"I'm not going to step down, Sage. Not that easily."

"No," Sage said. "You *are* going to step down. Or I'm going to cut off your head and hang it next to your daddy's in Mousafeld. I'm sure Damian will be pleased."

"I don't understand you," Louis said angrily. He leaned forward, and the energy he let off captured the attention of everyone in the room. No one tried to hide it now—everyone was point-blank staring. "It's like you're obsessed with this guy, almost to the point that you worship him as a god! Do you hear yourself?!"

"I do," Sage hissed. "And I'm not speaking lies, Louis. There is an obvious difference between you and Damian, but we're not here to talk about the latter because he's *dead.* And you know what? You fucking coward—you killed him on purpose, didn't you?"

Louis' jaw dropped. "How could you think that was me?!"

"Because it was. Nova is no idiot—she's had years to perfect all her serums and she would never in a million years give Damian a faulty one. Nova loved his daughter from Mousafeld—respected him way too much—to do something as half-ass as inject him with a serum that would turn him into a monster. That was *you* who tinkered with it on purpose—or bribed Nova to do it or whatever—and I'm sure you fucked it up to kill him."

Sage gritted her teeth. She clenched her fists. "I swear that the only reason I haven't killed you right now is because I actually care about my soul. I believe there is a God watching us and every decision we make, and I'm not talking about fucking Squids. The right thing to do would be to let you admit to everyone in Diamond City what a complete asshole and reckless ruler you've been, and that's exactly what you're going to do or I really will kill you. Then, if God asks me why I did what I did, I'll have plenty of good reasons to give him."

Louis continued to gape at her. "Are you crazy?"

"Maybe I am," Sage said icily. "But that's how it's going to be. If you have a problem with that, then it looks like you're in trouble. And don't even think about sending Tyrus and Herman after me, because I'll cut them down faster than you can brush your stupid hair."

Sage slammed her book closed, picked up her bag, and left the restaurant. She had eyes staring at her on the way out, but she didn't meet any of them.

"Sage!" It didn't take long for Louis to follow. He reached her side. "What's going on? Why are you so aggressive lately?"

"I'm tired of the bullshit," Sage said. "Now leave me alone. I'm going to say bye to my husband, who's dead because of you."

Sage left Louis standing in the middle of the sidewalk like an idiot. It was a long walk to Damian's nest, but she welcomed the distance as well as the solidarity it offered. It was winter time again, so the cold was brutal out here. Sage's jacket wasn't near enough, but she didn't really care much for her wellbeing at the moment. Damian would have scolded her, but he didn't have a mouth to scold her with anymore, so fuck him.

Strangely, the nest stiffened as soon as Sage entered it. Was that Damian's way of showing her he was angry? Sage didn't really care.

Sage left him the poetry book at her usual spot next to one of his trunks. Then she looked up into the mess of spindly flesh that didn't have any rhyme or reason. It was hard to hold all her emotions inside. She would have never dreamed that the beautiful Warlord she had met in Mousafeld would become *this*. A shapeless monster. A true, cruel joke played by Louis.

"I thought about it," Sage whispered to Damian. The nest stopped rummaging. All was stiff, as if Damian was fighting to hear every word she uttered. "I thought about it, you know. Killing him and ending his life, like we should have done so long ago. If it weren't for Louis and my naivety, you would still be here with me."

Sage took a deep breath. She clenched her fists. The wind didn't reach her here so there was nothing to blow the hair from her face. She shoved it back angrily. She had told Pollux her bangs were too long.

"How did you do it?" Sage croaked. "How did you go thirty years without me? I can't even go one without you! I-I'm not as strong . . ." She wiped her eyes. "I'm nowhere near as strong as I thought I was. You once told me that you envied my resistance and willpower. Well, I have none, Damian. Look at me . . . I'm a mess."

A tendril crept over the ground and toward her left foot ever so slowly. Sage fought for control of her emotions so she could tell Damian what was about to happen next.

"We're going into the city," Sage said. "And I'll be taking charge. My sister and all her mutant monsters have to die . . . and then the Lolligo do, too. You were right all along, Damian: they want to kill everyone that's non-human."

The tendril wound around Sage's leg.

"I'm going to fight again," Sage whispered, "for Diamond City. Just like I did in the Unification War. It seems to be my mission in life . . . but I can't complain." She wiped her eyes again. "If I can save my loved ones one last time . . . give our sons a brighter future . . . then I will do it."

Sage stopped when she heard movement. She whipped around as Damian let her go. She edged out of the nest and froze at whom she saw approaching her.

Faye?

What the fuck?

"O-oh." Faye stopped at the sight of Sage, too. She was properly dressed because Samson had probably inspected her clothes before letting her leave the lab. He used to do the same with Sage.

Sage snorted.

"Sage." Faye cleared her throat. This was the timid, soft-spoken Faye now that Samson didn't lie dying on a table. "I wasn't expecting you to be here so early in the morning."

"What the fuck are you doing here?" Sage spat. She checked

469

Faye's hands for any matches or lasers, but they were clean. "Get the hell away from my husband, you bitch."

Faye closed her eyes and took a breath, as if exercising patience like she had been taught by her yoga instructor. Sage wasn't in the mood for this—she drew her new sword in Faye's face, making her stumble back in fright.

"I said back the fuck up!" Sage exclaimed.

"Please!" Faye whimpered, hands up. "I didn't come here to antagonize you! I was actually here to retrieve another sample for Samson. He's been trying really hard to save Damian!"

Was this supposed to be some sort of redemption? An apology for all the games and lies?

"*What?*" Sage breathed.

"Sage, we never meant any disrespect, nor did we mean to make you believe that we were going to wipe out hybrids—"

Sage raised her sword and brought it down in the wink of an eye. Faye didn't even notice her severed hand on the ground until she looked.

Faye screamed. Blood spurted out of her stump.

Sage grabbed Faye by the coat and shook her. She hissed at her like a snake, eyes glowing a bright amber.

"Stop fucking screaming and listen! You are going to tell Samson that he needs to leave this city *immediately*. And he is not to lay a single fucking hand on Damian, whom he wanted dead just a few months ago. Is that clear?"

Faye sobbed. "M-my arm . . ."

"I SAID IS THAT CLEAR?!"

Tendrils shot out from behind Sage and wound around her arms and legs. They came from all the fleshy trunks in Damian's nest. They yanked her back from the crying Faye.

Sage wasn't afraid to use her sword and she did. She sliced off all of Damian's tendrils and watched them land with a plop on the snow.

"This is my last siege," Sage said to them quietly. They twitched with life. "I am done fighting. I am done with this miserable life."

She brushed the tears from her eyes. "I am done having my heart broken again and again. No matter how hard I fight . . . I can never seem to achieve what I've always wanted. The love of my life is dead, Samson's betrayed me, and my city is in ruins. At the very least, I will take back what's mine, and then do what I should have done so long ago."

"Sage?"

Sage sheathed her sword because she had no intention of battling Samson right now. She was too damn exhausted and she had to save her energy for the true fight in Diamond City.

"I changed my mind," Sage said, more to Faye. "You fucks can do whatever the hell you want with Damian. Here." She picked up one of the tendrils and chucked it at her face. She did Samson, too.

Samson looked like he was about to cry again. Clutching Damian's fleshy appendage, he fell to his knees beside the weeping Faye.

"Mother?!"

"Mom?!"

Castor and Pollux were here. They had sensed Sage's distress from miles away.

"Mom, what's going on?" Pollux gaped at Samson and Faye on the ground.

"Nothing," Sage said, stepping right past them. Castor and Pollux stuck to her sides.

". . . Don't leave her alone . . ."

Sage didn't look back at Faye, but Castor and Pollux did.

"Don't let her out of your sight." Faye choked on another sob. "She's going to kill herself."

That could mean so many things: Sage was going to kill herself fighting; Sage was going to exhaust herself completely; or this was going to be Sage's toughest fight yet. No one thought she was suicidal, and Sage wouldn't be thanks to Hayes.

This was all going to end in Diamond City.

That's where it had all started.

CHAPTER 31

The Unification War

S tar, are you ready?

That was August's text on Tuesday, June 5th, 2632. 135 years ago. The Diamond City calendar hadn't existed yet. The Overseers in each of the districts were still using Old World dating systems, trying to keep old traditions alive. They swore they were doing the best they could as rulers, to pull people from the debris left behind by Nuclear Devastation, but were they? Truly? Not a lot of people, of course, bought those lies.

Sage breathed in and out shakily. For a long time now, she had known she was different. It wasn't just her mother who reminded her that she was half Lolligo—it was her jaw-dropping times on the track-and-field team. She was proud to say she had brought home the championship this year. She had medals and trophies to display on her shelves, but those weren't going to help the people struggling with their day-to-day life.

If Sage listened closely enough, she could hear gunshots. People were shouting. Crowds gathered around medical facilities where they swore loved ones had been taken. August knew all about government experiments because his mother, who had suffered from myocarditis, died from faulty medication.

Tonight, August was making a stand . . . and Sage supposed she would help him.

With another deep breath, Sage threw on a jacket and pants. She tied up her ankle boots. The only weapon she had was a dagger she had bought from an antique shop. The blade itself was pretty blunt, so Overseer Callus probably didn't think it could be used as a weapon, but Sage had already fixed it herself. Now, it could slice through wood like butter. Anything else would require a bit more effort.

And that was it. No guns for Sage because they were loud and boisterous. Her strategy was speed and stealth. She had no training whatsoever, but she relied on her instincts a lot. That's why she never asked Wyatt out on a date—she knew he wouldn't say yes.

That didn't stop Sage from drooling over him, though, or being a creepy stalker and cutting his picture out of the yearbook and putting it up on her wall. She had a collage of hot guys she was rather proud of.

Sage and August were a thing . . . sort of . . . but August wasn't the most pleasant person to look at. At least he was reliable, though, and determined to do something about the Cut District's misery.

Sage threw up her hood. The best way to escape the house was through the window, so she slid that up as quietly as possible. Her mother had already returned from her nighttime ventures and she was in the room next door.

"Sage?"

Aurora. Of course.

Sage turned her head. She looked over her shoulder at her frightened, peeping sister. Five years younger, but Aurora was her best friend in life, ready to start high school in the fall. Sage wanted to make sure that Aurora didn't spend her best years worried about being kidnapped for experiments.

"I'm going," Sage said. "I'll be back."

"Please come back . . ." Aurora whispered. Her large eyes shined with tears. She wore the cutest little pajamas to bed. "Please... don't leave me."

Sage blew her a kiss. Then she patted her Star Raider tattoo on her right wrist. It was an "SR" inside a green circle, the symbol of the most powerful superhero in *Defenders Unite!* "I won't."

Sage couldn't hesitate and she didn't. This wasn't her first excursion in the middle of the night, but it was her first operation against the Overseer's forces. According to August, there was a whole stash of weapons in a warehouse a few miles from their school. Sometimes, students reported military driving to and from there in plain sight. Overseer Callus wasn't afraid to show off his might or the fact he was keeping a close eye on everyone.

Home of the Cavaliers. Her Alma Mater. It was time for Sage to live up to her promise as a graduate, to "brighten the future with her sword in hand."

Sage's home was in a rural, isolated residential area, so there wasn't a lot of security here. If a car did drive by, it was easy to hide behind a tree, in a shrub, or next to a pair of dumpsters. There was a curfew in place for all residents. Anyone who got arrested was never seen again. That's why Sage's mother, after her jobs, usually stayed at her clients' places until morning.

It was the heart of the Cut District that was a lot harder to navigate. Commercial centers, school campuses, and hospitals were crowded with officers. Ambulances carried patients all hours of the day, but the injured and sick weren't the kinds of people Overseer Callus was worried about.

Sage made it to The Black Cat. It was the gambling hub of the Cut District, but it was also the place where people purchased drugs. Some carriers were able to get their hands on legitimate medicine from the Overseer's stash and sell it for cheap, while others were up for experimenting and promising their clients a good high. Tonight, carriers were offering Cells like they were candy.

Allegedly, Cells transformed humans into Enhanced, super beings that some scientist in a private laboratory had created. There was talk of a massive coup against the Overseer and all his corruption. No one knew details, but everyone knew that this stuff worked, because it hit Sage's nose like a ton of bricks.

It smelled different. Not that people here stunk, but it was a different kind of scent from the usual sweat and cheap bath soap. Sage likened it to a dog detecting one of its own across the street, in between a pair of humans. These people in The Black Cat weren't human anymore.

Their bodies were bigger, muscles more defined. Their eyes were an odd amber color. Veins popped out of their skin, engorged with a power that wasn't human. Those Cells must have given their recipients a boost in confidence because everyone was grinning, drinking, and talking loudly.

"Sage!" August bumbled over to her right away. Despite his new powers, he was still a bit on the chubby side. His dreams of becoming a professional fastball player had been dashed, but at least he had his lucky Wooly Socks on. Sage had hers on, too. They looked a bit ridiculous, but no one was looking at their feet right now. "You made it, girl!"

Sage embraced him. She loved nestling her head into his soft chest. She could smell lavender, but it was faint. August hadn't showered since this morning, and it had been a long day. Sage had kissed him goodbye when they parted ways at school. Just another day of finals, and they'd be official Cavalier graduates.

"All right, so." A tall, muscular guy with a goatee stepped forward. His name was LL. He didn't go to Sage's school, but he was definitely a local who hit the gym for hours at a time. Sage would have to do the same in the future. She felt her body was too skinny and frail to last long in a siege like this, and others must have been thinking the same. They eyed her up and down. "This is ... ?"

"Star," August said quickly. "My friend. And trust me—she's strong."

"We don't have time for this, August," snapped another guy with a mohawk, KK. "We need warriors, not fucking dolls!"

Sage noticed that there weren't any women here at all. The only exception was this quiet chick in the back with blonde braids, but she looked like she could bench press all these men and throw some hand grenades while she was at it.

"Trust me, she knows what she's doing," August snapped back. "Now can we just get on with it? We need all the help we can get, don't we?"

No one had time to complain, so they got right down to their mission tonight. Group A (consisting of AA-LL) would take the street, while Group B (consisting of MM-ZZ) would take the high road. They explained all this using their secret language, Lucidum.

It was still a new language to a lot of them, but speakers got the hang of it quickly because it was based on the English of the Old World. It had the same letters (just different pronunciations) and same grammatical rules (just different words). For a lot of the districts in Diamond City, it was code. Now, these warriors could shout to each other and still communicate in secret.

Because Sage's name started with an S, she was SS, so she'd be in the latter group. August kissed her lips.

"Good luck, Star," he said. "And remember what we practiced."

Right. The dagger.

Sage took it out.

"Is that really all you're going with?" the quiet chick with the blonde braids approached Sage. She was RR.

"It's all I need," Sage said.

"You're fucking brave." RR smiled. "I look forward to seeing you in action."

Sage smiled back. "I hope for a better future."

"Me, too. My prom date asked me to marry him a few weeks ago, and I intend to. He was captured by the Overseer, taken because of his 'condition.' Well, I'm going to free him."

Everyone in this group had some reason for fighting. August's was purely out of revenge for his mother. The lot was motivated without a single fear of death. With Cells in their veins, why would they be?

It was time to go, and Sage didn't wait for anyone to follow. Her mission was to lead this band of Enhanced to the warehouse in the northernmost point of the Cut District, right next to the Color District border, and that's what Sage was going to do. Everything else ceased to matter—her art final tomorrow, Aurora's eighth grade graduation, and her mother's failing health—except for that squat warehouse down the street.

Sage jumped across rooftops as if she had been born to do this. The Enhanced were still gathering their bearings and getting the hang of their new abilities, so a lot of them were clumsy and slow, struggling just to stay hidden beneath the dim street lamps. That was fine, because the first hit was the most important, and that was up to Sage.

She leapt right into the fenced-off perimeter, as nimble as a cat, scaled the tallest tower to the officer keeping watch above, and took him out with a slit to his throat.

Sage got control of the machine gun and she fired at every militant below. No time for thinking—no time for remorse—Sage had already said all her prayers, asked God to forgive her, sought out other methods of taking out the Overseer peacefully, but there weren't any.

Group B was here. They jumped right over the fence as the militants frolicked over what the fuck was going on up on the tower. In the commotion, Group B held a ton of momentum and were able to open the gates and allow Group A to flood in.

That was Sage's cue to join them below, but not without taking the gun. She gave it to the closest person next to her—RR—then led the charge to the warehouse for the rest of the weapons.

Every Enhanced watched Sage burst through those doors and get sprayed with bullets. Not that any of that stopped her—her broken bones, blood, and torn ligaments didn't exist in the rush. Maybe Sage saw her arm dangling or a bone sticking out of her knee, but as long as she could move them and weave through enemy lines, she didn't pay them any attention. Her mind didn't allow her to, as if it knew she'd freak out and abandon the mission. Survival was at stake here.

As Sage fought off the militants in the warehouse, she confiscated guns and threw them back at her crew. By the time she reached her last foe on the second floor landing, her comrades were armed and quickly taking control of the base. When Sage finally defeated the last sniper at the top of one of the buildings, she collapsed, but not for long.

"Star!" August was right behind her and pulled her up to her feet. He was panting, sweaty, and dirty, but no wounds. A lot of their people were unharmed. In fact, everyone was alive except for—

"RR!"

Sage peered over the rail. There were bodies down there, blood pooled like someone had spilled water in class, but nothing took her breath away quite like the sight of her comrade who had taken a wayward bullet to the brain.

RR was dead.

"Sage!" Aurora croaked as Sage clambered back into her room through her window. Had Aurora been waiting for her here the whole time? It seemed like it. "S-Sage! Y-you're hurt!"

Maybe. Sage wasn't sure if her wounds had healed or not. She had cut and bruised herself so much growing up—even stuck her hand in the garbage disposal when she had dropped Aurora's ring in there by accident—and she had never had to sport a bandaid. Now, for some reason, she felt really banged up.

Aurora helped Sage into the shower. With shaking hands, she took off all of Sage's clothes and sponged all the blood from her body.

No wounds.

"Oh, thank God . . ." Aurora breathed as she scrubbed a particularly deep stain of blood from Sage's lower back. "God, what happened, Sage?"

There were bullets on the shower floor. They had either been in Sage's clothes or lodged in her body.

"Well..." Sage said dismally, staring at the tiles. "We won. We... accomplished our mission."

"August?"

"He's alive."

RR wasn't.

Suddenly, Aurora sobbed. She threw her arms around Sage's waist and bawled into her back. "I-I'm so happy you made it home!" she cried. "I prayed so hard for your return... What would I have done if you hadn't made it back?"

Aurora was getting soaked. Her cute pajamas were hanging off her body. She didn't care, though—she must have relished at the feel of Sage in her arms because she didn't let her go.

Eventually, they both made it back to bed. It was already four in the morning and it'd be time to wake up soon. *If* school wasn't canceled. Sage could hear the pounding wings of helicopters and the frantic calls to "find the hoodlums!" outside. She and Aurora both laid there, eyes wide open, with minds racing at a hundred miles per hour.

This was crazy.

Strangely, there was absolutely no word of the siege the following morning. Insane. Just when Sage thought the entire district would be locked down, everyday activities carried on as usual. Aurora spent countless hours scrolling through her phone, wondering when headlines were going to reflect the militant massacre from last night.

Nothing?

"Maybe the Overseer doesn't want to let us know something's wrong," Aurora whispered to her as their mother quietly cooked them their eggs.

Sage stared at the castle painting on the wall. Her mind always soared to unreachable heights at the sight of it, taking her to another place and time, when she'd be a queen and wear pretty dresses all day. Well, maybe not all day—those things were so limiting. At prom, Sage's range of motion had been shit. So she wouldn't wear the dress all day—only when she went out to dinner or posed for the cameras. She'd like to see herself dressed up . . . it'd certainly beat her school photo. Her mother had one pinned on the refrigerator. Sage's hair was a frizzy mess.

"What was going on out there last night?" her mother asked, looking out the window. "Did you girls hear all the guns?"

"Yeah." Aurora kept her head down. Their mother had been pretty aloof lately, but she could still read lies like a seasoned detective. "Nothing on the news, either."

"This world's going to hell, I'm telling you. I've already taught you girls how to survive: you keep your heads low and let the crazies blow themselves up."

It was terrible advice. Sage wasn't sure she could ever stand by and watch someone else get killed, but that was just her. Aurora, on the other hand, was only human.

After breakfast, Sage and Aurora were ready in minutes. They donned their school jackets and grabbed their backpacks. They took the same bus since they went to the same school. There were K-12 centers everywhere in the Cut District, since officials liked to indoctrinate children from a young age.

As Aurora continued to scroll through her phone for any news updates, Sage looked out the window. She couldn't see the warehouse from here, but she could still see some smoke. There were even more militants out and about now.

When the bus arrived, August was waiting for Sage by their usual tree. A stream of black and gray were making their way through the front doors of the school. The colors fit the mood perfectly. Students kept their heads down and lips sealed. August wrapped a thick arm around Sage's waist and kissed her cheek. He and Sage had lime-green Wooly Socks on today.

"Hey, August," Aurora squeaked.

"Hey, kiddo. Everything good?"

"Yeah." Aurora wasn't allowed to mention anything about last night, surrounded by so many students and so much security. She did speak in general, though. "Everything is pretty good. I'm glad nothing too serious happened last night."

"Did you hear?" August said.

Sage noticed a few security officers looking their way. They didn't work directly for the Overseer, but important information might promote them to higher places. They seemed hopeful these young students would give some indication as to who was behind last night's siege.

Aurora nodded her head. "All night."

"Crazy, isn't it?"

Eventually, Sage and August had to part ways with Aurora. Sage kissed her little sister on the forehead and fixed her bow. "Stay out of trouble," she said to her.

Today was a short schedule because of finals. Sage had World History for first period. The final was pretty easy there. Then she had Art History for second period and *that* was a whole other monster. The teacher sucked and the final was going to be hell. Sage was terrible when it came to artists and what styles they were famous for.

"We've received word," August said to Sage as their teacher passed out their exams. She was a no-nonsense bitch who liked to snarl at students. Sage liked her. "There's a coalition in the Color District. We should go."

"How are we going to jump the border?" Sage asked.

"Star, please. You should know by now that we have underground channels everywhere."

Sage breathed in and out. "It means I'll have to leave home."

The horrifying part was Sage had to leave home anyway. Because as soon as she and Aurora got home, she had to knife down a bunch of militants who had been on the verge of arresting her mother. They were all over the neighborhoods like roaches, dragging people out of their houses and pushing them around like criminals. It looked like Overseer Callus wasn't taking any chances and seizing whoever got in his way. A few of Sage's comrades stayed to take care of the citizens in the Cut District, but the rest used the tunnels to make it to the Color District.

Sage had never been to the Color District before. She hadn't even heard rumors or seen any live footage on TV. Districts were isolated and the Overseers ensured it stayed that way. Someone had taken initiatives, though, by creating those underground networks. So while August met up with some of his buddies, Sage jumped on her chance for a stroll through these *very* colorful streets.

There was a lot to do in the Color District. Shops, shows, concerts, and naked races were enough to keep tourists here for months. For an area populated by those who loved to use their hands and put their creativity on display, they came to a consensus on one thing: the Overseer had to go.

Unlike the Cut District, the people here weren't afraid to show their distrust or hatred of the government. The Overseer might not have been abducting people for experiments, but she was ignoring a lot of issues and taking advantage of those around her by increasing taxes and allowing inflation to run amok. Poverty, homelessness, and bankruptcy were the results of that. Without funds, creativity crashed and burned.

August showed Sage a scandal from just a few weeks ago. Someone in the Overseer's council had leaked a problematic million-Diamond transfer directly into the Overseer's bank account. No one knew the whistleblower's name, but Sage had a feeling they weren't alive anymore.

Sage loved art. She appreciated every facet of it. That's why she let August take care of the political, rebellious stuff and spent most of her days exploring the streets. She peered at the shops that were open and lamented the ones that were boarded and closed. She found a few that sold fabrics and designs. Sage wasn't savvy enough to know how to put any of that together and she was fucked if someone asked her what time period they were from.

"And who are you, young girl?" asked one of the store managers standing out on the sidewalk as Sage walked by. The sign read,

"Georgina's Bracelets". Sage guessed that was Georgina herself. "I'm afraid I've never seen you around."

"I don't usually come here." Sage knew better than to admit she was from the Cut District. No one was supposed to be crossing the border without permission, and if this woman happened to work for the Overseer, then Sage would have security on her in a heartbeat. She had no papers or ID. "But my mother's working late and my friends are doing their own thing, so I decided to take a walk."

"A bit dangerous, don't you think?"

There were shouts from protestors in the distance. "*Take her down! Take her down! Take her down!*"

Sage nodded her head. "Definitely."

"Come in." Georgina waved her inside. "I've got something for you."

Sage took a look at all the bracelets out on display. They were made with thin, thick threads of all colors. Some of the patterns were crazy. Sage wished she were better with her hands.

"What are your favorite colors?" Georgina asked, taking a seat behind one of her crafting tables. There were needles and threads out everywhere, but she seemed to know her mess well.

"Red and gold," Sage replied, still looking around. She noticed all the colors hanging on the wall, as if this woman paid tribute to them every day.

"Where would we be without colors?" Georgina said. "Where would we be without diversity? Life would be pretty boring, wouldn't you agree?"

"Yes, ma'am. For sure."

"I hope we can unite the districts."

Sage held her tongue. Saying that was mighty dangerous in public. Georgina seemed trusting enough of Sage, though, and maybe she was tired of hiding it in general.

Georgina picked up gold and red threads. With needles, she started weaving them together expertly.

Sage walked over, impressed. She stood aside as the woman used her hands to create an intricate bracelet that Sage could wear.

"Your left wrist, dear," Georgina said. "Since your right holds an important tattoo." She smiled. "Star Raider, eh? From *Defenders Unite!* The fourth season ended with a bang, wouldn't you say?"

Sage nodded. "It sure did."

"Have you heard of the Enhanced?"

"I have," Sage said.

"They say that the show is supposed to market them. It's a secret call to get people to join in the fight against the Overseers. All of the districts have had enough. We won't survive much longer."

Georgina presented the bracelet. Sage took it with a bow.

"Here you go, ma'am." Sage paid her twenty Diamonds. Perhaps it was a bit much for a bracelet, but Sage felt it was the right thing to do.

"Oh, dear," the woman lamented. "I can't possibly accept this."

"Please do. I honestly don't need money right now." Sage nodded her head in assurance. "All I need is a dagger. I have many battles ahead of me. For my services, the coalition gives me everything that I need."

Georgina arched a brow. "Is that so? So you are an Enhanced?"

"I suppose you can say that, yes."

The woman took Sage's hands and kissed them. "Please don't forget me, Star. My name is Georgina ... but my daughters' names are Candice and Olivia. I fight hard to make sure this store survives ... for them." Tears welled in her eyes.

Sage bowed again. "Don't worry, ma'am. I will do what I can. Honestly, I have a good feeling about all this. I think there are a lot of people who want change."

And because of that, the Color District overtook their Overseer in just a matter of months. Three, to be exact. Thanks to August's campaign, the coalition was over ten thousand strong.

There was no new government yet, but Color swore to help the other districts with their Overseers as well. There was already talk of an Allseer floating among them, some guy by the name of Marchello, who was eager to unite the districts and fight government corruption. There were a lot of snorts, eye-rolls, and protests.

The coalition wasn't about to kick out Overseers just to give power to another, but then they learned that Marchello was from the Clarity District. That's where all the pious, holy people dwelled. How dangerous could they be?

It was dead quiet in this district. People were holed up in their churches, praying to the Lolligo for help in these very dark times. Sage swore it was the Lolligo behind the corruption to begin with, but there were many who believed that the humans in charge, by nature, were just greedy and evil. So far, Sage had yet to meet a single Lolligo.

"Star!" August hissed at her, sticking his head out of the abandoned church a group of them had managed to hole themselves into. Like Color, it didn't look like Clarity was doing too well economically, either. At this point, people were forgoing religion in lieu of making sure there was food on the table. That meant looting and stick-ups. Crime rates were climbing. There was graffiti all over the walls. "Where are you going?"

"Just for a walk," Sage said, zipping up her jacket. "I'll be back."

There was a library down the street. Sage and Aurora were fascinated by the people in Clarity, who walked around in pure white robes and wore crazy masks. Aurora claimed she wanted one for her wedding. Sage just wanted to see one up close, but priests and pious worshipers weren't crawling out of their hiding spaces until the "time of reckoning" was over.

"Damn it." Sage knocked on the library door, but no one answered. The windows were opaque, and there didn't seem to be any movement inside. Perhaps people were hiding in the basement or attic. Sage wasn't one for vandalism, knowing this was someone's business she was destroying, which meant she wouldn't be forcing her way in.

Sage turned around and noticed the church across the street. The door was ajar. She heard crying from inside. A couple, perhaps?

"Why hasn't he come back?" a woman's voice croaked.

"I'm sure he took a walk to clear his mind."

"He was devastated! That art school meant everything to him!"

"We told him that the Color District wasn't going to accept a worshiper! You know how arrogant they are—filthy freaks—"

"We have to go after him!"

"It's too dangerous out here!" the man exclaimed. "There's no one out here—"

The man, who was also the preacher of the church, opened the door some more and spotted Sage. Clearly, she was an outsider. As soon as he saw her, he slammed the door closed.

Sage kept walking in fear that they would call security. She quickly reassured herself that even if that happened, she'd be long gone by the time anyone came. Most of the Clarity District's defenses were dealing with the Overseer. There definitely wasn't as much fighting out on the streets as there had been in the Color District, which was a relief for Sage, whose hands were still shaking.

Suddenly, Sage smelled blood. The coppery scent hit her nose hard, making her head snap up in its direction. It was coming from down the block. Then she heard a light sobbing. Not cries or wails, but a miserable exhale.

Sage took off. She wondered if someone had gotten knifed or shot and needed help.

She turned into an alley and didn't see anyone at first. That's because the person in distress was behind the dumpster. Sage jumped onto the lid and looked down at the body sprawled against the wall.

Both arms were outstretched. Both hands were limp. One had a piece of bloody glass. His white robes were stained. Sage didn't have to look anymore to know what had happened.

"Hey." Sage clambered off the dumpster. She got to her knees next to him. "Can you hear me?" She got a good look at his face, more for signs of life than because she wanted to know what he looked like. His pupils were extremely dilated and his skin was pale from the blood loss. His mouth was slightly parted, sucking in little bits of air as his vitals slowed.

Sage ripped the sleeves of her jacket. As she wound them around the young man's wrists to stem some of the bleeding, she noticed smooth, sharp features. The young man had a long straight nose with full lips. His hair was a lot longer than a Claritian's should be, and it was a miracle he had been able to keep it at this length without consequences. Sage knew that Claritians always went for a clean look, just in case the Lolligo descended upon them and passed judgment. Not that this young man looked dirty, though . . . In fact, he was pretty handsome.

The dark eyes crawled up to meet hers. Before they saw too much, Sage was already lifting his body into her arms.

She didn't hesitate to jump out of the alley and then dash down the street until she came across the nearest hospital. It was just a few miles away, thankfully. It was two stories—small—but it was taking people in. Sage made sure to go through the emergency side for immediate help. The doctors didn't ask too many questions because their number-one focus was saving lives. Sage appreciated that.

"Are you all right, ma'am?" the ER doctor asked Sage in the hallway. He was about to join his team in the operating room. It looked like they were going to have to stitch the young man's wounds together.

"Y-yes," Sage stammered, craning her head to keep her eye on him. She glimpsed him on the table inside. "Is he going to be fine?"

"We'll do what we can, but it seems you caught him in time," the ER doctor said. "His vitals are weak, but steady. With enough blood and some medication, we'll be able to bring him back."

At the very least, the healthcare here was adequate. Sage hadn't thought it would be, as these people were holy and pious and relied more on Lolligo miracles than actual medicine, but maybe the Claritians weren't as slow as some people thought. Maybe that's why Marchello was gaining so much steam as a potential Allseer.

Sage sat down in the waiting room. There were only a handful of people here, more proof that protests were at a minimum. August was texting her, but Sage told him she wouldn't be returning to their hideout until she made sure the young man was fine.

A nurse came with a change of clothes. Sage got to use the showers to clean the blood from her body. She hadn't realized just how much of it she had on her until she saw the dark red water swirling around in the drain between her feet.

Sage cried. She didn't know why, but she sobbed in the stall. She couldn't get the young man's look out of her head. So blank and empty ... like someone who had lost everything. RR had died fighting for her fiancé ... but that young man had nothing to fight for.

That wasn't true, though. There was *always* something to fight for.

Sage donned her white robes with a tie at the waist. Her skirt covered her legs entirely. It wasn't her preferred wardrobe, but it was snug and comfortable because it was new and clean. She buckled her boots and then went to see the young man in his room after doctors finished stabilizing him.

Both of his wrists were bandaged. His head was slightly to the side, hair covering most of his face. Nurses had changed him into a hospital gown, and now he was just resting. His vitals were good and his IV was delivering blood back into his body.

Sage pulled up a chair. Before she sat down, she leaned in and kissed the young man's forehead. She brushed back some of his hair.

"Do you know who this young man is?" asked the nurse in the corner. She was recording data on her tablet, but she also seemed to be searching for the young man's identity.

"I don't," Sage admitted. "I found him behind a dumpster."

She felt bad admitting it. Her heart broke all over again. She took the young man's hand and brought it up to her lips for a kiss.

"No ID, so I guess we'll ask him when he wakes up," said the nurse before stepping out.

It was quiet minus the beeping of the young man's vitals. Sage stayed by his side until she saw him open his eyes. She didn't want to leave without offering him hope, without giving him something to fight for.

"You're fine now," Sage said to him, smiling warmly. She squeezed his hand for emphasis. "Things are going to get better. The Enhanced are forming a coalition across all the districts and we're going to unite Diamond City."

The young man gazed into her eyes. His own welled with tears.

"There's always something to live for," Sage said. "There's always something to fight for. And if there isn't . . . then let me be that something. Diamond City will be one again, and you'll have an opportunity to move to whatever district you like. You can become whatever you want."

"And what do you want?" the young man whispered weakly.

Sage sighed. "I know it's not practical, but I want to live in a palace. I want to wear different dresses every day and see myself in different ways. I don't like attention, but I'll make the sacrifice if it means photo shoots. When I'm not trying on dresses, I'd like to see the world. Wouldn't you like to know what's out there?"

The young man smiled. "I would like to, yes."

"It'd be awesome to leave Diamond City in prosperity and then spread that prosperity to other places. I like to see people happy, you know." Sage kissed the young man's hand again. "What's your name?"

The young man hesitated. He glanced at the door, as if checking for eavesdroppers, then looked at Sage. "Have you ever killed someone?"

Sage kept a straight face, even though she caught on to what he was implying. He had some skeletons in his closet, ones he couldn't afford to expose if he wanted freedom. "I have," she said softly. "Quite a lot of people, actually . . ."

"Do you feel guilty?"

"I do." Sage didn't realize she was kneading the young man's knuckles.

"I had to . . ." The young man croaked. "Or he . . . was going to kill me . . ."

It seemed that was all the energy the young man had. His eyes drooped closed again, although he kept a tight hold on Sage's hand.

"Promise me you'll fight," Sage said.

The young man nodded. ". . . Yes . . ."

"Promise me you'll fight and maybe one day we'll see the world together."

He nodded again.

"Your name?" Sage asked.

"...Damianos...but...don't tell..."

"Sage," Sage said, although she had a feeling he hadn't heard her.

Regardless, Sage knew Damianos would fight...and that was all that mattered.

age! said August's vicious texts. *Get back here! Marchello is here!* Right. The guy who was supposed to be the Allseer. Conveniently, he worked at the Overseer's office itself, so he knew exactly where to strike and how to lead the coalition to victory.

Sage didn't really pay attention in any of those meetings because she always expected August to fill her in afterward. Instead, she sent secretly-coded messages to Aurora about her safety.

She never told her sister about the young man, Damianos, though. After the meeting, she told August, who just brushed the whole incident aside.

"Do you know how many people want to commit suicide in this district?" August said, eyeing the white robes Sage was sporting. "Should it really take you by surprise?"

Perhaps, but the Clarity District was definitely a big win for the coalition. It was by far the easiest to overcome in their struggle for control. Because Marchello had so much insight, it didn't take them long to barge into the government building and join the rebellious Claritians against the Overseer. Sage led the charge in this final push, but she came to a stop in one of the dark offices when she... sensed something.

"Sage?" August said, stopping in the hall.

"Go on," Sage said to him, pushing through the door. "I'll be right there."

She still didn't know what had drawn her to an empty room. She looked around at the bookcases, the lone table, the computer in the corner, and then what looked like a knapsack on the desk. Inside was something white.

It was a huge egg.

Sage furrowed her brows. She couldn't help the occasional glance at the Lolligo portrait hanging on the wall. His name was Luminator and he was the Clarity District patron. His picture was everywhere in this district, so the egg right beneath his frame couldn't be a coincidence. No, it looked like someone in the office had left the egg behind on purpose. How could anyone forget an egg that big?

But what the fuck was in that egg? It was the size of a small watermelon.

Sage pictured an ostrich when she picked it up, but there was no way this had come out of a bird's body. It was too heavy. Sage kept it in the knapsack, which she slung over her shoulder. She didn't tell anyone about it, and August didn't ask her, either, when he saw her at the end of the hall with a new bag in her possession. There was no telling who that belonged to, either.

"Sage!" he choked. "I think we did it! Marchello's in the Overseer's office!"

The battle for the Clarity District was finally over. The nastiest one was going to be in the Carat District where multiple tight-knit gangs ran the streets.

By then, though, Sage's coalition would be nearly a hundred-thousand strong. So many Enhanced. Sage always looked for Damianos among new faces, but she never saw him again. It was possible he was still in the Clarity District and its leftover campaigns.

Regardless, Sage knew in her heart that Damianos would live on. And perhaps, one day, she'd get to see him again. Just like she got to see her sister as she marched back into the Cut District with her Enhanced in tow.

Her biological sister.

Wren was standing on a runway next to an aircraft. She was in a straitjacket, long coffee hair blowing out in the humid breeze. A whole year since the Unification War had started, summer was upon them once more. To Wren, however, a little humidity didn't do a thing. She rejoiced in the world she had never gotten to experience. She grinned at Francis Kilstrong standing next to her, guiding her into the aircraft. To think that was Marchello's brother up there . . .

Sage's eyes returned to Wren's.

Wren grinned at her. She didn't talk because she was too far away, but she did make Sage a promise.

I'm going to live my life, too, sister.

CHAPTER 32

Queen of Diamonds

Clapping.

Low, sophisticated clapping.

It filled the entire Color Dome even if there was no one in it. It came from that person sitting in the front row and didn't stop as Sage stepped down the aisle. He was tall, colorful, and handsome like anyone from the Color District would be.

"Oh, Wren!" sang the man despite the roars outside. The Mutatio were in distress. "Your sister is here."

Sage was, indeed, "here". She was standing at the entrance to the biggest, most famous theater in all of Diamond City. Who wouldn't give their entire life savings to stand on that stage beneath the beautiful kaleidoscope? With the right amount of sunshine, there'd be color in every corner. Even beneath the moonlight, there was no escaping the reds, greens, purples, blues, yellows, and oranges twinkling across the stage. Sage missed Fido's pups desperately, knew that they were still alive in Emerald City thanks to their Cells, but, unfortunately, she couldn't afford to think about them much longer. Not when she was gazing into the eyes of her twin on stage.

"Welcome," said the man royally. "Oh, Queen of Diamonds." He had dirty-blond hair, a hooked nose, and dazzling teeth. They looked fake. Damian had nice teeth, too, but they didn't shine like a lighthouse beacon.

Sage clutched her sword. After cutting through Mutatio for an entire three weeks without shower or rest, she was positively disgusting. Bloody. Clothes torn and ripped everywhere. But at least she didn't have any wounds.

Sage took a deep breath. She studied the man standing near the stage a bit longer. She knew immediately that he was a hybrid. God, where were so many of them coming from? She hadn't seen that guy in Elysium and she suspected he wasn't from there, either. All the hybrids from Elysium had either fled or gone into hiding. This guy was way too glitzy and colorful to have suffered at the hands of Elysium's corrupt Prime. He had never lifted a single weapon in his life.

"Gorgeous," the man breathed, eyeing Sage from head to foot. "No offense, my beautiful Wren, but your sister certainly does have a . . . spark. Just look at those muscles and look at those eyes. She'll bite the penis off of any man who challenges her."

"I don't bite penises," Sage spat. "I cut them off with my sword."

"Oh!" the man purred. "Feisty. Just like you, Wren."

"Please, Nathan." Wren scowled. "Can you stop comparing me to my sister? It's not much of a compliment."

"How can you say that, darling? This is the *Optimum*. I watched her fight from the sidelines during the Unification War."

That was a grand possibility, although Sage didn't remember Nathan at all. Like the other hybrids that Emerald City had planted in Diamond City, he didn't jump to action unless he really needed to. Unification of the districts wouldn't have changed his life one way or the other—fashion was clearly his passion. What would Laetus, the Color District Lolligo, have had to say about that, Sage wondered. The Forefathers had created a hybrid in hopes they'd amount to something more than just crazy sociopaths. Their mission was to create a better world, not destroy the little of it they had left. Nathan seemed like a pretty useless piece of shit.

"But she's annoying." Wren tilted her head up. After so much time lounging around, there was an ethereal glow to her skin. Her hair was long, silky, and shiny. Nathan had knitted that costume himself. Cerulean blue with black trims and intricate frills.

Damian would have hated it.

It was too blocky. The colors were too stark. Plus, blue and black weren't his favorites. If he wore blue, he always paired it with silver. He also hated frilly sleeves because they took attention away from the hands. Fingers and nails were too elegant to hide. Cuffs were a must.

Sage fought hard to shove Damian out of her thoughts. That stage right there would have been where they'd exchange vows and become husband and wife in front of thousands of people. While there wasn't any damage to the Color Dome itself, it was empty. Mutatio didn't have free will, but that's the way Wren liked it.

"Sage, darling," Nathan said sweetly, licking his lips. He must have been wondering what it was like to have twins in bed. Wren was devil enough between the sheets, but Sage? Those two would demolish him. "Why don't you come in and have a seat?" His arousal grew larger by the second. "Wren is going to put on a show for us. She's been dying to show the world just how graceful she can be on stage, since she never really got into fighting. Perhaps show-biz is in her blood."

Sage raised her sword. "Shut up. I'm not here to watch anyone's show, asshole. I'm here to kill her, and now it seems like I have to kill you, too."

"Oh, dear! Such violence! Has the Warlord not pleasured you enough in bed? You look like you're in need of a good climax. We can help you with that—"

Sage flew forward, ready to slash this bastard to pieces. Nathan moved so quickly that Sage didn't see him until he was standing in front of her, clutching her wrist and holding her blade before it sliced anyone in half.

"No, Sage!" he chortled. "Not in front of the child!"

And then Sage's heart dropped. Her eyes immediately found the bundle in the front row.

"Isn't she just incredible, sister?" Wren twirled around on stage, bumping into one of the large tree props. "I gave birth to her all on my own! Well, Nathan helped me." She cleared her throat with a grin. "He had to yank her out of my belly."

"The cocoon would have killed her for sure." Nathan forced Sage's sword down. "So why don't you act civilized for once and say hello to your new niece?"

Sage could hardly believe what she was seeing. *Another* hybrid. And while this one wouldn't be able to spawn Enhanced like Castor and Pollux, she still carried Wren's blood. What sort of destructive desires would she develop over the years?

"*Your* blood." Wren frowned at Sage. "Your blood, too, sister."

"Blood doesn't mean shit!" Sage exclaimed. "I would never consider you my sister, Wren, when you've done nothing but kill people! You turned Francis into a fucking monster because you could, you played games with Rhett at Elysium and created a bunch of freaks, and now you're having sex with the only hybrid who will look at you!"

"And what's wrong with that?" Wren said coolly. "Everyone else ran away from me. Or rather." She grinned. "I killed them."

"You're fucking sick!"

"And why do you think that is, Sage?" Wren stopped her prancing. She let the bell of her dress settle around her ankles as she straightened her shoulders and looked up into one of the highest ceilings in Diamond City. So many colors. "Why am I 'sick', and not you? Why did I become a lab rat while you went to school and dated any guy you wanted?"

"I was lucky," Sage said quietly. "But that didn't stop me from experiencing the hell of war. I didn't have scientists poking me all day, but I did have to fight and I did have to watch people die. That doesn't mean I'm going to take it out on people who don't deserve it."

"You grew up with humans!" Wren hissed like a snake. "With people who loved you, dear sister! I am just starting to understand what it means to be truly loved." She smiled at Nathan. "He loves me for me."

"Bullshit!" Sage exclaimed. "He loves you for your baby!"

"Just like your precious Warlord?" Wren grinned, sharp teeth flashing. She glanced at the double doors. "Where is he, by the way? I was hoping to see him again. He was in his Mutatio form in Elysium, but then you told me he wasn't doing so well in Ruby City. Is it because he has too many Cells? Where did he get them?"

"LEAVE HIM OUT OF THIS!"

"But he is a part of this," Wren said patiently. "He is a part of the New World, Sage. That's the age we're living in. And it all started in Diamond City. Don't you see, sister, that Diamond City was never meant for humans? It was meant for *us*."

"It was never meant for us!" Sage yelled. "Humans were here first—we were created to help them take it away from people who abused power and played games with their own citizens!"

"Do you see why there's no talking to her?" Wren whined to Nathan, who was shaking his head. He looked ready to scold Sage for sticking glue in her friend's hair. "She's the most selfish bitch I've ever met. Always raining on my parade with her spiels of righteousness when she's an even bigger killer than I am!"

Not true. Sage was no killer. And she wasn't going to let Wren tell her otherwise. She had lived too long not to know the truth, and no one else's accusations were going to take away her confidence. Sage tightened her grip on her sword, ready to fight to the death. Nathan gave a small step toward her.

"Stop," Wren said to Nathan.

Nathan eased his shoulders. Wren drew a sword instead. It must have been over four feet in length. She must have procured that from Elysium.

"*I* will settle this." Wren scowled. "My sister has been a thorn in my side for long enough. She prances around pretending to be human, and I've had quite enough. If she's not going to conform to this new way of life, then she can go to hell."

Nathan actually obeyed. Sage didn't know what it was about Wren, but men seemed to listen to her. They seemed willing to do anything for her, and Nathan didn't even share her blood. He was no monster that Wren had spawned, either—only one that she had manipulated with her tits and pussy.

So it was Sage versus Wren. Their swords crossed right there on stage, the shockwaves knocking over some of the props. Those weren't the cheap flimsy ones, either—those were sculpted or made of metal, thick and heavy. Sword to sword, Sage and Wren battled for dominance. They held it there for a few moments, using raw strength to shove each other back, until they both jumped and reset their stances.

Sage was confident as hell in the face of her sister and that's probably why she lost her momentum. Not that Wren was able to land a hit on her, but Wren was surprisingly skilled with a sword. She met Sage's every blow and dodged ones she couldn't block. All of Wren's feats made Sage question her own abilities, and that's why she started to slow down.

Of course, Sage had expended a hell of a lot of energy to make it here. She had spent weeks battling Mutatio alongside her sons and Damian's rebels. Emerald and Ruby City forces were all trained, too. The guns Samson had provided them were a great aid against the Mutatio, but they weren't miracle workers. It took a tremendous amount of effort to kill one.

And Sage was at an extreme disadvantage. She didn't have Slainium in her weapon anymore, which was how she wanted it. Wren's weapon, on the other hand, was pure Slainium.

And that was fine. Even when Wren cut her across the chest, Sage didn't long for a better weapon—she used the horrible burn from that gash to motivate her.

Sage had to do better. She yelled at her sons for it all the time and now she had to do the same.

Sage started with slowing down her heart rate and breathing. If she could get them under control, her mind would be a lot clearer. She'd be able to analyze her sister's movements a lot better. If she followed her own advice, she could very well pull off the win.

Wren didn't realize what Sage was doing—she thought Sage

was simply exhausted. She rode that momentum hard, springing forward with a swift slash that Sage ducked.

Sage didn't attack yet.

Wren swiped again—Sage ducked.

Not yet.

"What's the matter, sister?" Wren cooed, never letting up on her assault. "Getting a bit tired? You do look quite miserable covered in all that blood. Does it belong to my babies?"

Sage kept dodging. A few more, and she had a good idea of what Wren's next moves were going to be.

"Say, where *is* that beautiful man of yours? I don't believe for one second that he's out of commission. Overdosing on Cells can lead to some pretty extreme reactions, but we adapt, dear sister, and it's already been a year."

"Adapt"? What did Wren mean by that?

Wren laughed. "I know that we're fighting to kill each other, but I honestly wish to see him again. I'm surprised he's not here to cheer you on. Did you guys fight? Or did he finally break your heart like I told you he would?"

All talk, and Wren failed to catch on to what Sage was doing—that's why she got a blade through the chest.

Nathan gasped loudly. Wren looked down at the pommel sticking out between her boobs. Sage never let go of the hilt—she pulled the sword right back out then followed up with another slash that Wren barely deflected. Her wrist was off and she lost her sword because of it.

Wren looked up, confused. "What are you doing, Sage?"

"Killing you!"

"Without Slainium in your blade?"

Sage grabbed her sister's weapon from the ground. "I have my Slainium now."

And Wren had her share of surprises as well. She shape-shifted her arm into a blade and thrust it right into Sage's chest.

Sage's surroundings turned dark. It felt like she was swimming underwater, so she wasn't sure if she heard someone shout, "MOTHER!"

No Slainium in that strike, but . . . damn, she was tired. Sage fell to her knees. She bent over onstage, swords falling from her hands. She watched blood drip onto the beautiful laminated floor, staining it forever. The blood didn't stop for some time.

Wren growled. She looked more annoyed that her frilly dress was ripped and ruined than the stab wound in the middle of her chest. "Did you seriously come here without a shred of Slainium? How do you expect to beat me?"

Sage smelled something was off. Without looking up, she knew that Wren was morphing. At first, she swore she was hallucinating, because she had only seen Damian do this. And the only reason he had been able to was because of Louis' "cure" . . . Of course, Wren had been exposed to so many serums at Elysium, so this shouldn't have taken Sage by surprise, but it did. Since when did Wren do all the fighting herself? Where was cheerleader-Wren from the Junkyard or the palace at Heart?

It caught Sage totally off guard. Wren wasted no time slamming right into her with a bulky body that was no longer human in its figure. With a thick clawed hand, she grabbed Sage by the ankle and flung her out of the Color Dome.

Like a bullet, Sage crashed through all the stained glass before making contact with the hot summer air outside. The sun wasn't up, but it was hard to breathe. Raindrops were coming down steadily, blurring everything around her. It was one big thick swirl of blue, gray, and black, like the backdrop of David's painting years ago, when Damian had been a monster. That hesitation cost Sage another hit from Wren, who smashed her straight into the ground.

Sage rolled on the sidewalk before Wren could follow up with a blade. She gritted her teeth and looked into her unruly sister's amber eyes. Everything about her sister at that moment was vile, from the saliva dribbling all over the floor to the long spindly arms that seemed to dangle just like her breasts. She looked like a mutant bat, far from the Wren Sage knew. Just what the hell had Wren done in order to transform like this?

Wren flashed forward, striking Sage in the face. Then she palmed Sage's chest, breaking her sternum. A kick sent Sage across the street, crashing into abandoned cars and traffic lights until she rolled to a stop on the concrete. Wren never let up—she was back on Sage in seconds. Like a wild gorilla, she pummeled Sage into a bloody pulp. Bones cracked and blood sprayed in all directions. Wren didn't have any Slainium at her disposal, but her ruthless attacks were enough to destroy Sage.

"THIS IS MY CITY NOW, SAGE!" Wren roared. "You were too much of a coward to defend it!" She kicked Sage across the ribs with her thick shins. Even her feet had claws. That slit in her groin must have been her vagina. "You're crumbling, sister, and that's not how a hybrid should behave!"

Sage curled up into a ball. A few of her teeth were on the ground next to her. She cried.

"Oh?" Wren said. "Why are you crying, Sage?"

Sage hid her face with her hands. Her fingers were twisted, some of them crushed. As if she were a child, she sobbed. She was so tired . . .

Wren hesitated for a moment. Perhaps she hadn't been expecting the great Optimum to crumble like that. It was a bit pathetic, actually, to the point that Wren must have felt sorry for her. She seemed sympathetic enough to say, "I don't want to fight, either. But you give me no choice when you continue to be a nuisance."

"Damian . . ." Sage choked. She hugged her knees. One of her kneecaps was shattered. "Damian . . ."

Perhaps Wren was starting to catch on to the fact that Damian was dead. It slowly sunk in. By the time she realized it, a huge body came out of nowhere and slammed right into hers.

This time, it was Wren who got caught off guard. She skidded across the street until she found her footing again. When she looked up, she locked eyes with Samson, who was back to confront the very hybrid he had kidnapped over thirty years ago. Wren might have been a victim then, but she was nightmare fuel now.

It showed on Samson's face, the grimace on his features. He tried so hard to keep his brows drawn and the gun in his hands steady, but fear of death was quickly rising in his chest like a wave. Little beads of sweat, even though he had no skin, started to trickle down his temple. He had a huge wet spot in the center of his jacket, too. That wasn't the rain, either—Sage could tell when Samson was about to shit himself from fright.

It was a bit ironic. To Sage, it was strange to see the seemingly invincible Samson quivering in his boots. They trained like this all the time—to the death—but Samson never engaged in combat he might possibly lose. He was comfortable around Sage, knew that she would never try to kill him, an intent that Wren clearly didn't have.

"YOU!" Wren shrieked, more talons erupting out of her arms. "YOU JUST DON'T DIE!"

Samson met each of Wren's attacks blow for blow. Sometimes, he used the gun to block, and others, he used his own thick forearms which he could harden into steel.

"I should have never delivered you to Elysium!" Samson snarled in between clashes. "I knew I should have just killed you when I had the chance!"

"Stay out of the way, Squid Man!" Wren exclaimed.

Sage whipped around when she heard shouting and grunting from the Color Dome. To her horror, she very quickly remembered that Castor and Pollux were fighting Nathan after she had told them to stay the hell away from her. The rest of their crew was littered throughout the city, tackling Mutatio, and the twins were supposed to be *leading* them. What the hell were they doing with Nathan?

"SAGE!" Samson cried, grabbing each of Wren's arms with his bare hands. He'd do this to Sage so easily, yet he looked like he was about to crumble against Wren. "SEE TO THEM!"

Wren, apparently, wasn't the only one who could transform

into a Mutatio—Nathan could, too. He sprouted wings and took off into the air. From afar, he looked like a rocket launching off into space, cocoon baby in his arms. Castor and Pollux must have given him one hell of a time if he was fleeing from battle.

They jumped up after him. Like the impeccable team they were, they used each other to leap like frogs into the air. It was the craziest stunt Sage had seen them do yet. The two were as sophisticated as acrobats. Once they reached their desired height and were close enough to their target, they whipped out their Slainium swords to take him down.

Sage didn't have hers since losing it onstage, but she did shape-shift despite the horrible state her body was in. She didn't transform into a Mutatio, but she fired her arm into the sky and wrapped it around one of Nathan's legs.

Thanks to that, Castor and Pollux were able to land each of their uppercuts. The attacks were strong enough to cast Nathan to the ground much like Wren had with Sage.

Nathan used his body to cushion the landing for his cocoon. He didn't spring onto his feet right away, either. He curled up, shaking like a leaf, in clear frustration.

Castor and Pollux stepped forward as Sage finally made it to the scene.

"Please..." Nathan croaked, cowering before the trio. He used his bat-like wing to shield his body. He still had scraps of his glamorous costume on his arms and hips. "Don't hurt her..."

"Then stand DOWN!" Pollux barked, pointing his sword. "Stand down, damn it!"

Castor let Pollux do all the talking. The two approached with caution, swords raised. For a moment, they held their breaths in hopes Nathan was going to comply.

Unfortunately, that didn't happen. When the twins were close enough, Nathan lashed out like a rattlesnake. He managed to shape-shift one of his arms into a large talon, which he would have used to cut Castor in half were it not for Sage who threw out her own blade. Nathan struck her instead and the force of it created a massive shockwave. It actually cracked another few bones in Sage's body.

"Mom!" Pollux wheezed.

Sage wasn't going to let a few fractures stop her—she struck Nathan with the blade on her other arm. She was relentless as she drove him across the street, ducking, jumping, and swinging until she had him tumbling to the ground. She nailed him to the asphalt with her blades, then Castor and Pollux confiscated the cocoon from his weak hands.

Nathan roared. He turned even more monstrous at that point, completing his transformation into a Mutatio. Unlike Wren, though, he didn't stop growing. He swelled to the size of a mini building, over fifty feet tall, with so many arms he might have been a centipede.

Sage stepped back. The clouds blew in, and the rain came down as hard as ever in Diamond City. The droplets were pelting and they burned the hell out of all of Sage's open wounds. There were so many that were still struggling to regenerate thanks to the Slainium in her blood.

"What the fuck?" Pollux breathed as Nathan morphed into a monster even more grotesque than Venus.

It was three against one now, but the one was loaded with Cells. Sage suspected that Wren had made good use of Rhett's body back in Elysium and taken every bit of blood. Amidst sex, she must have shared some with Nathan. It was the only explanation.

Sage could admit that seeing these monsters never got easier. There wasn't anything more horrendous than Cell Land, but she still felt bile stir in her gut in the face of this thing. The rain strengthened, to the point it became impossible to see anything. This was one big nightmare and there was no hope of waking up from it. In between these vicious winds, all Sage could do was feel her opponent's vibrations, movements, and energy. All three were much grander than her own.

"Mother," Castor croaked.

Was he worried for himself? Or for her? Sage must have looked pretty pathetic. She was on her knees, actually, arms flaccid before her. She couldn't even hold a blade anymore. Her sword was nowhere to be found. It looked like her sons were going to run the show now.

Like the jumping beans they were, they devised their own strategy to slay this great monster. The twins' advantage was their agility, whereas Nathan couldn't do much moving. He did have tentacles to swat at them, and a few snuck out to try to reel in the cocoon Pollux had left under a car.

Sage got to her feet. As Castor and Pollux buzzed around Nathan like annoying gnats, using their swords and then guns to blast parts of him away, Sage reached the cocoon.

"NO!" Nathan roared, swiping at Sage, who jumped back with the bundle in her arms. "DON'T HURT HER!"

Castor and Pollux landed on a nearby traffic light. They both turned to watch their mother. They must have been wondering what on earth she was going to do with the cocoon now. Was she really going to crush a baby?

"Surrender," Sage said quietly.

The rain was still coming down. It was hard for Sage to describe what was happening at that moment, holding what would be her niece to her bosom. She kept her eyes on Nathan's amber ones, waiting for him to follow through with her command.

Nathan's body sagged with a thud. Anyone could have mistaken it for thunder. He lowered his head in submission.

"Come here," Sage said to her sons.

The both of them were frozen with sheer terror. They peered into her eyes. Theirs were so dark and glittery, swimming with fear. They were just like Damian's, but held none of the conviction. They didn't have the authority that Damian did, and they shouldn't have had it, either. They were too young and Sage was their mother.

Plus, it was time to end this nightmare.

Sage gave Castor the cocoon. She took their guns in turn. Yes, those were Samson's guns ... but Sage felt she was quite over her grudge at the moment. Before this fucking monster destroyed any more of the Color District, Sage was going to blast his ass straight to hell.

With both guns charged and ready, Sage tore two enormous holes into Nathan's body. The lasers burned everything they touched, incinerating Cells like fire on gasoline. At this point, there was nothing Nathan could do to regenerate. His remains continued to burn long after his heart stopped beating. The smell made Pollux throw up.

Sage turned around. She faced Castor, who was holding onto the cocoon. She glared at it. Her hands tightened around the guns. Instinct told her to make it quick.

"Mother," Castor said carefully. "You're not going to end the cocoon's life, are you?"

Of course Sage was. That was Wren's fucking child. Sage was goddamned done with anything having to do with her sister.

There was a snarl from afar.

Sage, Castor, and Pollux looked up.

Samson.

"Stay with the cocoon," Sage said to her sons.

Still clutching the two guns, Sage ran. There were cars, debris, and random body parts all over the streets. Sage had no idea where she was going—she just followed the scent of blood. It was light, but present beneath the pounding rain, and took her right back to Samson and Wren.

When Sage reached them, she saw her sister hunched over Samson on all fours.

At first, Sage didn't quite understand what was happening. Samson's gun was lying on the side of the road, discarded. Light wisps of smoke were still coming out of the barrel, so it was used recently. By whom, though?

The answer became apparent when Sage noticed the gaping hole in Samson's side. Blood was flooding onto the asphalt, creating a pool of red. Wren wasn't a fool—it was feast time.

She was as monstrous as ever. In just a short hour, her body had managed to morph even more: her arms and legs were twice as long as before, heavily jointed like a spider's from hell; her long beautiful hair looked like burnt twigs; and there were tentacles flailing back and forth from just beneath her armpits.

Sage started shaking. She was frozen in place, watching Wren tear into Samson's body like a stack of barbecue ribs. There was still so much about Cells that Sage didn't know, but she did know what it did to humans thanks to Enhanced. She also knew what happened when Enhanced took in too many—it turned them into Mutatio like Taz. And now she knew what happened when a hybrid overdosed on the very Cells they gifted to others.

At last, Sage understood why hybrids were so much more dangerous than Lolligo.

Hybrids were unpredictable. Hybrids were part *human*.

"Get the fuck off him," Sage said.

"Sage . . ." Samson's eyes welled with tears.

"I SAID GET THE FUCK OFF HIM!" Sage roared at Wren. A powerful blast from one of her guns threw Wren right off the dying Samson. Sage flew across the street and smashed into her sister's body. She might not have had Samson's blood or his strength, but she did have his guns.

It should have been easy with all this Slainium at her disposal, but this was the hardest fight of Sage's life yet. Wren moved like a goddamn spider on steroids, ducking, flipping, and twirling through the air as if she could manipulate gravity.

Sage didn't let any of those fancy maneuvers distract her, though—she kept shooting her guns. The lasers flashed a bright blue every time she did. Ten minutes in, the guns started to run out of power. In the corner of her eye, she saw a blinking red under *energy level*.

"DIE, SAGE!" Wren roared like a banshee. She unleashed thirty tentacles at Sage, who rolled to the side; it was her turn to duck, flip, and twirl around those masses of flesh. In fact, Wren didn't stop morphing. As the minutes ticked by, Wren's body broke and twisted, as if the Cells in her blood were replicating at the speed of light. At that rate, Wren was going to be larger than the highest skyscraper in Diamond City.

Sage took a step back. All she could do was stare at Wren and think of Venus . . . of Damian . . . of Nathan . . .

". . . Sage . . ." Samson rasped from behind her.

Sage looked at him.

Samson smiled at her. He coughed up some blood as he said, "The blood of a Lolligo . . . was never meant for a human . . ."

Right. Wren had just consumed Samson's Cells. A lot of them, too, based on how much Samson was bleeding. Like with Enhanced, too much of them in the body of a hybrid was catastrophic.

But wait. At Elysium. The Lolligo had used Wren to create more hybrids . . . but those hybrids had also consumed the Cells of a Lolligo for nutrition. Wasn't that what Reinforcement shots were?

Ilan was still in his human form. And so was Sage, who had consumed Samson's Cells on more than one occasion, too. Perhaps she hadn't consumed anywhere near as many as Wren had now, though.

But then what about Damian? He had never drank Lolligo blood, had he?

Suddenly, Sage knew the answer to that.

Tyrus and Herman. Nova must have used their Cells to create that special serum. And Louis must have done something to fuck up the dose because Damian's Cells hadn't stopped replicating since. A whole year later, Damian's nest was nearly the size of a forest.

And that's exactly what was happening to Wren. She was growing rapidly, appendages and tentacles bursting out of her like stars exploding in the sky.

Seemingly, that's what had happened to Venus, too. According to Jared, she had consumed a Lolligo after escaping Diamond City. She had also eaten a ton of Enhanced in Cell Land. Yet, when she fought Damian, she had regained her human form . . . so did that mean the same was going to happen to Wren?

Perhaps not for a while. First, Wren was going to destroy all of Diamond City. Castor and Pollux were already grabbing Samson's body, but Sage wasn't going to budge.

This was her city. This was *her* city, damn it.

"Mom!" Pollux cried.

"Mother!" Castor cried.

The twins already knew what Sage's mission was and they weren't going to stop her. They threw her their swords, and Sage caught them in each hand.

Then she looked up at Wren. Her grip tightened on the warm hilts of her sons' weapons three times before she was ready.

Last battle, Sage thought to herself. *Last battle*.

She had to do this one last time. How hard could that be, when she had been fighting since high school? Since August had shown her how to throw a punch? Since Sage had discovered a talent for reading her opponents and cutting them down while expending as little energy as possible? That's what she had to do now in the face of a one-hundred-foot monster.

Sage closed her eyes. She wasn't fearful. Not at all. She wasn't nervous, either, because she knew what she had to do. Jump, slice, and kill . . . even if she could very well lose her life. That was fine. For Diamond City, Sage would do anything.

"Sage!"

Sage stopped. She turned around.

Gertrude, Tate, Sonia, L, Tai, and Sword Devil were here. They weren't alone, either—more of Damian's rebels like Margaret, Ramon, Eric, Shane, Bernard, and Cecilia ran into the street. There were others Sage had never met before from Emerald City ready to help and end this nightmare in any way they could. They had all been fighting alongside her. They had all sacrificed their lives to save this city.

"You're not just fighting the Optimum!" Gertrude exclaimed to Wren. "You're fighting her best warriors!"

When they all blasted her at once with those powerful lasers, it was easy for Sage to finish the job. She had complete and total access to the heart of Wren's body. Two swords, both laced with Slainium, would finish this bitch. If Wren had already suspected this would happen, Sage didn't know, but Wren couldn't put up much of a fight now anyway.

Sage flew straight to Wren's body, sliced up and across, then jumped. She landed on the closest tentacle, stabbed it with a sword, then swung down to slice another in half. A hand came out of nowhere to swipe at her, but Gertrude blasted it and Sage was able to follow up with a slash. She landed on one of Wren's knees, jumped to the other side of Wren's body with her swords out, and let them cut through whatever they touched like butter.

That was it. Wren was in two pieces. On top of that, she was full of holes that were hissing smoke. Slowly, she slumped to the ground.

Blood continued to spray all over Sage. Unlike water, it was so thick and coppery. The smell burned Sage's nostrils, but most of the stench was coming from the disintegrating flesh around her. The rain helped to quell some of it, at least.

"Sage!" Tate called out, but Ramon held him back.

Sage gazed into the center of the mess. She could see a body.

Wren.

Wren was quivering. Her skin was bubbling. Her limbs were twitching, as if they were fighting to come back to life. Her hair was growing, too. She looked like she had just crawled out of her mother's womb. Perhaps that's what the mess all around her was: excess parts. A cocoon. And the body on the ground was what it had given life to. Wren had transformed.

Wren had adapted.

Sage stepped over to her sister, two swords in hand.

"What do you think would have happened..." Wren whispered to Sage, "if Mother had never sold me? Would we have been best friends?" Her teeth were sticking out everywhere. Her face was still configuring itself.

Sage exhaled a shaky breath. She clutched her swords. "I don't know," she whispered.

"Would we have conquered the Overseers together?"

"I don't know."

"Would we have started the pizzeria and called it 'Three for Pizza'?"

Sage shook her head. "I don't know."

Wren chuckled wryly. "So I guess . . . neither of us . . . gets our fairy-tale ending . . ."

Sage smiled. It was a horrible, twisted, sad sort of smile. "No, Wren. Neither of us."

Sage stabbed Wren's body with both swords. She slammed those blades through flesh and ground alike, skewering her sister like a fish.

Wren didn't jump or groan. She just looked up at Sage and said, "Look for it."

Sage didn't understand.

"I don't know what a fairy-tale life is . . . but look for it. On behalf of your sons . . . and new niece."

But that couldn't be. Sage couldn't look for anything right now because she was supposed to die here today. That's the part she didn't have enough time to tell Wren about.

Perhaps it was better that way. Wren closed her eyes and died with a peaceful smile gracing her lips. Her arms were by her sides, legs stretched out in front of her. Her old body continued to burn and crumble around her, but at least she was whole and recognizable now. Her teeth had shrunk back to normal.

She looked like Sage.

Sage withdrew her swords. When she looked up, she found Hayes pointing a laser at her.

"I'm going to do it," Hayes said quietly, stepping out of the shadows.

Gertrude and the others, who had looked about ready to celebrate, froze. It was all eyes on Hayes now, who had come out of nowhere. Wasn't he supposed to be with Jamie and Bruce some-where in the capital? Samson stared at him from in between Cas-tor and Pollux, who were doing an incredible job of holding a three-hundred-pound body.

"I'm going to kill you, Sage," Hayes said more loudly this time. "But you're going to tell them why you want me to."

CHAPTER 33

Reasons to Live

Everyone on the street froze. The Color Dome looked like a crypt from here. The rain came down hard. There was broken glass everywhere. The district so full of life and flair was so dark and gray now.

"Tell them, Sage!" Hayes choked, hands shaking around the gun. "Tell them how you coerced me into this fucking deal of ending your life after everything was over!"

"S-Sage?" Gertrude sucked in a breath. She was as confused as everyone else. This was definitely not like the Sage they knew. Was this some sort of joke? Not funny after all the hell they went through.

But, no, this was no prank. They just didn't understand. Or maybe they did and they were just too selfish to recognize she had to die. All of them wanted her to live because they loved her, but they didn't understand what could happen if another force out there captured her and used her blood to create more Enhanced or even her DNA to make more hybrids.

That's what Elysium had done with Wren. The other hybrids like Ilan didn't have the same powers. Only Emerald City had perfected the hybrid, and the ones they had sent to Diamond City were all dead . . . except for Sage.

"All the Emerald City hybrids are dead . . . except for me," Sage said quietly. "Ilan . . . and the other hybrids from Elysium . . . can't create Enhanced. But I can. My biggest strength has always been my humanity, the fact that I look human. It's how I've been able to live incognito. Without that, I'd probably hide in a hole like the Lolligo have all their lives."

Sage snorted. She put her weapons down on the ground. Slowly, she got to her knees in between them. She lowered her head.

"But you know what I look like," Sage said quietly. "You know what I am and what I can do, both on and off the battlefield."

The rain came down as hard as ever now.

"I don't want to be used as a weapon."

Louis, Geoffrey, and the rest of the Diamond City military found them at last. They ran right into the scene, confused, perhaps, at the mound of burning blood and guts, but even more perplexed by the sight of Sage on her knees.

"I hid from this life for so long," Sage went on quietly. "After the Unification War, I dreaded it. I made Marchello swear he wouldn't go looking for me and he kept his promise. He never mentioned my name to anyone in the capital because I stayed out of the Warlord's Rebellion. I didn't betray him. He knew I put him in power, so he honored that.

"Damian and Blackburn, though, knew the Optimum was out there. They might have pursued me for their own reasons, but they wanted to seek me out nonetheless—expose me. And I was stupid enough to get involved in palace affairs and do it myself. Or maybe it was my own nephew who sold me out first, since everyone already knew who I was before I even set foot in the palace."

"Sage," Louis said softly.

Everyone looked at him. It wasn't every day that Louis had the balls to step forward and speak his thoughts. Perhaps he had yelled at Damian a time or two, but the infamous Warlord always struck fear into his heart and kept him quiet. Louis had lost an entire opportunity at love because of it, but now it was his turn to talk.

"No one here sees you as a weapon," Louis said. "And even when you didn't know who the fuck you were, I never touched a hair on your head." His eyes welled with tears. "I just wanted to see you happy. That's why I kept you away from Damaris, because I knew as soon as he saw you, he'd drag you right back into his affairs!"

"Fucker," Pollux hissed. "That's not true! Diamond City was already a shithole before my father knew it was my *mother* you were keeping all to yourself in the palace! *You're* the one who endangered her!"

"Keeping her confined to the palace wouldn't have saved her," Castor snarled. "Jared and Venus had already gotten out—on your watch, I might add."

"The point is," Louis growled, without looking at the twins, "that everyone respects you, Sage. Maybe there are assholes out there that want to use you, but not us. We'll fight tooth and nail to ensure you live the life you deserve."

Sage looked over her shoulder at Louis. She was horrified by the look she found on Geoffrey's face.

His big hazel eyes, just like Wyatt's, were huge. They were swimming with tears, that his Optimum was on the floor, waiting to die, and that fucker, Hayes, still hadn't put down the gun. They shined with all the amazing memories they'd had together. Number one on that list was the Silver Gears concert. Geoffrey had come down with Red Fever, but that was part of the fun. To think they'd never do it again—that after thirty years of waiting for Sage to wake up, it was all about to come to a screeching halt.

"This is your city, Sage," Louis said, projecting his voice over the pitter-patter of the rain. "You might not want to be Allseer, but you've fought so hard for it. Wouldn't you want to see it up and running again? D-didn't you want to get married in the Color Dome?"

It was ironic and hardly funny, but Sage laughed. "That place brings back nothing but bad memories now."

"Fine, but it doesn't have to be that way. Not anymore."

"Why are we talking about a goddamned city?" Tate snarled. "What about her goddamned sons?! Did you think about *them*, Sage, when you made this bat-crazy decision to have Hayes kill you? Or your new niece? Who's supposed to raise her now?"

"I am thinking about them," Sage said quietly.

"Don't you fucking get it?!" Tate stomped over to her. "Whether you live or die doesn't make a damn difference—there are *always* going to be people out there ready to take advantage! Life isn't one big fairy tale with no opposition—you're always going to have to fight for yourself and for the ones you love! But giving up isn't going to solve anything!"

Sage lowered her head. Tate grabbed her by the shirt and shook her.

"Look at me, damn it!" he exclaimed. "I'm fucking talking to you! I don't know what pity party you're trying to have—and at the end of the day you do what you want—but I want you to think real hard about how you dying in front of us is going to affect us.

"Is this really the way you want to go? You, the one who saved Damian's life, who told him to live on when he had nothing? Well, you have something and you still don't want to live on, so that makes you a spoiled brat *and* a hypocrite. There is always something to live for in this world, and you have plenty of it. Those were *your* fucking words."

Tate shook his head. He threw Sage on the ground and stepped back. "I'm not going to watch this," he said out loud. "I think there's something wrong with her fucking head. Samson, you might want to give her a brain transplant. Oh, but wait." He waved his hands. "Castor and Pollux are supposed to kill him and every Lolligo out there now, right? Well, what are you waiting for, boys? Kill the damn Squid! Let's all fucking die here today and screw everything we've worked so hard for!"

Sage cried. She curled up into a ball next to her swords and sobbed.

Samson, as wounded as he was, stepped forward. He got to his knees next to her and wrapped an arm around her body. He brought her close to his chest, full of blood and all. He was looking like shit, but it seemed he hadn't been hit with his own gun, after all. Perhaps he had let Wren tear into him on purpose. Part of the master plan? Maybe.

"Sage," Samson said against her temple. "Please . . . please stop crying. You know how much I hate it when you cry."

"Samson!" Sage choked. She clutched his body with her hands. She sobbed into his chest. "I'm sorry . . . I-I'm so sorry . . . but I'm just so tired . . ."

"But it's over," Samson said to her. "It's over now. Don't you see? Rhett, Venus, and your sister are dead. We can pick up with our lives now."

"Don't you want to kill me?" Sage croaked.

Samson broke down. He sobbed.

It was such a strange sound, too. Nasally, as if Samson were scooping up all the phlegm in his sinuses. But he wasn't doing it to be funny or to put on a show in front of the dozen or so preachers that arrived at the scene.

Leave it to Preacher and his squad of worshipers to the heart of the battlefield. They raised their hands in reverence.

"Praise the Forefathers!" they all chanted at once. Had they practiced that? "Diamond City, at long last, has been liberated! Human, hybrid, and Lolligo have finally joined forces to accomplish the peace we have sought for so long!"

"Of course I don't want to kill you, Sage," Samson croaked against her head, completely disregarding the preachers. "How could I want to kill you? Faye was being a bitch—we can all agree to that—and I was being unreasonable when I said we should abandon Damian, but I didn't know what else to do. I know you didn't want to fight . . . despite the fact you cut down all those Mutatio practically single-handedly. But that in no way meant I wanted to kill you." He squeezed her tightly. "Although I do think about it when you leave your goddamned boots on the floor."

Sage couldn't chuckle.

"Mother," Castor said.

"Mom," Pollux said.

The twins stepped over to her. They got on their knees, too. Castor had surrendered the cocoon to Sword Devil, so he and his brother could take Sage's hands.

"We know what you've been through," Castor said. "Father told us everything. And so we understand it feels hopeless. But we want to assure you it isn't. So long as we live, we will continue to fight on your behalf. We have learned so much from you. Most of all, we have learned how to be brave and confront our enemies. For that reason, we will face every challenge that comes our way with confidence and dignity. In the meanwhile, people can pick up again—as Enhanced now—and live long, wonderful lives. Wasn't that what you and Father always wanted?"

Sage supposed it was. She rubbed her eyes against Samson's ripped jacket. She smiled. "Yes."

The thought of Damian started a horrible burning in her chest. It felt like someone was ripping her heart out. But Sage had to ignore the feeling and caress the beautiful faces of her sons. Then she had to wrap her arms around Geoffrey. Then Margaret actually beat Gertrude to Sage and threw her arms around her. Sonia and L bumbled over to hug her, too (L was reluctant). Then the rest of Damian's crew took their turns, with Sword Devil wondering when the cocoon would hatch and if they could teach the newborn how to play with swords. And then Louis and the rest of the Diamond City military chanted her name.

"*OPTIMUM! OPTIMUM! OPTIMUM!*"

Sage laughed.

From the other side of the street, so did Hayes.

He finally put the gun down.

Sage had finally gotten her new life.

It had stopped raining, too.

CHAPTER 34

Living the Dream

Sage woke up to Hamilton's tongue on her face. That meant he was either hungry, needed to pee or poop, or wanted a run around town. Possibly, all of the above.

Sage smiled and patted Hamilton's head. His whole torso was on the bed, paws on her shoulders. His coat was so shiny, muscles tight. He was definitely the most handsome Doberman Pinscher in all of Ruby City. All the lady dogs went nuts whenever he walked by.

"All right," Sage said, stifling a yawn. "I'm up."

Hamilton jumped back as Sage sat up. She patted her hair, which was a damn mess from the pillow. It had grown quite a bit. It was now in the "unruly" phase, as Pollux had put it. In other words, it had become that much harder to manage. It couldn't be the rain, either, because Ruby City had nothing but bright days all year round.

Always a little hot, but doable. Fall was coming, and the trees were already turning a bright crimson. It was quite beautiful. Sage was learning how to appreciate nature a bit more.

After brushing her teeth and donning her jacket and joggers, Sage secured her pouch. She always grabbed some breakfast from

Jo's Yo-Go. Later, she was accompanying Candice to a doctor's appointment. The baby was coming along incredibly well.

There'd be two Sages in the world soon. Sage couldn't wait to meet her little niece.

"All right, let's go." Sage opened the door to her room and Hamilton trotted out.

They were still at Crystal Light. A lot of Diamond City residents had already moved back home, but a lot more had decided to stay in Ruby until repairs were complete. It wasn't just the Color District, either—Wren had made quite the mess everywhere. It was a lot, but Louis and his council had jumped on it right away.

As soon as reconstruction was done, Louis was stepping down, though. As Sage had proposed, there'd be elections in Diamond City by the end of next year. District officials were already discussing who their candidates would be. It was a bit crazy to think about, but Preacher was going to run for office. They had already had their first debate just last night in one of Ruby City's auditoriums.

"And so the Lolligo have endowed me with the strength and wisdom to lead Diamond City to prosperity!" Preacher exclaimed to his opponents and moderators. "I have been by the Optimum's side and witnessed her battles! I have also received the blessings of the Lolligo Prophet himself along with his two trusted companions! The Wise Three would never lead me astray."

Sage laughed. "The Wise Three" were supposed to be Samson, Jamie, and Bruce. Vince was still the size of a toddler, so he didn't have many revelations to offer humanity yet. Regardless, the four were heroes thanks to their feats: they had saved humanity from bloodthirsty monsters. Despite their popularity in Diamond City politics, however, the Lolligo were perfectly content in Ruby City, where they were still experimenting with Surgium and building all sorts of breakthrough technology. Samson's Robo was a huge hit here. The little robots rolled down the streets every night, picking up trash and cleaning windows. Paige and Pedro, who had decided to switch genders again in honor of Sage's success, swore by them.

Sage took a deep breath. She looked out into the horizon. The sun was rising. It was going to be another great day. After some quick stretches, she started her jog.

There were only a handful of people on the streets at this hour. They all greeted Sage with a smile and wave. Hamilton never strayed far from Sage's side, although he stopped to examine some bushes on the way to the *Luse* on the south side of town.

It was exactly five miles away from Crystal Light. The Lolligo never came out of their cave, so Sage didn't expect them to greet her. Once in a while, she'd see Faye hanging out by the bushes or watering the plants.

They hardly ever made eye contact, but when they did, they both bowed to each other. Faye would have a submissive look on her face, while Sage would apologize for her hand. Sure, the Lolligo had put it back seamlessly, but it wasn't the injury that bothered her—it was that whole encounter. Admittedly, it was one of the worst of Sage's life.

Faye wasn't here this morning. Once Sage touched the ship's door, glad that it was still intact after two years, she jogged over to Jo's Yo-Go for breakfast.

"Aunt Sage!" Olivia exclaimed, standing from her seat immediately. "You're here!"

Sage smiled at her niece. They had plenty to catch up on, but Sage got her order in first. She went for the Breakfast Special today: two boiled eggs, hash browns, and bacon. Hamilton had the usual Berry Goji Getaway since it was his favorite.

"Do you always go jogging in the morning?" Isadora asked her.

"I do," Sage said happily, taking a seat at their table. "And at night, too. After I finish kicking Castor and Pollux's ass in training."

"Your strength is incredible. I wish I could be more like you." Isadora frowned at her belly. "Ever since I moved to Ruby City, I've gained a ton of weight."

"That's because you work in an office now," Olivia said. Her plate was packed with protein. "And are no longer running for your life and surviving hell."

"But you always look good."

"Of course. I'm a model—I have to look good on the go."

Olivia was the center of attention everywhere she went for a reason. She wore the right clothes to show off her round shoulders, shapely breasts, and thick thighs. Sage couldn't get them that big even if she tried.

"I do like it here," Isadora admitted, swirling the whipped cream into her frappuccino. "But I am kind of looking forward to seeing Diamond City. Candice and Olivia want to show me your pizzeria, Sage. Are you excited to go back?"

"I suppose I am," Sage said, squeezing ketchup all over her hash browns. "Pizza is in my blood, after all."

"Candice wants to have the baby there."

Sage nodded. She definitely had her hands full. Castor and Pollux planned on attending the birth of their cousin, too. Sage worried about Emerald City, which she had yet to actually see, but according to the twins, Jarka and Josiah were managing just fine. Those two were Damian's second-in-command.

"So." Olivia cleared her throat. That indicated she was about to bring up a touchy topic. She always asked about Damian and if there had been any changes.

"No," Sage said softly. "There haven't."

Hamilton looked up at her. His lips were full of purple slush, but his tongue made quick work of it.

Sage never lost hope, of course. In addition to the leather jacket, Paige and Pedro had made him an undershirt, pair of pants, and some boots. Sage wrote him a poem every day much the same way Damian had drawn a picture of her every day.

"Don't give up hope, Aunt Sage," Olivia said tenderly, touching her hand. "If Venus and Wren were able to restore their bodies, then why not Damian? All three of them overdosed on Cells, so if the first two were able to evolve and return to their human forms, then there's a good chance Damian will come back."

That was Samson's theory. Seemingly, hybrids who consumed or contained too many Cells "exploded." Their bodies grew to monstrous proportions until they were able to stabilize themselves. Hybrids were that incredible, adapting to whatever changes or excesses they were exposed to.

But there was still so much on Cells that they didn't know … and Sage wasn't sure she cared so long as people were Enhanced and happy. There was no other reason to pursue Cell experimentation.

Sage finished her breakfast and then it was time to meet Candice at the clinic.

This clinic had been in operation for nearly a year now. Doctors, nurses, and office assistants from Diamond City were all running it together. Even Dr. X had joined the team to help out. He was an old Enhanced who knew a thing or two about physiology regardless of the species.

To Sage, Dr. X was still a creep. She made sure to stay the hell away from him ever since Damian had brought him here. But she felt a twinge of sadness every time she saw him because she thought of Damian. To think these two had met in school over a hundred years ago.

"Aunt Sage." Candice embraced her as soon as she saw her in the lobby. The nurse was waving her in, so Sage was right on time.

This wasn't Sage's first time supporting her niece through one of these grueling physicals, and she thanked almighty God she wasn't the one on that cold, hard table. All the white uniforms, freezing air, and antiseptic smells gave Sage the shivers. She was grateful that her pregnancy hadn't been a traditional one, and although she could have done without slicing her belly open and yanking out cocoons from her womb, she preferred that over what was waiting for Candice in three months.

A baby … coming out of her vagina.

Sage crossed her legs as Dr. X performed his exam on Candice. She tried not to look and focused on the human anatomy poster on the wall instead. She knew every bone thanks to Samson, who had broken them all, and every artery just in case it was life or death on the battlefield.

Candice laughed. "Aunt Sage, why do you always look like you've swallowed a lemon when you're here?"

Sage cleared her throat. "I think you know the answer to that."

Dr. X snorted. His hair was darker and nicer now that he had access to stylists (Pollux refused to touch him), but his glasses were as thick as always. He checked each of Candice's reflexes. "Your aunt is a bigger child than you might think. Just like Damian."

"I'm not a child," Sage snapped. "Just cautious."

"More like foolish. To this day, you still refuse to allow me to examine you."

"There's nothing wrong with me."

"And you can't truly know that, can you?" Dr. X said coolly. "Just thirty years ago, you went into hibernation, and just a year ago, you were dying from Slainium poisoning. You have no idea what sort of state your body is in."

"Yes, I do," Sage said. "I know I was 'reborn' and that I'm young again which is why I look like a college student. I know that I've recovered a lot of strength and stamina, which I started losing in my previous life as I got older. Sure, I've been in a lot of battles now that have fucked me up, but I've recovered and I feel good."

" 'Feeling good' does not mean you are well!" Dr. X sputtered.

"I think it's a big indication," Sage said. "I live in my body, therefore, I definitely know it better than you do."

"Last I checked, you were not a medical expert."

"No, but I know my body and you don't."

Dr. X huffed at her. "You know nothing about diseases and genetics or what can potentially happen to you." He put on his stethoscope.

Sage snorted. "Does it count if I can still kick your ass and not feel any pain while I'm doing it?"

Candice laughed. That was the reason she brought Sage with her everywhere. Geoffrey was too much of a pussy for entertainment.

With his patient in a fit of giggles, Dr. X couldn't dream of auscultation. He glared at the culprit. "How on earth does he put up with you?"

"How does he put up with *you?*" Sage spat. "Don't tell me your dick is that outstanding. Please—it can't be that big."

"Aunt Sage!" Candice rasped. She sounded like she was dying on the table.

"If you are going to be that disrespectful, then I am going to ask you to leave!" Dr. X barked.

"But before I do, I want you to explain it to me, *Doctor,*" Sage sneered. "Because Damian swears you have the nicest penis he's ever seen. Well, what's so great about it? You can piss and ejaculate all the same, can't you? If it squirted gold, *maybe* I'd want to see it, too."

"I really don't care what Damian thinks about my penis and I especially don't care what you think!" Dr. X snapped over Candice's guffaws. "Your mannerisms are horrendous for a lady, and indeed I am concerned over the growth of any child around you."

Sage shrugged her shoulders. "Candice and Olivia are just fine. The bigger mystery is how you and Damian were ever a couple."

They were polar opposites, for sure. But maybe Sage and Damian were polar opposites, too, and that's why they got along so well. Dr. X was done with this conversation.

"Please leave, Optimum."

"I want to see my niece," Sage said coolly.

"Then wait outside until I am done examining my patient and the technician comes in for the sonogram."

So Sage waited in the hall. There, she got to watch passing doctors and nurses. She smiled a bit at her banter, and she snorted with laughter when Dr. X stepped out of the room with a huff and she still heard Candice laughing inside.

There were definitely many reasons to live. And at that moment, there was an infinite number of them for Sage. Her heart longed for Damian, but she couldn't complain when she was looking at her little niece on the monitor. They had 3-D scans of her, too.

"The new Sage," Candice said happily with tears in her eyes. She held Sage's hand. "I can't wait! And I especially can't wait for you to come back to Diamond City with us."

Sage couldn't, either. She held Candice's hand on the way out of the clinic, too. She reminisced on all the nieces and nephews she'd guided through child-bearing. It was always exciting to raise a new human being, especially in the good times that lied ahead.

"Sage!" Sonia came bumbling out of nowhere. She jumped onto Sage's back, hugging her from behind. Her hair was always blonde and short, but today it was dyed all red in honor of fall.

She and L, as well as the rest of Damian's rebels, were taking it easy in Ruby City. Gertrude and Tate were taking a much-needed vacation at the Tall Hotel on the west side; Margaret was hitting every shop because it was time for a "new look"; and Cecilia, Bernard, and Shane were starting a food blog.

"Did you hear?" Sonia asked excitedly. "Tai and Sword Devil are getting ready to play some fastball."

"Can you not choke her?" L snapped at Sonia.

"Let's play!"

It was a bit unpredicted, but Tai and Sword Devil had taken custody of Wren's cocoon baby. Sage had learned that Sword Devil had her uterus yanked out of her in Centerfeld when she declined sex with Lex. It was a disturbing thought, one Sage couldn't stop whenever she saw the baby carriage. It looked like Tai and Sword Devil were serious about adoption and retirement once they got back to Emerald City. It wouldn't be long before the baby hatched.

Sage had to say hello to her little niece before anyone else. She remembered what it was like to stare at Castor and Pollux for hours and wonder what they looked like inside that hard shell.

"And how are you doing today, Anastasia?" Sage cooed. She made sure to sprinkle some blood over the cocoon. Only a hybrid's blood could quench an offspring's hunger. Unfortunately for Sword Devil and Tai, theirs wasn't potent enough. Sage definitely didn't mind. Everyone was a little wary that she would go into hibernation again, but Sage was confident she wouldn't. She had given blood to a lot of people without consequence, so why would this be any different? Besides, it's not like she was the one who had given birth or carried the cocoon in her womb.

Damian's sperm had totally killed her.

"Hey, Ma!" Pollux swept her into his arms and devoured her with kisses.

Sage laughed and hung on tightly for the ride.

Castor was way more mannered. He took her hand and kissed the back of it gently. "Good morning, Mother."

"Don't the two of you look comfortable," Sage said. It wasn't every day that Castor and Pollux were in casual button-ups and jeans.

"We heard there was a fastball tournament going on and you were playing in it." Pollux clapped his hands excitedly. "You're making me a lot of money today, Mom!"

"It's just a scrimmage," Sage said.

"Doesn't matter—it's a well organized scrimmage."

"You know that Pollux cannot control his urges or resist temptation," Castor drawled. "I, on the other hand, will not be losing any more money to this fool."

Pollux elbowed him. "I told you to bet on Mom."

"No offense, Mother." Castor kissed her hand again. Sonia was laughing. "But I am still not confident in your fastball abilities. Now, if this were a duel, I'd bet my whole life savings and my collection of model airships that you'd win."

Sage rolled her eyes and grumbled. Candice and Olivia came up behind her and patted her back.

"It's all right, Aunt Sage," Olivia said happily. "Can't be good at everything."

"I *am* good at everything . . ." Sage grumbled.

"Don't listen to these losers, Mom." Pollux picked her up in his arms. He beamed at her. God, he looked just like Damian. He had red highlights in the long part of his hair, too. "I believe in you."

"So do all of us," Castor snapped. "Just not in fastball."

"I think she's pretty good," Faye declared.

Sage was a bit surprised to see her here. She had already apologized so much for her tirade, but she wasn't sure how to fix the awkwardness. Faye had just found a way to amend her own cruel comments. Of course, Sage had a sneaking suspicion that this was mostly Samson's doing.

Sage's own fastball uniform. It was a tank top with the name "Arpine" and the number "18". The shorts were nice and comfy, too. The Wooly Socks, though, set Sage's heart soaring.

"Wow," Sage said as Faye bowed her head. "Thank you, Faye."

"Go on," she urged. "Why don't you try it on?"

So Sage took a bathroom break. When she came out, her family and friends clapped. More people had joined the circle.

"Excellent!" Paige and Pedro beamed.

"Wow," Randall said.

"You look fabulous, darling," Jasmine said; Travis nodded in agreement.

Sage blushed. "Thanks."

"Ready to kick some ass, Ma?" Pollux wrapped an arm around her and directed her to the stadium.

Tai and Sword Devil were playing against each other on the court. This was like any other scrimmage match, but Sage noticed that the seats were starting to fill up. That's because all the district's best players were here for some friendly matches before they all returned to Diamond City.

Including the professional teams.

The Cut Porcupines.

And Sage was invited.

Holy shit.

"Go on!" Sonia said happily, pushing Sage toward the court.

The crowd burst into cheers and applause. Sage's cheeks burned a horrible red.

"This is it, Sage!" Hayes said happily, clapping alongside Micah and Kendra. "The fastball match you were waiting for!"

In other words: it was the closest Sage was ever going to get to playing in a real game.

Indeed.

In Sage's head, it was Royal Academy versus Cut University all over again. Ten versus ten. Even some of the previous tournament's best players hadn't made it onto a team. Sage didn't feel like she deserved it, but Tai and Sword Devil reeled her to their side.

"We've got to win six," Tai said to his teammates. Sage's heart was pounding so hard.

No one wanted to go up against Number 18, Feodor Petrov. He was a Cut University graduate who had turned pro. Sage would have betted her money on this guy easily, but it looked like she'd be playing him now for the win now.

Sage played in the sixth match, so she had some time to meditate. If not, she'd be a nervous wreck and become a laughingstock in front of hundreds of people. There was no way she could be the Optimum and lose in some silly fastball match. Little Man always said that fighting and fastball were completely different animals, and while Sage agreed with him, not everyone else did.

The crowd was on its feet. The fastball court was ready for its first match. Twenty-four meters long and eight meters wide with a net across the middle. The floor was smooth, shaved concrete in neutral gray. The crowd brought the colors and the pride: red and gold for Diamond City and red and silver for Ruby City. It probably looked beautiful from up above, but who the hell cared?

No way. Sage couldn't stop to look at anyone other than her opponent. All that mattered was him and the court.

"*Optimum, Optimum, Optimum!*" cheered her fans from pretty much every corner of the stadium. Sage could see all their handmade banners. There was one that said, "Crush Them Like You Did Diamond City!"

Had people really been expecting her to play today? Apparently, or else they wouldn't have spent so much time putting those signs together. It lit another kind of fire in Sage's chest, to see all her support. She couldn't wait to show everyone what she could do.

She had to get to ten points first. That was it.

Sage's team had lost the first five matches, so it was totally up to her to keep them alive. Tai was the match right after hers, but it wouldn't matter if she didn't win. The crowd went crazy.

It was Sage's time to shine!

Sage stepped forward onto the court. She already had her attire, so all she needed were her wrist wraps. They helped steady her fists, which she'd need to blast that ball across the court. Seven inches in diameter and made of plastic that felt like steel sometimes. Depending on the opponent, it had the potential to fly at the speed of light. Sometimes, Sage couldn't see the ball—she had to feel it.

When she thought too much about this, Sage lost her concentration, so she stopped the tirade in her head before she psyched herself out. She walked out to her opponent and shook his hand.

Feodor squeezed it. Hard. His grip was a clamp, but so was Sage's.

"Ready to lose?" he teased her.

Sage said nothing. She called tails for the coin toss and won. She always served first. The referee gave her a ball, and Sage took it back to the serving line.

"*Optimum, Optimum, Optimum!*"

Sage looked out at the crowd. At their chanting. She had heard it so many times in her life. From the Unification War all the way until now. Sage was the Optimum in their eyes. She had always hated the name, but she didn't fight it anymore.

She had given her life to fight corruption, oust terrible Allseers, fight hybrids, and defend Lolligo from persecution. And she would continue to give her life for many years to come. That was Sage's duty: to keep these people safe. She had to fight for all their sakes.

And yours, darling, Sage said in her mind with a smile. *Always for you.*

She had his name tattooed on her right arm. Her sons were on her shoulder. Elias and Johanna Westbrook were on her ankle. She hadn't gotten her old tattoos yet, but she didn't need them. She knew who she was and the life she had lived before this one.

"Sage!" Hayes hissed from the sidelines. All her teammates were watching her. "Hey! Come on! Concentrate!"

Sage looked at the ball in her hand. Right. She had to win this. She had to stop daydreaming. This was no fantasy—this was a *real* game. She had to serve just like Tai had taught her and she had to win.

Bam!—Sage blasted that ball to the other side of the court. She jumped back, ready for the counter, and here it came—*Bam!*—she hit it back again.

Feodor shot to his right, so Sage knew it was coming for her right, but Feodor knew that she was waiting for it there, so he went left—Sage was ready—she dove for the left, got a good angle, and hit it to Feodor's *right*, switching it up on him like he had her—

She got the point!

"FUCK YEAH, MA!" Pollux pumped his fist. "100,000 Diamonds, here we come!"

Sage gasped. 100,000? Just how much had Pollux bet on her? That was a fucking lot of money! From the look on Castor's face, he hadn't known the amount, either.

Oh, shit. Sage got super nervous with all that money on her shoulders. It was her turn to serve again, but her hands couldn't stop shaking.

Calm, she told herself, taking a deep breath. *Calm, Sage.*

When Sage calmed down, her surroundings got blurry. She entered her own little world. She thought of herself making a pizza or greeting customers. She thought about that stupid Silver Gears concert when Damian had painted everyone's body black and silver. So ridiculous.

"Sage!" Hayes hissed again. He knew when she was daydreaming a bit too much. "Concentrate!"

Sage couldn't think of pizzas, concerts, or Damian, who was standing by the entrance to the stadium. She pictured him so well that it actually looked like he was there, dressed in the leather jacket, pants, and boots she had gotten him. His hair was long and silky, fluttering in the wind, but it wasn't all loose. Sometimes, Damian wove patterns into it or tied certain strands into braids. He had a million and one hairstyles, while Sage had to keep pushing flyaways out of her face. She didn't like headbands because she thought they looked stupid on her.

All right, round two: Sage served again. She liked to change it up, so she went for Feodor's left, even though she favored her right.

Feodor was ready for her this time and he hit the ball back to her with precision.

Sage intuited every move and kept the volley going for five minutes straight. Stamina was her strength, so she wasn't going to tire out. She just had to keep her eye on Feodor and what tactics he was up to. At some point, fatigue would strike him down. He was pretty hefty with all that muscle he had, but Sage never underestimated her opponents.

"UGH!" Feodor slammed the ball right back to her side of the court.

Sage was ready—she hit it again!

Pollux was biting his nails. Castor was smirking.

"Come on . . ." Hayes clenched his fists—Sage saw him in her peripheral.

She also saw Damian, though. He was still by the entrance, but Candice had her arms around him now. Olivia and Isadora, who were in the front row, were grinning, watching him over the rail. Geoffrey was pushing people out of the way to get to him. Candice started crying, and Damian chuckled as he rubbed her pregnant belly and said, "Congratulations!"

"Her name's Sage," Candice said happily.

Damian guffawed. "Isn't one enough?"

What the fuck?

This was no daydream. Sage was losing her concentration and fast because she couldn't stop staring at Damian. She swore she was going crazy, but then Geoffrey embraced him next. She couldn't be imagining all that, could she?

Feodor hit the ball and just barely got it over the net. Pollux had 100,000 fucking Diamonds on this match, so Sage dove. She scraped up her knees big time, leaving a trail of blood on the court, but she hit the ball right back to Feodor's side. She wasn't supposed to have gotten that, so Feodor was ill prepared for any rebuttal.

"Wow!" the referee called. "It's a point for the Optimum!"

"YES!" Pollux grabbed Castor and kissed him in the mouth—Castor shoved him back into an elderly couple. Pollux landed on the old lady's lap, but he still waved and pumped his fist for Sage. "GO, MA! Just eight more points to go! Remember all your training with Tai—you got this!"

Right. Sage got back to her feet; a few medics went out to check on her, but she waved them all back. Her wounds closed, but there was still all that blood on the court. Attendants would have to clean it later.

"You better step away," Damian said to the medics, coming closer to Sage's side of the court. He was as snide as ever. His eyes glittered and his lips curled into a smirk. He truly did look like a fairy god gracing them with his presence. "She already threatened to kick Dr. X's ass, and who knows what she'll do to you if you touch her."

This was definitely a daydream, but this was the most vivid one yet. Sage stared at the beautiful Damian standing by the sidelines. But—wait—if Hayes was gaping like that, then Damian had to be real ... right?

The crowd stiffened and held its breath in the presence of the Emerald City Allseer. Many craned their heads for a better look. Others like Castor and Pollux composed themselves; the latter immediately got off the old lady's lap and cleared his throat.

"Damian?" Sage said, as the referee gave her the ball again.

Damian chuckled. "Aren't you going to come give me a kiss, darling?"

Sage chucked the ball at him. Hard. Meant-to-break-a-few-bones hard. That was the only way to know if he was real or not, and sure enough, Damian hit it right back to her like a pro. Sage wasn't about to let that arrogant bastard get the best of her, so she made sure to smash it right back into his face. Damian was no pushover and he was ready for another hit.

And then, amazingly enough, they started a volley. Amazing because no one had ever seen the Warlord play fastball. It was incredible that he could actually keep up with Sage. They eventually moved on to the court, with Damian pushing Feodor to the side, and made use of the net. They turned it into a real match.

"If I win"—Damian rushed to the corner to get that sneaky shot—"we go on the honeymoon of my choosing, just you and me."

"And if I win"—Sage dove— "you'll sing for me in front of an entire auditorium."

"You're on, darling."

"You know…" Sage got the next hit easily. "The honeymoon sounds amazing. Let's do that, too."

"Fine, that was a terrible bet." Damian had to run fast for the next one and he nearly crashed into the net. "How about if I win, I have to paint your body how I want to and you have to walk around like that in public."

"But if I win," Sage huffed, "then I have to do that to you."

And she'd really make him look ridiculous on purpose. Idiot.

Damian agreed. "All right, then."

"There's more than just paint at stake here, though," Sage said as she went for another hit. "I have to beat you or else Pollux will lose 100,000 Diamonds—"

Damian gasped. He whipped around to Pollux and located him in the crowd instantly.

"Hi, Dad!" Pollux waved with a grin.

The ball hit Damian's side and rolled out of bounds. Damian had lost.

"What a doofus!" Sage laughed. "I can't believe you fell for that one! Although the bet was on my match against Feodor, not yours—"

Damian marched across the court and toward the stands. Pollux very strategically started sliding through the crowd toward the exit.

"I told him that gambling was strictly off limits!" Damian snarled. "After he lost all his savings on the Emerald Cup, I banned him from ever making another bet again. I don't care how old he is—he is not allowed to touch money. That's why I appointed him a financial advisor for life." He shook his head as he started climbing up the stands. Pollux couldn't get away fast enough. Damian looked over his shoulder at Sage. "That, by the way, he gets from you."

"My gambling is strategic," Sage huffed as the referee gave her another ball. It was time to continue the match. "The highest I ever bet was ten thousand Diamonds and I actually won because I knew the players, statistics, and my chances. And then I donated over half of it to charity."

With that money, she had bought all of Two for Pizza's fancy decor. Gambling was addictive, though, so she tried to control herself. Pollux, obviously, had to work on that, but Sage let Damian handle it.

"Come here, boy!" Damian exclaimed as he prowled through the stands to reach Pollux.

It was hard to tell what was more entertaining: father and son or the fastball match that commenced below.

Right now, Sage had a match to win. So, after apologizing to the referee and to an annoyed-looking Feodor, she served. It was round three, and she was going to win.

She felt it in her chest, in her very soul. She was doing more than just playing fastball.

She was living her dream.

Epilogue

There were a lot of colors. That was really all Sage pictured for her wedding celebration. The Color Dome, newly remodeled, with its beautiful kaleidoscope of colors, sucked her into another place and time that wasn't on earth—that wasn't anywhere, really—but that was in her head. On this stage, Sage's mind took off into space, into the unknown.

Once in a while, she glimpsed the crowd. The people—all her family and friends and anyone else who had purchased tickets—were sitting all around her, watching Sage and Damian put on the show of a lifetime.

It was just Sage and Damian on the runway in matching fabrics, suits, costumes, and dresses. Their makeup was in sync, their hair was in similar styles, and their expressions were stoic. They didn't smile at each other, but they didn't need to.

Their eyes said it all.

Smoldering love and passion. A promise to carry on what was now their hybrid creed: to use their powers and abilities to ensure Diamond, Emerald, and Ruby City were secure and protected from the world.

Samson was a married person now, but he and the Lolligo were already taking trips around the Outskirts in search of more life. They had grown bored tinkering in their lab in Ruby City, so it was time for some traveling. Faye had respectfully declined and chosen to work at Two for Pizza. Hayes, however, was all up for adventure. Sage would have gone with them, but she had her own honeymooning to do with Damian, who claimed he had so much to show her.

First, they'd elope. Damian wanted to go on his own little adventure with Sage. He had heard of a beautiful moonlit city called Opal City and he was dying to see if it really did sparkle like stars in the night sky. The catch was that it was just a rumor. No one had ever traveled that far south from Diamond City. It was all speculation, but Damian swore it existed. And so, that's what he wanted to find.

After that, they'd go to Emerald City, of course. Sage had yet to see the city she had heard so much about in school and everyone held in such high esteem. That would be just her and her sons as promised, so no Damian allowed. Besides, he had political issues to discuss with Josiah and boring meetings to attend. Sage was lucky enough to bypass all that because she had no ties to the throne— she could pretend to be a tourist and forget about governing. Castor said that the Carat District there had tons of museums and Old World collections, while Pollux said that the gambling sector was to die for. Sage had to keep an eye on her sons, as Damian instructed her every chance he got, because the two were devious as hell. It sounded like he was disciplining her, too, though.

While a lot of Diamond City citizens had moved to Emerald, and some had stayed in Ruby, there was hope Diamond was going to make a comeback with Preacher as its new Allseer.

It was crazy, but true. A year later, election results were in.

Preacher had won.

By a landslide.

Sage would have never guessed that Diamond City would unite in its decision to elect another zealot into office. The Color District, especially, after all their hardships with Marchello, but Preacher had promised equal opportunity and prosperity for all, regardless of how passionate he was about the Lolligo. He claimed the praying and blessings part was his job—everyone else could carry on, abide by the law, and do the right thing in order to live prosperous lives.

In the meanwhile, alongside her family and Faye, Sage had gotten Two for Pizza up and running again. She had introduced Baby Sage to her life's biggest accomplishment and taught Anastasia how to sprinkle cheese.

"You see?" Sage cooed to the cute baby in her arms. "Not too hard, right? It's actually kind of fun!"

Hamilton, clad in his chef's hat and apron, whole-heartedly agreed with a reassuring bark.

Candice, Geoffrey, and Micah were living in Sage and Samson's old apartment at The View since the three had inherited it. Olivia was out in the Color District with Isadora and Sage was back in her old home.

Her mother's home. Aurora's home.

Sage had spent some time and money fixing it up herself. Damian had been planning the wedding and Castor and Pollux had been at Heart, tending to Preacher.

Of course, everyone was at Sage and Damian's wedding now.

It was the month of Faith, year 135. So far, it was Diamond City's coldest winter yet. It was freezing outside, but it was so warm in the Color Dome.

And, pretty soon, Sage would have Damian all to herself. Not that they hadn't spent every morning and night having sex (except in her period month), but today would be different.

The fairy tale was for real now.

After their last walk, Damian held Sage on stage. He cupped her cheeks and peered into her eyes. He had all kinds of red and gold eyeshadow on his face. It went so well with his white creamy skin and full red lips. The costume was low cut, showing off his pecs, and tight around the arms, showing off how defined his muscles were. His waist was trim, and his pants had a bunch of cuts in them, too.

Sage was in the exact same costume. She had already seen herself in the mirror before hitting the stage. But now, she was looking up at Damian, who had captured her heart and soul from the very moment she laid eyes on him during the Warlord's Challenge and never let go. All that existed was him and his beauty. Always. And now, his voice as he sang, smooth and full of melody and power:

"You're my end and my beginning
Even when I lose I'm winninvvvg
So tell me when you hear my voice, can you feel all my love for you?
It grows greater by the day, like a balloon in my chest
All the things that we've done, all the things we've yet to do
I will wait for you, darling, because I know you'll make it through

"Darling dear, I'll hold you for an eternity
I'll make you feel my love through the pain and adversity
When the evening shadows and the stars appear
I'll drive away all your fears
When the sun rises and the light shines
I'll kiss your lips, our bodies intertwined

"From the first time I saw you, I knew that you'd be mine
From the first moment we spent together, you filled my heart with joy
You gave me the confidence to finally see
That if I worked hard enough, together we could be
One day, I'd ask you to marry me and you'd say yes
We'll be together always, to the world I profess

"Darling dear, I'll hold you for an eternity
I'll make you feel my love through the pain and adversity
When the evening shadows and the stars appear
I'll drive away all your fears
When the sun rises and the light shines
I'll kiss your lips, our bodies intertwined

"I could sing a thousand songs about you but what good would that do?
They'd all say the same thing: I can't do this life without you
There's something in your smile that gives me strength to carry
on
And there's something in the way you used to look at me that lin-
gers even when you're gone."

Damian smiled when he finished.

Sage did, too.

They kissed and embraced as the whole crowd erupted with cheers, loud whistling, and hooting.

Sage closed her eyes on Damian's shoulder as she relished in this moment.

This time, it'd be forever.

Acknowledgements

This section seems to get longer and longer with every book I write. For that reason, I'll cut down personal journey stuff and just focus on the people who have been incredible contributors in my career.

To my cover artists: Kira and James. Everyone loves these incredible covers. You have done my series some serious justice.

To my formatting team: you make the inside look pretty. Thank you Mayfly Design team!

To my incredible arists: Kiwi Byrd and Reign! You guys have brought my characters to life.

And now . . . here it comes . . . I'm going to get teary-eyed.

To my incredible, loving, engaging, helpful, supportive ARC/ street team. Oh my goodness. I love and appreciate all of the random messages about random topics that bring a smile to my face every time.

Kari (lostinthebooks_byk), Valery (valeryarchaga), Hannah (hannahshardcovers), Kelsey (kcreads1), Kaitlin (justkait_and_her_books), Trisha (whitson.trisha.booklover), Cass (cassleareads), Nora (nbbookery), Jenn Hogue (jenn_n_things), Shandy (shandy-bereading), Marissa (booklovermarissa), Micmic (pinkbibliophile), Leah (leigh.heart.books), Zarina (redheadsreadingsmut), Christina (one.more.chapter.4), and Danielle (danielle_reads_): you guys are a forever part of my street team. You have been with me from the very beginning of *Diamond City*'s journey.

Ashley (justanotherbook10), Alisha (bemybookhangover), Liz (lizslostlibrary), Adriana (last_page_yyc), Becky (book.lover.1986), Kez (booklover.kez), Chloe (lolosbookblog), Brit (literary_dystopia), Brooklyn (brooklynlwolves), Carmen (carmens.book.corner), Cat (catsbooksta_), Mathew (matthatterreads), Alex (thecoffinbookshelf), Gia (librosentrelazos), Heather (tea_in_velaris), Heidi (bookingitmyway), Holly (turning.thepageswithme), Jennifer (dorianhellfire), Anna (ani.reading.by.starlight), Cindy (ciin_leest), Jessi (thebookdragon.jessi), Kat (bookkat), Lindsey (always.find.me.reading), Mia (mama_mia14), Morgan (momosbooknook), Pishi (between_dah_pages), Sam (reading.with.sam001), Vanessa (letmereadbooks), Whitney (whit.nicole.books), Amanda (magneticice), Ashleigh (_ashleighreadsbooks), Shay (shays.readss), Devon (prose_princess), JBell (bell.of.the.books), Nathalie (bookish_nathalie), Nautica (tika.readss), Penni (bookdragon_1982), Rachel (rachel_readsnow), Sapphyre (yggdrasil_dreams), Tara (tarasbookrecs), Lorayne (storiesonmeadowood), Maéva (meevreads), and to ALL my ARC readers:

I am officially crying.

I love you guys.

Aris, you will continue to always be an influence in my life and storytelling. I'll never forget al of our brainstorming!

Cassandra, you are so far from me now, but you were the one who gave me this crazy idea! I love you!

Andrew, you never fail to tell me (even through your always-smile) that hard work pays off.

Ronald, you are the superman from Steelhouse. I think I've said that in every acknowledgement.

Carlos, you are the greatest gym buddy in the world. You teach me that it's not just about hard work in the gym, but in real life.

Soolmaz, you know you're an inspiration to me.

Danny . . . you gave me some options a long time ago and I pick "Option C: All of the Above!"

ACKNOWLEDGEMENTS

Mom, you keep me on track. I lose sight of things sometimes, but you're there to put me back on it again. That's what moms do.

Richard, you play sax no matter what because it's what you love. I want to be like that, too.

Robin, you are my prince charming.

Readers, you are my everything. You are the reason why I do this. I love it when you message me and accuse me of emotional damage!

And last but not least, all my thanks and love wouldn't be possible without my Heavenly Father, Lord Jessus Christ, and Mother Mary, who have given me the opportunity to write. That's what I will continue to do.

Stay tuned!

About the Author

Astrid Cole has a Master's in English Literature from Florida International University. Although she enjoys all subjects, she started writing fiction in high school and hasn't stopped since. When she's not plotting her next novel, she's teaching students history and hitting the gym. A former bodybuilder, running and exercise are a part of her daily routine . . . and so are playing video games and watching horror movies. *Diamond City* is her first published novel.

Coming Soon

Look out for the next installment in the *Diamond City* series, *Opal City*, coming in summer of 2025!

After the devastating ordeals in Ruby City, Sage can finally put the past behind her and move on with her life. That includes raising the newborns in her family, running her pizza shop, and marrying the man of her dreams. She and her new husband elope on the honeymoon of a lifetime, and what better adventure is there than an excursion in the Outskirts?

Unfortunately, not every town and city out there are friendly. Tales tell of a mysterious Lightbringer who harvests a strange power and can bring the dead back to life. After a close call with some freaky worshippers, Sage realizes that Lightbringer is no friend-- he's the leader of a cult who shuns foreigners. And when Sage gets a little too close to Lightbringer's glorious Opal City, she and her husband are captured and it's time to fight for her life all over again.

Honeymoon dreams shatter as Sage finds herself in a struggle against yet another power-hungry warrior. Physical struggles, however, become the least of Sage's worries when her PTSD flares up and mental trauma wins the battle over her sanity. Sage is in danger of not just losing her life, but everything she ever worked for: her family, her pizzeria, and her marriage.

Check out my website www.astridcolebooks.com for the latest news, special editions, and future books!